The field of daffo... ...my mind some twenty ... ...started to the creek to see those magnificent golden flowers. With the help of a steady breeze, their heady aroma greeted me halfway along the dirt path.

Sitting by the creek bed each day after school, I listened as the melted snow of winter's fury made its way downstream, and marveled at the flowers that had fought their way up through the barely thawed ground. Hardy and determined–nothing could suppress them; so different from my life. I never took home a single flower from that field however; my worlds could not mingle.

At the creek, I pushed aside my life and the world as I knew it. The beauty surrounding me quelled my constant fight or flight response, allowing me to let down my guard and take note of things most people wouldn't give a second glance. Subtle details became acute in the absence of distraction. Although I didn't know it then, it was the beginning of my writing career–developing a gift for perception out of a need for survival.

They say that hindsight is 20/20. While working on, *While the Daffodils Danced*, I had no idea why I was writing it, but I knew I'd been given a story to tell. Once I started writing, I couldn't stop. I doubt it's a coincidence that the daffodil is a symbol of hope and renewal.

Twenty years later, I'm no longer that young girl sitting at a creek bed trying to escape my life. I've arrived at another beautiful place, a place I'm happy to call home.

Cathi LaMarche

What people are saying about
Cathi LaMarche's

While the Daffodils Danced

"A beautifully written book by a new voice in contemporary fiction."

~New York Times and USA Today
Bestselling Author Bobbi Smith

"While the Daffodils Danced drew me in on the first page and never let me go. Cathi LaMarche paints a dazzling literary picture, one that is characterized by heartrending emotion and stunning imagery. A starkly beautiful story and a truly remarkable debut. This is a book that will appeal to every woman. I loved it."

~New York Times and USA Today
Bestselling Author Elizabeth Bevarly

"This book touched a place in me that I don't normally allow access to. The elegant prose and vivid imagery is breathtaking in such a spectacular way. Cathi LaMarche not only touches the reader with her words, she enfolds you with the emotion of each beautiful moment. An truly inspiring novel of hope."

~Alexis Hart, author of
Dark Shines My Love

Cathi LaMarche

While the Daffodils Danced

To Laura —
Best of luck on the
upcoming birth of your
baby. I hope you enjoy
this book on motherhood.

Blessings,
Cathi
LaMarche

Echelon Press

This is a work of fiction. Names, characters, places, and incidents are products of the author's imagination or are used fictitiously and are not to be construed as real. Any resemblance to actual events, locales, organizations, or persons, living or dead, is entirely coincidental.

Echelon Press
56 Sawyer Circle #354
Memphis, TN 38103

Copyright © 2005 by C. LaMarche
ISBN: 1-59080-402-3
www.echelonpress.com

First Echelon Press paperback printing: May 2005
Cover Art © Nathalie Moore
2005 Ariana Award Winner

Photography © Barbara J. Kline

Printed in Lavergne, TN, USA

Dedication

For my husband, Michael,
who taught me how to laugh, to love, and to live.

And for Holden and Piper,
who brightened my life with the joys of motherhood.

In memory of Philip Scharf,
who instilled in me the value of hard work.

Acknowledgements

I am grateful to my publisher, Karen Syed at Echelon Press, for having faith in me and this novel. A special thanks to my editor, Kat Thompson.

Heartfelt gratitude goes out to my research assistants. Suzy Wert taught me more about daffodils than any gardening book. Adrienne Rosen not only shared her artistic talents, but also how to look at the world through an artist's eyes. Attorney Jim Ford kept me straight on Family Law in Michigan. Dr. Mayra Thompson and Barb Dam, R.N. provided me with the facts on ovarian cancer. Sam Vance shared his firefighting experience and Mark Minges guided me through funeral planning.

I couldn't have done it without my critique group, Liars, Ink. Thanks to Kevin, Michael, Kirk, Amy, Shawn, Terri, Glen, Richard, and Michael P. for their honest and sometimes painful insight.

My early readers muddled through unedited copy to give me first impressions. Thanks to Christine, Judy, Carol, Liz, Nancy, Shari, Christina, Sally, and Katie for your feedback. And special thanks to my fellow author, Dana Taylor, for all your support.

And my infinite gratitude to my most cherished critic, Michael, for your writing expertise, ongoing support and love. I would have quit fifty times over if it weren't for your unending words of encouragement and belief in me.

And then my heart with pleasure fills,

And dances with the daffodils.

William Wordsworth

An Old Wives' Tale

A woman with a notebook clutched to her chest walked into the hospital room. Her buttercup linen suit tugged me toward spring's joys, but my heart remained slumped in winter's past. She closed the door and the room shrank two sizes.

"Hello, Ms. Robertson. I'm Mrs. Appelbaum from the Social Work Department," she said. She brought the notebook to rest on her hip and made her way to the bed. "Did they tell you I was coming?"

"Yes," I choked out, staring at that oversized notebook filled with tales of despair, knowing that my own story would join them.

She pulled a chair alongside the bed, then reached for my hand. "This must be a difficult time."

I nodded.

"Have you seen the baby?"

Sleep had given me a short reprieve from the truth in the nursery down the hall. Now it was time to talk about my child, the child I had never seen.

On April seventh, I became a mother. I told them upon my arrival at St. Elizabeth Hospital that I didn't want to know anything. The doctor obliged by discreetly handing the newborn to the nurse as if it were a drug deal going down. Then the nurse cradled the infant, pausing at the door an extra moment, giving me a chance to change my mind. She looked back over her shoulder and I knew what she must have been thinking. *How could you not want to see your own baby?* She dared not say it, she didn't have to. The truth was that I couldn't be bothered with gender, eye color, and hair color, because of a much bigger question. Would I survive from this day forward? Then with one shake of my head, the door snapped shut, and my baby was gone.

Now I had to answer to Mrs. Appelbaum for my decision. "There's no way I could...it would be difficult to..."

She leaned toward me. "Cara, do you have any doubts about

proceeding with the adoption plan?"

"No. Absolutely not." The words slipped out so easily they were almost believable.

She opened her notebook and pulled a pen from her pocket. "Did your attorney explain the process to you?"

"Process? Oh, you mean the plan. Yes."

My attorney and I first met to discuss the adoption on a cold day last November, overcast with dampness so thick that it clung to me. I didn't complain about the weather; it felt only right to be dismal both inside and out. My father had arranged my meeting with his law partner, Henry. After making sure no one had coerced me into the decision, Henry informed me of Michigan adoption law and assured me that he could not share any information with my father due to attorney-client privilege, a term that had been thrown around our family for years. Something I never fully appreciated until now.

The plan was simple. Henry had a colleague a few towns over from Mission Bay with clients thought to be a compatible match, though the couple was somewhat skittish due to a prior bad experience where a teenager backed out at the last minute. This time, they were looking for a more mature birth mother. I suppose they were thrilled to hear that I was twenty-four. They didn't know that I still struggled with my decision.

"You chose a closed adoption process, is that right?" Mrs. Appelbaum asked.

The word closed had never sounded covert before now. I felt the need to explain.

"I thought it best for all involved that we not know the other party. Since I wouldn't be staying in touch, I wrote a letter for the baby to read later on. I needed to...to explain the reasons." But would my child understand them?

There was the timing issue. My father had reminded me of the obvious. "It's hard to raise a baby on your salary, Tulip. You're fresh out of college. You've yet to establish your career, and that will take quite some time as an artist."

Mother pointed out that it was not the natural order of things. "How would you ever find a man willing to marry you, dear, with all that extra baggage you'd be carrying around? Men don't want to raise someone else's baby. Can you blame them?"

And my sister. "Who would want a baby with *his* genetic influence? It would be damaged from day one," Steph asserted. "Not to mention the jerk left you the moment you told him you were pregnant."

A more self-centered approach came from my best friend, Tory. "How would you ever find time to paint with a baby to look after? You don't want to be stuck working at the gallery all your life, selling other people's work, do you? And think of all the dates you'd have to pass up."

There were many excuses, but my hand had hovered over that paper for hours, unable to write a single word. Later, I rewrote each paragraph in an attempt to justify my decision, but the words that came forth never satisfied my conscience; guilt oozed from each page like a puncture wound in need of a bandage. The letter started out innocently enough. The first line simply read, *A letter to my baby, with love*, just like a valentine. I looked at the pyramid of crumpled papers at my feet and thought it a shame that the candy company never put the words *adopt me* on any of those little, colored hearts.

The following day I handed the letter to Henry and he promptly stuffed it into a business envelope. Then his secretary typed *Adoption Letter* on the outside, cold and proper.

Henry winked. "Don't want it to get thrown out accidentally."

I knew what he was really saying–it was a business transaction, a negotiation between two interested parties. The emotions needed to be tucked away in a lined envelope to protect everyone.

Mrs. Appelbaum squeezed my hand. "I hope the letter has brought closure for you."

Didn't she know that a simple letter wasn't going to solve anything? What was I thinking? The baby deserved nothing less than a book of at least three hundred and sixty-five pages, a page of reassurance for every day of the year.

"Now, how about the father? Is he in agreement with the adoption plan?" Mrs. Appelbaum asked.

"He doesn't know."

"Doesn't know? Well, he needs to be notified. What's his name?" Her pen went to the notebook and began to bob up and down as she fished for the truth.

"I'm not sure who the father is," I blurted.

Her hand came to rest. "Oh, well, that's different. So, you're not naming a father."

"Right."

Withholding the father's name was not something that came natural to me because I had always been true to Mitch. Henry must have had faith in my character since he asked several times if I knew who the father was, but I never wavered. Mitch didn't deserve to be named after tossing a mere *good luck* over his shoulder as he walked out of my apartment for the last time. As twinges of pain still crawled around my mid-section, I was certain I had made the right decision.

The social worker glanced at her watch. "Your attorney will join us at four o'clock to proceed with the adoption process. There will be papers to sign for temporary placement of the baby with the adoptive parents."

I noticed how carefully she chose her words. Using adoption plan and adoption process so neat and precise. Never once did she slip and say, "You're giving your baby away to total strangers because a baby would be a total inconvenience and put a damper on your future plans."

She must not have read the letter.

Mitch had conveniently been on vacation when the pregnancy test confirmed that my morning queasiness was unrelated to the previous night's dinner. He'd been gone for two weeks, but was due back into town the following morning. With stick in hand, I called his office at nine o'clock sharp. His secretary answered and told me that he was not available, that the father of my baby was having breakfast with his wife.

The need to know overrode the necessity to breathe.

"He has a new wife?" I managed to squeeze out, before struggling for air.

She laughed longer than necessary, then said, "It's the same old wife he's always had. He shouldn't be gone too long. Can I take a..."

I dropped the receiver, then fell to my knees and watched it spin clockwise, then counter-clockwise until the dial tone reminded me that I was in this alone.

I hadn't known Mitch Sanders was married all the while he was on top of me, under me, and inside me throughout the year and a half we had dated. I suppose it should've been obvious, the way we'd drive twenty-five miles to catch dinner and a movie because he was tired of the same old thing. How Mitch always came to my apartment where we'd have more privacy because his roommate didn't like company. The way he'd call me from his office first thing in the morning before I had the chance to call him. Such suspicions were easy to explain away when he looked into my eyes so lovingly and called me his one and only, the love of his life. In the throes of passion, there was little time for doubt.

He had been the frat boy, the All-American college football player that could have had any woman, but he chose me. I just didn't know that I was second string and would eventually be cut from the team altogether.

My friend, Tory Parker, took a seat beside the hospital bed. She foraged around in her purse and pulled out a silver tube along with a mirror, then re-applied the red lipstick that accented the small gap between her two front teeth, just wide enough to be sexy. She puckered to check for evenness and zipped her tongue across her teeth.

I knew the answer, but decided to ask anyway. "Do you think I'm horrible?"

She glanced up and snapped the compact closed. "Of course not. Do you have to ask? By the way, how was the meeting with the social worker?"

"She wanted to know if I had any doubts."

"You told her no, right?"

I looked out the window.

"Cara, you're doing the right thing. For God's sake, you've barely been able to take care of yourself since Mitch walked out on you. How many times have you called me in the middle of the night crying your eyes out, unable to eat, to sleep? You can't take care of a baby right now. And it's not like your family will be of any help."

I choked back my tears. "I know. But I didn't realize it would be this hard."

"It's the best thing...for both of you. You can get your life back in order and the baby will have a good start...a stable life, just like you said in that letter."

The letter. I closed my eyes and searched for a reason, any reason. *Ah, yes, my baby deserves better.*

Tory stood and pressed out her jeans with her hands and her multiple bracelets fought for better positioning. "You should get some sleep. I'll go make a few phone calls. Want me to try to reach Mitch?"

I bolted up in bed. "God, no! Did you forget the part about him being married? Besides, he's probably with her."

More than likely they were eating breakfast at the local pancake house. I pictured them seated on the same side of the booth, placing their need for closeness over comfort. He ran his fingers down the center of his wavy, black hair while deciding whether to go with the blueberry syrup or stick with maple–her decision based solely on whether the word light was involved. He held his coffee mug with a firm one-handed grip, the same way he drank a beer. His wife hugged hers with both hands; gently tipping the cup to her lips in short bursts of energy as if to show moderation in all areas of her life.

Tory scooped her leopard print purse off the floor. "I'll be back shortly."

"Don't," I said.

A smile inched across her scarlet lips. "Don't what?"

"You know."

"Do I?"

"I think you do."

"Sleep. You're exhausted. I'll be back in a bit," she said before trotting out the door.

A clicking noise from her heels followed her down the hall, trying to catch up with the rest of her body. As I closed my eyes, my thoughts drifted back to the pancake house and I prayed that he got food poisoning. No, that *they* got food poisoning.

My head hit the pillow and I soon found myself in an old schoolhouse; a sweet, fruity smell swirled about my head. A thick layer of dust covered the desk. I swiped it with my index finger and put it to my lips.

Mmm...orange, my favorite.

The schoolteacher was a plastic Pez dispenser with an elephant head, but for some reason I never questioned her authority. She walked over, flipped her head back, and coughed up a test.

I straightened in my desk chair. That's funny, I didn't recall any mention of an exam.

The other students smiled and placed their hands in front of them, accepting the paper as eagerly as their First Communion. With heads bowed they set to work, the confident scratching sounds from their pencils magnified my lack of preparedness. I had not studied. Not for the stupid math test, the pregnancy, the birth or the adoption. I was going to fail. Fail the test, motherhood, and life.

The first question: One baby minus one baby equals blank.

It didn't seem logical, but I knew I had to put something down on paper, so I leaned to the right to copy off the girl sitting next to me. As my neck stretched outward, a trunk firmly tapped me on the shoulder.

"Don't you know that cheaters never prosper?" the teacher warned, in her candy-scented breath. "If you don't know the answer by now, you never will."

Suddenly, the school bell rang. While the other students ran out to the playground, I fell out of my desk spiraling downward three stories, stopping just short of the faculty parking lot.

I shot up in the hospital bed and gasped for air, then suddenly understood the real test had yet to come. Tory stood at the foot of my bed with a man. I furiously rubbed my eyes in hopes of erasing him.

She cringed. "I know...I know. I thought Mitch would at least want to see how you and the baby were doing."

He stepped from behind her. I had forgotten how his shoulders filled a room. His extra large shirt tapered down to his thin waist, tucked neatly into jeans that were neither too old nor too new.

"Oh, Christ, Tory!" I said.

The thought of killing her on the spot flooded my mind. The coroner would hover over her lifeless body. "Yep, she's dead all right," he'd say, giving a quick nod to solidify his diagnosis. His assistant would zip the body bag closed and they'd hoist it onto the metal gurney. Fortunately for her, I was armed with nothing more than a plastic spoon on my food tray.

Mitch turned to Tory. "Can you give us some time?"

"Sure. Just be nice, Mitch. You promised, remember?" She spun around on the spikes of her shoes and left the room.

It was awkward, just the two of us. There was a time when I would have given anything to be alone with him. Now I longed for an interruption. He made his way toward the bed with that casual walk of his; hands stuffed deep into the front jeans' pockets as if flaunting my inability to hurt him.

"Cara, I know you must hate me."

Throughout my pregnancy and labor, I had thought of a million reasons why I hated him. As he stood there in front of me, looking more handsome than I ever remembered, not a single one came to mind.

"But I knew you'd make it on your own," he said.

Now there was a reason. I stared at the crucifix on the wall and longed for him to suffer like that.

"Please, say something." He shifted his weight from right to left and back again.

"Why did you come here?" I held my head steady to prevent tears from spilling over onto my cheeks.

"Guilt, I suppose. I'm not sure, exactly."

"Really now," I said through my clenched jaw.

He took a step closer to the bed. "I know you won't ask your parents for money, so I'll help what little I can from a financial standpoint. It wouldn't be much, but..."

I bit my bottom lip to stop the trembling. My heart grew cold as I realized that it was indeed guilt that had brought him to see me. "I don't want a dime from you. What I need...what I *needed*...was a father willing to help raise the baby."

"I can't do that."

Why do things you already know hurt worse when said aloud?

"Did you ever love me, or was I just a fling for you?" I grabbed the side rails of the bed to brace myself for the impact of his response.

"Do you have to ask?"

"Did I have to ask whether or not you were married?"

He glanced toward the door, but decided to stay. "Look, I should've told you, but I can't change that. Whether you believe me or not, I care about what happens to you."

"Don't. I'll manage just fine without your concern. Spend it on your wife."

He cleared his throat. "I went to see her."

"Your *wife*?"

"No, the baby."

My hand cupped my mouth. *God, it's a girl. A little, baby girl.*

Then I saw her for the first time. Chestnut hair and dark brown eyes. My eyes, to see a world filled with beauty to capture on canvas. Not his useless blue eyes that could not even see how much pain he caused us.

"I knew she'd be beautiful. She looks like me," he said.

His narcissism jolted me back to the issue at hand.

"You better hope your wife never sees her."

"Well, I certainly don't plan on...anyway...I hope you know that I won't cause you any problems. I won't pursue custody rights."

Did he really believe that he had such a right? I tilted my chin up and fluttered my wet eyelids as I did every time I watched a sad movie in a theatre full of strangers.

The word old wife infiltrated my mind again. I had no choice but to hurt him and searched for just the right words, truth or no truth. *Now I'm the teacher. Don't you know that cheaters never prosper?* I looked deep into his eyes. "I'm not asking a single thing from you, Mitch. In fact, I'm not positive the baby is even yours."

He forcefully exhaled as if he received a blow to the stomach. "What?"

"You might not be the father."

"You're lying."

"Nope."

"Cara..." He yanked his hands from his pockets. "Are you serious?"

If you don't know the answer by now, you never will. "I swear."

He pinched his eyes closed with the tips of his fingers and swayed back and forth like a boxer who'd been dazed, then shook his head as if to throw off the punch. "Well...I guess we're both guilty then."

"I guess so." Relief settled in as I swallowed the last of the lie.

"I'm sorry it had to be this way," he offered, staggering toward the door.

"Me, too."

The door closed behind him and a deafening silence hovered overhead. I closed my eyes and felt myself spiraling downward once again. I had never felt more alone.

My beautiful baby girl lay in the nursery down the hall.

Scales of Justice

A cry from the room next door ripped through me. A shrill, piercing wail that unsettled my nerves no matter how many times I heard it. The sound came out of nowhere, unexpectedly; the first cry as intense as the ones that followed, never allowing me time to build up a tolerance. Then the screaming came to a sudden halt; mother's milk held the power to calm, even I knew that. My breasts ached with every swallow.

There was the melody. The *Brahms Lullaby* played throughout the hospital every time a new baby arrived. I stopped what I was doing to listen and pictured others doing the same. The elderly couple held up the cafeteria line as they reached for each other's hand and recalled the birth of their first baby fifty-five years ago. The doctor in the emergency room had a glimmer of hope that life goes on, before making her way to the waiting area to give the family the bad news about the heart attack victim now covered with a sheet. The woman next door to me shed tears of joy that the song announced to the world that she was a new mother. They had not played the song for my baby, out of respect for my feelings, I suppose. Too bad they had forgotten that I was still in the building with each subsequent cradlesong.

I leaned back in bed and watched the rain hit the window. It was a light, sideways rain that left streaks of moisture across the glass. The people in the parking lot below hunched over and scurried to and from their cars, caught off guard by the sudden sprinkling. Didn't they know that April in Michigan was unpredictable? Those with umbrellas took all the time they needed. Then I saw it, the oversized golf umbrella with the Lady of Justice on each of the panels. She stood tall with a sword in one hand, the Scales of Justice in the other, and carried not a hint of embarrassment that her breast was semi-exposed. It was Daddy's prize for a hole in one at the four-man scramble he had played with his colleagues a few years back. Mother never could stand that umbrella, claimed the message to be overbearing.

"Justice is something to be assumed, not advertised," she'd say. "And honestly, she should cover herself up a bit. A little modesty never hurt anyone."

The umbrella folded up out of sight. I was not surprised that Daddy came, just shocked that it was on his lunch hour, the time of day he usually reserved for a romp with Rachael, one of the young paralegals in the office.

I quickly ran a brush through my hair and straightened my gown. He never did like people who wore the lasting effects of a crisis.

He eventually poked his head into the room. "Is anybody home?"

"Yeah, Daddy, come on in," I said.

He walked to the bed and handed me a bouquet of freshly cut daffodils. "Hey, Tulip, how are you?"

"Fine." I placed the jonquils to my nose and smiled for the first time since going into labor. "From the creek?"

"Where else would I find such beautiful flowers?"

They were in bloom now, self-sowing daffodils whose perimeter had widened substantially over the years. The daffodils never let me down, reappearing each spring like an old friend wanting to share a cup of coffee. They bloomed, they died, and they bloomed again–that simple. If only my life was that simple.

Daddy shed his suit coat and leaned over me. He firmly held his Brooks Brothers tie against his heavily starched shirt, not allowing it to mingle with the shame of my hospital gown. "So, Petunia, is everything settled? There weren't any problems?"

My script had been written years ago. I never deviated from it, no matter what the subject. "No problems. Everything is going as planned."

He leaned back, his shoulders relaxed. "Good. The last thing we need is a change of plans."

"Right." I straightened the blanket covering my legs, smoothing each wrinkle, out of the need for something to be in order.

"That ex-boyfriend of yours isn't being difficult, is he?"

"Nope." Daddy never cared for Mitch with his useless degree in physical education and go nowhere job.

Daddy brought his hands together with a clap as if cheering Mitch's good sense. "Great. We certainly don't need difficulty."

"Yep, that's the last thing we need."

He patted my leg. "I know you feel awful, but in a few months this will all be behind you."

A few months from now it would be fall, a time of dormancy followed by hibernation. He knew little about the seasons, and even less about me.

"Yes, it most certainly will be," I assured him.

"I have to get back to the office for a deposition. You and Henry will be meeting with the social worker to start things in motion, will you not?"

"Four o'clock."

He checked his watch. "It's best to get the papers signed right away. The last thing we need is legal problems down the road."

"Absolutely. No legal problems needed here."

"No reason to drag this out any longer than necessary."

I nodded. "The sooner the better."

The nine months of pregnancy, the labor and delivery, the new life that I helped to create was reduced to a single signature in his eyes. The swipe of a pen resolved everything, no further obligation on my part. I could go back to my life as it was prior to the blue-lined stick, prior to the first kick, prior to the first cry. It made sense to him. To Daddy, things were either black or white: alibi or no alibi, evidence or no evidence, keep the baby or don't keep the baby. That mindset had earned a prosperous income over the years.

If only he had declared me not guilty before leaving the room.

Viewed from the outside, other than painful breasts and a few stitches, I could have been mistaken for your average, slightly overweight, smelly person; the inside was a different story.

The hospital gown fell to the floor and I gave it a kick as if it were somehow responsible. While the hot water from the showerhead trickled down my back, and tears streamed down my cheeks, my thoughts drifted to her. Had she been aware of her fate all along? Did she notice the way I kept my hands from rubbing my belly in greeting? The way I ignored her kicks and pokes? If only I could have told her the distancing was out of necessity. She had to know that if I had given in to the joys of motherhood, her fate would have been worse; raised by a single mother, living in an efficiency apartment, attempting to survive on an artist's salary.

I had dreamed of the adoptive couple being royalty or heirs to a fortune, able to give my baby everything. At night, my imagination carried me off to sleep. Their castle, set into the hillside and surrounded by a thick forest, was camouflaged unsuccessfully as both children and adults climbed trees for a glimpse of a lifestyle they could only dream about. The guarded entrance left no doubt that visits were by invitation only. Or, perhaps the couple lived in nothing more than a two-story colonial with a few shrubs and a no soliciting sign on the door. At the very least, they could offer my child a father, so I stuck with the plan, royalty or not.

Soon she would enjoy the benefits: a two-parent family, the house with a fenced yard, or the castle complete with moat and dragon, whichever the case. But here's what I needed to know—what was the benefit for me? For me and all the other birth mothers who stood in this shower, shedding tears over their lost babies. It wasn't fair that our hopes and dreams swirled around with the soap at the bottom of the shower.

At four o'clock, Mrs. Appelbaum sat next to me. The wrinkles in her suit outlined her every move throughout the day.

Henry took a seat across the table. He folded his hands as if in prayer, asking for absolution for being an accomplice to my crime. "We'll try to keep this brief."

Brief? This meeting will be part of my every waking moment for the rest of my life.

My throat tightened as he pulled an official looking envelope out of his black leather briefcase. The papers were suddenly a reality, no longer just a process.

My baby deserves better, I reminded myself.

When we finished reading the last page, Henry offered me a pen. "You can sign now."

The reasons, remember the reasons. She'll have a wonderful life. I reached across the table to Henry's outstretched hand, but Mrs. Appelbaum grabbed my arm and brought it back to my side.

"Cara, do you have any questions?" she asked. "Anything we can explain further before you sign?" She obviously had informed consent on her mind, or maybe she couldn't believe that I was really giving my baby away.

"No," I whispered. I took the pen and put tip to paper. *The flow. I just need to get into the flow.*

As I wrote the letter C, the sickening rhythm of selfishness echoed throughout the room. I forced each letter like a kindergartener learning to write for the first time. When I finished, I dropped the pen on the table. She needed a father. Was that selfish of me to believe that?

April seventh, I became a non-mother.

Henry picked up the papers, slid them into the envelope, and dropped the package into his briefcase. He pushed the lid down into place. The click of the latch sounded like a prison door slamming shut. Barrier after barrier now separated me from my child.

Tears streamed down my cheeks. But she'll have more than I could ever give her, I remembered.

Henry stood. "Cara, I'll take care of things from here. I'll call the adoptive parents' attorney when I get back to the office...oh, and Mrs. Appelbaum, if you could assist with the baby's release from the hospital that would be helpful."

Then Henry walked out of the room with my baby securely locked inside his briefcase.

April Showers

Sleep was supposed to bring relief from the pain that had settled deep inside my chest. Instead, it tore at me. Jagged little gashes, like the kind I used to get when stumbling into a patch of greenbrier. Sharp pricks stealing bits of flesh no matter which way I turned; the warm trickle of blood down the length of my thigh, proof of my struggle.

The knock at the door brought me back from the wilderness and I sat up in bed. A woman made her way over, her white uniform crinkled with every step.

"Hello, I'm Sarah, your evening nurse. How are you feeling?" she asked. With every turn toward the light, her cross pendant necklace glistened like freshly fallen snow in mid-December.

"I'm fine." I drew my lips taut to stop the trembling.

"Really?"

I cupped my face in my hands, the tears pooled in the middle of my palms. The bed groaned under her weight as she sat down beside me. She sighed, then brushed the stray hairs from my face. "I'm not sure about your religious beliefs, or if you even believe in God. But I have to believe there's a reason for all this. You may not know that reason for many years. Or you may never know. God will decide that. There's one thing I do know." Her hand came to rest on my forearm. "You gave that baby life and your baby may give someone else life one day."

It was time to ask. "Is she healthy? I mean, okay and everything?"

"Yes, she's doing fine."

Words that ordinarily brought comfort doused me with guilt. Perhaps a sickly baby would have been easier to give up.

Sarah stood and completed the physical assessment. Did I have any pain? Had I used the toilet? Was I getting around without difficulty? The questions were insignificant to a woman who'd given her baby away.

When finished, she put her arm around me. "I am sorry for your loss."

Your loss. The words were not profound; nothing more than an acknowledgement that something bad had happened. For me they were more. Someone finally realized that my baby meant something to me.

Sarah leaned in close. The cross dangled in front of my eyes, begging me to have faith.

"What a wonderful thing, to give someone life," she whispered, before leaving the room.

I looked through the window at the storm that had gathered strength, the rain hard and steady. Mothers in the wild shielded their young from such harsh elements. My baby didn't have her mother to protect her, but she was alive. Something she could be thankful for on days when there was nothing else going in her favor.

My mother had a knack for acquiring personal information without appearing nosey. She played by country club rules–be polite, but don't dare leave empty-handed. Most of the time people never noticed the questioning camouflaged as small talk. By the time they did, she was on to the next topic. My sister Stephanie had an altogether different style. Straightforward–*bam*! People knew exactly what she was after, but she said it in such a way that they were afraid not to answer, a sort of gossip by intimidation. Different styles, but the same outcome. They both walked away with dirty, little secrets tucked inside their coat pockets.

"So dear, how are things?" Mother asked.

"Fine."

She patted her freshly styled hair into place. "Things went well then?"

"Sure."

"That's good to hear." She sighed. "No surprises?"

Like a buzzard at the side of the road, she waited patiently. Seeing that I'd just given away something much more important, I decided to continue with the generosity and stop wasting everyone's time.

"Which part do you mean? The hellish labor and delivery, the visit from Mitch, or the heart wrenching decision to give my baby away to strangers?"

She gasped and drew her hand to her throat. "Goodness. All of those things, I suppose, dear."

Steph pushed her aside and lunged toward the bed. "*He* stopped by? Does his wife know about the baby? He's not going to get involved, is he?"

"No, he's not getting involved," I shot back. Please don't be greedy, I prayed. Just take what I gave you and be satisfied.

Steph's hands landed on her bony hips. "What makes you so sure?"

Mother sighed the way she always did when something was clearly evident. "Men don't walk out for that long, only to walk back in."

"So, did you let him have it?" Steph wanted to know.

"It?" I asked.

Mother leaned forward. "Oh, for the love of God, he wants the baby? I wouldn't think that with him being married and all that he would even dream of such a thing. Honestly, what on earth could he be thinking?"

"No, Mother. He doesn't want the baby, for God's sake," I said.

She settled into a chair. "Oh, well, that's certainly a relief. Surely, the missus wouldn't have allowed him to keep it anyway, do you think?"

"Well?" Steph waited for an answer.

I thought back to my monstrous lie. "Yes, I did let him have *it*. Can we please not talk about Mitch anymore?"

A sound similar to that of a young boy throwing a handful of pebbles at a window drew my attention outdoors.

"Oh my, hail," Mother said. "Probably not many visitors in this weather, right, dear?"

Such a simple inquiry on the surface, but I knew an underlying question when I heard one. Even though I lived more than twenty miles away, Mother feared the ladies at the country club would get word of my condition. "What would they think?" she'd said throughout my pregnancy. "You not being married, him being married, but not to you."

Daddy once joked that in the event someone discovered my pregnancy, Mother carried a list of responses in the back of her pocketbook along with the weekly grocery list.

- ✓ *Pancake mix*
- ✓ *Artificially inseminated as part of a clinical trial for medical research*
- ✓ *Vanilla extract*
- ✓ *Surrogate for an infertile, handicapped cousin*
- ✓ *Marinated artichoke hearts*
- ✓ *Impregnated by aliens*

I decided to test her. "Oh, the bad weather hasn't stopped them. I've had hoards of visitors. Of course, all the ladies from the club said the baby looked like a Robertson."

Steph and I chuckled.

Mother blushed. "Honestly, you two."

I nodded toward the daffodils. "Tory left, then Daddy brought me the flowers, that's all."

Mother pried her hand off her chest. "That's nice."

"Yeah, he came on his lunch hour."

"Well, why wouldn't he come on his lunch hour?" she asked. Her denial didn't stop at my pregnancy.

Steph swatted my arm. "Hey, I brought something to cheer you up." She dug into her purse and handed me a small envelope.

"What's this?" I asked.

"A year membership to the gym. It shouldn't take you long to whip yourself back into shape. My personal trainer has offered to help you out."

"Can it wait a day?"

She waved her index finger about like a pistol. "Of course, but don't let yourself go too long. You don't want everything going south on you."

I discreetly felt my navel, which happened to be a good two inches down from where it was before the pregnancy. "Right."

Steph knew what she was talking about when it came to fitness.

She placed second in the local triathlon last year. All year long, she rationed food like a squirrel preparing for winter and never skipped a day at the gym. She kept herself too thin if you asked me, a number two pencil with extremities.

I looked at Mother. "I'll probably be going home tomorrow. Can you pick me up?"

"Of course I can, dear. Oh, but it will have to be in the afternoon. Tomorrow morning is tennis with Mrs. Whitehead."

"I wouldn't want you to put your plans aside for me, Mother. I'll just call Tory."

"If you feel that would work better."

The sarcasm in my voice had lost its effectiveness years ago.

Mother tapped Steph on the shoulder, then pointed to the door. "Well, Cara, I suppose we'll go and let you rest." They each gave me a kiss on the cheek. Before reaching the door, Mother turned back. "Oh, one more thing. This won't be announced in the paper? You know…the baby's birth…your name?"

"Of course not, Mother," I said.

Steph hit her arm. "Jesus. Why'd you have to go and ask that?"

My eyes followed the reflective stripes of Steph's jogging suit out the door. I picked up the bouquet of daffodils and closed my eyes. Their heady aroma carried me off to a distant place where large oak trees lined a creek embankment. Throughout its watery bed, rocks unearthed themselves and beckoned me for a game of hopscotch. I tried to hop, but the weight of my guilt wouldn't allow it. I eventually made my way to the opposite side of the embankment and walked toward the field awash with yellow–the flowers swayed in the spring breeze, always the first sign of life at the creek. My hand brushed over my empty womb searching in vain for any sign of life. While the daffodils danced about in my head, I could do nothing but weep.

A small ray of light slithered under the door and illuminated a narrow pathway to the bed. Outside the room, people rushed about and talked way too fast. It reminded me of when my Aunt Kate used to say that people never slowed down to appreciate the beauty that God put on earth. Nature's miracles she called them. "He wouldn't have put them here if He didn't want us to take notice," she'd say.

As a child, I considered her an expert on such miracles. Aunt Kate and I jumped in the car every Sunday afternoon for a trip to the countryside. No agenda. We just stopped when the mood struck, pulling over to enjoy golden wheat fields spread out over several acres, heavy headed sunflowers that struggled to stay erect, and small blackberry patches in the middle of an otherwise barren field. Sometimes we buzzed past something beautiful alongside the road and Aunt Kate periodically looked back over her shoulder for the next mile or so. Then, without notice, she'd slap her arm across my chest, pinning me to the seat and call out, "Hold on, honey!" while she threw the car in reverse. We weaved from side to side leaving a trail of dust in front of us, eventually making it back to the point where the car should have stopped in the first place.

To Aunt Kate, beauty knew no season. Fresh snow covering an orchard of apple trees in the winter was as magnificent as the blossoms that covered them in the spring. She swore God loved Michiganders best to have given them such variations in the weather. "Who would want sunshine every day? What about the snow and the rain? Aren't they just as pleasing to the eye?" she'd ask.

I gave Aunt Kate and our Sunday drives credit for my love of nature. For years, I'd made it a habit to carry my art supplies in my Jeep, lest I miss an opportunity to capture such a miracle on canvas.

Although Uncle Joe had died several years earlier, I'd always hoped Aunt Kate would live forever. The day she died had been the saddest day of my life, until now.

After the noise outside my room had quieted, I followed the streak of light to the door and grabbed the handle. A firm push and a few steps down the hall was all that was needed to see one of nature's miracles, my baby, the greatest gift from God. How had I kept myself away from her beauty all this time? I longed to press my nose against the nursery window to study her every detail. Instead, I turned around and headed back in the opposite direction, going against everything Aunt Kate ever taught me. As I climbed back into bed, the door swung open and light panned across the room.

"Cara," a familiar voice said, "you're not my patient tonight, but I wanted to say goodbye before you went home in the morning." I looked up to find Sarah, the night nurse, beside the bed.

"I appreciate that. Thank you."

She took my hand into her soft grasp, her touch as gentle as her words. "God will watch over both you and the baby. You have to have faith." She took the cross from around her neck and pressed it into my palm.

"I couldn't possibly…"

"Please, I want you to have it."

"But…" The chain wove in and out of my fingers, unsure whether to stay or go.

She took the necklace from my hand and secured it around my neck. After it settled over my chest, she patted it into place. That night, I fell asleep tucked in by Sarah's faith.

Morning brought with it a sense of relief. I was leaving the hospital, the place where new mothers spent hours learning to care for such things as umbilical cords, circumcisions, and delicate skin; where swaddling infants in cotton receiving blankets sent college-educated women into sheer panic and the mention of the word breastfeeding made even the most confident feel inept. They had not a moment to relax. My free time was a constant reminder that I had abandoned such obligations.

I looked at the clock. It would be two more hours before Tory arrived to take me home. My backpack sat at the foot of the bed. Unlike the women who brought a baby journal, camera, and sleeper, my bag held nothing more than a drawing pencil and sketchpad. I set up my workstation and looked at the flowers on the bedside table. There was a perfect angle for every picture; finding it was the challenge. One of the jonquils bent slightly downward, held apart from the others. I took its offer, and began to draw.

"Cara," Mrs. Appelbaum called from the doorway, "sorry to interrupt. I wanted to bring support group information before you left today." She handed me a piece of paper.

The groups appeared to be listed in no particular order: compulsive gamblers, riskaphobics, sexaholics, sexaphobics, parents without partners, partners without parents, and a myriad of other groups for those suffering from mental and physical afflictions. Then

I saw it–*Adoption Support Group For Birth Mothers*; my category, my affliction. They met on Wednesday night at seven o'clock, the same night as the bipolar people and those who recently stopped smoking. A manic-depressive who had given up both a baby and cigarettes had quite the decision to make. Lucky for me, I had only one problem from which to recover.

"Thank you." I tucked the sheet into my backpack.

"Now, the days ahead may be rough," she warned. "With the exhaustion from the labor and delivery, you may have yet to feel the full impact of what has happened. There's still the court appearance to permanently relinquish your parental rights. That will most likely be the hardest day of all. If I can help in any way, please call."

Why the hell did she have to say all that? A mere goodbye would've sufficed.

She left the room to attend to someone else's shattered life. I picked up my drawing pencil and looked back at the daffodils. They were hardy flowers; able to withstand whatever nature threw at them. If only humans were that strong.

The wheelchair sat in the middle of the room. Hospital policy mandated that I leave as an invalid. I climbed in without objection.

The nurse unlocked the wheels. "Ready?" she asked before pushing me to the door.

Tory followed close behind. We stopped momentarily in the doorway, and then turned right.

Right? Was this the only way out? I gripped the arms of the chair. Why would they force me to go past the nursery? Windows that showcased God's little miracles soon replaced walls. Behind them, a row of bassinets lined up like small freight cars with cards exclaiming, *It's a girl!* and *It's a boy!* I closed my eyes so I would not see the card at the foot of her bassinet–*It's an outcast!* With the name Baby Jane Doe written underneath.

When we reached the lobby, it was safe to open my eyes, but gone was my chance to see her. Passersby glanced in my direction and politely nodded. Surely, they had no idea why I had been hospitalized; I carried not a hint of childbirth. Gallstones maybe? Appendectomy?

I waited for Tory to pull the car into the circle drive. It was a dry, sunny day, but the tears streaming down my face felt as though I had been caught in a sudden April shower. I sat hunched over, wanting to scurry across the parking lot. Where was Daddy's umbrella?

Tory drove up and the nurse helped me into the passenger seat, then slammed the door shut. As we pulled from the curb, my empty arms ached as if holding a pile of bricks.

Starving Artist

As a preschooler, I used a paintbrush better than a spoon. My kindergarten year was spent transforming the sidewalk into a work of art with nothing more than an old, stiff brush and a bucket of water. The sunshine and the hot, summer breeze often erased my masterpiece before I could finish, but that didn't matter. I just dipped the brush into the bucket and started over. Well-meaning neighbors and relatives walked up the drive and asked, "What's that you're painting?" I'd say, "It's a horse in the field eating clovers!" Then I'd frantically point to the fading parts of my creation in an attempt to show them. "Oh," they'd blurt before making their way to the door.

On my fifth birthday, Aunt Kate gave me an easel and a set of real brushes. It was the best gift I had ever received. The celebration continued around me as I flipped the paper up over the top of the easel and imagined the picture; a dark brown horse with a coarse, black tail who munched on greens with tiny, yellow flowers. My heart raced trying to decide which color I'd use first. I ran the bristles of the large brush over my fingertips and then my cheek to get the feel of the new tool. I wanted the party guests to leave so I could start painting. Somehow, I managed to smile throughout the birthday song, and the cake and ice cream. As soon as the last guest pulled out of the drive, I locked myself in my room. Within a half hour, there wasn't a clean sheet of paper left.

Years later, I stood with brush in hand and announced to my family that art was my planned course of study at the university.

"Those poor, starving artists," Mother said with a sigh as heavy as her heart.

"That's just a silly phrase," I tried to assure her.

"There has to be some truth behind it, dear, or they wouldn't advertise those sales at the Holiday Inn."

Mother pictured me in a rat-infested apartment, a mattress on the floor, eating beans out of a can. She tried to convince me to seek a noble profession–a stockbroker, physician, or attorney like Daddy. When her pleading failed, she cut the want ads from the daily newspaper and placed them into two separate piles. The artist pile and the anything other than an artist pile. "See, other people don't think artists are necessary either," she said, pointing to the empty spot. Of course, my chosen pile remained barren for months, but that still didn't deter me.

Steph heeded Mother's advice and pursued a business degree. After graduation, she opened her own sportswear store–The Sport Port. You wouldn't find *Fruit Of The Loom* sweats on her racks. She carried designer sweats for the people who felt the need to be fashionable while marinating in perspiration; the type of clothing that netted her a two-hundred percent profit even after being marked down. My parents were thrilled when she married Andrew Braun, the accountant. He was the perfect accompaniment to her store.

Mother once asked me, "Why must you paint?" She might as well have asked, "Why must you breathe?"

Breathe. Remember to breathe, I told myself as I walked to my apartment carrying nothing more than my backpack.

"I can stay if you'd like," Tory said.

I shook my head. "No, I'm fine. I think I'll just get some sleep."

After she left, I stood in the center of the room surveying the frayed sofa, the mismatched end tables, and 19" television sitting on a stand made of pressed wood. It wasn't much better than the life Mother had envisioned for me years ago. Except for the fact that I had a box spring for my bed, a small spare bedroom, and ate beans out of a Crock Pot rather than a can. Everything in my apartment screamed single, underpaid, recent art graduate. Whenever Mother came to visit she'd say, "Are you sure we can't buy you a few things? Touch things up a bit." Each time, I declined out of pride.

The light on the answering machine blinked at me. I went over and pushed the play button.

"Hello dear, it's Mother. Just checking to see if you made it home from the hospital. Perhaps you can come over to the house soon for dinner. Call us."

Message number two: "Hey Cara–Steph. I would've called

earlier, but things are just crazy here at the store. Everyone wants to shed those winter pounds. I'll see you at the gym, right?"

Number three: "Cara, Henry here. We should be able to get into court soon to finalize the adoption. I'll call you with the date and time when I get notified. I'm sure you're anxious to get this over with."

The light stopped blinking. I had hoped for a fourth message that went something like this: "Hey darling, it's Mitch. There's been a huge misunderstanding. I'm not married after all and I'm ready to be a father. I'll be over shortly with the baby."

There was no fourth message. My baby wasn't with Mitch, but rather safely tucked away in her new home. More than likely, asleep in a sleigh crib with colorful, Laura Ashley sheets. Across the room, the valance above the window complemented the bedding. Her closet was stuffed with dresses and matching hats from the children's boutique, and rose-colored sleepers were folded neatly in a dresser lined with paper that carried the fresh scent of baby powder.

I dropped to my knees. I should have been thankful that she was being well cared for. Instead, I was drowning in sorrow.

Spring, a minor season nestled between two major ones.

People in Mission Bay yearned for spring, not for what it had to offer, but for what followed–summer. That was what they were really after. They couldn't be bothered with basking in the joys of new life when they'd rather be basking in the sun on the beach. But spring never took offense and offered its beauty year after year. Perhaps realizing it was much better than fall, the prelude to the dreaded winter.

There was a special place to appreciate this rebirth, so I gathered my art supplies and drove the twenty miles to Oak Hill Lane. My parents' home was nearby, but I couldn't get myself to visit quite yet. Instead, I parked on the side of the road and walked the old dirt path, merely stepping through one of the breaking points in the barbed wire fence. A weathered sign stapled to the fence post read, NO TR SP S ING. Just like a child, I planned to plead ignorance.

Each new pothole offered proof that winter had come and gone. Looking down the path that resembled a piece of Swiss cheese, I convinced myself that a stroller would not have been practical anyway. But the discomfort and fatigue that accompanied every step reminded me I should have been pushing one.

When I was a child, this place seemed a thousand miles away from civilization, but it was only a mile as the crow flies from my childhood home. The adventure would begin when I left our backyard, walked across the neighbor's yard and continued through the apple orchard. When in season, I'd pluck a Red Delicious right off the tree. Then a left at the vineyard, where each September the smell of grapes made my mouth tingle. Next, through Farmer Jensen's asparagus field.

He tended his land from atop his red tractor with his border collie Scout running alongside. He always tipped his hat, nodded, or gave a slight wave of the hand as if to say, *Glad you could pass on through.*

I knew his tractor sat idle today. He'd as soon let the fruit rot off the trees as work on the Lord's Day.

When I'd reach the big maple with the dilapidated tree fort in its boughs, it was exactly twenty-six skips through the tall field grass to reach the creek. Today there would be no skipping. "Slow and easy for a while," the doctor had said.

This time of year, the bed was filled with the melted snow of winter's fury. Bunched piles of leaves and branches interrupted the flow. Courtesy of a few large rocks, I made my way over to the daffodil colony, flowers that Baby Jane would never get to see.

The southwest corner of the field of flowers grabbed my attention. In the early morning hours, the daffodils' necks bent downward as if in prayer, while the trickle of the creek provided a rhythmic incantation. I waited, and waited some more until the morning sun warmed the air and they lifted their drowsy heads. Nature was in charge and it was useless to think otherwise. At ten o'clock, I pulled out my viewfinder to locate the perfect patch of jonquils.

"There," I said.

There were eight of them, golden perfection, still glistening from the morning dew. I went over and set up my French easel and laid out the colors on the edge of my palette.

With petals now spread open, the daffodils invited me into their lives. I knew their parts as intimately as my own body: the corona, the six pollen-bearing stamens, the three-lobed stigma, the dark green stems reaching down to the bulbs sitting in the rich soil, drawing out nutrients that made them whole. For years, I had painted in this field, and each time captured something fresh, creating a new mood, a different harmony; never tiring of the yellow flowers that were spring's messenger. "Except for an occasional cold snap, the winter is over," they'd announce.

I worked quickly to sketch their details before the lighting changed; my canvas was now ready to accept a light wash of raw umber, and color soon followed. Titanium white mixed with cadmium yellows–the perfect combination for the color of a jonquil. And just like that, the flowers came to life.

I suddenly realized why my loss was unbearable. The daffodils remained clear in my mind, even after closing my eyes at night, and they could be called up at a moment's notice throughout each day. Their sweet fragrance followed me everywhere. With Baby Jane it was different. I grieved for the unknown, with nothing to draw from memory. What would I miss most? Would it be her little toes that curled under, her small fists clenched to her chest, or her new baby scent? It would be easier to let go, if I knew what I had given away.

As I folded the easel and placed my supplies back in the bag, I remembered one last thing I needed to do. The tip of a brush became a new tool. Moving throughout the colony, I took pollen from the anther of one flower and placed it on the stigma of the next, performing this delicate procedure over and over until I grew weary. My job was finished. Now nature would form seedpods with enough weight to bend the heads of the flowers down so the seeds would tumble out onto the ground and take hold. A few years from now, I would be partly responsible for this new life. For the first time since her birth, I felt free of the intense pain that held me in its powerful grip.

Spring, a major season trapped between two minor ones.

Two more weeks passed before I gathered the courage to visit Mother and Daddy. I pulled into the drive and sat for a moment, my hand rested on the keys still in the ignition, momentarily giving me the impression that I had a choice. Daddy opened the front screen door and waved me inside.

They had renovated an old two-story farmhouse to meet their contemporary needs. Butterscotch siding with a caramel-colored door made it as delectable on the outside as on the inside. Surprisingly, it hung onto its character and charm even after the swarm of carpenters, plumbers, and electricians pulled out of the driveway. Screen doors on both sides welcomed a breeze on hot days, and a wooden swing hung from the wraparound porch. Throughout my childhood, I'd sat on the swing, pushing off from the floor to get that perfect rhythm down before settling in to watch the fireflies drop in and out of sight. *Reek, err, reek, err,* the swing chanted; the sound as pacifying as a lullaby.

My parents had no interest in tilling land or planting a garden; they hired out help to perform all tasks related to the outdoors. They purchased their country home in the small town of Laurel based on Daddy's proclamation that if he lived far enough away from his office, when he left for the day, it would seem like a vacation. We all knew that he hadn't been on holiday in years. Mother went along with this charade. Maybe she didn't argue because miles of farmland now separated him from the beautiful women at the office.

Mother loved everything about the house, except the small kitchen. Daddy thought it plenty big enough. For as long as I could remember, heavy sighs echoed out into the living room whenever she prepared the family meals, along with the unnecessary banging of pots and pans, and dropping of utensils. Her way of saying I told you so. When things got too noisy, Daddy made his way into the kitchen and offered to put the house up for sale, knowing full well that she'd rather cook on a campfire in the backyard than move. He'd smile while the noise level returned to normal.

On this particular night, I was late and missed out on the usual pre-dinner show. I took my seat at the table just as Mother placed a bowl of angel hair pasta with clams and marinara sauce on the table. She always broke out the carbohydrates when someone's mental health was in jeopardy. The question tonight—was it hers or mine?

She twirled the pasta around her fork. "How are things, dear?"

"Good," I said, then grabbed for my glass of water to wash down the lie.

Daddy took a slice of freshly baked bread. "So, Petunia, when are you going back to work at the gallery?"

As usual, my back straightened. I placed my hands neatly across my lap and slid my legs together as if sitting on the witness stand. He never quite shook that attorney look, not even while sitting around the family table dressed in jeans and a Polo shirt.

"I talked to Mr. Farnsworth this morning. He said I could return anytime, as long as I felt up to it. I don't have much sick time so I need to go back soon."

"I see," he said. "It certainly wouldn't hurt to get a job with better benefits since you don't have a husband to provide you with such."

I shook my head. "Daddy, please...not tonight."

Mother jumped to her feet. "Seconds, anyone?"

"No thanks," he said.

She pointed toward the kitchen. "Can I at least freshen your drink while I'm up?"

He nodded and she promptly left the table. Throughout the evening, she filled his glass several more times, cleared his plate, and brought him dessert on cue as if rehearsing for a part in a play.

Daddy put his fork down. "Oh, before I forget, Tulip, Henry wanted me to tell you that the court hearing will be next Thursday."

My glass hit the table with a clank just shy of a shatter. "Next week? But that's...so...so soon."

"Henry's well liked down at the courthouse. He pulled in a favor. It's best to get things taken care of before anything unforeseen happens."

My throat tightened. "Unforeseen? Like what?"

"You never know what can happen within the legal system. That's why there are lawyers to–"

"Coffee, anyone?" Mother interrupted. Anything to keep Daddy from making his 'why we need lawyers' speech.

After Mother and I washed the dishes, I said goodbye. On my way home, I wondered if one of Daddy's girlfriends ever placed a baby for adoption. Suppose he'd been through it several times. Maybe that was the reason he talked about mine as if it were an ordinary occurrence.

I stood at the bottom of the long stretch of steps–twenty-eight to be exact. As a child, I played games on those steps while my father talked to colleagues just outside the courthouse doors.

One, two,
Buckle my shoe;
Three, four,
Knock at the door;
Five, six...

"Come on," Tory said as she gently placed her arm under mine and led me upward. I didn't recall it being so hard to climb to the top.

We entered the courtroom and I sat next to Henry. After several minutes, Judge Klugman entered the room. He had a neatly trimmed beard and his matching white hair looked as though it had been ironed into place. Daddy had warned me that this judge liked his courtroom just as orderly.

I suddenly questioned my appearance. Had I made the right choice? Dressing for court hadn't seemed like such a big deal, until I stood in the closet thumbing through my wardrobe. Then I remembered Daddy's suggestions to his clients. He'd even bought ties now and then for those who didn't own one. "First impressions are everything," he'd say. "You don't want to alienate the judge before you even open your mouth."

I had pulled out the five dresses that I owned. Black seemed melodramatic, flowers frivolous, and pastels too lighthearted. Paisley was motherly and might raise doubts about my ability to follow through with the plan. In the end, I chose a simple, navy dress, not so much for its significance, but because it was the only thing left.

Throughout the trial, Henry tapped his fingers on the table, fidgeted, and rearranged his legal pad. Every once in a while he looked over and gave me a half-smile.

Across the way sat the adoptive couple's attorney. Since it was a closed adoption, the new parents would not be present; he represented their interests. Their attorney leaned back in his chair with his hands folded neatly across his mid-section and waited patiently for his turn to speak, occasionally scratching his baldhead with the tip of his pen.

Why did he look so calm? Could he see that I wasn't going to change my mind?   Did the navy dress make me look too coldhearted, businesslike?

As the judge addressed me, the shame and guilt that loomed overhead at the hospital returned.   And there was something else hauntingly similar–the lack of a partner. Mitch didn't have to stand in open court and explain why *he* didn't want her. I should have claimed him to be the father, then his name would have been attached to the social disgrace just like mine.

I had prepared for the worst by tucking tissues inside my pockets, up my sleeves, and an extra stash in my backpack just in case. The words permanently relinquish jolted me each time I heard them.   Somehow it all seemed, well, so permanent.   Tory stood behind me and placed her hand on my back whenever such emotional words or phrases spewed from the judge's lips. Luckily, minor child and adoptee didn't carry the same impact as baby, or I would have run out of tissues.

Throughout the proceeding, I felt a step behind. Henry tapped my arm and nodded; my prompt to agree with what the judge had just said. I was too busy trying to suppress my overwhelming desire to run out of the building.   Then with a strike of his gavel, Judge Klugman granted my wish. With the hearing now over, she was gone–permanently.

Henry gave me a couple of firm squeezes on the shoulder. "Well, you made it through. Good job. I'll be seeing you." Then he motioned to the adoptive parents' attorney and they walked out together.

The judge returned to his chamber and I remained standing underneath the slight hum of the fluorescent lights. It all happened so fast. Why hadn't I objected to something? Anything. I stared at the wet tissue in my hand, now wadded into a giant ball.

"Cara, it's time to go. I'll get you home," Tory said.

She took my arm and led me through small clusters of people waiting for their turn in court. We went through the revolving door, and into a world that continued on despite my loss. People laughed while strolling down the sidewalk, vehicles whizzed past, and the sound of car horns, a distant train whistle, and a church bell echoed in the cool, spring air. We started to descend the steps.

> *One, two, three, four, five,*
> *Once I caught a fish alive.*
> *Six, seven, eight, nine, ten,*
> *Then I let it go again.*
>
> *Why did you let it go?*

A Woman Named Adelaide

The Farnsworth Gallery sat in the heart of Stony Harbor, three towns over from my apartment in Mission Bay. An affluent area with lakefront property and specialty shops, Stony Harbor drew shoppers from neighboring towns. Storefronts were filled with things not needed in the least, but appreciated by those who could afford them. Lampposts lined the roads along with BMWs.

Oliver Farnsworth, the gallery owner, made only occasional appearances. It was not his primary source of income; more of a hobby, an admission ticket into the art world. While he embraced the art community by attending shows, openings, or charity balls most every weekend, his employees ran the business. But to his credit, he filled the gallery with original works from fine artists, allowing for some limited editions, but never touching mass productions.

I hesitated outside the door. The thought of facing the regular customers who had followed my pregnancy month to month made my stomach churn. How would I even begin to answer their questions? The chime of the bell greeted me as I pushed the door open. Erin, my co-worker, looked toward the front.

"Cara!" She put her coffee cup down and ran toward me, her arms outstretched. She squealed while lifting me off of the floor.

"Hi, Erin."

She let go and my shoes touched the ground again. "You look great. God, it's good to have you back."

"I'm glad to be back."

"It's been nuts around here with all the vacationers. Not to mention, the temporary help didn't know a thing about art. I mean, who can't tell a watercolor from an oil?"

"You...when you first started." I laughed.

"Oh, yeah."

I hung my backpack on the hook behind the counter and studied the room. A few paintings had sold, a few new ones acquired during my absence. My painting of a bouquet of Barrett Brownings was missing from the wall.

Erin smiled. "Yep, it sold."

We worked all morning without one word about the baby. I couldn't blame her for not asking. Even I hadn't been able to say the word since the court hearing. Many customers looked me up and down as if they knew something was different, but couldn't quite figure it out. They'd go to speak, then give the never-mind head shake.

Mrs. St. George noticed everything. Her keen sense of observation was reflected in the artwork she bought, pictures of city life so detailed that even the alleyways had names. She needed a special piece for her foyer, and decided my first day back was the day to indulge.

"So, you obviously had the baby. A girl or a boy?" she asked.

"Girl." I rang up her purchase.

"And what did you name her?"

"Oh, I haven't named her." It was neither a lie nor the complete truth.

"Ah, still waiting for a name to come to you. Baby names *are* difficult." She patted my arm. "Take your time, honey. Once you're named, you're stuck with it for life."

I glanced at her Visa card. A woman named Adelaide had to know what she was talking about.

The rest of the day brought more inquiries. I delicately sidestepped questions without being too evasive or unfriendly. Just as we closed for the day, Tory rushed in. She wobbled over to the counter, her heels unable to keep the pace.

"Are you free for dinner tonight?" she asked.

"Sure, everything okay?" I said.

"I have to talk to you about something. How about The Crow's Nest at six-thirty?"

"Great. I'll just finish up and meet you there."

She darted back into the street without a glance in either direction.

Erin laughed. "Is she always in such a hurry?"

"Tory was born before her due date and she's kept the same

schedule ever since."

I quickly rearranged the artwork to fill the gap left from Mrs. St. George's purchase and locked up the gallery. I needed to get to the restaurant. Tory had important news; she never moved that fast, not even when chasing a man.

The Crow's Nest carried the largest selection of beer on tap in town, enticing the locals to indulge after a hard day at the office. The customers who stood waiting for a seat ducked as platters filled with assorted sandwiches, salads, and soups whisked by their heads.

Tory raced over to the booth, her mouth cockeyed as she chewed her bottom lip.

"What's wrong?" I asked before she even sat down.

She grabbed my hands and jerked me halfway across the table.

"Jesus, this must be serious," I said. "Is it your mother? Did she fall off the wagon again?"

"She's off more than she's on, Cara. Do you think that would be earth shattering news?"

"No, I suppose not."

Tory had become so used to her mother's frequent distress calls that they hardly registered as a crisis. Apparently, the only stretch of time her mother had remained sober was during her pregnancy. Bernice proclaimed victory from her fascination with the bottle those few months and decided to name her daughter accordingly.

Our gazes locked. "So, what is it then?"

"I don't know how to tell you this," she started, "but I ran into Mitch today."

Relief settled over me. "It's okay, Tory, I'm pretty much over him now."

"No, Cara...listen. He was with his wife–"

"Um," I interrupted, "I know about that too, remember?"

She pounded her fist on the table. "No. Cara. Listen. He was with his pregnant wife. His *very* pregnant wife."

"What?" I broke free from her grip. His old wife was very pregnant?

My back slammed against the booth, and the background noises fused together into a giant roar, rising and falling into a distinct pattern of chaos.

Tory had to be wrong. Maybe his old wife was just fat. Very fat.

She patted my hand. "I didn't want to tell you, but I thought you'd find out sooner or later. If you found out that I knew..."

Even in disbelief, I understood her need to keep the best friend allegiance intact.

"That certainly explains a lot," I said as I gazed out the window.

"What an asshole," she said. "Well, we might as well eat while we're here. You'll have plenty of time to worry about it later."

She handed me an open menu as if I still had an appetite.

A Walk in the Park

She was a slender blonde with big, brown eyes and looked part Labrador Retriever and part anyone's guess. Her leash was secured to the fence post, a note attached to the dog collar.

My name is Sadie and I need a good home. Please take care of me. God Bless.

While I paced at the side of the road, kicking rocks with my boots, contemplating what to do, she wagged her tail and stirred up dust. I made my second mistake (the first was stopping my Jeep), by reaching down and tweaking her ear. She looked at me with old, tired eyes.

"Come on, girl." I untied the leash and walked her to the Jeep.

She jumped into the passenger seat as if she'd been riding there all her life and we headed for the pet store and groomer. Later that night, Tory came to see my new roommate.

"So, what'd you name her?" she asked.

"Her name is Sadie. I'm going to keep it. She's not a pup so she's probably used to it by now."

Tory glanced at my new dog that had taken up residence on the sofa. "I suppose she looks like a Sadie."

"And what if she didn't?"

She shrugged. "Then I guess we'd have to change it...to Lucky."

I sighed. "Luck had nothing to do with it. It was fate. She needed me and I needed her."

"Oh, Christ." Tory rolled her eyes.

"There's nothing wrong with believing in fate. It provides for a natural order. Why else do things happen?"

Tory simultaneously folded her arms and crossed her legs. "Because they have to. You know action–reaction. The dog sat there–you picked her up. That's all."

"Well, you can believe whatever you want." I reached over and patted Sadie on the head. "She came to me for a reason. It's a new start for both of us."

Tory chuckled. "It's more likely that she's yours because fifty other people drove on by." She hit my arm. "Hey, speaking of driving by, I heard David is back in town for summer break."

"Really? When did he come back?"

"I'm not sure. He hasn't called."

"Oh, he will," I assured her.

Although, we both knew that when it came to David Wilkins there were no guarantees. He was a drifter in the nicest sense of the word, traveling around the world at his leisure, mostly when classes were out of session, but sometimes not. Spring break had been known to fall in January. Nepal, Paraguay, and Tanzania were not too remote for his interests. He drifted in and out of Tory's life as easily as he did the country, but she never seemed to mind. She loved him. The problem being that every time she planned to tell him, he left before the alarm went off the next morning. Goodbye was never said, just assumed. She dated other men between his vacations into town, but these substitutes never compared to David. She claimed they were not as smart, enlightened, or free-spirited.

"I think *lazy* is the word you're looking for," I would say.

The fact that Tory was happy whenever he came to town was cause enough for me to like the guy, lazy or not. This time, Tory vowed to keep him stateside, even though it was officially summer break.

After Tory left, Sadie followed me around the house the rest of the night. I climbed into bed and slapped the mattress. She hopped up, circled three times, and fluffed the blanket with her paw before collapsing beside me.

I turned out the light and rubbed the back of her neck. "Don't worry girl, you've got a home now. I'll take good care of you."

While I drifted to sleep, I wondered if Baby Jane's new owner had said those exact same words.

The moment Sadie noticed the collie ahead of us, she tugged on the leash so hard that I had no choice but to follow. Once we reached the dog and its owner, she pranced around with her tail at high mast. *Sadie, you big flirt.* I looked up to begin my apology speech. "I'm…"

I started.

There were many ways to end that sentence. "Sorry" being the most appropriate, but "attracted to you immediately" was more accurate. Suddenly, English became a foreign language.

His eyes were unable to settle on any particular shade of brown as they absorbed the last of the evening sunlight. I pictured my palette filled with paints. Burnt sienna was surely their natural color.

He smiled and extended his hand. "Hello, I'm Noah. Noah Meyer."

I surrendered my left hand to his. "Um...I'm Cara Robertson."

He patted his dog's head. "And this is Amadeus."

The strands of sandy brown hair that drifted across Noah's forehead reminded me of the wheat stalks that Aunt Kate and I stopped to admire. He looked toward the end of my leash.

My gaze followed his. "Oh...I'm sorry. This is Sadie."

"A pleasure to meet both of you." His smile registered somewhere between boy and man.

"You, too," I said.

Jesus, what was I doing? I just had a baby. A man should be the last thing on my mind. It wasn't like I had committed myself. I could break off the conversation by simply tugging at Sadie's leash and proceeding in a forward direction. Yes, a snap and release would do it.

Then Noah's eyes met mine.

"There's only a few more minutes left of this beautiful day. Would you like to join me?" he said, pointing to the park bench.

I nodded, then snapped and released in his direction. We sat down and Sadie squeezed in alongside Amadeus who had settled at Noah's feet.

Noah turned to me and said, "I usually go to the park on the other side of town, but I'm finding this one to be much nicer."

That explained why I hadn't recalled seeing him before.

"So…" we both said.

"Go ahead..." we said again, then laughed.

Darkness quickly settled in, producing a chill in the air. He glanced to the sign on the left that read, *Park closed at dusk*.

"An hour earlier tomorrow?" he asked.

"Yes, that would be nice." *Cara, you big flirt.*

As we made our way to the park entrance, I wondered if he could hear my heart beating.

It was five-thirty when we met for the second time. Noah and I made our way around the walking path, the breeze to our backs, Sadie and Amadeus at our sides.

He stopped walking. "I hope this doesn't seem forward, but I would like to go on a real date. You know, without the dogs."

My heart lurched. "When?" Then I instinctively sucked in my belly. Could I lose ten pounds by Saturday? A more disturbing thought–did he think this was my usual weight?

"Saturday night?"

"Great."

We followed the path around the small, man-made lake. Joggers whisked by, a stark contrast to those in paddle bloats in the center of the water who had given up and now floated lazily back toward the dock.

"How about if I call you from the school tomorrow so we can make plans?" he asked.

"School?"

"Yeah, where I teach."

"Oh, that's where you work. I thought you might be a student."

He laughed. "Perhaps we should get to know a little about each other."

We walked over to the park bench and sat down.

"I guess we're doing things backwards," I said.

"That's not always a bad thing...impulsiveness, I mean." Aunt Kate would have approved of him already. "So, what type of work do you do, Cara?"

"I work in an art gallery a couple towns over."

"Let me guess. It pays the rent so you can fulfill your true calling...painting."

I smiled. "Exactly."

"I've been known to take on a few piano students to pay the bills while I try my hand at composing. Whatever it takes to pursue your passion."

Pursue your passion. *Oh, my God. Did he say that, or did I?*

He looked at his watch   "Ah, I have a student coming for a lesson in less than an hour.   Before I leave, I'll need your phone number for tomorrow."

"Oh, yeah.   Right."   I grabbed a piece of paper out of my backpack and jotted the number down.   "Here."   I placed it in his hand; our fingertips brushed past one another producing a chill I had not felt for so long.   Why did it seem so right even though the timing was so wrong?

We made our way to the parking lot.   There was that awkward moment–a goodbye was not enough, yet a kiss on the lips too much. He opted for my cheek, lingering, as if deciding whether to round the corner.   I drove home with my hand firmly pressed to the side of my face.

Shopping with Tory was a challenge.   She liked sparse and tight; I favored layered and loose.   I frantically searched the sale rack and took an armful of clothes into the dressing room.   Tory and I had our usual disagreement.   The boutique was closing and we needed a compromise.

I stood in front of the mirror.   "I think this is it."   I placed the oversized, lavender silk shirt over the white cotton tee to hide the remaining evidence of my pregnancy: the few extra pounds, the stretch marks, the little pooch that still dominated my mid-section.

Tory burrowed her way into the dressing room.   "Lose the shirt. The tee is sexier all by itself."

"Did I say I wanted to be sexy?"

She straightened the collar.   "You're going on a date.   What else would you want to be?"

I looked at my expanded waistline.   "I'm just hoping for presentable.   The shirt stays."

She sighed.   "You can always take it off back at the apartment."

"We won't be going back to the apartment.   This is a first date, remember?"

I turned to the mirror; the dark gray skirt came to rest just above my ankles.

"The slit could be higher," she said.

"It's fine."

"By the way," she said, "I can't believe you're already back into a size seven. A few weeks and you'll be your old skinny self. If I didn't know any better, I would've never known that you even had a baby."

"Gee, that certainly makes me feel better."

"Just an observation." Tory twirled me around and puckered her lips like she did whenever she wasn't quite sure about something. "So, when do I get to meet this so-called musical genius?"

"When I feel he's ready to meet you."

"What's that suppose to mean?"

"Well, you know, you're kind of...how should I say it...direct. I don't know how he'd take your forwardness. Remember the first time you met Mitch?"

She laughed. "You mean when I told him his hair looked plastic from all the hairspray?"

"I think your exact words were helmet head. Not that it wasn't true," I said.

"How'd you ever get into the bathroom with him hogging the mirror all the time, anyway?"

"I'd tell him someone was breaking into his Firebird and he'd make a run for it."

Tory looked at the floor, then slapped my arm. "Hey, speaking of running...what about shoes?"

"Oh, God." I pointed at my hiking boots. "I guess these won't work, huh?"

"Heels," she said.

My hands went to my hips. "Have you ever known me to wear heels?"

"It wouldn't hurt you to try a pair," she muttered as she left the dressing room. She returned with a pair of crisscross, woven shoes and handed them to me. "Against my better judgment, I might add."

I slipped them on. "Perfect."

"They're flats."

"Like I said, perfect."

I paid for my purchases and we headed out the door, giggling like schoolgirls on the way to the prom.

"So," Tory said while walking to the car, "you think you'll introduce this one to your parents?"

"Music teacher."

"Say no more." She unlocked her car door. "Follow me."

"Where to?"

"The salon. You don't think I'd let you go out on a first date without a makeover, do you? My treat."

I knew better than to argue. I just hoped that Noah would still recognize me after Tory was finished with me. We zigzagged through town and pulled up to Rejuvenation Station. Tory jumped out of the car and motioned me to join her. I followed her inside and sat down in the waiting area while she talked to the receptionist. The woman behind the counter consulted her computer screen and Tory nodded. I watched as women walked around doing half-hearted mummy impersonations and wearing sandals with cotton laced between their newly painted toenails. Some carried cups of tea or coffee while dressed in white, cotton robes, looking as comfortable as they would in the privacy of their own homes. I suddenly realized this was Mother's life: Monday–manicure, Wednesday–waxing, Friday–facial. "Easier to remember that way," Mother said. Daddy said it was a good thing that they didn't offer a Turkish bath or Taiwanese Massage or she'd be there all week.

Tory eventually made her way back over. "Okay, this is the itinerary."

"Itinerary! Geez, we need a schedule?"

"Well, they can't do everything to you at the same time."

I jumped up. "What do you mean everything? You said it was just a haircut and makeup."

She grabbed my arm and pulled me back into the chair. "So, I added a manicure and pedicure. I didn't think you'd mind. Besides, miracles are worth the effort."

"Do I *need* a miracle?"

"Relax. You like this Noah guy, right?"

I nodded.

"I'm going to make damn sure he stays around then. We don't need another Mitch on our hands."

"It's not like Mitch left me because I didn't wear eyeliner or because my toenails weren't painted."

"No, but have you ever thought that maybe his wife *did* all those things. Look, I'm going to run some errands. I'll come back when they're done with you."

"But…"

"You'll be fine. Trust me," she tossed over her shoulder.

Customers came and went as I waited for my miracle to occur. They entered the salon plain and tired like me, and left beautiful and rejuvenated. I pictured the new Cara, my hair more of a blunt cut and the makeup just enough of an accent to leave people wondering if it were natural beauty. My nails were polished with a shade of deep lavender to coordinate with my new outfit. But even after the makeover, there was still something unsightly, troublesome.

"Cara Robertson," the stylist called.

I darted toward the woman in the long, white lab coat in hopes of being transformed. Perhaps if I hurried, I could add the guilt reducing therapy treatment.

The Waterfront restaurant was known for its magnificent view of the lake. Built on Wyndham Bluff, one could clearly see the lighthouse on the right, and to the left, a long stretch of beach houses in an assortment of pastel colors. At night, their porch lights lit up the beach like an airport runway. Beyond the houses sat the marina, where people paid an exorbitant amount of money for a boat slip; something viewed as a necessity rather than a luxury.

I was running late, so I met Noah at the restaurant. As soon as I arrived, Ethan Clark, the owner, led Noah and me to a table in front of one of the large picture windows. Ethan pulled out my chair. "I think this table will be to your satisfaction. Enjoy your evening." He turned on his heel and made his way to the front of the restaurant.

We sat down and I looked at Noah across the candlelit table.

"My God, you look fabulous," Noah said.

"Thanks. So do you." The khakis, navy blue sport coat, and brightly colored tie wore his body well.

"So," we said.

We laughed, then he pointed at me. "You first."

"Okay. Have you taught at the school very long?"

"This will be my third year. It's my first job since graduation."

I took a hard look at the Crème Brulee at the table to the left, knowing full well that I wouldn't be ordering dessert tonight, then drew my attention back to Noah. "Oh, and where did you study music?"

A trail of steam swirled up around us and Noah waited for the hissing platter of mussels to be carried out of earshot before he answered. "Julliard," he finally said.

My hand quickly covered my mouth to stifle a laugh.

He smiled. "What, may I ask, is so funny?"

"From New York to Michigan. I just find it odd that you ended up here of all places."

"Actually, I had other plans. A good friend of mine was going to open a private music school in Vienna, and he wanted me to help him get the school started. Unfortunately, his dream was delayed and this job was available. So...here I am."

"This is certainly a far cry from Austria."

"I don't mind. I was tired of the big city. When I came here to interview, it looked like a perfect place." He pointed to the lake where the orange sun hovered above the water as if testing the temperature before diving in. "With a view this gorgeous, how could I say no?"

A single line of boats made their way toward the no-wake zone. The serious boaters were notorious for using every moment of daylight, relying on the sunset to provide just enough light to dock. Once in awhile their timing was off and they'd have to rely on instinct.

"So, what about you, Cara? What keeps you here?"

My trips to the countryside with Aunt Kate came to mind. "Oh, for the contrast between the seasons, I suppose, especially the arrival of spring. Nothing can beat the slight chill in the morning air when I paint out in the field."

The waiter came over to take our order.

"Cara?" Noah said.

I was starved. "Oh...um...just the Caesar chicken salad for me." I would have to make myself a bigger meal later, or stuff my purse full of fancy crackers for the ride home.

He looked up at the waiter. "I'll take the rainbow trout."

Throughout the evening, Noah talked about his love of music and his respect for the talented students in his class. His eyes widened and voice quickened whenever he spoke of his true passion– the piano. I understood this love; it was the same ardor I felt whenever I picked up my brush. He listened to me talk about the way the smell of turpentine and linseed oil made me spontaneously smile, and the way that my palette was merely an extension of my arm. I had met a man who not only understood me, but also the artist within me, something I had waited for all my life.

After dinner, he walked me to my Jeep.

"It seems we have a lot in common. I enjoy your company, Cara."

This time there was no awkward moment. I stood motionless as he bent his head slightly to the side and moved toward me. The fresh scent of shampoo drifted past, while I closed my eyes and accepted his warm, moist kiss. Our lips parted, then eagerly met again, as if for the first time. I reluctantly pulled away to catch my breath.

"Can we see each other again?" he asked.

"Yes," I said, startled by my lack of hesitation.

"When?"

"Tomorrow."

"Great. I look forward to it."

After he left the parking lot, I reclined the driver's seat and looked up to the starlit sky, knowing this was how it was supposed to be. I still smelled the clean scent of his hair and felt the warmth of his mouth on mine. Best of all, I recalled the fervor in his voice when he talked about his passion–his music.

Noah let me choose the activity this time. He climbed into the Jeep and watched out the window, heaving a sigh of contentment every few miles. I pointed out the old, gray barn minus the door; its one side nearly parallel to the ground, but the words Mail Pouch Tobacco still held steady. "Those advertisers surely got their money's worth, wouldn't you say?" Aunt Kate would ask every time we drove past.

The empty, roadside produce stands reminded me of what was

soon to come. "You haven't lived until you get a bushel basket of fresh peaches from the Watson farm," I pointed out.

Noah nodded. "I suppose you'll have to bring me back for a sampling."

I rounded the last corner with the usual anticipation, then pointed to the dirt path as I parked. "Look, there it is!"

Noah opened his door and stretched out his leg. "After the fifteenth mile or so, I thought you were kidnapping me. Not that it would be a bad thing." He looked at the road sign. "Oak Hill Lane. Now doesn't that conjure up pleasant thoughts?"

"Just wait."

We walked to the fence and he stopped at the NO TR SP S ING sign.

I stepped over the wire and motioned him to follow. "It's all right. I do it all the time."

He shrugged and stepped over the fence and we walked toward the creek. "Wow, how'd you ever find this place?" he asked as he looked across the field.

A day I'd never forget. "When I was nine years old I decided to run away from home. So, I packed a small bag and started walking. I thought I'd hide over there in the tall field grass until my parents became sufficiently worried. Like until dinnertime."

I pulled the folded blanket from under my arm. Noah grabbed the opposite corners and we spread it out under the oak tree.

"But I wasn't planning on a huge swarm of grasshoppers flying at me. I ran out the other side of the grass and ended up here."

"You went back home, I take it."

"Yeah, to grab my canvas, brushes and paints."

He laughed. "So much for your parents being worried."

"Oh, on the contrary. To them, spending all my time painting was more worrisome than my running away!" We sat down and I pointed to the left. "The daffodils bloom in that field." Their season was now over and their wilted stems were parallel to the ground. I swept my hands out in front of me. "This is how I picture Heaven."

He placed his hand upon my cheek. "Me, too."

"My place to ponder life's most serious questions."

He stood and pulled me to my feet, leading me over to the tall field grass. "Hey, I've got a serious question for you."

"And what might that be?"

"Would you mind if I kissed you again?"

I shook my head and he cupped my face in his hands, pressing his lips into mine. A deep longing for his touch pushed aside thoughts of the past. He wasn't like Mitch, I told myself as the grass whipped back and forth against my legs with each gust of wind. The birds sang their songs and the creek trickled in the background. All things in nature continued on despite our presence, reinforcing my belief that we were as natural as the landscape that surrounded us.

The bell on the gallery door chimed. Erin and I looked toward the front. A gentleman began browsing at the paintings near the entrance. His tortoiseshell glasses made him look more intelligent than anyone had a right to be. Erin nodded toward his feet. Even his shoes matched his perfectly tailored suit. His charcoal hair reminded me of the color of my drawing pencils.

I nudged Erin. "This one's yours," I whispered.

"What? You're giving this one up so easily?"

"Yep. Not interested."

She hopped off the stool and walked over to him. "Can I help you find something, sir?"

"I thought I'd just take a look around, thank you," he answered without shifting his gaze from the artwork.

"Great. Just let me know if you need anything." She slinked back behind the counter and we watched as he leaned in to each picture for a closer look.

"Serious buyer," she whispered.

"Or jerk," I murmured.

The bell chimed once again. "All yours," Erin said.

"Thanks."

An elderly woman held a cane in one hand and large envelope in the other.

I walked to the front. "Hello. What can I help you with today?"

"I'm hoping to get this photograph framed." She stuck the cane under her arm, her legs temporarily gaining independence while she slid the picture out of the envelope. The photo had at least twenty people crammed together, smiling with arms around one another like a high school class reunion. "You can frame this, can't you?" She handed it to me.

"Sure. Is this your family?" I asked, noting the resemblance.

"Yes, ma'am. Four generations of the McKnights." She pointed at a little boy wearing a double-breasted, wool suit that appeared to be squeezing the joy right out of him. "That's my great grandson, Kyle. Isn't he a peach?"

"He certainly is. Why don't we make our way to the counter and we can work on the frame selection?"

I pulled several different moulding samples and mat corners from the wall, while Erin's attention remained glued to the mysterious man winding his way through the gallery.

The woman tapped the counter with her cane. "You look familiar. Do I know your mother?"

"Maybe. Do you frequent the Fenwick Hills Country Club?"

She laughed. "Doubt they'd take an old woman on Social Security."

I placed a cream-colored mat around the picture, then looked up to find the man standing in front of the painting next to the counter.

She glanced down at the picture. "Oh, I like that color. Neutral's good from what I hear. Flashy colors take away from the picture, isn't that right?"

"Yes, that's right. Less is more," I said while staring at the gentleman's diamond cufflinks.

She shook her finger at me. "Now, what did you say your name was?"

"Actually, I didn't. But it's Cara. Cara Robertson."

"Robertson...now where have I heard that name? By golly, I bet your father is Sam Robertson, the man in the plumbing business. Been around for years. Must be good money in it. His radio advertisement made me laugh every time I heard it. What was it? Wait now...it'll come to me." She smiled. "Ah, yes, I have it now. 'We'll put on the rush, when we know that you can't flush.'"

"Well, that's certainly a great jingle. But, my father is an attorney in Laurel."

The man looked up as if about to speak, but instead, he turned and made his way to the back of the gallery.

I grabbed two more moulding samples from the wall and placed them on the corners of the photo.

"That's a far cry from a plumber," the woman said. "Though, I'm certain there are similarities between the two jobs these days, with the justice system going down the commode and all."

"I'm sure my father would agree." I pointed to the picture. "What do you think?"

"Why, it looks lovely. Almost has an antique quality to it, wouldn't you say? We do go back several generations, you know. Seems like every year one's dying and another one's being born."

I looked at the photo again. Young and old stood next to each other blurring the lines of the past and the future by merely enjoying the present.

The woman chuckled. "Funny how life goes on regardless whether or not you're here, isn't it?"

"Yes, how true."

Her hand came to rest on mine. "You've been most helpful, honey."

"So have you." I handed her an invoice. "We'll see you in a week."

She walked out of the gallery humming the plumbing jingle.

A few minutes later, the gentleman approached the counter and turned to Erin.

"The artist who paints these flowers...this Cara Robertson. Would I be able to leave my business card for her to call me? I didn't see exactly what I was looking for, but her work intrigues me."

"Well, I don't know." Erin tilted her head back and forth in my direction. "She's awfully hard to get in touch with."

I extended my hand. "Hi, I'm Cara Robertson."

"Jack Templeton. Nice to meet you."

"So, what exactly are you looking for, Mr. Templeton?" I walked out from behind the counter.

He led me to the painting of a bouquet of Poeticus. "Something similar to this, but much larger. I want it to be the focal point of the room."

"What type of room?"

"The living room, over the mantel. I plan to buy a house soon."

I laughed. "Don't you think it would be a good idea to get the house first? To make sure the art is congruent with the architecture?"

"You don't want my business?" He turned toward the door.

I grabbed his suit coat. "No…it's…it's not that at all." He looked down at his arm and I pulled my hand away in embarrassment. "Sorry," I said.

"I'll work around the painting," he assured me. "When I see something I want, I grab it."

My fear of him leaving empty-handed subsided. "I'm sure we can work something out, Mr. Templeton. What time frame are you looking at?"

He handed me his business card. "Call me, tomorrow morning at ten o'clock." Then he promptly left the gallery, the chime of the door his goodbye.

Erin said, "Good God! There aren't many men with a backside as nice looking as their front."

I glanced at the card in my hand. "Oh, great. An attorney. He'll probably sue me if he doesn't like it."

She sat down. "My, aren't you the lucky one? You have a commissioned painting by a gorgeous man. An attorney nonetheless. So, do you still think he's a jerk?"

I smiled. "Even jerks can have great taste in art."

According to the card, the firm of Derby, Dunn, and Whitaker specialized in corporate law and real estate. With industrial growth at an all time high, the firm thought it best to add another associate, or so my father had heard. That associate was Jack Templeton, a Stanford Law graduate who'd been practicing on the West Coast for a few years prior to coming to town.

"Dunn wooed his nephew's hotshot friend here from California, supposedly to groom him for partnership," Daddy said. "Apparently, Templeton had been promised partnership at his last firm, but was passed over. He must be a hell of an attorney for Dunn to recruit him."

Quite a compliment coming from Daddy.

"I have to give it to Dunn, the old bastard. He stays aggressive, something his clients seem to appreciate." A look of concern swept across Daddy's face. "Why do you ask?"

"Oh, it's nothing important. It's just that Mr. Templeton came into the gallery and commissioned me to paint a picture for his new home."

"That certainly sounds important to me, Tulip. If you get enough private clients, maybe you can open your own gallery and stop giving all the profits to Farnsworth. This Templeton must have good taste."

"I'd certainly like to think so." I looked around the room. "Have you seen Sadie?"

"She's sunbathing out back with your mother."

I walked outside and found Mother resting near her rose garden with Sadie at her feet. "Hi," I called from the patio.

She sat up and readjusted her straw hat atop her head. "Oh, hello, dear." She took off her sunglasses and looked me up and down. "Cara, have you lost weight?"

"Well, yes, a few pounds. Speaking of lost weight, has Steph been over lately? It seems like I haven't seen her in forever."

"She stopped by a couple of days ago after her doctor's appointment."

I plopped down in the wicker chair and swung my feet onto the ottoman. "Doctor? Is she sick?"

"I wouldn't call it sick, exactly. It's more like..." She picked at her clothing as she always did when a topic of discussion showed the slightest promise of confrontation.

"What is it, Mother?"

"It seems that she went to see some infertility specialist. She waited sometime before making the appointment. You know your sister. She hates to think that her body functions at anything less than perfect."

"And how long has she been trying to get pregnant?" My feet dropped to the floor and I leaned forward, my eyes welling with tears. "I didn't know she wanted a baby."

"Well, she is married, and that's the usual order of things." Mother took off her hat and looked at me. "Oh dear, you're crying. I knew I shouldn't have mentioned it. That you might take it the wrong way."

"And how am I supposed to take it?" Then it hit me. *Who would want a baby with his genetic influence? It would be damaged from day one*, Steph had said. She had never even considered it.

"You don't actually feel as though she should've taken your baby, now do you?"

"No, of course not," I said, trying to ignore the increasing pressure in my chest.

"I didn't think so. Besides, that would have been rather awkward, don't you think?"

Of course it would've been awkward. Steph never was one to accept hand-me-downs.

Business as Usual

Pier Pointe was the gathering place for community activities. Fundraiser walkathons, festivals, and outdoor concerts shared this park along the lakefront. The townspeople of Stony Harbor took recreation seriously and put up the tax dollars to prove it. Noah and I spent nearly every weekend there. Once, we even attended a cherry spitting contest and a wood carving demonstration as an excuse to spend time together.

The beach was within walking distance from the park. As we strolled along the shoreline, tourists sizzled under the hot sun like rows of kielbasa on a grill. Windsurfers defied the law of gravity while their triangles of candy apple red, canary yellow, and sun-kissed orange panned across the perfect backdrop of sky blue. Behind them, cigarette boats with their sleek lines grazed the water's surface as they raced to the marina. The roar of the engines could still be heard long after they were out of view.

"Simply amazing," Noah said as we sidestepped sandcastles along the lakefront.

We made our way farther inland and spread a blanket over the sand.

"So, Noah," I said, "you never told me how you first became interested in music."

"It was my parents' suggestion. They felt I had a gift for music and suggested I make a career of it."

"Wait, let me get this straight. They actually *encouraged* you to pursue a degree in the arts?" A twinge of jealousy shot through me. "I suppose they made sure you had the means to practice?"

"I took lessons from a neighbor lady." He laughed. "But, believe it or not, most of my studying took place in the crawl space of our home."

He recalled every detail. How the light made its way from one corner to the other throughout the day, telling him which meal to expect next. The distinct pattern of squeaks in the floorboards from pacing back and forth to the tempo of the classical music coming from the record player in the middle of the room. In the smallest area of his family's Cape Cod home, Noah stood on a stool for hours, a chopstick for a baton, and conducted the musicians of his imaginary orchestra.

"Mom and Dad eventually bought me a piano. Used, of course," he said. "The middle C stuck and it was in desperate need of a tune-up, but I didn't mind."

I pictured his hands flowing effortlessly over the black and white keys as if that was the only thing they were made for.

The crawl space remained his favorite place to write music whenever he returned home. Noah admitted that he could have chosen a larger area in which to work; however, he believed that music written in such a compact place yearned to disperse itself amongst an audience before the first note was ever played.

Later, we sat under the glow of the moon and watched as the waves dragged the sandcastles out into the water. Noah shook his head. "Good thing the people who built those don't know what just happened to their masterpieces."

While the activities along the shore were entertaining, Noah said they couldn't compare to the weekly concert in the park. The outdoor band shell was perched at the top of the grassy hill. Every Wednesday afternoon, the local symphony performed. The sounds of Handel, Mozart, and Tchaikovsky floated out over the lake, much to the delight of the boaters anchored nearby. Noah and I enjoyed the concert from the hill overlooking Lake Michigan.

He stretched out with his head in my lap, his eyes closed to avoid distraction from the landscape that surrounded us. Each time music burst forth from the orchestra, I was quick to start, but he didn't flinch.

"Ah," he said. "*Allegro Spiritoso*." He smiled without opening his eyes.

I watched as Noah breathed in every note, keeping the tempo with his index finger. While he conducted the musicians, I studied his handsome face. Just as Noah took in every note as he would his own music, I studied every line and crease as if it were my own face;

memorizing how his eyes were the perfect distance from his nose and how his angular jawbones firmly held his cheeks in place.

As always, the corners of his lips turned upward in anticipation of a strong finish; my cue to stop staring at him and look toward the water. He opened his eyes and we held hands while the sun turned crimson in color and dropped to the water's edge.

"Will it be like this forever, Noah?" I whispered.

He folded his hands across his chest and looked skyward. "I hope so."

His words carried a hint of a plea.

On my way over to the restaurant to meet Mr. Templeton, I practiced my sales pitch aloud, anticipating his questions as if campaigning for political office. I lined up rebuttals to possible concerns he may have about my artistic abilities. Yes, this was my first commissioned painting, but I had years of experience and a Master of Fine Arts Degree from the University of Michigan, graduating with honors nonetheless. No, I had never won a juried show, but that is not necessarily indicative of good painting. In desperation, I could mention the first place ribbon I received for a 4-H exhibit as a youth, but I hoped it wouldn't come to that. I took a deep breath, straightened my skirt, and headed into the restaurant clutching my portfolio.

While I waited for him to arrive, men in suits huddled around tables and booths, with briefcases afoot, discussing the best way to invest their money. Closing numbers for the Dow Jones and the NASDAQ reverberated within the walls of The Mile Post Inn. There was not a casual conversation to be heard. Perfect. Just the message I wanted to send to Mr. Templeton—my painting was serious business.

After thirty minutes, the sales pitch streaming through my head had lost its freshness. I was no longer a gifted artist, but a tired, irritable, hungry woman who would be lucky to draw the color wheel. I gathered my backpack and portfolio to leave. Then I saw him walk through the door, and quickly sat back down before he caught a glimpse of my impatience.

He came over to the table. "Sorry I'm late. Business. Can't seem to get away from it."

I nodded. "Hello, Mr. Templeton."

"Please, call me Jack."

"Okay...Jack."

He folded his hands and placed them on the table in front of him. His sharp-edged knuckles were so different from Noah's smooth hands. "So," he said, "we're here to discuss the painting."

"Yes, you can look at my portfolio." I reached to my side to grab it.

His phone rang and he waved off my suggestion as he mouthed, "not necessary."

"Hello," he answered. "Yes, the hearing is at two o'clock. I'm fully aware of that. I'll see you then." He put the phone down and looked at me. "Now, as you were saying?"

"I have some photographs of some of my previous works if you'd like to take a look. It depends upon whether you prefer a landscape or a still life–" my sales pitch was interrupted by a ring.

"Yes," he answered. "Not there yet? It was mailed three days ago. It has to be there. Look again and if it's not, call my secretary." After he hung up, he stared off in the distance.

"Jack?" I said.

He ignored me like an all too familiar train whistle.

I tapped his arm. "Um...the pictures."

"Oh, yes. Where were we?"

I cleared my throat. "Personally, I think a still life would be nice. A bouquet of white Poeticus in a bronze vase would make a striking contrast."

He shrugged. "Anything would be fine. Whatever you decide."

"Well, it is your painting. I prefer that you have a say in the matter."

He raised his hand and motioned for the waitress. "You're the artist. The expert. I trust your judgment."

"It's not a matter of judgment, Mr. Templeton. You're the one that asked me to paint the picture. You need to..." *Shut up, Cara. Shut up, shut up, shut up*. No wonder Daddy said I'd make a horrible witness on the stand. I swallowed my annoyance and decided to take a different approach. Talk of money was sure to get his attention. "Do you want to know what I charge for such a piece?"

"I'm sure you'll be fair."

I fell back into my chair exhausted from the effort. "I certainly don't feel that I've given you the information you need to make an informed decision."

"I know all that I need to know."

He didn't notice the irritation in my voice.

Meanwhile, the portly waitress wobbled across the room like a washing machine on the spin cycle with an uneven load. Jack placed her on hold and answered the phone again. While he chatted about buy-sell agreements, piercing the corporate veil, and non-dischargeable debt, I turned to the server and ordered a double steakburger, fries, and a big, fat, chocolate milkshake. Maybe he would notice *that*. He remained on the phone for the next twenty minutes while I stuffed myself. I had no idea why Jack Templeton had commissioned me to paint a picture. The only thing I did know was that I had a stomachache.

Noah wanted to go back to the creek before summer's end. I chose a spot under the largest oak tree to shade us from the hot sun, while he brought the picnic basket from the car.

"Are you ready?" His hands pushed down on the lid of the basket as if to keep the food from jumping out like a Jack-in-the box.

I nodded.

He opened the top. "We've got Pita bread, hummus, and a bottle of pinot noir to start. Followed by roasted baby vegetables and tortellini salad. Lastly, pineapple, papaya, and mango fruit salad."

"What a nice selection, Mr. Meyer."

"Thank you, Ms. Robertson. I long for your approval."

We started the meal off with our table manners; using the correct utensils and dabbing the corners of our mouths with the cloth napkins he had tucked away in the bottom of the basket. It didn't take long before we resorted to using our fingers to feed each other in between giggles. Pineapple juice dribbled down our chins, which made us laugh even harder. Soon we were holding our sides, unable to eat another bite.

"Let's go for a walk," he suggested, then pulled me to my feet. "This is your territory, so you lead the way."

I led him down the dirt path, our hands woven together. Sadie and Amadeus entertained themselves by chasing squirrels and jumping in and out of the creek bed. We turned to our usual talk of painting and music. He stopped and twirled me toward him.

"Cara, I have something to tell you," he said.

I smiled. "Yes, Noah."

His touch on my cheek felt urgent, desperate.

"I'm...I'm..."

"Noah? What's wrong?"

He pulled back, pausing briefly as if to speak. Instead, he shook his head, then placed his mouth on my neck and kissed down the front of my throat. We fell to our knees, while kissing in between deep breaths laced with passion. Suddenly, memories of bright lights, stirrups, and sterile tools robbed me of the pleasure to come. I pushed him aside.

"I'm sorry," he said. "I shouldn't have. The timing...it wouldn't be right."

My God, he knows about the baby. Why did I think I could fool him so easily? Tears streamed down my cheeks. "I should've told you earlier."

He pulled back. "What? But I'm the one that should have–"

"Asked? No, I should've been honest. I didn't mean to keep it from you. I've wanted to tell you for so long."

A puzzled look flashed across his face. "Cara?"

I turned to the creek to find the strength to say the words that I had not repeated for so long. "I got pregnant a while back by an old boyfriend. When he found out, he left me." I bowed my head. "I placed her for adoption...never even saw her." Tears dropped into my lap. "I have no idea where she is."

He tilted my chin upward and stroked the back of my hair. "God, I'm so sorry. I would've never..."

"I left the hospital with nothing but a backpack, Noah. A stupid backpack. I was terrified to tell you. God, I hope this doesn't change anything between us."

He looked at me as a tear made its way down his face. "Of course not."

It was no longer a dirty, shameful secret. I now had the freedom to tell him how I longed for her in the middle of the night, and peered into every stroller, hoping to get a glimpse of what I had given away. He would know that when the pain became unbearable, I grabbed the five-pound sugar bag from the kitchen cupboard and gently rocked it in my arms. I fell onto his chest and we sat under the summer sun for the longest time, and he never once suggested that we move somewhere cooler. From that moment, I not only had the freedom to be Cara, the artist, but also Cara, the grieving mother of a baby girl.

The day the nurse wheeled me out of the hospital empty-handed, I had vowed never to return. But when Steph's husband called there was no choice but to go. My breath quickened while recalling the trip past the nursery, the ride down the elevator, and pulling away from the curb. I took a deep breath and forced my way over to the information desk.

Just keep breathing, I reminded myself, as I approached the receptionist. "Can you tell me what room Stephanie Braun is in, please?"

She scrolled down the computerized list. "Room three fifty four. Take the elevator at the end of the hall."

I got off on the third floor and saw Andrew getting coffee in the visitor's lounge. His unshaven face and wrinkled clothing told a story I didn't want to hear.

"Andrew," I called, "how is she?"

He ran his fingers through his disheveled hair. "They don't know yet. She lost a lot of blood."

I gasped. "Blood? From what?"

"Ectopic pregnancy. One of her tubes ruptured."

"My God, I had no idea she was even pregnant."

"Neither did we. This was how we found out."

How cruel to discover your baby, then lose it in the same day. "Can I see Steph?"

"She's still in recovery. They're supposed to let me know when she gets to her room."

"Are Daddy and Mother here?"

"On their way."

A woman in scrubs walked over. "Mr. Braun, your wife is

stable and should be moved to her room in about an hour."

"Oh, thank God. So, she's all right then?" he said.

"She's alert and talking. The doctor will give you more details. But, yes, she's doing rather well." The nurse turned and went back to her workstation.

I looked at my watch. "I think I'll run down to the pay phone and call the gallery to let Erin know I'm here. Do you mind?"

"No, go ahead. I'll be in the room."

I rode the elevator down to the first floor and walked toward the lobby. A few cars sat parked in the circle drive. Then his car pulled up. I knew that car anywhere. Mitch kept his red Firebird shiny enough to catch his reflection each time he strolled past. In the center of the lobby, my muscles froze. People darted around me with wheelchairs, canes, and portable oxygen tanks. I stood motionless with clenched fists, nails cutting into my palms.

For months, I had wondered what his old wife looked like. To ease the pain, I pictured her Grimm Fairy Tale ugly. Her hair dull and unmanageable. Overweight with acne, she waddled into Walgreens at midnight to secretly purchase depilatory cream for her upper lip. The truth on the other side of the window was far from what I had imagined. Even after childbirth, her clear, bronze skin glowed in the sunlight and her shiny hair remained styled to perfection. I doubted she ever stepped foot in a Walgreens. Her beauty nullified the satisfaction I felt every time I thought of him being stuck with her for the rest of his life.

Mitch put away the camcorder and loaded the suitcase into the car. Then he tugged on the infant car seat to make sure it was secured into place before taking the pink bundle from his wife's arms.

A girl. I struggled to hold back my tears.

He gently lowered the child in, buckled the safety belt, then tucked her in with an additional blanket. Next, the new mother got out of the wheelchair with help from the nurse. He stood on the other side, lightly touching his wife's arm to make sure that she kept her balance. After she climbed into the front passenger seat, he closed her door, shook the nurse's hand, and hopped in the car to drive off to Happy Land. It was exactly how I had pictured it to be if I'd left with my baby.

Worlds Apart

By the end of August, tourists left town by the carload and headed south for home. Even though the local merchants needed the increased sales, the town seemed to breathe a sigh of relief, freed from the extra weight it had carried over the past few months. The townspeople would get their favorite parking spaces back and could reclaim their usual booths at restaurants. The long line at the local ice cream shop was reduced to a grandfather treating his grandson and a police officer grabbing a sundae between calls. The beach no longer accommodated towel-to-towel sunbathers, but rather a scattering of locals, as if some celestial artist had taken a paintbrush and splattered the sand with a shake of the wrist. I suppose Floridians felt the same way when snowbirds returned north at the first hint of spring.

It was entertaining to watch people cram their vehicles with inflatable rafts, oversized beach umbrellas, and fishing poles that they purchased while on vacation. The fathers pounced on the trunks and wondered why they didn't have the same problem when packing for the trip. Cars burdened with boats, bikes and canoes gassed up one last time at the Amoco station on the corner. The cars pulled back out onto the road with children pressing their hands against the back windows as if reaching out for one last moment of fun.

Steph had recovered from her hospital stay and appeared not to have given the failed pregnancy another thought. She busied herself changing her clothing line from short sleeve to long. While the end of summer was disheartening for some, I considered it one season closer to spring. Noah would return to teaching soon. He surprised me with a last minute dinner invitation at his apartment.

"Something smells good," I said, following him back to his kitchen.

He held up a bottle of Chardonnay. "Wine?"

"Sure."

His kitchen was simple; the counters held nothing more than a toaster, coffeemaker, electric can opener, and microwave. Mother would deem it a typical man's kitchen. "They're just limited when it comes to preparing food, dear," she'd often say, then quickly cut Daddy's steak for him, as if to either prove her point or make sure he stayed that way.

"Please, sit down." Noah gestured, before placing the tuna fillet, couscous, and asparagus in front of me.

"This looks wonderful," I said. "I thought we could plan dinner with my friend, Tory, soon. She's been asking to meet you for a while."

He looked up, nodded slightly, but said nothing. Throughout dinner, Noah ate little and spoke even less. The distance between us was inescapable. I had to ask.

"Noah, is something wrong?"

He rearranged his food without looking up. My heart quickened with each scrape across the plate. When he finally raised his head, his eyes were moist. "Do you remember when I told you that I might have an opportunity to teach in Vienna?"

"Yes," I said, my throat narrowed. I gripped the arms of the chair as he got up and walked across the floor to his desk. He returned and placed a letter on the table. My attention could not get beyond the Vienna postmark.

"The music school's finally up and running. Hans wants me to come and teach."

I stared at the envelope. *This is not happening. He has to say no.*

"Cara, say something. Anything."

I love you. Please don't go. I'm begging you to stay. I can't live without you, was what I wanted to say. I lifted my head and stared straight ahead. "Well..."

"God knows I don't want to leave," he said, "but this is an opportunity of a lifetime. It's Vienna. I may never get another chance like this. Cara, do you understand that's why I can't pass this up?"

The truth of the matter was that I did understand. It would be the same reason I couldn't refuse a job in France to teach art, but I wasn't going to admit that to Noah. Instead, I longed to drop to my knees and hang from his leg, letting him drag me around the apartment while he filled his toiletry kit.

He reached for me, but my hands grew rigid, unyielding as I noticed the date on the envelope. "You've known for weeks."

He brushed the hair back from my face. "I'm sorry, Cara. I meant to tell you sooner. I planned to tell you during our last visit to the creek, but it wasn't the right time. I must have tried a hundred times since then and–"

"So, when do you go?" I interrupted, feeling both his betrayal and loyalty.

"Tomorrow."

There is no way this is happening. Not Noah. He can't leave me. "Jesus." I dropped my fork. "But...but, what about your students here?"

"The school had a replacement in mind, so they didn't mind the short notice."

"Well, I don't have a replacement and I *do* mind." My tears splattered the envelope. If only they could wash away this so-called chance of a lifetime.

He came to my side and placed his arms around my neck, pulling me close. "I'm sorry, Cara. I wish the timing were different. You know that."

Bad timing–I knew all about that. Sadness won out over anger, followed by a flash of hope as I glanced around the room. There were no boxes, packing tape, or thick black markers.

"But you're nowhere near ready to leave tomorrow," I pointed out. "Nothing's packed. You can't possibly go so soon."

"My parents are coming in the morning to get Amadeus. They'll pack everything and put it into storage until I get back."

I turned sharply toward him. "Back?"

"Well, yes. You didn't think I was going to stay in Vienna forever, did you?"

"How long?" I asked in desperation.

"I'm not sure at this point. Two years, maybe three."

"Two...years?"

"We'll get through this." He scooped the letter off the table. "You said it was fate that you found Sadie and fate that Sadie found

Amadeus in the park that day. I have to think this is fate as well. For some reason, I've been called to Vienna."

Fate–the word now used against me. How ridiculous it sounded.

Clergy sold blind faith from pulpits on a weekly basis, and reminded their flocks to trust that whatever happened to them was in their best interest. "Don't ask why," the pastor warned. "Just believe." I gripped the cross that hung around my neck and felt for the reason behind Noah leaving me, but found none.

As Noah held me tight, I knew that I'd never allow myself to love this way again. With our cheeks touching, his tears became mine and mine his. The words I love you rested on my tongue so long, I tasted their sweetness. But, because of ill timing, just as Baby Jane, he would never hear those three words leave my lips.

To say that a Poeticus flower was splendid was like saying Michigan winters were chilly. One only had to walk a short distance down the creek bed from where the jonquils bloomed to see the Poeticus field, a smaller colony, but their beauty more than made up for it. Appearing later than the jonquils, the two never competed for my attention, nor could they be compared. The jonquils possessed a simple beauty. Their solid yellow color had an uninterrupted flow; the entire flower taken into the eye at once. The Poeticus were more complex with their virgin white petals and vibrant dash of green and yellow added to the center of the disc-shaped corona. But it was the red, crinkled rim that captured the eye and drew you in. Not a meek or timid red, but Coca-Cola can red. God knew what He was doing, for no bee could resist this magnificent flower.

I made my way to my easel in the spare bedroom. Over the last several weeks, I had sketched the flowers onto the canvas. Next, shadow work, then roughing in the colors. My palette started with titanium white, pure and unspoiled like the first snowfall to cover the ground each winter, followed by the others: cadmium yellow, yellow ochre, viridian, cerulean, cobalt blue, cadmium red, burnt sienna, raw umber, Payne's gray. I flipped through my notebook that reminded me how to repeat that perfect hue or tone whenever I stumbled upon just the right color by adding and subtracting, mixing and remixing. No right or wrong, just a shade or two lighter or darker. Perhaps that was why painting was so much like life–no absolutes.

I looked at my brushes lined up next to me: rounds, flats, brights, and filberts. "They all look the same," Mother would say. Little did she know how they created dramatic differences: broad strokes or finer detailed work; sharp, angular lines, or a softer effect.

"I always knew that size mattered," Tory would joke. And I'd have to agree. These brushes would give the petals their velvety softness, while my palette knife would provide the ball-shaped anthers with a rougher, raised appearance.

Three hours later, I leaned back and studied the canvas slowly coming to life. If only Jack Templeton knew of the painting I had in store for him, he might have feigned the slightest bit of interest.

The sky darkened as the fall winds summoned the gray clouds out of hiding; the daylight hours shorter now that winter approached. Drizzle replaced dry air and leaves crunched underfoot as I walked Sadie in the park, finding comfort in the knowledge that my daffodils were busy rooting underground in the cool, October rains in preparation of their arrival next spring. But that was my only comfort. I glanced at the bench where Noah and I had first sat nervously waiting for the other to speak, and the park sign nearby that reminded us that dusk was something we never wanted to arrive. There stood the gate to the front entrance where I left my heart each time we parted. Everywhere I turned there were memories.

I found myself going to bed earlier, unable to fight fall's deception. Sometimes as early as eight o'clock, I pulled the covers up under my chin and motioned for Sadie to join me. She didn't seem to mind. Thoughts of Vienna that accompanied me during the day were pushed aside, and it was Baby Jane who came to me in the middle of the night. Sometimes as a four-year-old, standing next to my bed.

"Mommy, can I have a drink of water?" she whispered.

But it was me who was thirsty.

Other times, she appeared as a school-aged child wearing little pink dresses, ruffled bobby socks, and white Keds, the familiar blue rectangles on the heels symbolizing innocence. No longer a baby, it only seemed right to call her Jane. She climbed into a swing on the playground and slowly built momentum. When she reached the desired speed, she let her feet dangle and sang *A-Tisket, A-Tasket.*

But it was me who longed to pick her up.

One night, she appeared as a grown woman, attempting to explain to her children why they did not know their grandmother.

But it was me who didn't know them.

Miraculously, when I awoke, the pain was not as raw as it was in the murkiness of the night, allowing me to still function during the day. It had been six months since I had brought her into the world. She'd now be settled into her new home, comforted by the faces of her mother and father. I could not blame her. It was only natural to seek solace in the things you know best. One would have to look no further than Jack Templeton's painting to see my consolation.

Holidays in Laurel were the same every year, right down to the smell of the orange-cranberry mulling spices that gathered at the door to welcome me home. I would say, "Mother, why don't you change things a bit...you know, surprise us." She'd say, "Why mess with perfection, dear?"

She had a point. The coconut shrimp, pate, baked goat cheese, and French bread wound their way around the living room, matched with Daddy's bottle of Rhone Valley Condrieu that he had saved for the occasion. "The French know how to make a good wine," he'd say, before pressing the glass to his lips. Then he'd close his eyes as if the elimination of one sense would heighten another. He set a second bottle aside for the family toast that preceded dinner, the speech in which Daddy highlighted everyone's major achievements. If we did not have any, he simply told us what he thought we should have accomplished.

Mother spent most of the day preparing food. She refused to accept the fact that we were a family of four, plus one in-law. She broke out industrial-sized serving bowls and large utensils resembling gardening tools. Mother made a turkey and a ham because she could never decide on one or the other. "Well," she'd say, "nothing wrong with Monte Cristo sandwiches for lunch tomorrow, is there?"

She spent as much time constructing her dinner sanctuary as she did preparing the meal. Vases of fresh cut mums–burnt orange and gold in color, along with brass candleholders–anchored the family heirloom tablecloth that had belonged to her great-grandmother. "Still not a stain on it," Mother would say as she eyed Daddy scooping the cranberry chutney out of the bowl. He'd answer her stare with his free hand immediately finding its way under the ladle. Mother even set out place cards as if we were visiting the house for the first time and might not know where to sit. We'd play along, circling the table, "Excuse me, that's my chair," "No, I think it's mine," "Oh, look, you're right, I'm over there."

Sadie had taken her rightful place underneath the dinner table to wait for her share of holiday spirit, while Mother played chess with the serving bowls, striving for that perfect presentation. We stood in the living room and waited for permission to enter.

"Oh Lord, the sweet potatoes. How could I forget?" Mother said as she rushed back to the kitchen.

A knock at the door sent Daddy across the room. He opened it and extended his hand out into the cold. "Hey, come on in."

I glanced up to find Jack Templeton standing in the foyer of my parents' home on Thanksgiving Day.

Daddy led him over. "Cara, I believe you know Jack."

"Yes." I glared at Daddy. "What a coincidence. I wasn't aware that you and Jack knew each other."

Jack looked at Daddy. "Yes. Through business, of course."

"Of course, business, how else?" I said.

"Seeing as Jack is relatively new to town and didn't have plans, I thought we might extend him an invitation," Daddy said.

"I think we're about ready," Mother announced from the kitchen entryway.

Daddy motioned for her. "Gail, I want you to meet Jack...Jack Templeton. He's with Lyle Dunn's firm."

Mother smoothed out her apron with her hands and swept the dangling strands of hair back from her face. "Why, yes, Jack. It's certainly a pleasure. Welcome."

"Thank you for the invitation, Mrs. Robertson," Jack said.

Everyone walked over to the table and glanced at the place cards out of courtesy to Mother. Jack stood until Mother grabbed his card out of the china cabinet drawer and placed it on the table to the left of my chair.

Steph leaned over to take a look. "Does it say Daddy Junior?" she whispered in my ear.

Mother's hand went to her forehead. "Oh Lord, I forgot the gravy." I followed her into the kitchen.

I grabbed her forearm and whispered, "Since when do we have guests for Thanksgiving dinner?"

"Why, I suppose I'm taking your advice after all these years. How did you say it? I've decided to change things a bit, to surprise you. Now find your seat, dear, before dinner gets cold."

Mother placed the porcelain gravy boat in the center of the table.

"Nothing like a boatload of calories," Steph chortled. Andrew patted her arm to show support for her intolerance of holiday indulgences.

Daddy poured the wine, then held up his glass. "Here's to Mother and the wonderful dinner she has placed before us. To Steph and Andrew on their successful business." He turned to me. "To Cara and her blossoming career."

Now I was the budding artist, thanks to Mr. Templeton.

Daddy faced Jack. "Congratulations on joining such a fine firm."

"Here, here," we said, confirming Daddy's observations as each glass met with a clink.

In years past, I selected my food with an occasional glance over the shoulder. Eating in the same room as Steph was nothing short of going to confession. Transgressions usually lined my plate; butter, salad dressing, and gravy were the mortal ones. Bread, whipping cream, and brown sugar passed for venial sins. With every bite, I'd feel the need to ask her forgiveness for my weaknesses. But today, I was eating light and Steph gave me an approving nod as I passed the gravy without lifting the ladle. Daddy took my share and then slipped his hand under the table to give Sadie a piece of turkey.

"She shouldn't eat table scraps," I reminded him.

"Everyone deserves a treat on the holiday, Tulip. Hell, even prisoners get a special meal. Right, Jack?" he said, as he tore off some ham and dropped his hand below the table.

Throughout the evening, my thoughts drifted over to Europe where Noah enjoyed a Viennese meal if he chose to celebrate

Thanksgiving away from the states. My mind wandered to the hospital cafeteria where Sarah squeezed her holiday meal in between caring for the sick and downtrodden. Lastly, to who knows where, as Jane celebrated her first Thanksgiving with her new family. It was too bad that on the day we should have all been together, we were worlds apart.

An eruption of laughter brought me back to our family dinner table. I watched as Jack Templeton eagerly joined each discussion, his cell phone off and never once mentioning business. Once in a while, his arm brushed against mine and gave me a little jolt, like one of Steph's metal clothing racks in the dead of winter. Under the table, Jack's legs touched mine, and he made no effort to move away, and neither did I.

After dessert, Jack turned to me. "Would you like to go outside for a walk?"

"Sure." I grabbed my coat forgoing my usual ritual of sprawling out on the floor, unbuttoning my jeans, and swearing that I'd never eat so much again. Only to immediately think about the leftovers I'd heat up in the microwave the next day.

"Well, Jack," Mother said. "I certainly hope we see you again."

"I'd like that very much," he said as we bundled up to head outdoors. Sadie tagged along. Jack shivered slightly as soon as we stepped outside. I stopped just short of laughing when I remembered it was his first experience with winter in Michigan.

"We can go back inside if you'd like," I offered.

"No, I'm fine. This is nice. Besides, I plan to stay here for many years, so I best get used to it."

Many years? "You don't miss the West Coast?"

"No. This is my home now."

We strolled down the sidewalk, sidestepping the cars that overflowed from each driveway and we listened to the sound of muffled laughter seeping out of the houses lining the street. Large snowflakes fell from the sky, dusting Jack's charcoal-colored hair with shiny crystals. He stopped at the street corner, took my hand, and I turned toward him. Without hesitation, his lips took possession of mine. And for some reason I didn't pull away.

He finally stepped back. "Cara," he whispered. My name fell

on my ear with wonderment, as if hearing it for the first time.

I looked up to find the streetlight illuminating both the snow and Jack Templeton.

Just the Facts

The letter bore a postmark from Vienna. I whipped off my gloves and ripped open the envelope without moving from the mailbox. My gaze bounced about the letter–beginning, middle, end, not able to concentrate on a single word. Eventually, I drew my attention back to the top.

Dear Cara,

Sorry I haven't written sooner. It's not that I've forgotten you. Just the opposite, really. Every time I pass an art gallery or a flower cart, I'm reminded of how much I miss you.

The job is everything I hoped it would be. There's so much to learn here. Sometimes I think my students are teaching me more than I'm teaching them. The children in Vienna accept music as part of their lives. More of a given, not just a possibility.

I hope the winter isn't too long for you. I know you're anxious for spring. One day, I'll be alongside you, admiring your daffodils in bloom.

Love, Noah

I had expected more. He must have been busy with the new students.

I ran indoors and grabbed a piece of paper along with a fountain pen from the drawer. My letter quickly filled with the things I would have told him if we were sitting on the grassy hill at Pier Pointe; details of Jack's painting, business at the gallery, Steph's recent trip to the hospital, how Sadie kept me company on cold winter nights. I even told him how the classical radio station made me cry.

Everything important that happened since he left was in that letter– except for how Jack Templeton kissed me on the street corner on Thanksgiving Day.

For as long as I could remember, whenever I was nervous, my inner voice whispered, "It's coming, are you ready?" The same voice whispered to me back in the fifth grade when the curtain lifted for our annual, school Christmas pageant. I heard it clearly as I made my way down the staircase of our family home to meet Ricky Mulhauser for my first date. It repeatedly nagged me during my senior year in high school whenever I entered a painting in the school's art contest and my eyes frantically searched for a blue ribbon hanging from the frame. However, on this particular night, the whisper loitered, swallowing up all other thoughts. Perhaps it was because the painting wasn't finished, and Jack might not be able to envision its full potential. Or maybe it was the thought that he might kiss me again, and I'd enjoy it. Whatever the reason, I couldn't escape the voice, not even with the hairdryer set on high.

I stood in the bathroom and made last minute adjustments–a thin layer of mascara, a hint of lipstick. The hem of my new, black dress was a couple of inches too high and the neckline too low. The tag may as well have read, *Designed by Tory*. She was sure to approve when we met her at the restaurant for dinner.

The doorbell rang and I slid on my new pumps. The fear of stumbling followed me to the door. "How does Tory walk in these things?" I mumbled. I pressed the front of the dress with my hands and ran a few fingers through my hair before turning the knob. "Come on in, Jack."

His business-casual wear sent a conflicting message. He glanced about the apartment, his gaze came to rest on the worn tan sofa in the middle of the living room, then darted to the laminated kitchen table. "I thought your father was a successful attorney?"

I laughed. "He is, but I'm not. Can I take your overcoat?"

He gripped the collar. "No, that's quite all right, thank you."

Was he cold or did he picture cockroaches eager to fill his pockets?

"Well, where's the painting?"

"Follow me." I motioned him toward the spare bedroom. "Now keep in mind that it's not finished, so you won't be able to get the full effect."

"I'm not one to pre-judge. Something they highly recommended in law school, by the way."

"Ready?"

"Absolutely."

When I pushed the door open, he wrinkled his nose, and drew back slightly. "What's that smell?"

"Smell? You mean the turpentine?"

"I guess that answers my next question as to whether you ever get used to it?"

"I had to get used to it. Something they highly recommended in art school, by the way."

I walked up to the easel and revealed the painting. "Here it is."

He took a step forward. "My God...it's fantastic."

"Really?"

"Of course."

"So, you like it?"

"Most definitely."

As he walked toward me, his cologne overpowered the lingering scent of turpentine.

"Almost as beautiful as you are," he said, pulling me against him. When I looked up to accept the kiss, he pulled away. "We have reservations. We better go."

My head bobbed, but the rest of my body fiercely disagreed.

Instead of moving toward the door, he reached behind my head and pulled me to his mouth. I fell against the bedroom wall, his body fitting into every niche of mine. Then there was the voice–a different voice–Noah's voice.

God knows I don't want to leave, but this is an opportunity of a lifetime.

Jack's lips made their way down the front of my neck, pausing momentarily at the curve of my collarbone.

I may never get another chance like this.

I felt the warmth of Jack's breath.

I wish the timing was different, you know that.

Jack pressed himself harder against me.

Noah will be back, he'll be back, he'll be back.

Well, yes. You didn't think I was going to stay in Vienna forever, did you?

"No...Jack." I ducked under his arm and stepped to the center of the room. "Really, we should go."

He pushed back from the wall. "You're right. We shouldn't be late."

Once outside, I quickly closed the door behind us.

Jack parked the car while I went inside the restaurant to find Tory and David. I spotted her alone at the bar.

"Where's David?" I asked.

"He changed his mind at the last minute. Decided to spend the evening lounging around our apartment."

"*Our* apartment...no! He didn't!"

She beamed. "Yep, he moved all of his shit in yesterday."

"All of what shit? You mean his backpack and passport?"

"Hey, don't forget his schoolbooks," she reminded me. "He told me that he could move in with me now that he's close to finishing his degree."

"Degree? In what?"

She laughed. "That's a good question. Hey, you look great by the way. I thought it was just business between you two."

I took out my compact and applied some lipstick. "Things changed a bit."

She pointed to my heels. "I'd say."

"I think I'm entitled."

"Hey, no argument from me. I've been saying that all along."

Jack walked over and Tory hopped off the stool with her hand extended in front of her. "You must be Jack."

"And you must be Tory." He shook her hand. "Where's David?"

"He wasn't feeling up to it," she said with an acceptance that had never wavered over the years. She'd been explaining away his absences for as long as I had known about him. At one point, I wondered if he really existed.

After finishing a glass of wine at the bar, we were seated at a corner table with a view of the lake.

Jack turned to Tory, "I hear you're an artist as well."

"Ceramics." She ran her tongue across her deep burgundy lips. "Obviously not as lucrative as oils, but I do okay teaching at the community college." She grabbed the menu off the table. "So, what are we having?"

"Lake Perch," Jack said, his menu unread.

Her fingertips lightly stroked her throat. "Aren't you going to even look at the choices?"

"No."

"Hasn't anyone ever told you that it's better to compare all that's offered before settling for the obvious?"

"I know exactly what I want." His hand came to rest on my knee.

I could not help but wonder if Tory wished she had chosen oils rather than ceramics.

She sighed. "Suit yourself." Her eyes traveled the length of the menu. "I suppose I'll have the grouper."

Jack turned to me. "Cara?"

I was starved. "Oh…um…the small chicken Caesar salad. Light on the dressing."

"What's with the salad? Aren't you going to order an entree? I've never known you to–"

"Salad is a complete meal," I interrupted.

"Let's have a toast," Jack suggested.

"This should be good," Tory said, pushing her wineglass toward Jack.

He poured the wine, then cleared his throat. "To friends."

Friends? Is that all we are–friends?

She ran her finger over the rim of her wineglass. "Don't forget a toast to the unexpected."

"That too, I suppose," he added.

"Yes, to the unexpected," I said, recalling his body pressed against me.

Tory immediately downed her entire glass of wine; unusual for even her.

"You okay?" I mouthed. She nodded.

When we left the restaurant, I didn't need to ask Tory what she thought of Jack Templeton. As with any guy she found attractive, she leaned in close every time he spoke, laughed at everything he said, and cocked her head slightly to the right whenever she answered one of his questions. I didn't take it personally. Tory was indiscriminate with her flirting. But for once, the man's attention was on me, not her.

Jack drove me back to my apartment and waited on the top step for an invitation.

We'll get through this, Noah had said. *I have to think that this is fate as well.*

I grabbed the doorknob and stepped into my apartment. "Well, goodnight, Jack." I quickly locked the door, the deadbolt preserving that fate for yet another night.

Jack came by early the next morning to drive me to Laurel. My parents had invited us to breakfast. Daddy wanted to talk to Jack about business and Mother wanted to talk to me about Jack. We sat down to an endless supply of eggs, pancakes, bacon, and pastries while Mother fretted over whether to add a fruit bowl.

"We're fine, Mother," I assured her.

She looked toward Jack for a second opinion. "Nothing else for me," he said. She added the fruit anyway.

"Breakfast sets the tone for the entire day," Daddy said every morning, for as far back as I could remember. No matter how busy his agenda, he never missed the morning meal. Whenever he won a case, he swore breakfast helped clinch it for him. The steaming skyscraper of French toast and the minefield of eggs was more than food to him. He never knew what to do with Steph, who desired nothing more than a dry bagel and half a grapefruit. He believed she was destined to make mistakes at the store. Steph had a different theory; since her body didn't have to waste energy digesting so much fat, her mind was free to give extra attention to her business. Both theories withstood the test of time with Daddy winning case after case and Steph making sale after sale.

Daddy enjoyed hefty conversation at breakfast as well. He

wanted to talk the minute we sat at the table. Was it this cold outside last year? Had we seen the price of gas lately? Would the Lions make the playoffs? It was like being on a game show while still half asleep. Our responses consisted of grunts and head bobs between yawns and the rubbing of eyes. Being new to the Robertson home, Jack was a willing participant.

"So, Jack, how are things at the firm?" Daddy asked.

"Real good, John. We've had a couple high profile clients sign recently."

"You don't say?" Daddy buttered his toast. "Do you like it here in Michigan? Probably not used to the cold, being that you're from California."

"I'm warming up to the place." Jack's arm slid around me.

Daddy stabbed another pancake with his fork. "Have your parents made it here for a visit yet?"

Jack's arm dropped from my shoulder and he pressed his back to the chair. "They're...they're…" Like an old truck in the dead of winter, it took him several tries to get started. "Both deceased."

Mother gasped. "Oh, dear Heavenly Father. We're certainly sorry to hear that, aren't we, John?"

What would be her first question? How, when, or where?

Jack kept rearranging himself in the chair, as if unable to settle into a comfortable position. "It was an accident, a house fire. I was away at college at the time," he answered before Mother had the chance to ask.

I struggled for something to say only to realize that there were stories so horrible, there was no correct response. I had a million questions–but yet, for some reason, didn't want the answers. Perhaps this was the reason people never asked about my baby.

Jack broke the silence by asking for more coffee. Mother immediately went for the kitchen while Daddy thought it best to dip into the pineapple. I just sat in silence and wondered how I hadn't noticed his pain. By looking at him, one would've never guessed that he kept such a sad tale within, and I was certain it was the same for me. We had more in common than I had first thought–personal tragedy doesn't announce itself the minute you meet someone.

* * *

Details poured out of Noah's letter. There was the fact that music could be heard anytime, anywhere: from the Vienna Philharmonic Orchestra that performed in the Musikverein Hall, to the Vienna Boy's Choir whose angelic voices were heard at Mass in the chapel of the Hofburg, to the everyday Viennese songs performed in the local wine taverns. Noah pointed out the fact that Mozart, Beethoven, and Brahm had ties to Vienna. He toured the homes of many famous composers and saw their original instruments and scores laid out as openly as a nightshirt on a bed.

He didn't forget to include the fact that the Viennese also took their art seriously. There was the Museum of Art History, the Museum of Modern Art, and the Hundertwasser's KunstHaus Wien art gallery to prove it. Many of the students from the Academy of the Fine Arts gathered at the Cafe Museum to discuss their paintings and sculptures over a cup of *Kapuziner*.

There were many interesting tidbits about Vienna that I didn't know until Noah put them on paper. The information I was looking for, like the fact he couldn't sleep at night knowing we were apart, that he desperately wanted to return home, or that he thought about me every moment of the day, was nowhere to be found. Perhaps he had met a beautiful Viennese woman and they kissed under a streetlamp on the Sonnenfelgasse, near the row of old houses with Baroque facades that he so elegantly described. Suppose he intentionally omitted that lesser known fact, just as I failed to mention I had kissed Jack Templeton. Maybe it was details like those that kept Noah tied to Vienna, and turned any previous thoughts of him returning to me to fiction.

A Day at the Spa

"I suppose I should have told you sooner." Jack handed me the newspaper clipping.

The headline read, *House Fire Claims One Life.*

Beneath it, a picture of what appeared to be a pile of charred rubble. The article had yellowed over the years, and was so worn from folding that some words were nearly illegible. But the smoke that swirled from the debris was unmistakable–so clear I could almost smell it.

There was the story.

Blevin County–Fire Captain Robert Stevenson claimed the two-alarm blaze at 1636 Hickory Lane to be the worst he had witnessed in nearly two decades of service. Two of his men in Rescue Company #3 were hospitalized with injuries.

"We mounted both an interior and exterior attack, but the fire quickly spread throughout the main floor," reported Captain Stevenson. "You get these old homes with balloon frame construction and no fire stops and the flames crawl right up the walls."

Ms. Leona Klein, a neighbor for sixteen years, saw flames shooting out of the house. "That's when I ran to the phone and called for help," she said.   "They're good people, the Templetons. Never bothered anybody. Kept to themselves, really."

A hospital official confirmed that Mr. Eugene Templeton, 43, died in the fire from smoke inhalation, and his wife Charlotte remains in critical condition at St. Luke Hospital with third degree burns over eighty percent of her body. The cause of the fire remains under investigation.

I quickly folded the article as if to tuck the sadness back inside.

Jack held out his hand to receive the piece of paper. "According to the investigator, the smoke alarm didn't have batteries. I would've sent them the goddamn nine volt." He said he didn't know whether to call it a miracle or a tragedy that he had decided to take summer classes at the university and wasn't home at the time of the fire, asleep in his childhood room. "Maybe I could've pulled them to safety," he said. "Or I may have died alongside them. Who knows?"

The cause of the fire was determined to be faulty wiring in one of the outlets in his father's workshop.

"I don't know how many times I told them to move out of that hellhole. They refused to even think about it." Jack glanced out the window.

Jack isn't from money? What would Mother and Daddy think? My parents wouldn't have to know, I decided.

"I was going to buy them a new house as soon as I made it rich. My best friend, Brian, told me he'd hook me up in his Uncle Lyle's firm–after I had a few years of experience. I wanted my parents to spend their remaining years in luxury."

That plan didn't work, but Jack made sure they were buried in the nicest caskets–solid cherry wood with rounded corners and elaborate, hand-carved tops.

"The funeral director felt sorry for me and gave me a big discount. Even the townspeople took up a collection. I paid the remainder out of the life insurance policy," Jack said.

I thought back to Aunt Kate's meager funeral. The plain casket with square corners–nothing fancy. We knew Aunt Kate would have wanted it that way.

Jack looked to be smoothing the air with his hands. "The caskets had velvet linings with roses embroidered on the panels and those swing-bar handles on the sides for easier gripping and…"

Daddy's words came to mind. "The fancier the funeral, the more guilt involved."

I feigned stupidity when Erin described Mr. Farnsworth's solitary eyebrow, but I knew he only got that mono-brow look when he had bad news to deliver. Like when he told artists, "Sorry, I don't think I'll be able to accommodate your work" or "Could you come pick up your pieces, they don't seem to be selling." The weight from the mere thought of confrontation caused the middle of his forehead to cave in on itself. Erin swore she saw it when he tacked up the notice for an emergency staff meeting.

I tried to reassure her. "The meeting is probably about planning a holiday sale."

"No," she said. "It's something serious."

I laughed. "Have you ever known Mr. Farnsworth to be serious about this place?"

"My point exactly."

Mr. Farnsworth arrived at the gallery at nine o'clock wearing a red nylon jogging suit, a black turtleneck, and Gucci loafers sans socks–Steph's ideal customer. He smiled and set his coffee mug on the counter. "Good morning, ladies. I suppose, we should...or I should, well, get this discussion started."

I nudged Erin and whispered, "See, he's smiling."

He dug through his briefcase and pulled out a piece of paper. Then without warning, his brows fused together into one long strip like a newly blacktopped driveway. I gripped Erin's hand underneath the counter.

Mr. Farnsworth looked down at what appeared to be a prepared speech. "When I purchased this property a few years ago, I saw it as a good investment for my retirement. I knew someday I'd, um...want to sell it. I just didn't know when, until…well, now, I suppose."

"Sell it?" I blurted.

"Yes, that's right. I have a buyer and the sale is…well, in the works, has been for sometime. We should close within a month or two. I know that probably seems a little sudden, probably very sudden, but I felt it was in my best interest to keep the sale quiet since I didn't want business to suffer. I'm sure you can understand. You ladies should have time to seek employment elsewhere. And I could possibly consider one month severance. Yes, I'd most likely be able to offer that to you."

I raised my hand like a kindergartner and he nodded in my direction.

"Who's going to buy the gallery? Is there any chance we could stay on as employees?"

"That's certainly a possibility. I'm sure you could fill out an application. They may be willing to train. I'm almost positive they would. Yes, I'm sure of it."

"Train?"

"It's going to be a…a…day spa."

"Excuse me?" I said loud enough to startle even myself.

"A prime location for a spa, from what the new owners have told me."

"But what...what about the art?" My gaze darted from wall to wall.

"I'm thinking a liquidation sale is the best route to go...I'm sure of it. That reminds me. Perhaps the spa could use a couple of pieces. I'll have to remember to give them first dibs. Yes, let me make note of that. That certainly would be a nice gesture." He scribbled on his paper. "Well, if there are no more questions." He grabbed his briefcase. "I'll keep you posted on the final closing date." The bell on the door chimed his farewell.

Erin stared straight ahead while I jumped up and paced in front of her.

"Can you believe the way he just walked in here and told us he's selling the place? No, 'I'm sorry', or 'Gee, what a hard decision it was.' Nothing! The pompous bastard." I pointed across the room. "Can you picture that wall full of mirrors?"

No answer.

"Well, can you?"

She turned toward me. "Do you think they'll need a shampoo lady?"

"Erin! Doesn't it bother you that the gallery is closing?"

"I'm not an artist, Cara. I just sell the paintings. I could sell facials and massages for that matter. Any job to pay the bills. You might want to apply at that poster store in the mall, at least it's something."

I never wanted to settle. I stood in the center of the room; the spot that would most likely become a manicure station. Heaviness filled my chest. I was not only losing a job, but also a place to display my pieces. Panic settled in with the realization that something far worse loomed overhead.   Mother and Daddy now possessed the right to say I told you so.

I was not sure why I ran to the mailbox everyday, searching for anything postmarked from Vienna. Maybe I believed that Noah and I had shared more than just time, rather a love for what we did best, fueling the passion between us. My heart lurched whenever I caught a glimpse of handwriting amidst the business envelopes, only to be disappointed. His letters had stopped. Had he forgotten me so quickly? Perhaps the Viennese woman I pictured him kissing under the streetlight was a musician and shared his passion. Not that he would have gone looking for her; she just popped into his life–like Jack walked into mine. I couldn't blame Noah. Who wanted to be alone?

I sifted through the mail one last time before making my way into the apartment. It was time to stop yearning for what lay thousands of miles away across a deep, dark ocean, and time to be thankful for what had been delivered right to my doorstep.

Once again, I turned to my studio for comfort. After Mitch left me I would paint for fourteen hours at a time. Tory brought me orange juice and snacks, afraid I'd collapse on the floor from smelling turpentine on an empty stomach.

"Cara," she'd say, "it's not good for you...or for the baby."

"What baby?" I'd ask, as if denial would bring Mitch back. Eventually, I put the palette down and shuffled to bed. The next best comfort.

Now the bouquet of ten Poeticus sprawled out over the 40x60 canvas. So lifelike, that if I stood there long enough, I'd forget they weren't real. The daffodils, their cups falling at different angles, were tucked inside a bronze vase that tried desperately to hold their splendor. The flowers' six white petals would surely feel like velvet if I could reach out and touch them. The burst of color in the middle of each flower; red, yellow, and green reminded me of nature's ability to produce colors not known to my palette, nearly impossible to replicate, but I had certainly come closer than I ever thought possible. As I stood before the painting, I drew breath from it, as it had drawn life from me; but it gave back so much more. Then I recalled the words that nurse Sarah had said months ago; what a wonderful thing, to give someone life.

I cleaned my brushes and turned out the light, certain that Jack would be pleased with the beauty stretched out across the once barren canvas.

It was nine-thirty, the time he usually called. Sadie hopped up and followed her tail three times before settling into her spot, then immediately stood and tried again. She had difficulty getting comfortable since arthritis set in and merely raised her head in response to the knock at the door. I tiptoed over and looked through the peephole to find Jack standing outside my apartment. My hand came to rest on a freshly washed face and then fell to my pajama top.

"Oh, God," I whispered.

He knocked louder.

I opened the door a few inches "Jack, I was waiting for you to call. I'm not dressed for a visitor."

He pushed the door open. "Is that what I am, a visitor?"

"You know what I mean."

"Got any wine?"

"Sure."

I went to the kitchen and grabbed the bottle, an opener, and a couple of glasses. "Let's sit in the living room."

"What shall we toast?" he asked, as he sat down and took the bottle from me.

"How about unemployment?"

"What?" He put the wine down. "You quit the gallery?"

"No! I wouldn't just quit. Mr. Farnsworth is selling the place."

"Jesus, did you even see it coming?"

"Not at all."

"It seems to me that Farnsworth could've given you more notice. Well, not to worry, something is bound to come along."

"Not worry? I still have bills to pay."

"What about your parents? Can they help?"

"I'd rather die than ask them for money. They're the ones who warned me not to become an artist in the first place."

Jack grabbed my hand. "I haven't paid you for the painting yet."

I laughed. "Please! My work doesn't fetch that much."

"How you underestimate your talent." He lifted my hand to his lips.

"It's finished, you know."

"What are we waiting for?" He pulled me to my feet and led me down the hallway to my studio.

"Just remember, it's wet, so you can't touch," I instructed him as I walked to the easel.

"I'll just look."

"Here it is," my hand sweeping in front of it like a game show hostess.

He paced before the canvas. Each step compounded my nervousness. He pressed his finger to his lips, then withdrew it. I waited, but he said nothing. I couldn't hold out any longer.

"Well?" I asked.

"Well, what?"

"Jack! You know what."

"Oh, that." He smiled. "Simply amazing."

"So, you like it?"

"I love it."

He grabbed my arm and pulled me to him. How I wanted him to kiss me again. I felt an anticipation that I hadn't experienced since Noah had kissed me. Jack finally cupped my face in his hands, bringing his lips to mine.

I listened closely for Noah's voice–for him to interrupt my new found feelings for Jack, my desire for Jack to sweep me away into another life. But the only sound was Jack's heavy breath along the nape of my neck and the small groan from deep within his throat.

Jack's hands made their way to my hips, pushing up my pajama top, finding my breasts. I struggled to pull the shirt over my head, then remembered the buttons. My hands might as well have been hooves as I tried desperately to shove the buttons through the tiny holes.

"Here, let me," he said. He released them one-handedly, giving the impression that he was an experienced lover.

Jack slid off my pajama bottoms. "Jack, we can't. We...we don't have..."

He ignored my protest and relinquished his pants; the clank of his belt buckle hitting the floor rattled deep in my chest. He placed his finger to my lips and reached into his pocket and pulled out a condom.

I was both surprised and relieved.

While Jack slid on the condom, my last ounce of reservation slipped from my mind.

"You're wet, I shouldn't touch," he whispered.

We shared a burning glance–a promise of giving more, taking more. Then his arm slid behind my back and he pulled me tight to his chest. I arched my back to accept him. Our bodies started to rock, then re-adjusted, finding that natural rhythm. His lips were hungry, making their way down my neck, and I, just as ravenous, lifted my back off the floor to consume all of him.

An unexpected moan seeped through my lips. I had forgotten how long it had been.

What a wonderful thing, to give someone life.

All Signs Pointed North

Everyone wanted to be part of the first wave of the liquidation sale at the gallery. The line snaked its way down the sidewalk and around the corner. For the first two weeks, the merchandise would be marked down twenty-five percent, the next two weeks–fifty percent, and eventually seventy-five. People gathered outside the gallery an hour before we were scheduled to open.

I looked over my shoulder at Erin making last minute adjustments to price tags. "Would you look at them out there?" I said. "If there would've been this much support on ordinary days, maybe Farnsworth wouldn't have sold the place." I flipped the sign, unlocked the door, and watched in disbelief as customers crowded each other to get inside. "People lose all etiquette at a sale, dear," Mother had warned.

"Would you set this aside until I make up my mind if I truly want it?" one customer asked. "Couldn't you just go ahead and mark it down from twenty-five to seventy-five percent now to save me the trip back?" a woman inquired.

The rudest were those who discussed the opening of the spa without regard to my imminent unemployment. The women rifled off their plans of self-indulgence. Mrs. St. George wanted the Himalayan Rejuvenation Treatment; Mrs. Thierry longed for the Aromatherapy Paraffin Manicure, while Ms. Huff yearned for a Sea Salt Glow. All three prayed that the massage therapist was a nice looking man in his early thirties, strong-handed, yet gentle for their aging bodies. They seemed overly excited that the salon was opening before the beach season and they could get a bikini wax. I nodded and secretly wished they'd get a rash.

At the end of the day, I flipped the sign to announce our closing, knowing that soon it would stay that way. Each night, Jack tried to comfort me. "Everything will work out. Trust me," he'd say. I'd tuck my head into his shoulder and forget about it for the evening while wrapped in his warmth.

Christmas Eve brought in customers I hadn't seen in months. Everyone wanted to look as though they spent a fortune on a piece of art for their loved ones. I was tempted to leave the discounted price tags in place under the giftwrap to expose the cheap bastards. I was exhausted when I left work, but Tory and I still upheld our yearly tradition of Christmas Eve Mass, followed by dinner. A few years back, she'd given up on her mother's empty promise of visiting during the holidays and we'd celebrated together ever since.

We didn't cook the standard holiday fare; no turkey, no dressing or mashed potatoes. Every year Mother would say, "Lobster! Who on earth eats lobster for their holiday meal? That's just not natural, dear." I suspect that was when she first started having concerns about Tory's influence on me. Mother felt better knowing that I would be coming to Laurel on Christmas day for a real holiday meal. This year, she was even more relieved; I planned to bring Jack.

When Tory put the water on to boil our crustaceans, the sacrifice weighed heavily on my conscience. If left up to me to plop them into the scalding pot, we'd be eating hot dogs, so Tory offered a deal. She lowered them to their death, while I put on music to drown out their screams.

She walked into the living room and gave me the nod, while Burl Ives reminded us that their sacrifice made our Christmas a little more holly and jolly. After dinner, we poured wine and sat around the coffee table to exchange gifts. Sadie settled in for the night at my feet.

"I'll go first," Tory said.

"No, I believe this is my year to go first," I reminded her.

"You went first last year, remember?"

"I don't think so."

"Oh, for Christ's sake, here!" She shoved the box under my nose.

It was wrapped to perfection with tight, level corners and invisible tape. The bow on top plucked the complementary colors from the paper. Every year she claimed to have wrapped the gift herself, but I knew a professional job when I saw one. To show appreciation for the extra money she had spent, I slid my finger under the seam and wiggled it back and forth, gently loosening the tape like a child peeking before Christmas.

"Just rip the damn thing!" she said.

I eventually made my way down to the box. Inside was a sterling silver bracelet with turquoise stones: green, aqua, brown. "It's beautiful." I secured it on my wrist. "Where did you find it?"

"Several months ago David called me from New Mexico. I told him to bring it back for you."

I smiled. "I guess his traveling came in handy for once."

Before I could pick up my gift to her, she grabbed it from the table. "My turn."

I laughed. "My, you're impatient. You never could wait for anything."

By the looks of my package, one could hardly tell I was an artist; the paper cut too short, a filler strip haphazardly tucked into place. The corners puffed out as if holding their breath. Tory once asked me how I could stand handing out something that looked so untidy.

"It's my day to take a break from the beauty I create the other three hundred and sixty four days a year," I'd told her.

Tory ripped open the package. "Oh, my God! Amethyst...my favorite." She slipped the ring on her finger, moving it back and forth across the light. "Jesus, would you look at the diamonds on the sides?" Concern flashed across her face. "But how could you afford this with the gallery closing?"

"My pieces are selling."

"I'm sure you could use the money for better things. You shouldn't have."

"You said you wanted a ring for Christmas and I had doubts about David pulling through. So now you have one." I took a sip of wine. "Speaking of David, what are the two of you doing tomorrow?"

"We're going to visit his family."

"Oh, where do they live?"

Tory laughed and slid down in the sofa. "You know, that's a very good question."

"It would be helpful to find out such details."

"Shit! I almost forgot. You owe me some details."

"About what?"

"The painting, how he liked it, the big event last night."

I sighed and took several sips of wine to gain confidence, knowing the pressures of talking sex with Tory. "Oh, that. He liked it." I leaned back. "But that wasn't the *biggest* event of the night."

"You didn't!"

"Yep."

"I don't believe it!"

"Do."

She leaned over. "Was it good?"

"The best."

She rolled her eyes. "Yeah, right."

"What?" I asked.

"Well, it's not that I don't believe it. All anyone has to do is take one look at the guy to know he's hot. But, I must point out that you only have Mitch to compare him to. And anyone has to be better than that idiot."

"You're doubting my ability to judge good sex?"

"All I'm saying is that it's a rather broad statement to make from such a limited sampling."

I crossed my arms and kicked my legs out in front of me. "And all I'm saying is that after Jack Templeton, I don't need any other samples–thank you."

"So," she leaned in, "cough up the details."

"You know I don't kiss and tell. Especially after you laughed at me for using the word fireworks a few years back."

"Well, *was* it fireworks?"

"Absolutely."

She hesitated for a moment, then said, "For some reason, this time I don't doubt it. The main thing is that you're having sex again. After the baby, I never wanted to bring it up." She gasped and grabbed my arm. "You did use protection, right?"

"Of course!"

"Just checking." She twirled the new ring around her finger. "It seems that Jack is exactly what you needed to get your mind off Noah and Jane."

"Don't they call that rebounding?"

"What does it matter as long as you end up in the right court? By the way, have you decided what you're going to do when the gallery closes?"

"If it were up to Mother, I'd marry a rich man," I said.

"It could happen, you know."

I held up my wine glass. "Hey, as long as we're dreaming, let's not only make him rich, but handsome *and* a great lover."

"To Jack," we both said, before lifting our glasses for a toast.

Jack had no problem confessing that his gift was professionally wrapped. He handed me the ornate box. "I think you'll find these useful."

Useful? Oh, God. I looked at the box that was the same size as a clock radio or an answering machine. *Just smile and look grateful.*

I unwrapped the package and peered inside. My lips were as taut as an overworked rubber band while I held a smile in place. "Slippers. Just what I needed."

"A little something to warm your feet," he said.

"*Mmm*, yes. Thank you."

"Aren't you going to try them on?"

I looked at the tag. "Size six. They'll fit."

"You need to try them on. Sometimes they're deceiving."

"All right, already." I slipped the right one on. "See, perfect," I said, holding my foot out for his approval.

"Now the left. We have to make sure the pair was made for each other."

"They're fine, Jack, really."

"Try it on." He held it out in front of me.

"Lord," I said. I slid my foot inside and my toes came to an abrupt stop. "What in the world is…" I took it off and pulled out a small box.

"A little something to warm your heart," he said.

I snapped the lid back. My jaw lay as wide open as the box.

"Jack…it's so…so…"

"Big," he offered. "Try it on."

I placed the diamond on my right hand and admired its beauty.

"No, other side," Jack said firmly, then moved it to my left ring finger.

I sat speechless and stared at the shimmering marquis larger than any of Mother's gems. Memories of Noah rushed back. Why hadn't he committed? Why hasn't he written? Would he really come back? There were no guarantees.

"Can I take your silence as a yes?" Jack said.

"Um…oh, of course."

Jack leaned in close for a congratulatory kiss. When I closed my eyes, all thoughts of Noah faded into the darkness.

I felt faint and blindly reached behind me for the chair, then lowered myself into the seat. "Now, tell me again."

"Which part, sweetheart?" Jack stroked my cheek.

"All of it."

"It's a great opportunity. I'll eventually be made partner in the affiliate office."

"Couldn't they send someone else?"

"I know that you don't want to move away from Mission Bay," he started, "but Piney Cove is only two hours north." He kissed me. "You can come back any time you feel the need."

"But I've never lived anywhere else, except while away at college. Even then, I knew I'd be coming back. I've made this my home, Jack."

"We can buy a house on the lake with a real studio where you can paint full-time. Isn't that what you've always wanted?"

"Yes, but the creek."

"*Shh*, darling. It will be a new start for the New Year. We'll come back here for the wedding this spring."

"This spring!" My hand swept across my forehead while I grappled for words. "A wedding takes time to plan. There's the dress, the cake, the photographer–"

He placed his index finger over my lips. "No need to worry, my love."

It all happened so fast, like I'd slipped down a flight of icy steps.

"Certainly you and your mother can pull it together by then," he said. "We can get married next to your beautiful daffodils."

I climbed into bed. "Really? You'd get married at the creek?"

Jack slid in beside me. "Of course. Everything will work out. Now get some sleep. We can talk about it tomorrow."

"On second thought," he said. His fingers released each button of my pajama shirt while I lay perfectly still, without a sound, praying that the opportunity of a lifetime that was knocking at the door again would be fooled into thinking nobody was home.

For the next two days, I sat in front of my easel waiting for a sign. Was the fact that I had painted most of the jonquils pointing straight up a signal that I should move north with Jack? Did I really see the word Piney outlined in the tall field grass in the picture, or was I imagining things? Of course, no one else understood my hesitation.

"What's there to think about, dear?" Mother had asked when hearing of the news. "You're pretty lucky to have found a man such as Jack after the likes of that Mitch fellow. Jack will be an excellent provider. Supporting such a career move will allow you to stay home to paint, will it not? You'll finally have a real future in art."

"Well, Tulip, it's certainly a great opportunity for Jack. He may not get another one like it," Daddy reminded me.

Steph couldn't resist adding her opinion. "What more could you ask for?" she had said. "Mother and Daddy love the guy. And why wouldn't they–he's Daddy revisited."

"He is not!" I objected.

"Hey, I'm telling you, if you marry Jack, you're golden."

"Now, what exactly is the problem?" Tory asked. "Most wives do relocate with their husbands."

"He's not my husband yet," I said.

"And if you don't go, he never will be."

"Well, then at least I could stay here."

"You'd honestly consider letting a man like Jack go just to stay in this nothing of a town we call home?"

"Maybe. Besides, I never saw you leave town with David."

She rolled her eyes. "Piney Cove is a little different than Bangladesh."

"I suppose you have a point there."

Needing direction from a neutral party, I got in my car and drove to the creek. This time of year there were no daffodils or field grass, just a thick blanket of snow covering the ground, threatening to steal my boots with every step. I stopped to catch my breath near the slight bend in the creek. Each spring, the water paused there momentarily before trickling over an old log's makeshift dam. I knew everything about this place: where the jonquil colony ended and the Poeticus began, how tall the grass would be at the end of each summer, which oak tree provided the best shade in the hot, afternoon sun. Winter's camouflage hid nothing from me. There was no hesitating, no guessing where to step, or wondering what pitfalls to avoid.

Continuing toward the Poeticus field, the snow swirled up around me with each small gust of wind; only to settle back down in a different place without complaint. I finally made it to the field.

We'll come back here for the wedding this spring, Jack had assured me.

I closed my eyes and my mind fast-forwarded to spring, the sun warmed my back and the flowers stood in full bloom. Daddy took my arm and walked me down the aisle and Jack waited patiently at the end of the runner. Jack and I vowed to love and to cherish, while the daffodils' spicy-sweet smell encircled us, the trickle of the creek provided a musical accompaniment to the pastor's words.

A house on the lake...a real studio of my own...a chance to paint full-time. All signs that pointed north.

A Means of Escape

The Plain Rapper newspaper served a three county area. I picked up the familiar brown paper sack and flipped through the local news, world news, sports, and comics to get to the engagement announcements. A summary of our lives hung beneath our photo.

Cara Robertson is a graduate of the University of Michigan's Master of Fine Arts Program. Jack Templeton, a graduate of Stanford University, practices law with the firm Derby, Dunn, and Whitaker. After the April 27th wedding, the couple will reside in Piney Cove, Michigan.

People all over town read about our marriage plans during breakfast. I could almost hear Mother and Daddy letting out a sigh of relief over the mound of eggs and runway of bacon strips sitting before them. I pictured Mitch shoveling in his pancakes, wondering how in the world I had gotten over him and managed to luck out and land myself an attorney, an attractive one at that. While Sarah sipped a cup of coffee in between caring for patients, she had affirmation that with a little faith, things worked out in the end. As for me, I believed it to be a combination of luck and faith. And just like Mother and Daddy, I too, let out a little sigh of relief after realizing that Noah didn't have to see my engagement to Jack Templeton splashed across the social page of the newspaper.

Jack drove us to Piney Cove in search of a house. He threw around the words escrow and balloon mortgage, along with acronyms such as ARM and PMI. I merely nodded and hoped that he wouldn't ask my opinion on the matter. All I knew about housing was the fact that I had to stick the white envelope marked 'rent' with a check for $425.00 in Mr. Schifano's mail slot by the third of each month to avoid a late fee of twenty-five dollars. Of course, I quickly learned that Mr. S. would let it slide until the sixth or so with a note vowing never to let it happen again along with an order of tiramisu from

Ciaccio's Bakery.   Jack continued to talk about lot size, square footage, and easements while I dreamed of what I might buy with my security deposit refund.

We pulled up to the Realtor's office. "Ready to find our dream home?" Jack said.

If only he knew that I'd never thought I'd own any home, much less my dream home. We got out of the car and went to meet the relocation specialist, Mrs. Annette Clayton-Harrington.

According to Annette, the town of Piney Cove was in a quandary. A place where the IGA manager knew the name of every resident and needed to expand to meet the demands of its growing population–a threat to the very nature of this quaint town along the lakefront. Annette's real estate office had never been busier, and the Million Dollar Sales certificates on her wall proved it. While she drove us around town, she pointed left and right while highlighting the attractions like a tour guide. "There's the shopping district to the left," she said.

All the specialty stores were uniform in prosperity with their forest green awnings, etched glass doors, and gourmet gift baskets decorating the windowsills. Boutique this and bistro that, were written in Edwardian script on the signs of the storefronts. We made our way north where bed and breakfasts the colors of swirled cotton candy lined the bluff overlooking the lake. Each of the Inns featured different amenities, some their view, others colorful gardens. Annette assured us that the waiting lists stood at a year for an available room; the regulars as loyal as the warm, summer breeze off the lake. "I don't think the new hotels popping up can compete with a bed and breakfast's hospitality."

On the outskirts of town, an industrial parkway drew in business. Annette said that it was a hot topic amongst the residents. Some figured it built the tax base, others viewed it a threat to the town's charm. Annette said, "Don't worry, the commissioner keeps a close eye on it. We don't want the area growing too fast."

Jack winked at me. If he had any say in the matter, new corporations would be sprouting up like wild mushrooms.

Annette stopped the car in front of a large building nearing completion. "That's our new convention center, Mayor Burton's pride and joy.   We're hoping it will bring in different groups and organizations to boost the local economy."

I pictured artists from around the country gathered there to display their work. "It's beautiful."

We eventually made our way to a planned community complete with golf course, clubhouse, tennis courts, and swimming pool and pulled up to 1255 Devonshire Court. Unable to take my eyes off the house, I slowly opened the car door and lowered my foot in search of pavement.

"I think we're home," Jack said. He grabbed my arm and we followed Annette to the front door.

She looked down at the MLS sheet. "This one lists for seven thirty-five, five."

I tugged at Jack's coat. "We can't afford that!" I whispered in his ear.

He waved off my concern. "Don't give it another thought."

"It's been on the market a while. They may be willing to come down in price a bit," Annette added.

Mature maple trees surrounded the Tudor home allowing the slate roof to hold onto a thick layer of snow, rendering the copper gutters useless. Annette opened the door to a vast foyer with ceramic flooring. A grand staircase invited us upstairs, but we resisted the urge; instead, we instinctively found our way to the large kitchen, confirming Mother's theory that it was the most important room in any house.

"Perfect." Jack ran his fingertips along the granite countertops and traced the edges of the cherry wood cabinets. "Of course, we'll have to change some of the décor to meet our needs."

"And what needs might those be?" I asked.

"Entertaining clients."

"*Hmm.*" My attention shifted to the sunroom to the right. The large row of windows overlooking the lake made it a perfect studio and there was plenty of wall space to hold the pieces I couldn't bear to sell.

Jack came up from behind. "Ah, your studio. See, Piney Cove does have something to offer you." He held out his hand. "C'mon, let's look at the rest." We followed Annette to the master bedroom.

"Jesus, this room is bigger than my townhouse," Jack said. He went and stood by the small sitting area with bay windows and French doors that led out onto a three-tiered deck. We walked outside and then back in through yet a different door, stumbling into the living room by accident, as if in a house of mirrors. Built-in bookshelves, displaying a large number of the classics, were on either side of the marble fireplace.

"The marble was imported from Italy," Annette said. Jack nodded as if he expected nothing less.

I pointed to the mantle. "Jack, that's where the painting will go. It'll be perfect."

"Painting?" he asked.

I let out a sigh and crossed my arms. "The Poeticus. Remember?"

"Oh, yes, of course." He turned and pointed at the staircase. "Let's go upstairs."

We walked up to the second level to find several rooms spread out in different directions. I followed behind Jack as he ducked his head into each of the rooms. He stopped at the last door on the right while Annette continued down the hall.

I stood on my tiptoes and peeked over his shoulder. "What's so interesting in…" Then I saw the crib.

He pulled me into the middle of the room. "We didn't even think of this possibility. Of course, we'll need a nursery."

Limoges, porcelain dolls, and wooden blocks that spelled E-M-I-L-Y lined the shelf on the wall.

I held my breath and ran my finger over the crib rail, then reached down and smoothed out the patchwork quilt that kept Emily warm at night. When I was finally able to breathe, I inhaled the unmistakable scent of pure skin and baby powder.

"Well, won't we?" Jack waited for my answer.

"Huh, oh...yes."

"Maybe we can fill all these rooms," he said as he slipped his hands around my waist. "Except for my office, of course. Can you see it now?" His hands panned out before him. "Templeton and Sons–Attorneys at Law. The five of us in our own firm. Wouldn't that be something?"

His dream sucked the air from my lungs. I backed out of the room, stumbling over a stepstool near the doorway and made my way down the staircase without looking back.

Jack leaned over the banister. "Four is a bit optimistic. I'm willing to negotiate," he called.

The new baby smell followed me out the front door. Jack came out of the house with Annette. "Have you seen enough?" she asked.

"Plenty," I said. We made our way to the car.

"What a beautiful home in which to raise a family," Annette added.

Jack reached for my hand. "Yes, it certainly is."

I tried to ignore the lump in my throat. *Of course, he wants children. Why would I think otherwise?*

"Did you notice the crown molding throughout the house?" Jack said.

How would I ever explain to Jack that we...that I...needed to wait?

"And the beveled mirrors..."

Would he put it all together and realize the secret I hid from him?

"The Tiffany swag lamp in the kitchen..."

There's no reason not to have children now, I reminded myself. I'll have money, a house, and a husband–things I didn't have before.

"...remote controlled awnings." Jack squeezed my hand. "We'll have it all, Cara."

I turned to take one last look at the house before getting into the car. Brick stretched out for what seemed like an entire city block. Its breathtaking proportions held dominion over the landscape. From a distance, it would surely be mistaken for a castle.

Once back at the hotel, Jack and I showered before ordering room service. We sat on the bed in white, fluffy bathrobes, the ones that every guest was tempted to steal. We crawled into bed and Jack still held onto the smile he wore at the home on Devonshire Court.

"Can you believe that house will be ours in thirty days?" Jack said.

"There's just one minor detail that we haven't talked about," I reminded him.

"Which is?"

"The price."

"Now, Cara, do you think I would buy a house out of our price range?" He turned up my collar.

"What exactly is our price range? And if that's it, where'd you get that kind of money?"

He laced his fingers throughout my hair. "Let's just say the market was very good to me. A few years back when it was a bull market, my stockbroker friend, Brian, tipped me off to a hot tech stock that ended up going through the roof. It paid off big–really big and I sold at top dollar. We'll have plenty to put down on the house. We'll use the rest for savings, retirement, and such."

"The rest?"

"Yes. I squirreled money away while real estate was booming in California. Not to mention, the settlements."

"What settle…" I quickly remembered the life and homeowners insurance, a result of the fire.

"My parents would be happy that I chose to invest their money wisely."

"Well, if any good could come out of it, I suppose."

A knock at the door announced dinner.

"Come in," Jack called.

The man pushed a cart lined with chafing dishes into the room, opened the wine, and poured two glasses.

Without looking up Jack thanked him with a twenty-dollar bill.

"Thank you, sir," the man said, before leaving the room.

Jack turned to me, untied the belt to my bathrobe, and ran his cool hand the length of my thigh.

I pointed to the cart. "Our dinner will get cold."

"We'll order again." His lips left a warm trail down my belly.

"But that will get cold, too," I whispered as his hands cupped my breasts.

"Let's just hope for a hot breakfast then."

Our fluffy bathrobes found their way into a pile on the floor.

I could not have three hundred people gather onto the creek

property for a wedding without permission from the owner. Neither Mother nor Daddy knew who owned the property next to the Jensen farm. Daddy offered to get the information from the courthouse, but I wanted to take a more personal approach.

Jack and I made our way up the weathered steps, sidestepping the rotted wood with holes large enough to swallow a foot, and forgoing the splintered side rail for fear it might collapse under the weight. I pulled off my mitten and rang the bell. The door opened a crack to yield a glimpse of a frail woman. She peered at me through the narrow slit, her sparse, gray hair falling just below her shoulders.

"Can I help you?" She squinted, then readjusted her thick glasses as if positioning would make a difference.

I stepped in front of the small opening to allow her a better look. "Um, yes. Are you Mrs. Jensen?"

She opened the door a bit wider and craned her neck. "Why, yes I am."

"I'm Cara Robertson. My parents live just up the road. I used to see your husband while walking to the creek to paint."

She smiled. "Why, of course you did. Please, come in. I've got water on the stove for tea. Why don't you join me?"

A dank, musty odor wafted out of the house, much like the smell that had barreled out of Aunt Kate's steamer trunk in her attic whenever I looked for treasure.

"This is my fiancé, Jack Templeton," I said as we stepped inside.

"Welcome, both of you."

The wood-burning stove hissed and crackled, working hard to dry out the walls and floors of the damp house. A border collie lifted his gray muzzle momentarily, but quickly decided we were not worth the effort. We followed Mrs. Jensen as she grabbed onto one piece of furniture then another, taking the longest, but safest route to the kitchen. She pointed to the butcher-block table. "Please, sit down."

Looking back over her shoulder, she said, "My husband talked about you often, Cara. He respected that you loved the land."

"The creek certainly is a beautiful place," I said.

She carried over a canister of assorted teas and put them down before grabbing the edge of the table and slowly lowering herself into the chair. Wrinkles streamed down both sides of her face and fused together at the corners of her mouth. Her eyes held a hint of brown underneath a milky film.

"Now, what is it that I can do for the both of you?" she asked.

"Well," I said, "I was hoping that either you or Mr. Jensen could tell me who owns the property next door. We would like to have our wedding ceremony there this spring. And of course, we need permission."

The kettle called and I patted her arm. "Please, sit. I'll get it." I came back with the steaming cups.

"You haven't heard," she said as I took my seat next to her.

"Heard?"

"Mr. Jensen has passed on. Complications from a stroke last summer."

I took her hand in mine, her skin was paper-thin with veins puffed like yarn. "I'm so sorry. I didn't know."

"Yes, sorry to hear that," Jack offered.

"I guess it was best that he died." She placed a tea bag in her cup. "He would've never been able to accept life as an invalid. That man hardly ever sat down."

I'd seen him many times thinning his peach crop with a whiffle bat and pruning apple trees with nothing more than a gloved hand, sometimes as early as six o'clock in the morning and as late as seven at night. Later in the season, he hauled the wooden crates overflowing with the peaches and apples behind his tractor, his reward for keeping his orchards in fine order.

"It has certainly taken a bit getting used to around here without him. My brother Frank will help me with the crops next spring, or make plans to hire the help out anyway. I suppose I'll be selling the place. My brother's widowed, too. His wife died three years ago following a bout of pneumonia. He never really recovered from her death. Was afraid I'd have to bury him alongside her." She pointed to a wheelchair in the corner of the room. "That's how I get around most days. We're talking about going into one of those retirement homes together."

I wondered how hard it would be for her to sell the property that helped to define them over the years.

"Just be sure not to settle for anything less than what it's worth,

Mrs. Jensen," Jack warned.

"Oh, I'm aware of how those people think. That I'm an old widow, needing to sell quickly–desperate. That's when they'll lowball me, pretending to do me a favor by taking the place off my hands. Why, it happened at the old Hubert place up the road. I'd just as soon die right here at this kitchen table as to let them rob me of all we've worked for."

"If you'd like some assistance with estate planning, give me a call." Jack slipped her a business card. "I'd be happy to help you. Free of charge, of course."

"Why, that's mighty nice of you." She tucked the card into her apron pocket. "Now, to answer your question, Frank owns that property next door. He never quite knew what to do with it. Was useless really, but he never got around to selling it. Until now anyway."

My hands began to tremble and I quickly searched for a place to lower my cup. "He's selling the creek property?"

"Yes, but not until next summer. You'll have plenty of time to have your wedding. I'll call him, but I'm certain he won't mind. In fact, go ahead and plan on it."

"How big is the property?" Jack said.

"Just a hair over five acres, if I remember right. Not large enough for crops, but large enough for a wedding. Of course, it doesn't help having that darned creek up the middle. No idea why he even bought the property."

She made it sound as if it was an oversight on his part, but I knew exactly why Frank had bought it.

"Cara, why don't you go warm up the car while I get Frank's number," Jack said. "We might have questions about logistics...parking and such." He dangled the keys in front of me.

I grabbed them and held back my tears. "Thanks, Mrs. Jensen, for everything. Keep April twenty-seventh open on your calendar."

My eyes blurred as I tried to make my way down the rickety steps, relying on memory to avoid the holes in the boards. I started the car and sat in disbelief. Who knew what the new owner would choose to do with the property. A few minutes later, Jack came out holding a little piece of paper.

He reached over and turned on the heat. "This might help in warming it up."

"Sorry, forgot." I stuck out my hand. "I'll call Frank next week."

"I'll take care of it. You'll be planning most everything else. I need something to do besides arrange the honeymoon. That reminds me," he said. "I've narrowed it down to either St. Lucia or a grand tour of Europe."

"Definitely St. Lucia," I blurted.

He laughed. "Well, you certainly fooled me. I thought for sure you'd choose Europe with all of its museums and art exhibits."

"Nope. Give me a beach and a rum punch any day."

"The beach it is." He pulled out of the drive.

He didn't know that I had already been to Europe. That I had toured every café, museum, and park, compliments of Noah's old letters and my dreams at night. There was simply no room in Europe for my future with Jack Templeton; it was too crowded with the past.

Jack parked the car. The NO TR SP S ING sign now hung by a single nail on the fence post. I needed to buy a new sign, a threatening one with all of the letters intact so the bulldozers that came to tear up my daffodils would take it seriously and leave.

We walked through the fence and followed the snow-covered path to the creek.

I pointed across the embankment. "That's where the jonquils bloom. We'll place the aisle down a ways to the left, where the Poeticus bloom."

"I see." His face held steady.

"I know it doesn't look like much. You really have to see it in the spring to appreciate its beauty. I'm sure it just looks like a big pile of snow. See, look over–"

"I trust you," he interrupted.

I was suddenly transported back in time to the driveway of my childhood home where I stood with a bucket of water and an old paintbrush, frustrated by those adults who refused to accept the beauty of what sat before them.

"Can you picture it, Jack? Can you see it?" I begged. "The

creek, the flowers, the field grass..." I pointed at all of them, as if playing connect-the-dots in the air.

He grabbed my hand. "I don't need to see it, sweetheart. If you say it's beautiful, then it is. Whatever makes you happy is fine with me."

"But I don't want you to just take my word for it."

He laughed. "It'll be fine no matter what blooms where. All I care is that we're married. Besides, I'll see it in the spring."

"You'll love it," I assured him.

"I'm sure I will. It's cold. Let's go back." He turned and walked briskly toward the car.

"Didn't you have a special place as a child, Jack?" I called, running up from behind.

"Special place?"

"Yeah, you know...a means of escape." I stopped, ready to soak up every detail as he intimately described his safe harbor.

Instead, he kept walking. "No. I guess I never needed one."

Dandelions

Piney Cove welcomed us to town with eight inches of new snow. The powdery crystals were pleasing to the eye, but surely disappointing to the neighborhood children hoping to build a snowman. I had experienced the same disappointment during my younger years. I'd throw open the curtains to my bedroom window to find the ground covered with a white blanket. Then, in a rush of excitement, I'd contemplate throwing my coat on over my pajamas instead of taking the time to change into long johns. One could argue that there wasn't much difference. Boots, hat, mittens, scarf were all for naught the minute I reached down for a big handful of snow and it sifted through my fingers like flour. I soon learned how to differentiate the flakes by looking at the street signs. If they were covered, it was the wet, heavy stuff–good for packing. And if the family car was nothing more than a heap of snow in the middle of the drive, even better.

The only activity in my new neighborhood was the scraping of shovels and the steady roar of snowblowers. The bitter wind cut through my down filled coat as if it was a spring jacket. Not ideal moving weather, but it was typical of winter in Michigan. I stood alongside the truck with clipboard in hand and checked off Jack's boxes as the moving men wheeled them past on a dolly. My belongings had fit into the back of the Jeep.

"I don't think that's the look we're striving for," Jack had said, glancing at my frayed sofa and mismatched end tables. "I suggest a charitable donation. We'll take the tax deduction."

I settled for bringing my art supplies, clothing, and a few kitchen items. Mother and Daddy made up for the light packing on my end by sending a new dining room set, entertainment system, and furnishings for four bedrooms; my prize for marrying the right man.

"Just a few things to get you started," Mother had said when she called to tell me of the delivery time.

Sadie made search patterns around the yard looking for wildlife. She ran back and forth, scooping up flakes on the tip of her nose, only to sneeze several times as if she had developed a sudden cold. Watching her brought both joy and heartache. The cold weather aggravated her arthritis. Tomorrow she'd pay dearly for her romp, but I delighted in her playfulness.

A sputtering sound drew my attention to the neighbor who was trying to get her blower started. She waited a moment, then with a sudden burst of energy, pulled several times in succession before letting the cord snap back into place. Clouds of frustration swirled about her mouth before disappearing with the winter wind.

Jack came out of the house and I handed him the clipboard. "I'll be right back."

I cut across the street and walked up her drive. She wore a white, knit hat that covered her entire head. There was no need to picture her with hair since her huge, brown eyes more than made up for any color it would have added.

She stepped out from behind the blower. "Hi, I was hoping you'd stop by." She motioned to the second story of her house. "I would've come over, but I couldn't leave my daughter–naptime." She extended her hand. "I'm Mary Rose Townsend."

"I'm Cara Robertson. Uh, soon to be Cara Templeton." I pointed across the street. "That's my fiancé, Jack."

"Oh, you're getting married! Well, congratulations. When's the big day?"

"April twenty-seventh."

"That'll be here before you know it." She adjusted her hat, and a few dark brown ringlets fell out. "Are the two of you new to town?"

"Yes, Jack took a position in one of the legal firms here."

"Ah, an attorney. Do you work outside the home, Cara?"

"I certainly hate to call it work since it's something I enjoy so much. I paint. I'll have a studio at the house."

"Gee, I've never met an artist before."

I laughed. "It's not like I'm famous or anything."

"Still, I'm impressed. God forgot to give me such talent."

"Everyone has a gift. It's finding it that's the challenge."

She pointed to the blower. "Right now, I'd settle for the gift of starting this darn thing."

"I'll send Jack over to help."

"Oh, thanks, but I hate to interrupt on moving day. I know how it is, unpacking all those boxes, getting to know your way around."

"I don't even want to think about all that. The move happened so fast that I didn't even have time to leave a forwarding address. I suppose everything will catch up to me sooner or later."

"Believe me," she said, "the bills will find you regardless. The post office is just up the road, by the way."

"Thanks." I turned to leave. "It was nice meeting you, Mary Rose."

She grabbed the pull cord. "Oh, by the way, do you like coffee?"

"Love it."

"How about tomorrow morning at my house? Around seven-thirty?"

"That would be nice."

I walked back across the street to find Jack scolding one of the movers for putting a small dent in the wall. "Could you go help Mary Rose?" I asked him, pointing across the street.

"Sure." He handed me the clipboard and whispered, "Watch these guys. They're rough with the merchandise."

Within moments, I heard the hum of an engine. Mary Rose gave Jack a thank you wave as she made her first sweep down her driveway. He came back to the house.

"Pretty impressive for a West Coast boy," I said.

"You'd think her husband could do that, or at least hire it out. By the looks of their home, I'd say they could afford it. What does he do anyway?"

"She didn't say."

The local florist pulled into the drive and handed me a bouquet of fresh flowers. The card read, *A little something to spruce up the place–love, Mother.*

Jack chuckled. "Like a single bouquet of flowers will make a difference in a house this big."

"If it's on canvas it would," I reminded him.

* * *

After the last truck pulled from the drive, I sat down amidst the sea of Jack's boxes and my parents' deliveries, immobilized by the mere thought of unpacking. Sadie curled up next to me and rested her muzzle on my leg.

"When do we have our housewarming?" I asked Jack.

"Not for a while," he said. "We have a lot of work to do before anyone steps foot in this house. Area rugs, new living room furniture, interior design…but I suppose we should start with unpacking."

"Where do we begin?"

"The bedroom's a priority. We'll need to put sheets on the bed and hang our clothes in the closet. And the kitchen is important if we want to eat tonight."

I sighed.

"What?"

"Nothing."

"You'd rather start somewhere else?"

"Do you mind?" I pointed to my boxes of art supplies.

He laughed. "It depends upon whether you mind painting naked and hungry."

"Not at all."

"Then what are we waiting for?" He scooped me into his arms and carried me into my new studio.

Mary Rose's country kitchen smelled of hazelnut coffee and blueberry muffins. They'd be a nice change from the bitter coffee and day old doughnuts from the corner convenience store. Sunlight spilled in through the bay window and onto the floor adding warmth to the already cozy atmosphere. Woven baskets of various sizes were tossed into a pile above the cupboards, and a white ceramic cookie jar in the shape of a rooster sat on the countertop along with bottles of homemade vinegars and oils. Copper pots and pans hung from a rack above the island, intermingled with bundles of dried herbs. I was certain her stove stayed on the majority of the time. I peeked my head into the living room and a magnificent piano caught my eye.

"Do you play the piano?" I asked while a sense of sadness swept over me.

"It's just for show," she called over her shoulder.

What Noah would've given for a piano like that. I turned back to the kitchen.

Mary Rose zipped alongside her marble counters and her long, dark curls bounced up and down. She reached into the oak cabinet and pulled out two oversized mugs. She winked. "Built-in refill."

"You have a lovely home," I said. "How long have you lived here?"

She brought the coffee and muffins to the table and sat down across from me. "Oh, it's been five and a half years now since Paul set up his medical practice."

"Oh, your husband's a doctor?"

"Yes, he was a cardiac surgeon." She brought the cup to her lips.

"So, he's no longer a surgeon?"

Her cup hit the table. Droplets sprinkled her hand, but she didn't flinch. "What?"

"Maybe I misunderstood. You said he *was* a cardiac surgeon. I thought he might have changed specialties or something."

"I'm sorry." She dabbed the back of her hand with a napkin. "I don't know why I thought you'd know. He died last summer in a car accident."

"Oh, Mary Rose, I'm so sorry."

She stood and grabbed a frame off the countertop behind her.

"This is Paul," she said, handing me the picture. "It was taken on our last vacation in Colorado. He loved winter sports." She glanced out the window at the large flakes that continued to fall and she smiled.

In the photograph, Paul had one arm around Mary Rose and the other around a pair of skis. His thick, black hair was in stark contrast to the white-capped mountains in the background, and his aqua eyes made me think that he should've been skiing on water rather than the slopes. She ran her finger over the photograph as if dusting the snow from his jacket, then placed it on the table.

"Do you have family in town to help you? This is certainly a big house to maintain," I said.

She shook her head. "No, I'm an only child and both my parents are deceased." She waved off her words. "Ah, well, I don't know why on earth I'm bothering you with all this."

"No bother, really," I said.

"It's tough being a single mother."

"I can only imagine. Where is your daughter now?"

She pointed toward the staircase. "She sleeps until eight-thirty or so."

I noticed the highchair in the far corner with the bib draped over the side, the chunky, alphabet refrigerator magnets, and a bowl of Cheerios on the countertop. I looked back at the photo on the table. Paul's death suddenly felt more tragic.

"Jesus, that's too bad," Jack said as he moved a few boxes around the living room. "Dead husband and then having to support a child on top of it. He must have left her some money, anyway."

"I think I'm going to invite her to the wedding," I said.

He laughed. "A bit soon, don't you think? You just met her yesterday."

"I know it sounds weird, but I think we're going to end up good friends. Besides, I doubt she gets out much since her husband died."

"Whatever you wish, love." He looked around the room. "What do you think?"

"It looks great. But you've forgotten one thing."

"What's that?"

I pointed to the mantel.   "The painting you so desperately wanted me to paint."

He snapped his fingers. "That's right."

He climbed the ladder while I grabbed the painting and hoisted it into the air. "Be careful. It can't be replaced," I reminded him.

"Anything can be replaced, darling. You'd just have to paint another one."

"Jack Templeton!   Art is not like that.   An original is an original."

"Everything an artist paints is an original, is it not?" He hung the painting and backed off the ladder. "You'd just have to paint me something else."

"But when you came into the gallery...I remember...you specifically wanted daffodils."

He came over and placed his arms around my waist. "I wanted you, my dear."

I pushed him away. "So, I could've painted dandelions for all that mattered."

He pulled me to him once again and his hands crawled underneath my sweater.

"Jack, I'm not in the mood." I swatted at him.

"*Shh*...darling." He lowered me onto the chaise and my anger started to melt from the warmth of his lips on mine.

I glanced up at the painting of the beautiful, white Poeticus as he gently lowered himself on top of me. With my eyes closed and the familiarity of him between my legs, I tried my best to free myself of any lingering hurt so he could fill me with pleasure. As he whispered my name into my ear, I looked up at the painting that hung above us. I suppose the fact that he wasn't smitten with daffodils wasn't so bad. After all, dandelions were the same color as Poeticus, before the wind picked up their feathery seeds and recklessly scattered them across the earth.

C is for Creek

Mother called an emergency meeting at the house in Laurel to make wedding plans. She brought over a box with Mother's Recipes inscribed on the outside and set it on the kitchen table.

"Recipes? I thought we were catering," I said.

"We are. This is just improvising," she said, taking a label with the word Wedding typed on it and placing it over the word Recipes. She left the word Mother's intact leaving no doubt as to who was in charge.

"Organization is critical since we have limited time, dear." She flipped open the lid. "Now, I thought we'd start in alphabetical order. There are no A's, well, unless you feel alcohol needs its own file card, which I'm sure some of your father's colleagues would suggest. I thought we'd put it under the C's for club, since they'll be providing the liquor."

I sat quietly.

"Honestly, Cara. It is your wedding. Don't be afraid to speak up." She shuffled through the box. "We'll start with the B's then." She wrote the word Bakery on a card, then wrote Perfection Confection underneath.

I couldn't argue since it was the best bakery in town. The small storefront in Stony Harbor had a wooden spoon for the door handle and their extensive list of pastries was carved into a rolling pin that served as the menu. The owner's Swedish accent only heightened customers' expectations for the baked goods.

"European Butter Cream is the only way to go," Mother said. She pulled out the P and the E file cards and placed them in front of her.

I shot her a quizzical look.

"Cross-reference," she said.

Next, she plucked the C card from the box. My heart raced with the sudden realization that the word church began with the letter C.

"It's been some time since we've attended Mass, but I'm certain we're still members in good standing," she said. "We've made it a point to mail in our weekly offering envelopes. I'll call Father O'Connor tomorrow."

Creek also started with C. At least she wouldn't have to switch cards. I cleared my throat. "Didn't I tell you that we plan to marry at the creek?"

Mother tapped the end of her pen on the table as if sending my transgression to God via Morse code. "And Jack...what does he think?"

"He's fine with the idea." Her pen hovered over the card. "I'm sure once he sees everything in bloom, he'll be even more thrilled with the decision," I said, trying to convince myself.

Mother looked to the cards, then wrote Church–see creek. On the second, Creek–see church.

I straightened in my chair and smiled. Planning a wedding with Mother wasn't so bad.

"Mrs. Whitehead's nephew is a member of the clergy, one of those Free Methodist churches of one kind or another. I'm sure he can help us out in a pinch." She grabbed a P file and wrote Pastor what's his name on it

Then came D for dress.

Mother threw a glance over her shoulder to make sure Daddy and Jack still sat in the living room. "Now, about the gown," she whispered. "It could become an issue if we're not careful. White would be dishonest, yet cream could raise eyebrows."

"Do you think people really care what color my dress is?" I whispered through a clenched jaw.

She let her pen drop. "Jack would certainly care, would he not? I suspect that's why you've never mentioned the baby to him."

I crossed my arms and fell back in the chair. "There's never been a good time, that's all."

"Nor will there ever be. Leave the past where it belongs, Cara. You'd regret the day you ever told him."

I rolled my eyes. "If you're that concerned about it, Mother, tell your friends that I chose cream because the white of the gown could never compare to the white of a Poeticus and the dress would look dingy."

She brought the pen to the corner of her mouth. "Why, that's simply brilliant, dear."

As Mother completed the cards for invitations, photographer, and reception, her warning shot through me. My mind wandered to the creek's embankment where I had told Noah about my baby and how he had taken the news so well, even holding me, comforting me.

I hope this doesn't change anything between us, I had said.

Or had it?

Mary Rose set the coffee cup on the table. "I remember the day Paul was brought to the hospital where we both worked. I was in a patient's room and my occupational therapist supervisor called me out into the hall and told me that Paul had been in a car accident and was in our E.R." Her finger traced the rim of the cup. "I was thinking, you know, a fender bender. That he'd need X-rays or something. When I got there, I knew that it was bad. The doctor looked nervous and he had the social worker with him...for grief counseling." Mary Rose bit her lip as a tear rolled down her cheek.

"The doctor said they did their best to save him, but despite all their efforts..." Mary Rose wiped her eyes with the back of her hand. "At first it didn't sink in. Then they asked if I wanted to see the body. Can you imagine? They didn't say husband or Paul. They said *body*."

I took her hand in mine. "I'm so sorry."

"I knew that if I didn't see him, I'd never accept his death."

I thought back to the nurse cradling my baby in the doorway. How I'd been given a chance to see her, but chose to look the other way.

"I walked over to the gurney," Mary Rose recalled. "The I.V. was disconnected...just hanging there. The cart with the paddles pushed to the side. The shirt I bought him for his birthday was cut up the middle. I told myself that a lot of people probably owned a shirt like that. But the wedding band...it was...ours."

She glanced down at her diamond ring. "I finally got the courage to slide it off his finger. And there it was on the inside– *Forever yours, Mary Rose.* When I had it engraved, I never knew that it would serve...to...you know...identify him."

I wiped my own tears with my shirtsleeve.

Mary Rose drew a quick breath. "I'm sorry, Cara. Here I hardly know you and I'm upsetting you."

"It's okay. You need to talk about it. Please…"

She closed her eyes and leaned her head back. After long moments of silence, she turned to me. "I must've driven past the scene everyday for months. I'd get out of the car and walk the length of the skid marks. When they were no longer visible, I counted the steps, trying to reconstruct what had happened. Did he even see it coming? What was the last thing that went through his mind? Did he suffer? But nothing haunts me like the fact that he was alone, that I never got to hold him...to say goodbye."

I gripped the arms of the kitchen chair and felt myself being wheeled past the nursery empty-handed.

"Can you imagine?" she whispered.

Jack warded off all visitors to our new home until a woman from Designs by Paloma could work her interior decorating magic. "We're just not quite there yet," he'd told Mother and Daddy when they asked to come to the house. "We want it to be perfect."

Mother accepted the explanation, but made it clear she wouldn't wait much longer.

Although Paloma had planned a three week holiday in her native Spain, she assured Jack that her assistant could consult long distance. Paloma assured me that the designer would work with my art, and my paintings would remain the focus of the rooms. Jack was on the phone with Paloma's assistant demanding additional swatches of upholstery and drapery fabric, while I slipped out the door to return to Stony Harbor to join Mother and my bridesmaids at the bridal salon.

Gabriella's was known for its designer gowns. There were no bargains, closeout sales, or women frantically grabbing dresses off the racks like over at the Bridal Loft across town.

"Don't worry about the price, dear," Mother said in a loud enough voice to get the owner's attention. "It's one of the most important days of your life."

Gabriella scurried off to gather an armload of dresses before herding me into the changing room. I put on the first dress and walked out, leaving the train back at the changing room door. My jury looked up.

"Too frumpy." Tory scowled.

"Ditto," Steph said.

Erin wrinkled her nose. "It's just not you."

Mother motioned for me to spin around. "I'm afraid I'd have to agree, dear. Not to mention the long train just wouldn't work out in the wilderness."

"It's hardly the wilderness, Mother," I said.

"I suppose the wooden floor your father has ordered will help with such matters."

The second gown drew the response, "too frilly." The third had a plunging neckline deemed too revealing by Mother and Steph, but drew applause from Tory. The fourth, with an Elizabethan collar, was voted ridiculously conservative by Tory, but received high praise from Mother and Steph.

Erin looked to the fifth dress and shook her head. "Where's the texture, the richness?" she asked. "Reminds me of watercolors, not oils."

Gabrielle zipped up the last gown. "This one is beautiful." She smiled before leaving the dressing room.

I had to agree. It was simplistic–a satin bodice, coupled with a tulle skirt. I twirled like a ballerina in *The Nutcracker* and stopped in front of the three-way mirror. My fingers swept over the pearl beading along the neckline, and then the waist, as I remembered Noah had always been partial to Tchaikovsky.

"Which suite is better, *Dance of Reeds* or *Fairies*?" he'd ask, then sigh. "Ah, the impossible question."

I stood on my tiptoes and curtsied. "Perfect."

"Are you okay in there?" Mother called.

I stepped out. "What do you think?"

After a moment of silence, Mother's hand went to her heart. "Breathtaking."

"Stunning," Steph said.

Erin nodded. "Wow."

"I suppose some men like demure," Tory mumbled.

We looked to Gabriella for the final word.   "Splendid."

Smelling a sale, she ran for her tape measure.

We moved on to the bridesmaids' dresses. After an hour of "You must be joking," and "I wouldn't be caught dead in that thing," and "Not in a million years," I took control, circling the rack until I found the iridescent top with a matching A-line skirt, pistachio in color. "There," I said, holding it to my body. I smiled as I realized how to seal the decision. "It will complement the green center of the Poeticus."

"Sure," Steph said.

"Great," Erin replied.

Tory nodded. "I suppose it will work."

When it came to daffodils, they knew better than to argue.

The coffeemaker sputtered, squeezing out the last drop of vanilla nut. Mary Rose pulled the lemon poppy seed muffins from the oven. Just as she turned toward the table, a high-pitched cry wound its way down the staircase.

"Oh, my," Mary Rose said, throwing off her oven mitt. "She usually sleeps through our morning coffee. I'm sorry."

"I've been looking forward to meeting her," I said.

Within moments, Mary Rose came back to the kitchen with a small child in her arms.

"This is Harper. Would you like to hold her for a moment while I finish?"

"Um...well...sure." I held my arms out like a forklift. How long I had dreamed of holding a child and now my arms wouldn't comply.

"Relax, there's nothing to it." Mary Rose bent me at the elbows and tucked Harper inside. "The first time I held her at the hospital, I worried she'd break in half. I soon learned that children don't care how you hold them, just as long as you do."

Jane was held by the nurse, I rationalized, and I'll bet her adoptive mother never put her down.

Mary Rose walked over to the counter and poured two cups of coffee. I waited nervously for Harper to cry, but she remained content to watch her mother move about the room. With Paul's black hair and Mary Rose's curls, the little girl surely drew attention everywhere she went. Looking into her blue eyes had to be comforting for Mary Rose; Paul's lasting gift to his daughter. Harper nestled into my chest and I instinctively wrapped my arms around her.

"How did you come up with the name Harper? It's so different," I asked.

"It's my maiden name. We wanted it to have special meaning." Mary Rose placed the mugs on the table. "So, tell me, how's the wedding planning?"

"We have a month yet." Bouncing my left leg up and down sent Harper giggling. "But if you listened to Mother, you'd think it was more like an hour. She spent weeks figuring out the seating arrangement for the reception, only to realize that Mr. Neilson once had an affair with Mrs. Boyce and she had them seated at the same table. Of course, this had a domino effect since Mr. Neilson has had affairs with most of the women in town. Poor mother thought she'd have to sit him up front with the wedding party. Then she worried that my friend Tory knew Mr. Neilson. Mother eventually placed him with the clergy and crossed her fingers."

"Oh, my. He could've sat with me." She laughed and handed Harper a cup of milk.

"I'm sure Mother didn't want to inflict him upon you. I've told her that we're best friends and I suppose she wanted to keep it that way."

"Tell her I appreciate that."

"What you'll appreciate even more is the coffee selection for the reception. Mother went all out on the imports. She knows we love our beans."

"Nothing but first class it sounds like. By the way, speaking of first class, how's the interior decorating coming along?"

My fingers wove in and out of Harper's loose curls. "Jack landed a big client, so he felt entitled to go all out. They're currently working on color schemes."

"They? I thought you were the artist."

"I told him what would work best, but apparently he needed a second opinion." I bent over and breathed in the gentle scent of baby shampoo and my cheek came to rest on the top of her head. "I suppose he'll consult me sooner or later." Harper started to fidget and

I moved her to the other side.

Mary Rose motioned for her. "How rude of me, making you hold her all this time. I bet your arms are just killing you."

If she only knew they had never felt better.

Tourist Trap

Jack stood at the front picture window and waited for the guests to arrive. Headlights sent him scurrying to the door, then back to the window when the car rounded the corner and continued down the street. He pulled back his jacket sleeve and checked his watch every few minutes as if it had lied to him just seconds before. Finally, a car pulled into the drive.

"It's about time," Jack said, giving the sofa pillows one last fluff on his way to the door.

Mother and Daddy were the first to arrive and Jack quickly offered a tour. Mother's "*oohs*" and "*aahs*" echoed down the hallway. She said, "About this Loompah woman–"

"That's Paloma," Jack interrupted.

"Why, whatever the name, she certainly had some marvelous ideas." Mother ran her finger across the custom, plaid sofa. "I've always loved red and gold color schemes, it gives the house a certain...what would you call it..."

"Richness," Jack offered.

"Coldness," I whispered as I draped shrimp over the rim of a glass. The only room with any warmth–my studio; a place in which Paloma and her crew had not gained admission.

I held a jumbo shrimp in the air. "A far cry from pork-n-beans, right, girl?" Sadie thumped her tail on the floor in either agreement or solicitation.

"You've done rather well for yourself, Jack," I heard Daddy say. "Your client base must be growing."

They all walked back into the kitchen. "I believe moving to the affiliate office to be the best decision of my life," Jack said.

"The best in your whole life?" I asked.

"Besides the decision to marry you, of course," he quickly added.

Voices trickled in from the foyer, then Steph and Andrew

popped into the kitchen.

"My, my," Steph said. "Looks like I'll have to open another store in order to keep up with Attorney Templeton."

Mother patted Andrew on the arm; her condolence that he was merely an accountant.

"Yes, quite the house," Andrew added, then immediately placed his fingers across his lips as if he had spoken out of turn.

Steph pointed to the *foie gras*. "Fattening. I hope there's something else to eat."

"Why don't I tour you," Jack said. "There's not one calorie involved. In fact, you may even lose a few pounds walking from one end to the other."

Steph and Andrew fell in line and Jack guided them through the kitchen, pointing out all the amenities to prevent any oversight: Vulcan stove, marble countertops, forty-two inch cabinets.

"This is the best," Jack said, pulling out a drawer. "Food warmer."

Steph nodded. "That wouldn't be practical for our salads and fruits, would it, Andrew?"

"Honestly, Steph," Mother said. "Today's a special celebration. You could give yourself a treat every now and then."

"Yeah, go hog wild, butter your roll," I said.

"Make fun of me all you want," Steph quipped. "I won't be the one crying when summer *rolls* around."

"Okay," Jack said, "why don't we move to the living room." Daddy tagged along for a second look and Mother took over kitchen duty. Her sighs grew heavier with the opening of each drawer.

"What now, Mother?" I asked.

"Cara, how do you ever expect to prepare a meal with things so disorganized?" she said.

"Disorganized?"

"Well, take your silverware for example. Not only is it two drawers down from the stove, but look inside." She motioned me over.

Rather than risk further ignorance, I stared at the utensils and waited for direction.

"Teaspoons and tablespoons are interrupted by dessert forks, and butter knives are lumped together with steak knives." Her fingers bounced about the felt lining showing me the correct order.

I was just thrilled to have a complete set.

Then she pointed to the spice rack on the countertop. "And don't even get me started here," she said.

I stepped aside. "Have at it. I know you won't rest until then."

Mother moved the Allspice to the front of the line, nudging the basil to the right. "Cayenne...cilantro...cumin...curry...dill…oh, forgot black pepper. But if we made that ground black..."

Hearing a knock at the door, I excused myself from the kitchen. Tory stood on the front step.

I waved her inside. "Just in time. Mother's in the kitchen."

"That's certainly trouble." Tory stepped into the foyer.

I looked over her shoulder to her car. "Where's David?"

"Oh, he's not coming."

"Everything okay?"

"He's a bit restless. Pulling out the World Atlas."

"Worried?"

"Not yet." She looked around. "Wow, you told me the house was big, but I never imagined this." She turned toward the staircase.

"Why, if it isn't the long lost friend," Jack said, his entourage following him down the stairs.

"I've hardly been lost. And if I remember correctly, it was quite the wait for an invitation," Tory reminded him.

"And well worth it, I hope." Jack grabbed her by the hand. "Let me show you around." He jerked her up the staircase before anyone else had a chance to say hello.

"He's certainly glad to see her," Steph said.

"Just another helpless victim that fell into the tourist trap. Wait until she gets to his office." I motioned a fake yawn.

By the time we made it back to the kitchen, Mother was all the way to yarrow. She nodded. "That about does it. Now, let's finish getting dinner ready."

Mother and I carried the serving platters and bowls to the table while Daddy played with the retractable awning on the back of the house, extending it outward. He clucked his tongue. "I'll be damned. Now, that's something."

Steph and Andrew looked out over Lake Michigan talking about her upcoming triathlon this summer. I was just about to call Jack back downstairs when he and Tory entered through the kitchen doorway.

"So, Cara," Steph turned to Tory. "How is your new friend, Mary Rose? From what Mother tells me, you've become best buddies."

Tory laughed. "If they were best buddies, I would think Mary Rose would be here."

"Maybe she's out searching for that perfect housewarming gift," Steph said.

"Actually, her daughter has the flu," I explained. "I told her not to worry, that I'd be over in the morning for coffee."

Tory turned toward me. "I didn't even know you liked coffee."

"She loves it," Steph said. "She must, since they meet everyday to drink it. Isn't that right, Cara?"

I pulled the pineapple-glazed ham from the oven and turned to Mother and smiled. "What do you think?"

"Oh dear, you forgot the cloves," she said. Her hands went to the spice rack, but stopped short. "It's too late. It was probably hiding behind the paprika. You shouldn't have that problem when Easter dinner comes around."

Daddy opened the wine. "Ready for a glass?"

"More than ready," I said.

Jack led us to the dining room with dark velvet draperies, a cherry wood table laced with Egyptian cloth, fine china, and brass candelabra. Mother nodded at the place card holders she had bought. "Impressive, dear," she said as she draped her napkin across her lap. "I've never had a ham without cloves, but I suppose I'll expand my food choices just as I preached to Steph earlier."

Tory turned to me. "You two have coffee *everyday*?"

I shrugged.

Steph heaved a sigh. "Okay, I thought I could keep an open mind, but why does everything have a glaze, or gravy? Ever hear of the word plain?"

Daddy poured the wine and held up his glass. "To Jack and Cara's success and their beautiful new home."

Jack placed his arm around me and lifted his glass. "But more importantly, to my beautiful wife and our upcoming wedding."

"Of course, to the upcoming wedding," Daddy finished.

"Why, yes," Mother said. "The wedding is more important than any old house."

I glanced at Mother who had never looked happier.

April seventh was the day Jane turned one year old. My weekly planner had nothing listed for that day. It should have read, Celebrate Jane's 1st birthday, then spelled out the last minute chores: pick up cake, get bags of ice, wrap presents. While her adoptive mother blew up balloons, hung streamers across the living room, and lined the kitchen table with trays of finger foods, I lay in my bed, closed my eyes, and invited myself to the party.

Jane donned a new birthday dress, white with a pansy print. She wore white barrettes in her hair.

"My, what a big girl you are," a guest said and patted her on the head. The birthday girl smiled before tucking her head safely between her mother's legs.

Jane's father stayed busy with larger tasks: setting up tables and chairs, arranging the charcoal, striking up the grill. Relatives from around the country flew into town, not only to celebrate Jane's birthday, but to congratulate her mother and father on their mastery of parenting skills over the past year.

While the guests dined on marinated chicken breasts, corn on the cob, and tossed salad, Jane ate simpler foods—chicken strips and fries—her favorite. She pointed over to the cake in between bites.

"After dinner, sweetheart," her mother said with the authority of an experienced parent.

When the candle was finally lit, Jane brought her hands together in a loud clasp, her eyes grew wider with each flicker of light. After the birthday song, her mother leaned forward and blew out the candle, but gave Jane all the credit. Just another example of her selfless love.

The party guests made their way over to the pile of gifts stacked four high. Jane's mother did her best to keep her little girl's attention, but Jane moved frantically from package to package.

"Looks like we've opened them all," her father said, picking up scraps of wrapping paper off the floor.

Even with my eyes shut tight, tears managed to slip down my cheeks. I had not given her a doll, wooden blocks, or a set of stacking rings. However, as Nurse Sarah pointed out, I had given Jane the gift of life. That had to be the best present, but I somehow doubted that I'd be getting a thank-you card.

Our morning coffee routine had been established. I'd stumble across the street in jeans, a sweatshirt, and hair that was styled overnight compliments of my pillow, while Mary Rose greeted me with fresh makeup and bouncy curls recently freed from hot rollers. She tried to convince me that if she had the luxury of working from home, she wouldn't be troubled with such, and I swore, in turn, that I'd fix myself up if I had to go one step farther away from home.

We alternated coffee, never drinking the same blend in a week's time. Robust coffee was saved for days with particularly hectic schedules. Even the weather played a role; rainy days brought out a darker roast, while sunshine warranted a lighter one. Mary Rose knew what blend complemented each of the morning baked goods. Cinnamon twists called for Mexican coffee, while apple streusel demanded espresso.

"I'll have to make spiced Madeleines one day," Mary Rose said.

"And what coffee goes with those?" I asked.

"They're best served with Viennese coffee."

"Really? I wouldn't have guessed that." I wondered if I could drink the coffee without crying.

"Missed you yesterday," she said, while placing the Irish mocha coffee, toast, and orange marmalade on the table.

"I just didn't feel like myself is all."

She gave a quick sigh. "After Paul's death, there were several months where I wasn't myself. I became depressed. Very depressed. There wasn't a day that went by that I didn't entertain the thought of suicide."

"How horrible that must have been," I said.

"I wanted to join him so badly. I'd spend the whole day just thinking up ways to kill myself. Accidental ways–just in case it was true that you couldn't get into Heaven if you did yourself in."

"Like how?" I asked out of curiosity.

"Oh, like taking a shower during an electrical storm, running up and down the stairs with a pair of scissors, or letting the car idle while filling up the gas tank. Silly, I admit, but people would have been sympathetic, said things like, 'How unfortunate, poor thing didn't even see it coming. What a tragedy...a freak accident' rather than to blame me. Then I thought of Harper." Mary Rose lowered her head. "She'd already lost her father. She couldn't lose her mother, too."

My need to share my loss rose up in my throat and a blanket of sadness fell over me.

"Cara, you okay?" she asked.

I couldn't leave her wondering. "Last year was difficult. I found out my boyfriend was married and his wife was also...I mean, um, she was pregnant. Then I met the man of my dreams, only to have him leave the country."

"That's awful. I can tell you that I would've killed the boyfriend." We both paused for a moment as if grabbing our weapon of choice. She leaned in. "Tell me about this man of your dreams and why he left."

"Noah," I said. The sound of his name startled me. It had been so long since it had touched my lips.

"Trouble with the law?" she whispered.

I laughed. "No, nothing like that. He moved to Vienna to teach music. We wrote to each other for a while, then the letters dwindled...eventually stopped. I can only assume he met someone else."

"I suppose long distance relationships are difficult to maintain, especially overseas."

"He couldn't guarantee when he'd come back. It was probably for the best. Besides, Jack and I have planned a great life together. A life that most women only dream about."

Mary Rose nodded and offered me more toast.

"We'll have a wonderful life here in Piney Cove," I added, grabbing a slice.

"I don't doubt it." Mary rose held up the marmalade.

"He's a good guy, you know."

"Seems to be."

I dipped my knife in the jar. "Mother and Daddy are nuts about him."

"That's important. Family needs to get along."

"Noah's leaving was nothing more than bad timing." I immediately thought of my other experience with bad timing–my pregnancy. There was so much I wanted to tell Mary Rose about Jane, my love for her, and the reasons behind the adoption.

I put down the knife and cleared my throat. "There's something I've been wanting to tell–"

"You don't need to explain, Cara," she interrupted. "It's only natural to have lingering feelings for someone that left without any closure. Like you said, nothing more than bad timing." She glanced to Paul's photo on the counter. "I understand such things."

Harper cried and Mary Rose bolted out of her chair. I knew she'd never understand the adoption.

Starting from Scratch

The dream started like a typical wedding; the crowd gathered at the creek to share in my joy. The string quartet played *Jesu, Joy of Man's Desiring* while the wedding party stood segregated at the end of the runner as if at a junior high school dance. Jane, now a little girl, was at the end of the bridesmaids' line in a satin, cream-colored dress and matching ballet slippers. She held a basket of Poeticus petals, scooping them up in her hand, then letting them fall between her tiny fingers.

Daddy stepped up beside me and I pulled down my veil, my vision now clouded by the netting draped over my face. While counting on him to get me to the final destination, I concentrated on combating the stiffness that made my first few steps resemble a wind-up toy. Before long, I took my rightful place next to the groom. The pastor started the ceremony with the familiar, "Friends and family, we are gathered here today…"

Suddenly, I tasted panic and struggled to breathe, the veil choking off my air supply. Something was terribly wrong. Had I chosen the wrong colors? Did I forget to invite someone? Was that thunder off in the distance? The anxiety of not stopping the ceremony was overridden by the fear of mistakenly disrupting something that should take place. I forced my worry aside as the preacher sped through the vows.

"You may kiss the bride," he concluded. When my new husband peeled back my veil, what was dreadfully wrong became ever so clear. He leaned in and kissed me, while I stood accepting my formidable fate.

The preacher cleared his throat. "I now present to you, Mr. and Mrs. Mitch Sanders."

There was an immediate tug at the back of my dress. "Mommy, I'm so happy you and Daddy got married," Jane beamed.

I wiped the perspiration from my forehead. "But...but…"

"Cara," a familiar voice dragged me out from my sleep. "Are you all right?" Jack said.

"Um...yeah." I ran my fingers through my sweat-laced hair. "Just a nightmare that's all."

"Don't you know you're not supposed to have bad dreams the night before your wedding? Now go back to sleep and think pleasant thoughts." He kissed my cheek before placing his head on his pillow.

While Jack fell back asleep, I folded my hands in prayer and thanked God that Mitch Sanders was already married.

The morning alarm brought about more prayers; for the courage to get out of bed, the ability to face Mother's onslaught of breakfast foods, and for the strength to walk down the aisle. I never recalled being so prayerful. Although we claimed to be on the side of religion, we'd never been what I'd consider a church going family. We attended Mass on the major holidays—Easter and Christmas, with Ash Wednesday thrown in as a bonus. An unexpected funeral Mass came our way every now and then. As a child, I had often asked Mother why we didn't attend more regularly. She proclaimed it wasn't necessary to attend to have Jesus in your life; this especially true if it conflicted with a double's tournament at the club.

Even though we didn't practice our faith regularly, we still clung to it at times. Daddy found pleasure in the fact that he could consult someone higher than a judge. Mother kept her prayers simple, "Oh Lord, please let my roast be tender," or "God, don't let Mrs. Whitehead be late for our tee time again." Steph asked for divine intervention upon notice that her new clothing line was scheduled for a late arrival.

I suppose it's too late to pray for Noah to whisk me away in the limo parked out front, I thought, while pulling myself out of bed. After my trip to the salon, my prayers sank to a lower level. "Please, God, *please* don't let me throw up," I whispered, with my head hung over the toilet bowl from pre-wedding jitters.

Mother knocked on her master bathroom door. "Are you coming out soon, dear?"

The nausea, headache, and clamminess made it difficult to stand. I reached for the vanity and pulled myself to my feet. I didn't have to glance in the mirror to know that paleness had seeped through the quart of makeup the salon applied just a couple of hours earlier.

Mother opened the bathroom door and pried the wad of tissue from my hand. "You need to get ahold of yourself. Perhaps you should've eaten a little more," she warned, fanning my face with *Wine Spectator* magazine, the breeze intoxicating. I closed the toilet lid and took a seat. My bridesmaids huddled around me in their pistachio dresses and I was suddenly drowning in a big vat of pudding.

"We can't have you passing out at the altar, or whatever you'd call it outdoors," Mother said. She grabbed my arm, leading me through my entourage and down the hallway to my childhood bedroom. "Your dress is in the closet. Let's get it on, shall we?"

"I just need a few more minutes, Mother. I'll call you."

"But dear, we don't have much–"

I shut the door and plopped down on the bed, leaning back against the headboard. How the room had changed since I moved out on my own. A queen bed with solid bedding replaced my white canopy bed with butterfly sheets, and a small table with a brass lamp now stood in place of my child-sized dresser with mirror. Mother stored my trophies, ribbons, and paint by numbers on the top shelf of the closet; my entire childhood wiped out with one spring-cleaning. Maybe Mother was trying to tell me something. I was now a woman in a world without ribbons and trophies to announce every win, that victories weren't always apparent at first glance, but revealing themselves over time. I needed to stop idealizing how things could've been if Noah hadn't left and focus on my prize–Jack Templeton.

"Are you almost ready?" Mother asked from outside the room.

"Just about." I walked over to the dress. As a teenager, I often thought about my wedding day and the beautiful gown I'd wear. How I longed to be so pretty, so elegant; something all young girls wanted.

I brought the gown to my body and the same thrill that ran through me at Gabriella's made its way down my spine. I could certainly pass for a bride with the dress, hair clips, shoes, garter, and hose. But something was missing. Something a teenage girl knew nothing about.

Eventually, I opened the door.

Mother rushed inside. "Thank goodness. I was afraid we'd have to postpone."

The women swarmed me. Tory and Erin held my arms out and I stepped into the dress. Steph zipped up the back while Mother patted the unruly hairs on my head back into place.

Mother sighed. "You look splendid, dear."

Erin nodded. "Radiant."

"Have I told you that dress has a great slimming effect?" Steph asked.

"I hope it has Velcro on the back for later tonight," Tory said.

"It's not like it's the first time for God's sake," I reminded her. "We've been living together."

"It doesn't matter," Tory said with a hint of authority. "Your wedding night is a clean slate, like starting from scratch." She elbowed Mother. "Isn't that right, Mrs. Robertson?"

"Well...I...I don't really recall," Mother said.

Tory shook her head. "That's certainly a shame. I thought it was something no woman could forget."

Mother pulled her shoulders back and straightened her dress. "Well, now that I think of it, yes, it most certainly is like starting with a clean slate." She grabbed the wine magazine and started to fan herself.

"Mother? You had a dirty slate before your wedding?" I asked.

Her wrist fluttered like wings on a hummingbird. "Not filthy, if that's what you're implying. A bit discolored perhaps." Mother glanced at her watch and threw the magazine to the floor. "Oh Lord, we're late."

She pulled me down the staircase before I could see if my tar colored slate showed through my cream dress.

When Jack's best man, Brian, hadn't made it to the rehearsal dinner the night before, Mother felt faint throughout the entire meal. "Perhaps you should think about a stand-in, just in case he doesn't show tomorrow," she said.

"Trust me, he'll be here. He wouldn't miss it," Jack assured her.

Jack was right; Brian made it. He didn't look at all like I had pictured him. I anticipated the stockbroker look; closely cropped hair with a touch of gel holding it firmly in place, his face freshly shaven with a bit of arrogance exuding from his pores. Instead, he looked as rugged as those cowboys on the cigarette billboards. I stood in the background as Mother instructed and constantly fought the force pulling me toward my only link to Jack's past. Brian caught me staring and made his way over.

"You must be Cara," he said. "Sorry about rehearsal dinner last night. Missed my connecting flight from San Diego."

"Those things happen. It's today that matters most," I assured him.

We both looked across the field where Jack and Tory stood talking.

"I have to admit, I've never seen Jack happier. He always wanted to have it all–great job–beautiful wife–big house. Looks like he wins on all fronts."

"*Hmm*...yes." I watched as Tory placed her hand on Jack's forearm and cocked her head to the right, flaunting her slender neckline.

"We even made a wager a few years back as to who'd get there first. It's my own fault that I lost the bet. If I hadn't introduced him to my uncle, Jack would still be waiting for partnership out in California and he'd never have met you."

"Uh-huh." Tory shot David a glance, but he never looked up from his pocket-sized travel guide. Then Tory leaned over and spoke into Jack's ear. They laughed, followed by his hand coming to rest on her shoulder. She looked at David who finally glanced her way and she responded by brushing her lips across Jack's cheek.

Brian watched the hired help make last minute changes to the aisle. The dirt path had been transformed into a wooden floor, complete with a white velvet runner. "Templeton's a lucky man to have come from nothing and now have all this."

Tory hiked up her dress and pulled Jack across the field. When they reached us, she handed him back to me as if he were a Christmas return. Jack started talking to Brian and Tory pulled me aside.

"Hope you don't mind my flirting. Just trying to get David's attention. He packed a few of his things last night. Claims he's getting organized," she said.

"Oh, no."

"You know what happened last time he organized," she said.

"Yeah, Lisbon, right?"

She shook her head. "No, Uruguay. Lisbon was the time he was thinning out for a garage sale." She rolled her eyes. "Garbage bag, free box, suitcase...what the hell's the difference?"

There was a tap on my shoulder. "Are we about ready, Buttercup?" Daddy asked.

Jack scurried to take his place next to Mrs. Whitehead's nephew, Pastor Fulton. Luckily, Mother was too busy worrying about the small gusts of wind mussing her hair to notice that Jack had seen me in my gown before the nuptials.

I clutched my bouquet of Poeticus tight to my chest to stop my trembling, while Daddy slid his arm through mine. Sadie settled under the big oak tree, tilting her head upward to catch the intermittent breeze. To my right, the daffodils danced to the tune of *Brandenburg Concerto No. 3* and I was transported back to the hillside at Pier Pointe where Noah's head had once lay in my lap and his fingers kept tempo with the same score. I closed my eyes and searched my memory for his face. The lines and creases that I had vowed never to forget were now fuzzy, opaque, like looking in the bathroom mirror after a hot shower. There was no use in wiping the mirror with the sleeve of my wedding dress; it would only make matters worse.

Andrew took Steph by the arm and they started down the aisle. Steph pulled and pushed at her gown, uncomfortable in anything other than Lycra. Then came Erin and David. She stood taller than David and he sported much longer hair. From the back, it looked as though they should switch attire. Tory gathered up her dress and latched onto Brian, the Marlboro Man. In an instant, the image was shattered; a real cowboy would've never considered walking down the aisle to *Sonata For Trumpet and Strings*.

Daddy rubbed the back of my hand. "Here we go, Petunia." He took a large step and I stumbled forward as if walking off a curb.

Left foot, right foot. Smile. Left, right, smile.

Once I got a rhythm down, I felt confident enough to raise my head. Mrs. Jensen firmly gripped the chair in front of her, while

Mary Rose stood directly behind her, waving and smiling. Henry stood two rows up from them. My gaze landed at his feet in search of that briefcase. Distant relatives, Daddy's clients, and Mother's friends from the club filled row after row. We finally made it to the end of the runner and Daddy turned me over to Jack. He took my hand and we faced the preacher together.

Jack leaned over. "Breathtaking," he whispered.

The pastor motioned for the crowd to be seated and opened his genuine black leather Bible; *The King James Version*, not *The Living Bible* that had been tampered with, paraphrased.

He cleared his throat. "Friends and family, we have been brought together today for a joyous occasion…"

My stomach growled. Tory nudged my arm and I shrugged. I realized that I should've indulged in Mother's hearty breakfast.

"Jack and Cara," the pastor started, "this wedding day is only the beginning. The words that you say today will most likely come easy. But nothing is harder than adhering to the vows that you will exchange before us on this beautiful day in April…"

Some of those little cocktail wieners smothered in barbeque sauce would be nice. I knew full well that Mother would never allow such a thing to grace the hors d'oeuvre table at a Robertson wedding.

Pastor Fulton turned to the groom. "Jack, will you take, Cara, to be your wife? Will you promise to love and respect her? Will you be honest with her all throughout your marriage? Will you support her efforts to live her life to its fullest for both the good of the family and her own happiness?"

Jack squeezed my hand. "I will."

Pastor Fulton turned to me and repeated the vows.

I instinctively glanced behind me. Wasn't this about the time Noah should run up the aisle and stop the wedding? I waited for a moment, but the only commotion was a stifled cough from the crowd, a child's cry, and my stomach begging for food once again. Mother appeared to be holding her breath and Daddy stood proudly. All eyes were upon me now, everyone waiting for my answer.

"Cara?" Jack said, squeezing my hand and I turned to face him.

Noah wasn't coming. I would marry Jack Templeton, pure and simple. "I will," I whispered.

Pastor Fulton took the rings and placed them on the inside of his Bible as if they would soak up the word of God. He turned to Jack. "By what token do you give of the vows that you have just made?"

"A ring," Jack said, prying my hand off my restless belly and slipping the ring on my finger. "I promise before God and these witnesses to be your loving and faithful husband. I promise to be your confidante, ready to share your hopes and dreams, as long as we both shall live."

Pastor Fulton asked the same of me and I answered, then placed Jack's ring on his finger.

"Jack and Cara, we have listened to you make a promise to each other that you will share your lives in the covenant of marriage…"

Noah, why didn't you come back? If only you had written…something…anything. Will you ever become a distant memory?

With a thump, the Bible closed. "Jack, you may kiss the bride," the pastor said.

Jack cupped my cheeks into his hands and kissed me.

Pastor Fulton addressed the crowd. "I now present to you, Mr. and Mrs. Jack Templeton."

Mrs. Jack Templeton. Cara Templeton. Mrs. Templeton. Mrs. Cara Templeton. If I rehearsed it enough times it would sound natural.

By the time the wedding pictures were over, my hunger had vanished; proving once again, that if something is ignored long enough, it simply fades away.

King Kokopelli

Mother stretched out the wedding celebration by having a post-honeymoon dinner. An array of bone china, crystal vases, silverware, and Egyptian cotton sheets lined Mother's living room, but Jack remained focused on the wedding gift from Mary Rose.

Mother held one of the copper candleholders to the light and looked at it from every angle. "No offense, Jack, but I fail to see what's so special about this little wiry guy...all hunched over like that, playing his flute." She set the gift back on the table.

"Well, Gail," Jack started, "I know it's not the most expensive gift, but you have to know the legend of King Kokopelli to appreciate him, right, Cara?" He elbowed me to enlist my help in his quest to win Mother's approval.

"*Hmm*...oh...right," I said.

"I'm not familiar with this Kokopop fellow," Mother said.

"Isn't he that fertility god?" Steph asked in a sharp-edged voice. She nudged Andrew. "And to think we've been wasting all of our money at the doctor's office when all we needed was a piece of Southwest pottery."

Mother patted her arm. "In due time, dear."

Jack cleared his throat. "Hopi legend suggests that Kokopelli played a flute while he traveled to pronounce his arrival to the villagers. It was a great honor to be the woman he chose as his companion. Apparently, many of these women bore children from the union and that's why he's regarded as the universal symbol of fertility." Jack picked up a candleholder, caressed it, and placed it back on the table.

Steph rolled her eyes. "Well, we already know that Cara is–"

"Not a big believer in folklore," I interrupted.

Mother shot Steph a warning glance, then said, "John, why don't you tell them what we have planned for tomorrow."

Daddy put down his fork and slid his last bite of tenderloin to

Sadie.

"I saw that, Daddy. I hope you didn't give her table scraps the whole time we were gone," I said.

"Of course not." He smiled. "I believe you will find our gift to outshine those candleholders. Mother worked hard getting the place ready while you were in St. Lucia."

"Place?" I said.

"That's right, Buttercup. We decided that a cottage on the lake would be a nice place for the two of you to unwind on the weekends."

Jack straightened in his chair. "I don't know quite what to say. Thank you."

"Yes, thank you." I picked up Kokopelli. "These candleholders would look great in a cottage."

"Oh, no you don't." Jack grabbed it from me. "They're staying at the house in Piney Cove."

"Remind me to thank Mary Rose for such a thought provoking gift," Steph said. "It has certainly entertained and enlightened us tonight. Speaking of Mary Rose, she seems like a nice person. A little more demure than your *other* friend."

Mother turned toward me. "What does Mary Rose's husband do for a living?"

I leaned back and folded my arms across my chest. "You can't compare Mary Rose to Tory. They are two totally different people."

"Thank God," Steph chortled.

"Mary Rose has a husband, no?" Mother asked.

Daddy looked around and said, "Some dessert would be nice."

I leaned across the table. "Why do you hate Tory so much? I don't recall her doing anything to you."

Steph sighed. "It's not what she does to me, it's what she does to you."

Andrew nodded as if it had been the topic of discussion many of times at their own dinner table. Jack outlined the intricate details of Kokopelli's flute with the tip of his index finger. I knew better than to elicit his help with an argument while he was busy daydreaming about mating rituals.

Mother looked at Daddy who had since settled for another biscuit and she said, "Perhaps her husband was sick the day of the wedding."

"Could've been," he said, reaching for the butter.

"What the hell does that mean, Steph?" I asked. "She does an awful lot for me. She's like a sister, in fact, better than a sister."

"Ouch, that hurt." Steph shrugged, then leaned back in her chair. "She holds you back, that's all."

Mother shook her index finger in the air. "A business meeting would be doubtful since it was the weekend."

I whipped around. "She had a husband! Had! He was a doctor. He died in a car accident last summer. Okay? That's why he wasn't at the wedding."

"Oh, well, that certainly explains it." Mother's face lit up the same way it did every time she was introduced to an important person. "A doctor, imagine that."

"Not just any old doctor," I wanted her to know. "A cardiac surgeon."

Mother tapped Daddy's arm. "A specialist at that, John."

He looked up. "Didn't I see you baking a pie this afternoon?"

Mother stood. "Oh, yes, if you'll excuse me."

"I'm heading upstairs," I said, pushing from the table. "I'll see everyone in the morning."

Jack smiled. "I'll join you." He grabbed the candleholders.

Mother pointed to the kitchen. "But what about the pie?"

Daddy laughed. "They're newlyweds, Gail. I think they have other things on their mind besides your dessert."

"Oh," her cheeks flushed. "Certainly."

Once upstairs, I slid into bed and Sadie hopped up and took her usual spot next to me. She whimpered while trying to get comfortable. "Yes, I agree, old girl. That whole thing downstairs was rather painful."

Jack placed the candleholders on the nightstand, then turned toward the bathroom. "I'm taking a shower. Want to join me?"

I waved him on. "You go ahead. I'm exhausted."

Jack shut the bathroom door and I looked at King Kokopelli, that stick of a man who taunted me, reminding me of my obligation to get pregnant now that I was married. I turned off the light and settled in before Jack ever made it to bed. While I drifted off to sleep, I swore I heard *Swan Lake Waltz* coming through that long, narrow flute.

Lake in the Woods was just what the name implied, set back from the road about a mile and a half into a thick forest. Unless you owned one of the properties, you'd never know the place existed. We followed Daddy's car to a gray cottage with rose-colored doors and shutters. Andrew and Steph pulled up behind us.

Mother started to swat at bugs the minute she stepped from the car. She was the farthest thing from a naturalist; her idea of roughing it was bad room service.

Jack glanced around the grounds, his eyes as sparkling as the water. "Beautiful. This is more than I'd imagined. Gail and John, you shouldn't have."

Mother placed her hand on his forearm. "The two of you deserve some rest and relaxation. Why don't we take a look inside? I've aired it out and tidied it up a bit."

We entered the cottage through the back door, something Mother would've never allowed in a real house. The kitchen table was set for six, complete with floral place mats and dinner napkins folded into the shape of swans. Small appliances lined the countertop. I was happy to see the coffeemaker would brew twelve cups.

"The cupboards have been stocked," Mother assured us.

The living room and bedroom held Mission style furniture, the closest Mother would get to casual décor. I glanced at the lighthouse and seascape paintings that hung on the walls. Why hadn't she asked me for a couple of paintings?

She must have read my mind. "Just until you get your pictures up, dear."

A couple of logs were stacked in the wood-burning stove and the wicker furniture on the screened porch sat at various angles to provide the best view of the lake. The cottage was nicer than any apartment I had ever lived in; a benefit of following Mother and Daddy's master plan for my life. I didn't know whether to be happy or angry that they finally accepted the choices I made for myself.

Daddy looked at Jack. "Are you up for a little fishing?"

"Sure," Jack said.

I laughed. "I never pictured you as the outdoor type. Do you even know how to fish?"

"I'm a quick study." Jack turned toward the door, then glanced back over his shoulder. "How about you, Andrew?"

Andrew looked at Steph.

"Sure, go have fun." She released him with a nod.

The men gathered the fishing gear stored in the wooden shed and rowed the aluminum boat to the middle of the lake. Steph and Mother sat in the screened porch to enjoy nature behind a safety net and I went outside on the dock. Just as my eyelids gave way to the warmth of the sun, a car barreled up the drive and honked the horn three times. Tory's signal. She got out and scurried toward me.

"Watch out," I called. "Don't get your heels stuck between the planks."

She plopped down beside me.

"How'd you find us?"

"I was a good eavesdropper at the wedding," she said. "Pretty nice place. Marrying Jack is certainly paying off."

I laughed. "To think I caught up with Steph with a single 'I will' and a kiss from the groom."

"And the honeymoon?"

"I went straight to the beach to paint while Jack befriended the concierge. The most important person on the island, Jack claimed. You should have seen the staff running around refreshing our drinks, bringing fresh flowers, and changing out the towels three times a day. It only confirmed Jack's belief in the power of the almighty dollar."

"At least he has money. More than we could say about Mitch who barely had two nickels to rub together. Which, I might add, will soon be reduced to one nickel. Rumor has it that his marriage is falling apart."

I shrugged. "Don't care."

"Oh, *please.*"

"Really, I don't." I turned away to hide my smile, then spun back and grabbed her arm. "Do tell!"

"I don't know the specifics. He wouldn't say."

"You mean you talked to him?"

She sat cross-legged on the dock. "Yep. He said he was getting a divorce. I couldn't help but to tell him all about your new life, your gorgeous husband, your fancy home."

My breath caught. "You didn't mention the adoption, did you?"

"Give me a little credit, would you? He'd go berserk thinking you didn't want to hold onto the tiniest piece of him. You know how much he loves himself. I think he'll be insanely jealous that you've moved on, that you haven't sat there, waiting for him to come back. And you know what happens when a man thinks you've moved onward and upward."

"What's that?"

"They want you back."

I slapped her leg. "Shut up."

"No, really, they do. Well, except for David. He'd never admit that he wants to come back."

My smile faded. "Whoa, wait a minute. Back?"

Tory looked out over the water. "He took a small trip–thought it best to take a few days off."

"Off of what?" I asked.

"Us, I guess."

I put my arm around her. "I'm sorry."

"It started when my mother asked for money again. He told me to cut her off and I told him to stay out of it."

"God, when's the last time you heard from her?"

"Three or four months maybe. She had a waitress job until she started to call off. You know the story."

"So, what did you do?"

"I mailed the check today. She said she's sober now. Just needs a few bucks to get her bills straightened out."

"Do you believe her?"

Tory shrugged. "Does it matter? She's still my mother."

We both knew that Bernice Parker's abstinence never lasted long. On more than one occasion, Tory offered to pay for the medical bills if her mother agreed to enter an alcohol treatment center. And every time, her mother's response was the same. "No thanks, but I sure could use the cash." Tory would write a check and place it in one of those Hallmark cards dripping with sweetness. I never asked why, nor did I try to stop her. Now, when Tory licked the envelope to that money-laced card, it gave me hope that Jane would continue to love me regardless of what kind of mother I had been.

"I think David was looking for an excuse to bolt," Tory said. "He thinks she's leaching off me. Kind of ironic. I should've never told him about her. Sometimes you're better off if people don't know your dirty secrets. Just be glad you never told Jack about your past."

I chuckled. "You know, that's exactly what my mother said."

"For once, I agree with her."

"On the other hand, if he knew my past, maybe he wouldn't be pressuring me to have a baby so quickly."

"Christ, he doesn't waste any time. Why so fast?"

"Oh, you know. Now he has the house, the job, the wife. It's the only thing missing. Not to mention, Daddy always said family men are more trustworthy in the eyes of clients and business partners."

"What the hell are you going to do?" Tory wanted to know.

I shrugged. "Stall, I suppose. I just need more time. Everything has happened so fast since Jane...Noah leaving, the wedding, the move."

"Don't wait too long. You don't want him losing interest."

"My God, you sound just like Mother."

"We both know a good thing when we see it," she said, stretching out on the dock. "Besides, sooner or later, you'll hear that biological clock start to tick."

I stretched out next to her. For the next hour, I heard the men's muffled voices float back to shore. Birds chirped, tree branches rustled overhead, and a couple of doors down some children laughed. "Five more minutes before you have to come inside," a voice came. Sadie's tags jingled as she readjusted herself beneath the oak tree on shore. I heard every sound but a ticking clock. I relaxed, surrendering to the joys of nature while the thought of pregnancy slipped from my mind.

As Jack brought the boat back ashore, Mother called from the screened porch, "I hope your trip was productive."

"Very fruitful," Jack assured her, holding up a string of perch. "You'd swear they were multiplying."

After the last guest pulled from the cottage, Jack grabbed my hand. "Come on." He hurried me down to the dock.

"But it's dark outside...and a little chilly," I reminded him. "Where are we going?"

He steadied the boat with his foot. "Hop in."

Jack held my hand as I searched for safe footing, then I made my way to the front bench. He untied the rope and sat down in the middle of the boat. A moonlit path opened before us.

"Where are we going?" I tried for a second time as the oars dipped into the water, drawing us forward.

"Does it matter?"

"Suppose not." I repositioned myself on the bench and settled in for the ride. The sounds of the night were different than those in the daylight: the hoot of an owl, the chirping of crickets, the lap of the waves on the boat.

The boat suddenly stopped, jolting me. "Damn it," Jack said. With each attempt to paddle, the smell of raw, decaying vegetation rose from the water. "We're stuck in this...this...shit." Suddenly, the boat gave way and lurched forward. "There. I'm getting out of this muck before we end up here all night. The smell is enough to kill me."

We finally settled into a rhythm and sliced through the darkness while fish jumped for their midnight snack, then slipped back into the lake.

Jack fidgeted, rocking the boat side to side. "You would think they'd make a more comfortable seat."

I lifted my chin skyward and breathed in the damp air– refreshing, like my nights on the beach with Noah. The lights from the cottages on the embankment cast a soft yellow glow that could only be detected between swirls of fog that now hovered above the water.

"Can't see where the hell I'm going," Jack said. "Maybe this wasn't such a good idea after all." He let the oars drop to the sides of the boat, then scooted to the front, taking a seat beside me. "This is far enough." He began tugging at my collar and tried to loosen my shirt. Then his hands crept into the waistband of my pants, pulling them down.

I grabbed his wrists. "Jack, we don't have...you

know...protection. Besides, we'll tip the boat over."

"*Shh*, we'll be fine," he said before taking off the rest of my clothes and placing them in a pile on the bottom of the boat. He wrapped me in a blanket.

I don't know why I didn't put up an argument. Maybe it was because I had always wanted to fool around outdoors. Make up for all those boys who never as much laid a finger on me at the drive-in movie or on a camping trip, for fear that Daddy would lock them behind bars. Perhaps I wanted to believe that Jack felt as comfortable with nature as I did.

Jack slid off his shirt and dropped his pants around his ankles. There was something about him undressing in the paleness of the moonlight; a shadowy, indiscernible figure. An outline that could be filled in with my imagination, an imagination that rowed me back to shore–to the grassy hillside at Pier Pointe.

Cemetery Ladies

The Gallery at Pines Crossing sat wedged between a fine jewelry shop and a custom furnishings showroom. A gourmet deli, Tiffany lamp emporium, and an antique place specializing in upscale, vintage clothing rounded out the strip. A dock at the end of the row provided easy access for boaters who had a sudden urge to spend money. Lanterns were mounted on each storefront and a bowl of dog treats labeled 'sea biscuits' sat tucked inside one of the doorways for any four-legged visitors. Standing outside the jewelry shop, I pretended to admire the emeralds, rubies, and sapphires while I settled my nerves. I hadn't the need to sell myself to Mr. Farnsworth. He allowed me to show my pieces as an employee benefit. Mrs. Calloway didn't owe me such a perk, my artwork would have to sell itself. I walked over to the gallery door, took a deep breath, and marched inside as if I'd done business there for years.

A woman looked up from her desk and walked over to greet me. A colorful scarf with geometrical shapes fluttered around her neck. Her glossy blonde hair knocked her black pantsuit down a few shades.

"Mrs. Calloway?" I asked.

"Yes," she answered.

I extended my hand. "I'm Cara Templeton."

"Hello, Cara. Blythe Calloway." We shook hands in that limp kind of way that gave no commitment on either end. She pointed at the leather sofa lining the wall. "Please, sit down. I'll make some raspberry tea."

I took a seat and placed my portfolio next to me. The gallery was much larger than Mr. Farnsworth's place. The equal distribution of oils and watercolors eased some of my tension. An entire row of paintings by the same artist proved that Mrs. Calloway opened her gallery to those she thought deserving. She came over and handed me a cup with wisps of steam.

"Thanks, Mrs. Calloway" I said.

"Please...call me Blythe." She plopped down on the sofa, tossed her head back, and heaved a sigh. "Please tell me you have more to offer than most of the artists in this town."

"I'll let you decide." I handed her my portfolio.

While she flipped through it, I tried to read her tight, little face, but detected not a hint of emotion. Daddy would have declared her an excellent jury member. I nervously sipped my tea until she raised her head.

"Welcome to my gallery, Cara. How many paintings do you have available?"

"Three."

"Great. If I like them, we'll sign a contract."

It was time to make a name for myself in Piney Cove. I brought in the paintings of jonquils, Jumblies and Lemon Glows.

She looked over the pieces, then grabbed a contract for me to sign. We ended our agreement on a handshake.

"Daffodils, the flowers of hope," she said. "And who on earth doesn't need a little of that?"

I had never met Paul Townsend, but I knew him from stories that I'd been told. During morning coffee with Mary Rose, I learned that Paul's favorite food was Pad Thai, that he loved to read true crime, and that he dreamt of buying a sailboat one day.

"You know," Mary Rose said, "he never planned on becoming a cardiac surgeon. His real love was pediatrics, but it broke his heart the way some of those kids wore black and blue as casually as they wore a T-shirt and jeans. During his rotation he heard all the excuses. Bruises explained away by parents. 'Oh, he's just clumsy,' they'd say. Or 'she's just shy.' And that emotionally labile child 'just didn't have a sense of humor.' But they couldn't fool Paul. He knew exactly what was going on in those homes–the same things that went on in his home when he was a child."

Mary Rose looked up from her cup. "You know, the memories never left him, not even after all those years. At night he'd bolt up in a cold sweat, gasping for air, sitting there for the longest time. I'd ask, Paul, are you okay? The bed shook right up until his head hit the pillow and he began snoring again."

"How awful," I said.

"Yes. Sometimes Paul envied his mentally retarded brother who'd been sent away to a group home. Paul was thankful that he was in good hands."

She reached for a tissue and dabbed her eyes. "Can you imagine Paul's mother calling out, 'Pauley! Help! Call the police,' before her husband grabbed her around the throat?"

I reached down and stroked my own throat. "Oh, my God. What did Paul do?"

"He was too afraid to stay put, but too scared to leave. If he picked up the phone, his father hit him."

"That's horrible."

"He'd see his mother sprawled out on the kitchen floor–her arms and legs bent underneath her. His father would step right over her without as much as checking for a pulse. Then he'd go click on the television with the same hand that struck his wife and son but a few seconds earlier."

"Did they ever try to leave, get away from that monster?"

"Paul claimed she was too afraid. She'd just get up, dust herself off, and go about cleaning the dinner dishes. Paul called it the 'eerie calm,' like the stillness that precedes a tornado. Then he'd sit and wait for that train whistle to announce the next round of violence."

I leaned back in my chair, sickened by imagining their pain. "No wonder you don't have any contact with his family."

"Exactly. We agreed never to subject Harper to that kind of abusive environment. I suppose we don't have to worry since they have no interest in our lives. A blessing, really."

I finished my cold coffee, saddened by the fact that his life ended as tragically as it began. I thought of his love for Mary Rose and Harper, taking some comfort in the fact that Paul had found a way to repair his wounded heart before he died.

I resisted King Kokopelli's charm for a couple of months by turning the holders toward the wall and never lighting the candles.

"You could at least dust the things," Jack would say. "Give them a little respect."

"Why are you so obsessed with them?" I asked.

"I'm not obsessed, just intrigued. Aren't you happy that I want to start a family? That I'm interested in more than just my career?"

When he put it that way it was hard to resist, and when the temptation was strongest, I'd tuck the King away in the hall closet, only to have Jack bring him back to our room. "Nice try," he'd say, placing the holders even closer to the bed.

Then something changed. It could've been Jack's storytelling of how Kokopelli scattered seeds onto barren land and played that little flute of his to bring warmth so they'd grow. "I'm sure he sowed daffodils," Jack said. Or it could've been the wine and the jasmine aromatherapy candles. Whichever the case, I now stood in the bathroom and stared at the test window for five minutes just as the directions stated. With the last pregnancy test, I was nowhere near ready for the result; and when the test had turned positive, I was even less prepared for the repercussions. This time I wanted a blue line to appear, but there was none. I sprawled out the instructions on the vanity and checked each step. Had I missed something that would justify starting over? A new test that might yield a new result. Sadie came over and sat at my feet, looking up with somber eyes as if she understood my disappointment. After ten more minutes, the window remained empty. I threw the test in the garbage and crawled back into bed.

Jack looked at me and I shook my head.

He stroked my arm. "Maybe next month."

The next month brought the same result. After Jack left for work, I pulled the test out of the garbage in hope of a delayed miracle, but it remained negative. I slid into the shower and cried. I didn't know why exactly, maybe because I wanted something that I didn't have. Or maybe it was that I once had something that I didn't want, but now did. It didn't much matter; either way, I was still empty-handed.

August sixteenth held little significance in my life, but to Mary Rose it was the day her world changed forever–the day Paul had died in that tragic car accident. We drove to the cemetery to honor the one-year anniversary of his death. The only other time I had been to a cemetery was the day we buried Aunt Kate. I remembered peeking at the older, more weathered headstones, subtracting the date of birth from the date of death. Surprise rushed over me, the number so low. Only twenty-two? Could that be right? When we came upon Paul's headstone, I quickly did the math–forty-one. The marker read, *In loving memory of husband and father, Paul M. Townsend.* The other side, *In loving memory of wife and mother, Mary Rose Harper-Townsend*, with no date of death inscribed. I wondered how strange it was for Mary Rose to see her name on a gravestone, knowing that by merely adding a few numbers her life would be over.

Harper reached out and traced the letters on the stone with her index finger. She walked around and around the marker, giggling with each step. Mary Rose knelt down and placed a bouquet of white roses tied with a red ribbon on his grave. She made the sign of the cross and bowed her head in prayer. Even with her eyes sealed shut, tears made their way down her face. I picked up Harper and held her as Mary Rose wept at her husband's grave.

"Cry," Harper said, sticking her finger into one of my own tears.

"Yes, cry," I whispered.

After a few minutes, Mary Rose repeated the sign of the cross and stood. "God, I miss him."

"I know," I said.

"I feel so close to him here, like I can almost reach out and touch him. I want to believe that he can see us...that he knows we're doing okay."

"Of course, he does."

We turned and made our way to the car. After a few steps, Mary Rose looked back over her shoulder. "Goodbye, Paul," she whispered.

Pulling out of the cemetery and onto the main road, I had a sudden panicky feeling as if I had accidentally left something important behind.

For Mary Rose's Christmas gift, I chose to paint a still life of Twin Sisters, white daffodils with tiny, yellow cups. Referred to as cemetery ladies in the south, they only seemed right given the peace she found at Paul's grave. The painting would cover the bare wall in her living room that nagged me during our morning coffee.

Crisp, autumn days brought steady rain, making ripples across the lake; no better time in which to paint. Day after day, I spent hours in my studio painting pictures to replace those that sold at the gallery. Blythe had been right when she told me the townspeople would welcome a touch of spring into their homes, especially during the winter months that were approaching; months when the snow piled up between storms with no melting period in between. Jack continued to bring in new clients with zoning work, real estate contracts–big land development money. One had to look no further than our custom home furnishings and Jack's new BMW to see his reward. Busy workdays took our minds off the absence of a positive pregnancy test. I tried not to worry, but still did. What if I couldn't have another baby? How would I live with the fact that I had given away my only child? Jack shot me the quizzical look about every twenty-eight days, give or take a day or two.

He walked up to my easel. "Are we?" he asked with a hint of impatience.

"No."

"Are you sure?"

I put down my paintbrush. "Yes, I'm sure, Jack. I would know."

He took my hand. "Do you think that you should go to the doctor? Maybe there's a reason you can't get pregnant."

I folded my arms across my chest. "I can get pregnant. There's nothing wrong with me."

"Obviously, there's something wrong. It's been five months now. Infertility?"

"If you insist on blaming someone, why don't you blame King Kokopelli?" I pushed back my chair and stood. "I assure you that it's not infertility."

"How can you be so sure?"

My anger intensified. "Because I've been pregnant before." Fear immediately replaced the anger.

He stepped back. "But I don't...I don't understand. Did you miscarry and not tell me?"

Mother's warning shot through me, but it was too late. "It was before I met you."

"I still don't understand."

"The baby was placed for adoption."

"Adoption? Wait a minute. You have a baby running around somewhere?"

"Had," I corrected him.

He paced the floor. "But your baby's still out there, Cara."

I glared at him. "You think you have to tell me that, Jack?"

"I can't believe you didn't tell me this before we got married."

"Jesus, Jack. You make it sound like you would've had second thoughts about marrying me." His silence confirmed my suspicion. "Well?"

Still no answer. I brushed past him, grabbed my backpack, and ran out the door. Sadie followed me to the Jeep. "Come on, girl." She hopped inside and we headed south to the cottage, a place void of people and questions.

While driving for the next two hours, I replayed the scenario in my head and wished that I had heeded Mother's warning and kept my past out of the present. Would Jack ever trust me again, knowing that I had kept something so important from him? Did he now question if I would be a devoted mother to our child after walking away from my responsibility to Jane? Could Jack accept the fact that I had once carried another man's child, yet failed to carry his own?

I called Sadie inside the cottage and started a fire in the wood-burning stove, then made my way to the screened porch. The abundance of stars and the light of the moon cast out onto the water, made it worthwhile to sit in the frigid air. Not a single light shone from the opposite embankment. The cottages had been sealed up in preparation for the winter months, something Daddy had planned to do for us last week. Thankfully, he'd gotten sidetracked with a high-profile case. Sadie burrowed her muzzle into my legs. My eyes grew heavy, until a knock at the door sent me to my feet.

"Cara, let me in," Jack's familiar voice called.

I cracked the door. "Please, not tonight. I want to be alone."

"I'm not leaving."

I knew that he meant it, so I stepped aside to let him in. "God, I've been worried sick. I called Mary Rose, Tory, your parents." He tilted my chin up, but I refused to meet his eyes.

"Of course, I would've still married you," he said. "I was just shocked...I couldn't think...that's all. I'm sure you understand what a surprise it was to find out now, after all the time we've been together."

I nodded, then buried my head into his chest. "It was such a painful part of my life, so difficult to talk about. I didn't want you to think I was this...this horrible person."

He took my hand and led me to the sofa where, for the next hour, he listened to the story about Mitch and Jane and even Mitch's old wife. I recalled minor details, like Mitch's smile when he thought that our baby looked like him, his wife's perfect hair and lustrous skin that glowed in the sunlight as she was wheeled from the hospital cradling their baby girl, and the way Mitch tucked her safely into her car seat before pulling from the parking lot; things that seemed insignificant if taken out of the context in which they belonged.

When I finished talking, we sat on the edge of the couch, teetering as though the slightest move would send us tumbling to the floor. The crackling of the wood-burning stove filled the huge expanse of silence.

Jack turned toward me. "I don't know what to say."

In place of words, we made love in the confines of our cottage just as we had any other night, before he knew my past. Mother was wrong. I had bared my soul and Jack understood.

Tory canceled our Christmas Eve plans because David wanted to go out of town for the holidays. She thought it best to accompany him to Chicago so he wouldn't get carried away at O'Hare airport and jump on the next plane to Suriname. Mary Rose gladly stepped in as a substitute.

"I've never had a night away from Harper," she said. "I won't know how to act...what to wear."

"Don't worry. Our goal is to relax and have fun. Who's watching Harper tonight?"

"One of my co-workers. She's staying home for the holiday and has a daughter Harper's age. She said she'd keep Harper for as long as I needed. Do you think a couple of weeks would be taking advantage?"

I laughed. "Like you could go without her that long." I pointed up the staircase. "Go get dressed. I'll be back at four-thirty."

We kept with tradition and attended five o'clock Mass. Mary Rose wouldn't hear of sitting in the back pew where Tory and I usually sat. Instead, Mary Rose pulled me up front where old ladies clutched their rosaries tighter than they would hold their handbags in a New York subway station. These same women knew all the prayers and didn't have to mouth substitute words like watermelon and pickle relish like I did. Now under scrutiny from the entire congregation, I dismissed the idea of darting out the door before Father McGowan served the Eucharist and I settled in for the duration of the service.

He started with the usual Christmas Eve homily. "We must remember the true meaning of the holiday, the birth of Christ, our Savior."

I suppose the message was worth repeating every year since dancing Santas pushed aside manger scenes at the local department stores. Unfortunately, most people had already decorated, even as early as the day after Thanksgiving. Something Mother couldn't tolerate. "Next thing you know," she said, "they'll just lump Easter and Christmas together. Make it one big holy celebration. We'll just hide the presents out on the lawn and be done with it."

Mary Rose eagerly recited the Mass prayers, charged through the Eucharist line, and wished all the churchgoers a merry Christmas after the service. When we arrived at her house, she held onto her leadership role by accepting the responsibility of the sacrifice. She plopped the lobsters down into the water without the need for background music. I suppose not having a man in her life hardened her. I opened the bottle of wine and we sat in the living room, waiting for the lobsters to cook.

Mary Rose nervously shifted her glass from hand to hand.

"You don't drink, do you?" I asked.

"How can you tell?"

I pointed at the glass and laughed. "You look as though you want to pass it off to anyone that happens to walk by."

"I'm sorry. You were nice enough to bring the wine. I hope it doesn't offend you."

"Of course not. We just won't be arguing over the last glass, like Tory and I usually do."

"It's all yours," Mary Rose said, handing me her glass.

"Thanks." I set it on the coffee table. "We'd usually exchange gifts after dinner, but I'm dying to give it to you now. Do you mind?"

She smiled. "You know, I was just thinking the same thing."

I brought out the present that I had wrapped before leaving for Mass. It was in the usual disarray; a bow on top that didn't quite match, the ends of the paper cut too long and twice folded over.

She felt around the four corners, then cupped her mouth. "You didn't."

I shrugged.

The paper fell to the floor. "Oh, my God. It's beautiful. It will be perfect in this room." She pointed above the recliner chair. "Right there."

"Exactly," I said.

She studied the painting. "I've never seen this variety of daffodil before," she said.

"Twin Sisters."

"Well, it has certainly felt that way since the day we met, hasn't it?"

"Yes, it has."

"I have a little something for you, too." She went to the bedroom and came back with two gifts, handing one to me. "This is from Harper."

The bow matched, but I detected a thin filler strip and I smiled. The small painting inside titled, 'The Artist' had been professionally matted and framed. The colors were smeared together more by accident than design, reminding me of my first pictures.

"One of Harper's finger paintings," she said. "I knew you'd appreciate it."

"I love it. I'll hang it in my studio."

She handed me the second gift. "This one's from me."

I opened the box and smiled. "Sable paintbrushes, a luxury."

"I hope you like them. The store clerk helped me pick them out."

"They're perfect."

Mary Rose motioned for the No. 6 filbert and ran the jet-black bristles over her cheek, then looked to her new painting. "It's amazing how something so dark can give off such light."

Don't Badger Me

The lack of a positive pregnancy test haunted me through the winter months and into spring. Looking out my bathroom window at the budding trees, green grass, and colorful flowerbeds, I couldn't help but think my odds were better during this time of growth and renewal.

"C'mon, c'mon," I chanted, standing at the vanity in my bathrobe. A blue line inched across the stick. Was it really blue? Why did I suddenly doubt my ability to recognize color? I was an artist for God's sake. With my judgment clouded, I called for a second opinion.

Mary Rose rushed over and placed Harper on the floor with makeshift toys: hand-held mirror, plastic toothbrush holder, headband. Turning her attention back to the stick, Mary Rose looked at it from several different angles, and finally declared, "It's positive!"

I ripped it from her hand. "Let me see that again." I squinted. "Do you think we should call the 1-800 number?"

"What for?"

"I don't know."

"Cara, you don't need a customer service person sitting at a desk halfway across the country to tell you that you're pregnant. I'm telling you, it's positive."

I sat on the edge of the tub. "I can't believe it. I'm pregnant. I'm finally pregnant." Relief and panic battled for my attention.

"When are you going to tell Jack?" Mary Rose asked while handing Harper a small travel case.

"Jack? Oh, yeah, Jack. God, he'll be thrilled," I said. "He'll be home in an hour, but our wedding anniversary is tomorrow, so I think I'll wait and surprise him in the morning."

"Can you wait that long?"

"What's one more day?" I held up the stick. "I'll gift wrap it."

"That'll be quite the anniversary present." She suddenly

clutched her chest. "Oh, no! I just thought of something. You won't be able to drink coffee."

"Decaf!" we said in unison.

She looked at her watch. "Well, I better go before Jack gets here because I can't promise I wouldn't blurt out the good news." She reached for Harper. "Let's go, sweetheart."

After they left, I gathered the wrapping paper, invisible tape, and a bow from the closet. I calmed my trembling hands before using a ruler to measure the paper, then folded the corners as neatly as sheets on a hospital bed. There was no room for error in wrapping this gift. My pregnancy would be announced in style.

I had barely eased into slumber before the jury came back from deliberation, a bad sign according to Henry. I gripped his hand as the group of men and women, both young and old, took their seats in the box. The judge accepted the slip of paper from the bailiff and read it, then sent my fate traveling across the room and into the foreman's hands. Henry and I stood at the judge's request.

"Has the jury reached a verdict?" the judge wanted to know.

"We have, Your Honor." The foreman looked a little too happy.

"And what say you?"

"In the matter of Cara Templeton vs. the State of Michigan, we find the defendant guilty of attempting to pursue happiness."

Gasps echoed throughout the courtroom. A commotion stirred behind me and I turned to listen.

"She really shouldn't have tried to outdo me," Steph told Andrew.

"Can't you pull some strings, John?" Mother asked Daddy. "You know the judge, don't you?"

Mitch laughed and turned to his old wife. "What made her think she could get over me?"

There was a tug at my orange jumpsuit. I looked down to see Jane with tears in her eyes. "Did you think that a new baby would make you happy, Mommy?"

Henry's hand came to rest on my shoulder. "I'll start working on the appeal. Don't talk to anyone. But more importantly, don't let anyone see you smile."

Tory raced over. "I told you life was too short not to wear heels." She whipped out a pair of three-inch orange spikes and handed them to me.

Jack came up behind her and shook his head. "I should've represented you. I would've done a better job, trust me."

Mary Rose dabbed her eyes with a tissue. "I'll leave a pot on for you."

The bailiff came over and cuffed my hands behind my back.

"Just a minute," Nurse Sarah called, running across the room. "You won't need this where you're going." She stripped the pendant from my neck.

The bailiff led me back to my cell. I sat on the edge of the cot and stared at the cold, gray concrete surrounding me. With good behavior, maybe they would let me paint a mural on the wall to brighten the place up a bit.

The alarm jolted me awake. Relieved to see drywall, I settled back under the covers while Jack made his way to the shower. I reached into the nightstand drawer for the wrapped stick and nervously waited for his return.

He came out of the bathroom dressed for work. "My, you're up early this morning." He leaned over the bed and kissed me.

"It's a special day."

"Special day?"

"Jack Templeton! Don't tell me you forgot!"

"Forgot what?"

"Stop."

"Stop what?"

"You know, our anniversary."

"Oh…that. Now, how could I forget?" He went over to the armoire and brought back an envelope.

A card? That's it? Did he really take the paper anniversary seriously?

He smiled. "Happy anniversary, sweetheart."

I swallowed my disappointment. "Thanks." I opened the envelope and pulled out an official looking document with the word deed across the top with an address below: 1090 Oak Hill Lane.

I looked at Jack, then back to the paper. "1090 Oak Hill Lane?

Where is…" Then I subtracted the address from my parents' house. "Oh my God, oh my God, oh my God!" I jumped off the bed and twirled around with the deed to the creek property pressed to my chest.

"Surprised?"

"I had no idea. I can't believe it! This has to be the most incredible gift in the world."

"Your fears of back hoes and dump trucks can be put to rest. The property is yours to do with as you please."

"Which will be absolutely nothing."

He brushed my cheek with the back of his hand. "I'm glad you like it."

"Like it? I love it!" In all the excitement, I had forgotten about his gift until he glanced toward the bed. I went over and grabbed his gift. "I doubt that it can compare to the creek, but I tried."

He felt the outline of the package. "Let me guess, a new fountain pen. Fitting for the paper anniversary." He tore off the wrapping and rolled the stick back and forth like a thermometer, trying to get an accurate read.

"Jack?" I finally said.

He glanced up with that hesitant lawyer look, needing more evidence before he was convinced. "Is this what I think it is?"

"Uh-huh."

He pulled me tight to his chest. "Now that, darling, is the most incredible gift in the world. Just think, he can take over my firm when I retire."

I pulled away. "He? And if it's not a boy?"

"What?"

"Maybe it's a girl."

He laughed. "I suppose that could happen."

Jack made reservations at The Wine Cellar restaurant just outside the small town of Cedar Hollow. He drove around the parking lot several times, stalking those coming out of the restaurant, only to be disappointed when they darted in the opposite direction from the one in which we were driving. "What the hell's going on here tonight?"

"Oh, I remember. I read in the paper that there's a conference in town. Michigan Meat Cutters Association."

"It makes sense. This restaurant does have the best steak around." He whipped the car into a newly vacant spot. "About time."

We made our way inside, only to find it more crowded than the lot. A singer, seated on a bar stool in the corner, entertained those waiting for a table with songs from the 70's. She had one of those raspy voices that made me want her to clear her throat.

Jack walked over to the *maitre d'*. "Reservations for Templeton."

The *maitre d* looked at the list. "Ah, yes. Right this way, please." He stopped at a table next to the kitchen.

"Is this the best you've got? It's rather noisy," Jack said.

"I'm afraid so, sir. We're very busy this evening. I can put your name back on the wait list if you'd prefer a different table."

Jack glanced around at the diners who looked nowhere near ready to leave. "This will have to do."

The man pulled my chair from underneath the table and I sat down. "Enjoy your evening." He walked back to the front of the restaurant.

"Damn badgers," Jack said as he spread his napkin across his lap.

"Excuse me?" I said.

He made the outline of a rectangle on his shirt pocket with his index finger. "Conference people."

"Oh, a name badge!" I laughed. "Well, I hate to say it, but it's because of those damn badgers that we're able to afford this nice restaurant. They do drive the new business in town. You should be nice to them."

"Whatever."

I leaned over the table. "So, are you going to tell me why we're celebrating?"

He placed his hands on the table, palms up, and motioned for mine. "I landed some huge clients this month. Even Dunn was impressed–not an easy thing to do. He was so impressed that he made me partner."

"That's wonderful news, Jack." I squeezed his hands.

"I told you that all my hard work would pay off. Our life is about to change significantly."

I dropped his hands and leaned back in my chair. "But...but I like our life the way it is."

"We'll have so much more. You'll see."

"We have everything we need. What else could you possibly want?"

"Look at your parents. They can afford anything. Your father is one of the most respected attorneys around. People envy him for what he has."

I thought about the price Mother paid for Daddy doing so well by them.

"There's nothing wrong with wanting it all," Jack said. "No need to feel guilty. If I hadn't set my standards so high, I wouldn't be married to you or be living in the beautiful house we enjoy. And the last piece of the puzzle will soon fall into place." He reached over and rubbed my belly. "We can buy the baby all those frivolous things."

I batted his hand away. "I don't like frivolous things. I like simple."

He laughed. "Darling, we surpassed simple a long time ago. Now that I'm a partner, we'll need to entertain clients in our home. Catered events, of course. Your energy will be spent socializing."

I recalled Daddy's dinner parties during my teenage years. Mother nearly lost her mind trying to get all those place cards in order; names that didn't make sense, like Wilson Hanley and Gallagher Bingham. "Why on earth do they have two last names?" Mother would say in frustration, crumpling the card and starting over.

She never allowed Daddy's gatherings to be catered. "Why, they'd think I couldn't cook and that your father is starving. They'd assume that's the reason he…"

She'd never finish the sentence. Mother truly believed that the way to a man's heart was through his stomach. She couldn't figure out why, even after the mammoth breakfasts and enormous dinners, he still chose to spend time with other women. I didn't have the heart to tell her it had nothing to do with quiche or chicken cordon bleu.

Jack demanded that we eat from the market price section of the menu to celebrate his good fortune. He looked at the waiter who now stood at our table. "I think I'll have the three pound lobster."

"But you don't even like lobster," I reminded Jack.

He laughed. "I know, but it's the most expensive thing they have."

"Lobster it is. And for you, ma'am?" the waiter asked.

"I think I'll have–"

"The same," Jack interrupted. "She'll have the same." He grabbed my menu and handed it to the waiter.

I looked at Jack. "I don't want the same. I want a pasta dish."

"Darling, you can get pasta any time. We're here to celebrate my success." He laughed. "You don't celebrate with pasta for Christ's sake. Hell, you and your friends even celebrate Christmas with lobster."

"Comparing your partnership to the birth of Christ, are we?" I asked.

"No, but close."

"Would you like me to come back in a few moments?" the waiter asked.

"No," Jack said. "We'll compromise. She'll take the twin tails with a side of pasta."

The rest of the evening, I picked at my food while Jack told stories of new land deals and all the money to be had in the condos sprouting up along the lakefront. Once we got home, I went straight to bed. Jack crawled under the covers, then on top of me.

"Not tonight," I announced.

He pulled up. "What?"

"No." I pushed him off and rolled over, proving to Jack that the simple pleasures in life couldn't be taken for granted, no matter what his income.

Please join us in celebrating Harper's 2nd birthday
May 22nd at three o'clock
1266 Devonshire Court

I put the invitation on the table and a wave of nausea rolled over me as I realized I'd forgotten Jane's birthday a few weeks prior.

Maybe it signified that I was moving ahead with my life, something natural, yet disturbing. Was it how Mary Rose felt when she rolled out of bed each morning following Paul's death?

"Is there anything I can help you with?" I asked Mary Rose.

"Nope. All you have to do is show up. We're just thrilled that you're coming. Last year, Harper and I had to eat the whole cake ourselves."

I laughed. "That was certainly a hardship."

Mary Rose stood and walked to the kitchen counter. She stopped to steady herself at the island, her free hand grabbed her side.

"You don't look so good. Are you okay?" I asked.

She laughed. "You'd think I was the one who was pregnant. I'm bloated, tired, running to the bathroom every hour. Must be sympathy pains."

"Maybe it's all the coffee we've had over the months."

"Could be. But why stop now?" She poured us another cup and came back to the table. "Oh, would you mind making a couple of posters for the upcoming occupational therapy conference? I'm on the local committee, but my handwriting leaves much to be desired."

"Sure. I'll make them now while we talk."

She handed me the poster board, markers, and the information sheet, then said, "Good thing we have the conference center in town. Otherwise, I wouldn't be able to go. I'd rather give up my restaurant seat and parking space to a badger in town, than to travel cross-country for a meeting."

"Jack feels altogether different," I told her. "Just the other day when he was late for work due to traffic, he proclaimed that Mayor Burton should declare it badger season." I stopped writing and looked up from the poster. "Do you think they know we call them badgers?"

"I'll announce it at the conference."

"Are you kidding? You have to spend two days with those people. I think I'd leave it a town secret." I finished the first poster and placed it on the table to dry.

Mary Rose picked it up. "Absolutely beautiful. Is this calligraphy or something?"

"No, just my style."

"Amazing. I have to say, I could pick your handwriting out in a crowd."

"There goes my chance of ever writing a death threat." I took a sip of coffee.

"Were you planning to do so?" she called over her shoulder as she got up and made her way to the oven.

"It depends upon whether Jack still plans to host his social events at the house while I'm pregnant."

She laughed. "In that case, I've never seen your handwriting before." She pulled the loaf of cinnamon bread from the oven. "I hate to take advantage, but are you up to making some name tags?"

I motioned for the rectangular stickers. "Why not? Those burrowing mammals help pay our bills." I chuckled. "According to Blythe at the gallery, badgers devour daffodils regardless of the fact they're poisonous."

Steph purchased her second store, The Annex, shortly after I announced my pregnancy. She gave up on the notion of having a baby. "Better you than me," she had said. "I don't know what I was thinking anyway…with my busy schedule and all."

I couldn't tell if she was serious or rationalizing, but either way it helped to alleviate my guilt.

The new store had a prime location, a couple of blocks from The Jungle Jym, the most popular fitness center in town. Steph had advertised her grand opening in the local paper and her loyal customers from The Sport Port made the trek across town to pledge support. They liked Steph because she understood their way of thinking; the need to skip the dessert tray at a five-star restaurant, to exercise on Christmas Day regardless of family plans, and to toss around carb load and carb deplete as if they were everyday words. They appreciated the fact that she stocked the latest equipment: gadgets to monitor heart rate while exercising, radios, water bottles that attached to the waistband for easy access, glow in the dark shoelaces for that midnight jog. I never knew that staying fit had become so complicated. My hands rummaged through one of the clothing racks, the closest I'd come to exercising.

Steph had ordered three dozen leopard print spandex pants for the special event. The moment I said, "Who on earth would buy such a thing?" a woman walked up and grabbed two from the rack.

While Steph totaled the woman's purchase, I checked out the refreshment table. The food reflected the clientele's lifestyle: Perrier, granola bars, vegetable trays, fruit salad, strawberry-banana smoothies. Daddy stood at the table, grief-stricken.

"My customers eat healthy," Steph reminded him.

Daddy slid his plate back into the pile when she wasn't looking.

"What a lovely turnout, dear," Mother said. "I'll have to tell the women at the club the next time you have a sale. You will be having a sale, won't you?"

"Of course," Steph said. "Everyone loves to think they're getting a bargain."

Jack plucked one of Steph's business cards from the holder on the countertop. "How did you come up with the name, The Annex? It doesn't have the same ring as The Sport Port."

"It's pretty obvious," Steph replied. "I couldn't think of anything better."

"Well, you didn't ask the right person," Tory said, stepping up from behind.

I thought of crouching down in the middle of the clothing rack to avoid the crossfire.

"I suppose you have a better idea," Steph hissed.

Tory nodded. "Simple. Lose Your Fanny Cranny."

"What?" Steph said.

Everyone, but Steph, howled with laughter.

"Don't Overcook Nook," Daddy said, glancing down the fat-free buffet table.

"I'd go for simplistic—Fit Pit," Jack offered.

"Wait," I joined in, "what about, Watch What You Swallow Hollow?" I winked at Daddy.

Mother flapped her arms like a fledgling learning to fly. "We can't overlook the Drop and Give Me Ten Den."

Steph rolled her eyes. "Real funny, everyone."

"Okay, on a more serious note," I said. "How are you going to manage both stores at the same time?"

"I have a couple of new employees starting tomorrow. One has experience in retail management. The other's a college student taking night classes. Seems reliable. At least she better be." The bell chimed and Steph looked toward the front of the store. "New customers, have to go."

"By all means," Daddy said. "We'll be leaving soon, anyway."

Mother looked at the clock with jogging feet in place of hands. "Yes, it's getting rather late."

After my parents left in search of the nearest restaurant, Tory elbowed Jack. "Congratulations, by the way. I can't believe Cara is having her *first* baby."

"Tory, he knows," I said.

"Yes, she told me everything," Jack confirmed.

Everything except for Noah.

Tory heaved a big sigh. "I have to admit, I'm certainly glad the charade is over. Putting on a front can be rather tiring."

My legs suddenly grew heavy and a wave of exhaustion swept over me. I looked at the chair by the fitting room. "I better go sit down."

The Next Train to Happiness

The bear-shaped sign on the front lawn announced that Harper was two years old. And if by chance people forgot, by the time they made their way to the front porch, the banner on the storm door would serve as a reminder. Inside, more evidence: streamers, hats, matching plates, all covered with the number two.

"Do you think I overdid?" Mary Rose asked, tying off the last balloon.

"Is that possible?" I asked.

"I suppose I'm making up for last year. I was still in shock over Paul's death and barely felt like getting up that morning, let alone celebrating." She pulled out a punch bowl and set it on the countertop. "God, I wish he was here to see how she's grown."

I looked up to the ceiling lined with dozens of silver and blue balloons, their ribbons falling down like confetti from Heaven. "He is here, Mary Rose."

Her eyes followed my gaze. "I think you're right."

She made last minute preparations, while I entertained Harper. A few of Mary Rose's colleagues trickled in. With each new arrival, Harper stuck out her hand for her gift.

Mary Rose shook her head. "Would you look at her. Queen for a day."

When it came time for the cake, Harper squealed the moment she saw the candles. She stared, her eyes growing wide.

"Blow them out, honey. Blow," Mary Rose coached her.

When Harper failed to give in to her mother's urging, Mary Rose and I leaned in, and on the count of three, the candles went out and two thin wisps of black smoke rose into the air.

Harper devoured the cake set before her. The guests laughed and she responded by shoving even more into her mouth.

I pictured Jane with frosting smeared on her cheeks, running her chocolate-laced fingers through her hair just like Harper. I suddenly realized I had to look no further than across the street to see how Jane spent her time, what she ate for lunch, the clothes she wore, and what milestones she had reached. For the rest of the party, I took in Harper's every move, her every word. Then I watched as she ripped open her gift from me and held up her new paint and brush set.

"I paint! I paint!" Harper rushed over and hugged my legs, spilling the tears that had welled in my eyes.

Jack hung up the phone and stomped into the living room. "A Tuesday, can you believe it?" he said. "They want me to settle for a Tuesday night. Who throws a dinner party on a Tuesday night?"

I stopped writing and looked up from my pregnancy journal. "What are you talking about?"

"The caterer–The Epicurean." Jack ran his fingers through his hair as he always did when short on patience. "They're booked solid. No Saturdays for the next four months."

"Why don't you just use a different caterer?"

He threw up his arms. "Because they're the best. Honestly, Cara, what are you thinking?" Jack marched back into the kitchen, dialed the phone, and accepted The Epicurean's proposed date. "I want dinner to be served at exactly seven o'clock. Not a minute later," he said, gaining back a bit of the control he had given away.

It didn't take long for Jack to push aside his anger when the caterer sent over the menu: arugula and pine nut salad, crab avocado canapés, veal roll with apricots in calvados, poached salmon with caper sauce, steamed baby artichokes and red potatoes, fresh stuffed peaches.

Jack had planned a flawless party to impress his partners. That morning, he explained the rules for the event. "Derby likes to hit the booze, so we need to instruct the wait staff to water down his drinks toward the end of the evening. When he gets toasted, it isn't pretty. God help any women in the room." Jack bent over and smelled the long-stemmed white roses in the crystal vase in the center of the table. "Dunn thinks he's a comedian, so you need to laugh at his jokes even if they aren't funny. And trust me, they aren't. Although, I'm sure he had to have a sense of humor at one time to marry that ditzy wife of his." Jack examined the white and burgundy linens, bone china, and silver, nudging the items to the left or right accordingly. "Whitaker's on the conservative side. No politics or religion or he'll go Rush on you. And who needs talk radio when you're trying to have a relaxing evening." Jack looked at me as I plucked flowers from the vase and placed them in different positions. "You getting all of this, Cara?"

"Every word," I assured him.

"Now, for the politicians. Commissioner Philips is a control freak. Let him re-arrange his silverware. Hell, even the furniture–I need to stay on his good side. You already know Mayor Burton. Let's not mention the word badger or I might say something I'll regret. That damn convention center is Burton's only accomplishment over the past four years, but the townspeople will still re-elect the bastard. Don't make the mistake of confusing the Aldermen. Rice, Hewitt, and Venture do look similar–all three are middle-aged balding men with beer guts and cheap, wire-framed glasses. The difference–Rice has a slight southern drawl, Hewitt wears loud ties, and Venture sports a cleft chin. Just be nice to them all and you can't go wrong."

"Is there anything I shouldn't do, Jack? You know, like pass gas...belch...run around the house naked?"

"Funny, Cara. Perhaps you should sit by Dunn. The two of you can trade jokes."

I crossed my arms. "Perhaps we will."

Jack retreated to the kitchen to oversee the caterer and I went to change into my party dress. When I returned downstairs, I found Jack stalking the wait staff, straightening their tuxedo jackets, picking lint off their shoulders. He reminded them that red wine was to be at room temperature and the white slightly chilled. They nodded politely as if they had never worked a party before. "Oh, absolutely, sir," they'd say.

I secretly pulled each server aside and guaranteed a larger tip to make up for Jack's obsessive behavior.

I thought about slipping outside and ringing the doorbell to push Jack past the anticipatory phase, but someone beat me to it. Jack made his way to the foyer every few minutes to greet his guests. Their responses were all the same. "What a lovely home," they'd say. "Oh, well...it does the job," Jack would offer. After all the introductions, we sat in the living room to enjoy cocktails and appetizers.

Mrs. Dunn turned to me. "Jack tells us you're a painter, Cara."

I beamed. "Yes, I am."

"I have to admit that I was a bit surprised. I suppose a job such as that could be stress relief. Sort of like mowing the lawn."

"Yes, it is rather soothing," I agreed, not exactly following her.

"Say," she said, "I'm thinking about painting my carriage house. Would you be interested in suggesting a color scheme and giving me a quote?"

I forced a smile that felt too big for my face.

Jack jumped up to diffuse the situation. "Ah, Mrs. Dunn, your sense of humor rivals your husband's. I'm sure Cara can appreciate your art jokes. In fact, I believe she's heard several throughout her career as an oil painter."

Mrs. Dunn blushed. "Of course, she has."

Jack smiled at me and pointed above the fireplace. "That's one of her pieces above the mantel."

"What a splendid piece," Mayor Burton said. "You'll have to gather all of your artistic friends from around the country for a conference here in town. We have quite the center, you know."

"Yes, we do," Jack said.

Mrs. Burton turned to me. "Cara, where did you get the inspiration for the painting?"

"Yes, I was wondering the same thing," one of the overweight, balding Aldermen said.

Then I noticed his turquoise tie with the assortment of sea creatures in orange, purple, and lime green. *Hewitt.* I suddenly found myself the center of attention, wanting desperately to share my passion, but unable to speak out of fear that I might say something wrong in front of Jack's elite social circle. Everyone stared at me, wanting an answer, even the wait staff had stopped serving.

Jack prompted me. "Cara, sweetheart, why don't you tell them about your beautiful daffodils?"

"Well," I started slowly, "that particular daffodil field is at the creek."

"Oh, a creek," several voices echoed.

"How lovely," Mrs. Burton said.

Their smiles gave me encouragement. "The creek where Jack and I were married."

Complete silence.

Jack hesitated a moment, then smiled with a glint in his eyes; the look that said 'watch me spin this'. "It's not your typical creek, by any means," he assured them. "And it certainly wasn't your typical wedding. Sure, we could've had the usual church wedding–boring. We wanted something people would talk about for weeks after. Cara is an artist, after all. We transformed the place–you should've seen it. We had a wooden floor put down and the chairs had these big bows across the backs, wrapped up like presents. Mr. John Robertson, the highly respected attorney from Laurel, would never allow his daughter to get married at a run-of-the-mill creek." Jack turned to me and winked. "Tell them, honey, how your mother planned everything to perfection...the string quartet, the engraved invitations." He laughed. "By the time she finished, you'd forgotten you were outdoors."

I couldn't believe Jack felt the need to oversell my special place, making it out to be something it was not. Even after buying the land for me, he was embarrassed by what it represented.

Jack turned to Mr. Derby. "Tell them Derby. You were there. Couldn't even tell it was a creek, right?"

Mr. Whitaker laughed. "Hell, if you served the right cocktails, Derby wouldn't know a creek from the Atlantic, would you, Derb? But I can vouch for you, son. It was a hell of a camouflage. Best damn cover-up I've ever laid eyes on. Believe me, in twenty-five years of practicing law, I've seen my share of cover-ups." He elbowed Jack.

The guests erupted with laughter. Jack joined in, but with a hesitation that told of lingering embarrassment. The dinner bell rang and Jack heaved a sigh of relief.

Sadie yelped as she jumped down from the bed and her back legs gave way to the floor. She tried to stand several times, but did not have the momentum to shift her weight from back to front. Eventually she gave up, placing her muzzle to the ground.

I knelt beside her and rubbed her ear. "What's the matter, old girl?"

I'd put off a visit to the vet for some time. Old age had settled deep within her bones, but the thought of having to make a fateful decision was more than I could bear. Her dull, lifeless eyes told me the time had come. Jack loaded her into the car and I waited for him to get in, instead, he shut the passenger side door.

I opened the window. "Jack, aren't you coming?"

He walked to the driver's side and peeked through the window. "I'd like nothing more than to be there with you, but I have back-to-back meetings. You understand."

"But I need you."

"You'll manage fine without me."

"I don't know if I–"

"Cara," he interrupted, "you're a strong woman. I'm positive you'll make the right decision."

No one had ever described me as strong before. And make the right decision–*me*?

He looked to the back seat. "She's in pain. You better get going. I'll call you later from the office." He patted the roof to send me on my way.

Once inside the vet's office, the technician took Sadie into a small exam room that smelled of rubbing alcohol and wet dog hair. Dr. Nichols came in with his usual tie, the one with the tiny paw prints splattered all over it. "Hello, Mrs. Templeton," he said, then knelt on the floor to examine Sadie. He moved her back leg and she yelped.

Dr. Nichols kept a dog treat in his front shirt pocket for his clients, a reward for good behavior. "It keeps them coming back," he'd say as if they had a choice. Sadie usually lifted her nose to sniff in that general direction, but on this day, her muzzle never left the tile floor.

"Well, Mrs. Templeton, I can't tell you what to do. Sadie is an old dog and she's in significant pain." He reached into his pocket and placed the bone in front of her. "Has she been eating?"

I shook my head.

"Incontinent?"

"Yes," I whispered.

"With all things considered," he said, "euthanasia wouldn't be out of the question. But only if you feel it's the right time."

Sadie's nose had yet to nudge the bone. I knew she would not be going back home. Aunt Kate would have supported this decision. She had determined the fate of many animals along the roadside, cradling an injured turtle or bird in her palm, evaluating the possibility for rehabilitation. She never blinked when it came to a mercy killing. "God brought me to this spot to help this poor creature," she'd say. Then she'd grab the shovel from the trunk of the car, stopping my heart in mid-beat with a thump that was loud enough to penetrate my ears, even when plugged with my fingers. "It's better off now...you know that," she'd remind me. An impromptu eulogy for the animal would follow. "He was a good, kind-hearted mourning dove..." she'd start out. After the last shovel of dirt, we'd go about enjoying the day as if the funeral were an ordinary interlude.

How I needed Aunt Kate to confirm that I was doing the right thing. I called the next best person. Mary Rose arrived within minutes and stood beside me, while Dr. Nichols filled the syringe. Mary Rose tightened her grip on my forearm and whispered, "You're doing the humane thing, Cara."

"You can leave the room if you prefer. The tech can assist me," Dr. Nichols said.

"No, I need to stay," I said.

"Ready?"

Would I ever be? My tears fell onto the back of Sadie's neck as I reluctantly nodded.

"Let's get her to stand." Dr. Nichols went down on one knee and pulled Sadie to her feet. "I'm going to place this tourniquet around her leg and then I'll give her the injection. Her lips may pull back into a grimace. Not from pain, but from relaxation of the muscles, then her legs will buckle and we'll lower her to the ground."

He raised the syringe, removed the cap, and lowered it toward her front leg.

I choked back the urge to stop him. Instead, I buried my head into Sadie's neck. Mary Rose's hand came to rest on my shoulder. "I'm sorry, girl," I whispered into Sadie's ear. My steady stream of tears dampened the thick fur around her collar.

Sadie exhaled the last sign of life and we lowered her body to the cold, tile floor. I reached over and closed her eyelids with my fingertips.

Dr. Nichols made a notation in the record. "I'll give you a few moments." The door closed behind him.

Sadness overwhelmed me, leaving my body trembling with a deep, silent cry. An emptiness echoed inside my chest similar to when Mitch had left me in the hospital, and when the nurse left the room with my baby, and when Noah hopped on that plane for Vienna. Tears for Jane, Noah, and Sadie all mingled together. I suddenly realized I had yet to rid myself of the finite number of tears for each of my previous losses. Hopping on the next train to happiness was much easier than remaining on the platform to finish grief work from the past.

I wept as my hand stroked the side of Sadie's face. I had put her to rest.

Mary Rose hugged me. "You gave her the most peaceful death possible."

I removed Sadie's collar that used to clank in the night whenever she moved or scratched herself. My finger swept over the word *REWARD.* How much I would have given to have her back. To have all of them back. I bent over and held Sadie one last time and like Dr. Nichols' tie, I had paw prints scattered across my heart.

"She died in your arms. That's the most important thing," Mary Rose assured me as tears streamed down her own cheeks. I hadn't even considered that Sadie's death might conjure up painful memories for her.

Mary Rose and I held each other and wept until no more tears came forth. A knock on the door sent us upright and we quickly dried our eyes. "Come in," I said.

Dr. Nichols entered and I turned to Mary Rose. "Do you think that we should wait until tomorrow and bury her when we can get help?"

"Can you call your father now?" she asked.

Dr. Nichols pointed to the door. "You can use the phone at the front desk."

Daddy stood waiting for us when we reached the creek. While Mary Rose and I watched from nearby, he buried Sadie under her favorite oak tree, the daffodils would add life around her each spring.

After patting the last of the dirt into place with the shovel, Daddy walked over and put his arm around me. "I'm sorry, Buttercup. I know how much she meant to you. How much she meant to all of us."

I buried my head into his chest, something I had not done since I was a young girl.

He stroked my hair. "It must have been difficult for you to make such a decision, to let her go."

I couldn't say what it was exactly; but I believed his words of consolation were for more than just Sadie. Maybe I was imagining things. It didn't really matter. I finally heard the words that I had needed to hear for so long.

Late summer brought the need for an ultrasound, the first glimpse of our baby. I sat in the doctor's office waiting room with my bladder so full that any sudden movement such as a cough, sneeze, or laugh would've sent me home for a change of clothing. Luckily, I was neither sick nor in a good mood. The hands on the clock inched closer to my scheduled appointment time and Jack had yet to arrive. Another woman without a partner sat across the room. I wondered why her husband was absent. It didn't matter, we were lumped into the same category–alone.

The door opened and a woman in scrubs stepped forward. "Cara," she said.

I took one last look out the window and into the parking lot. *Damn it.*

"My name is Becky. Follow me." She stopped and pointed to an exam room. "Will your husband be joining us?"

"He planned on it, but it looks like his court hearing ran over this morning."

Her eyes widened.

I quickly realized how that might have sounded. "Not for anything he did…I mean, he wasn't arrested or anything. He's an attorney."

She laughed. "You had me worried for a moment. I can wait a few minutes as long as your bladder can hold out."

"Could you? I'm sure he'll be here any moment," I assured her.

"I'll be back." The door snapped shut.

I sat at the edge of the exam table, while soft rock played in the background; the type of music you didn't notice unless you had nothing to do but listen. My anger intensified with each new song.

Becky popped back into the room. "I'm sorry, but we're going to have to get started. If I didn't have another appointment to follow I would–"

"It's okay," I interrupted, not wanting her sympathy.

She lifted my shirt and squirted the warm gel on my belly as I lay on the table. Then she started moving the wand in a circular motion as if coaxing a genie out of a bottle. Within seconds, my baby's heartbeat drowned out the soft rock in the background.

"Nice sound, isn't it? They tell me that you're due in January," she said.

"Yes." I squinted, trying to make out the image on the monitor.

Becky must have noticed. "Let me help you." She pointed to the screen with her free hand. "Here's the spine. And here's the skull."

I shook my head. "I'm sorry, I still don't see it."

She traced the outline of the baby with the tip of her finger. "Here, look at the leg…and the foot. See?"

Then I saw the baby kick. "Yes...yes...I see it now." My gaze followed the baby's every move, unlike the last time when I couldn't even look toward the same side of the room.

"Do you want to know the sex?" she asked.

"Um…oh God. I guess I should've thought it through beforehand."

Part of me wanted to know. To make an instant connection, something I didn't have with Jane. There were other advantages to knowing. I could call my baby by name while still in the womb, monogram the linens, and buy the proper clothing. Part of me wanted to keep the element of surprise. It would be a good surprise this time, rather than the unpleasant surprise of how hard it would be to give my baby away.

"That's okay," Becky said. "Many people can't decide. I'll write it down on a piece of paper. That way if you want to look later, you'll have it." She finished the ultrasound and pulled a notepad from the drawer. She scribbled onto the paper and sealed it with tape. "Here you go. It's up to you."

After she left the room, I started to open it, then changed my mind and threw it into my backpack before heading to my Jeep. A BMW greeted me as I stepped from the curb.

Jack hopped out of his car. "Oh God, did I miss it?"

"You did," I said, trying to calm my trembling voice.

"Damn it. I lost all track of time. After court, I stopped to talk to Crawley about our 401k plan. You know how that guy can talk."

"So it wasn't court that made you late?"

"Well, no, not technically. But our investment portfolio is coming along nicely." He walked over and put his arms around me. "I'm sorry, Cara. Can you show me a picture or something? I've got a great idea, we'll go somewhere nice for dinner tonight."

"You think a good meal will make up for this?"

"No, but it will give us time to talk. You can brief me."

I pulled away. "Brief you?"

"You know what I mean."

"I'm afraid I do." I dug into my backpack and pulled out the small piece of paper. "Here's your affidavit." I threw it at him, jumped in my Jeep, and tore from the parking lot.

Heartaches and Pancakes

I put down my paintbrush. A bulb waited patiently beneath the earth's surface; next to it, a green stem pushed up through the ground, followed by a bud closed up tight. Finally, a jonquil in full bloom. The mural on the nursery wall would honor the birth of my baby, the emergence of new life.

I sat in the rocker and spread my hands across my growing midsection. My baby responded with a nudge, something I would record in my pregnancy journal before going to bed. I glanced to the sleigh crib on my right with the yellow and green bedding, neutral colors for either a boy or a girl. Hardly a coincidence that they were the colors of a daffodil. Every now and then I wanted to ask Jack about that folded up piece of paper, but my pride wouldn't allow it. I thought about asking in clever ways, like, "Honey, what do you think of this train-shaped coin bank for the nursery?" Or, "Wouldn't this rose-colored tea set look nice atop the dresser?" I tried to read his face whenever I substituted he or she when referring to the baby, but his look held steady. Did he think I would later regret having known? Did he fear showing his own disappointment?

I went over and ran my fingertip down the crib rail, picturing the baby asleep with his or her mouth formed into a perfect little "O." The past two months, I spent hours leafing through drawers filled with baby clothes, pulling out socks and placing them on the end of my thumb. My fantasy continued as I fluffed the crib linens and spun the mobile. I needed to prepare myself for the birth. The fact that I would be a mother once again. Thoughts of Jane came flooding back and I couldn't help but feel both happy and sad. I focused on how things would be different this time. That I'd bring my baby home and place her in her beautiful bed, cover her with a soft blanket, and look forward to her cry of hunger so I'd have an excuse to hold her again. Sitting in the nursery, eased my anxiety.

Once in a while, I'd turn to find Jack standing in the doorway.

He'd walk up behind me and rest his hands on my protruding stomach, then work his hands either up or down, and the next thing I knew we'd be in bed. But, the last couple of weeks, I'd been too uncomfortable and warded him off with a flick of the wrist.

"Well…" he'd say and walk out of the room.

All remaining energy needed to be spent in my studio. Blythe had requested more paintings for the holiday shopping season. Jack and I decided to forgo our trip to Laurel and stay in Piney Cove for Christmas, since I was not up to traveling.

I took a night off from painting when Mary Rose and I celebrated our second annual Christmas Eve Mass followed by dinner at her house. This time, she agreed to sit in the back of the church and skip communion because she still had to put a pie in the oven. I spent Christmas day recuperating from our get-together the night before, while Mary Rose rushed off to church for a make-up session. Before I knew it, New Year's Eve had arrived and Tory called the house.

"Up for some company?" she asked.

"Sure. But aren't you and David back to–"

"No," she interrupted. "I'll be there in a couple of hours."

When she arrived, I waddled out to the driveway to meet her. Jack carried her suitcase into the house, then returned to his study to finish some work.

Tory and I sat at the kitchen table. Her eyes were distant and dark circles told the story of sleepless nights. "Got any wine?" she asked.

"Yeah, let me get some." I opened a bottle of Riesling. The fruity smell wafted upward, reminding me of how much I missed it. I handed her a glass.

"Thanks." She immediately took a few swallows.

"I'm glad you came. I miss you," I said.

"Sorry about the short notice."

I rubbed my giant belly. "It wasn't like we had much else planned. I'm so exhausted that I'm lucky to get showered these days."

She laid her head on the table and began to whimper.

"I don't mind…really," I tried to console her. "Most days I can at least put on deodorant."

She looked up, her eyelashes glistened with tears.

I suddenly realized that my personal hygiene had nothing to do with her sadness. "What is it, Tory?"

"He left me for good. Can you believe that shit?"

"Oh, my God. Are you sure it's not an extended vacation...a sabbatical or something?"

She shook her head, then downed the entire glass of wine and motioned for more. "All four suitcases and a note on the fridge."

I filled her glass. "But David never leaves a note."

"My point exactly." She sniffled as tears fell from her eyes. "Maui of all places."

"What? You've got to be kidding. The man who swore off any destination with indoor plumbing went to Maui?"

"Yep. The bastard went commercial on me. I'm starting to think his whole damn life was a lie."

"So, what are you going to do?"

"Find someone else, I suppose. I'm not about to spend my life alone while he's making it with some hula dancer, for Christ's sake. The only good thing, is that I get to keep everything. The guy brought nothing to the relationship." She motioned for more wine.

"Tory, please don't." I pushed the bottle aside.

"Fill the glass."

"But I hate to see you drink when–"

"Save it, Cara," she interrupted. "I don't need the lecture. I'm not my mother."

"I never meant to imply that you were. I'm just concerned, that's all."

Jack came into the kitchen and poured himself a glass of wine. "Mind if I join you?" He looked at Tory. "So, what's new?" he asked upbeat as if he hadn't noticed her puffy eyes, runny nose, and black trails of mascara down her cheeks.

"You wouldn't believe it if I told you." She traced the rim of her glass with the tip of her index finger.

"Try me," Jack said.

"David left for good."

Jack drew an exaggerated breath, then said, "I hate to say it, but I never did think the guy measured up."

Tory smiled for the first time since she had walked through the door.

"Are you sure he's not coming back?" Jack asked.

Over the next hour, she revisited the evidence to confirm her suspicion: the department store receipt for swim trunks, suntan oil, a copy of *Frommer's Maui*. How David failed to register for the next semester's classes and emptied his underwear drawer. Jack shook his head at key points during the story, more for his own safety, I believed, than out of empathy. They finished the bottle of wine just before midnight, while I nursed my allotted cup of decaf. The fireworks outside announced the New Year's arrival and we went out on the deck to watch the colors light up the cold, January sky.

"Just think, David's resolution was to leave me," Tory said. Then a large firework marked her statement like an exclamation point. "How could I have been such an idiot to think he'd stay put?"

After the grand finale, we went back inside and sat down at the kitchen table. I struggled to stay awake and eventually gave up when my eyes remained closed for longer periods than they stayed open.

Jack shook my arm. "Why don't you go to bed, Cara? Both you and the baby need rest."

I reached up and caught a yawn in my hand.

Tory looked at the kitchen clock. "Yeah, it's about that time for me, too. Right after I finish this glass."

I got up and pushed in my chair. "Jack, are you coming?"

He pointed to the dirty glasses on the table. "I'll be in after I clean up the kitchen."

Tory grabbed the empty wine bottle and threw it into the garbage, then rolled up her sleeves. "Let me help."

"Go, Cara." Jack waved me off with the back of his hand. "We'll clean up."

"Goodnight, you two. Oh, Jack, before you come to bed, show Tory to her room," I said.

"I can do that." He ran water into the sink.

"Oh, and get fresh towels out of the linen closet." I turned back. "And the nightlight…"

He sighed. "I can handle it, Cara."

Laughter followed me down the hallway. Jack must've said

something to lighten the mood. He was always good at that. After climbing into bed, I heard the clanking of glasses and muffled voices, thinking how sad it must be for Tory not to have a man by her side to start the New Year.

The baby gave me a swift kick before I drifted off to sleep.

How many times had Mother said, "For every heartache, there's a pancake. Nothing can ease the pain like flapjacks." Daddy didn't much care about the reasoning as long as they stacked up nicely on his plate. In my mind, Tory needed a big breakfast to ease her troubles. I went to the refrigerator to grab the eggs and milk and found a near empty bottle of wine on the shelf. Jack had broken open a second bottle, it was no wonder they were sleeping late.

While I mixed the pancake batter, he shuffled into the kitchen and headed straight for the coffee.

"Late night?" I asked.

He nodded.

"How's Tory?"

"How should I know?"

"You stayed up talking to her, didn't you?" I said.

"Oh, that. Well, yes. She went on and on about David. I thought it would be rude to cut her off."

I turned my attention to the stove. "She needs our support right now."

When the batter hit the griddle, it made a little sizzling noise like something important was going on underneath, something not visible until the pancake was flipped over to reveal the golden brown underside. The batter soon bubbled in the middle and the smell of freshly cooked pancakes spread throughout the kitchen.

I looked up to find Tory with suitcase in hand. "Aren't you going to stay for breakfast?"

"Not this time," she said. "I've inconvenienced you enough. Besides, I have to go back and fix this mess."

I pointed to the platter. "Can't it wait until after you eat?"

"Maybe she's not hungry." Jack motioned for her luggage. "I can carry that out."

"I really wish you'd stay," I said.

She came over to the stove and hugged me. "I'll call you soon."

Jack followed her outside. I quickly pulled the pancakes from the griddle and went to the front window to watch her leave. A large oak tree blocked my view. A few minutes later Jack walked back inside and went directly to the shower. He returned with his briefcase. "I have to go to the office. There are a couple of things I need to straighten out."

"But it's a holiday. I've made breakfast."

He kissed my cheek. "I won't be long." He walked out to the garage.

I looked down at Sadie's bowls that had yet to be taken up from the floor. She would've eaten pancakes with me. I set the entire platter on the kitchen table and drizzled half a bottle of syrup over them. While shoveling the pancakes into my mouth, I prayed that Mother was right.

That afternoon, Mary Rose decided to empty Paul's closet. She covered her bed with his suits and tucked white shirts neatly inside each one. She switched the colorful ties back and forth. Her hands stopped to caress a dark gray tie with burgundy geometrical shapes. "This one was his favorite."

"Keep it," I said.

She held it to her cheek for a moment before placing it on the dresser. "At least people will get some use out of these suits. They aren't doing anyone any good while hanging in the closet."

The rest of the afternoon, we hauled Paul's belongings to the garage. I never realized how many things a person could accumulate over a lifetime. Private stuff: letters, cards, photographs, old calendars. Luckily, Mary Rose didn't find anything unexpected, like a letter from a secret girlfriend or an illegal drug stash. Paul remained a marvelous husband even after all of his belongings were accounted for. Mary Rose decided whether to place a particular item into the save pile, the Goodwill pile, or the discard pile.

After we carried the last box to the garage, we went back in the house for coffee and cookies. She plopped down in the chair and let out a sigh. "You're probably wondering why I'm spring-cleaning in the middle of winter."

"I figured you'd sort Paul's things sooner or later," I said.

"It took me over two years to get to this point. Every so often, I'd peek my head through his closet door, but I could never go in." She took a sip of coffee. "He used to stand in there every morning and dress. I'd lie in bed and watch him put on his pants, left leg first, which I thought was odd since he was right-handed." She laughed. "Funny, the things I recall. We were married for ten years and what I choose to remember is how he put on his pants."

"But that's what made him Paul." I immediately thought of Noah conducting his imaginary musicians, something I found endearing.

She smiled. "You're right. So, have you picked a name for the baby yet?"

"The girl name is a given. If it's a boy, I'm sure it will be Jack Jr."

"What's the girl name?"

"Can't tell you. I want it to be a surprise."

Mary Rose nodded. "I can live with that. I kept the name Harper a surprise, too. I didn't want outside influence. Paul agreed to the name right away. We always thought alike."

I placed my cup on the table. "Do you think you'll ever find love again, Mary Rose?"

"Maybe, but not like the love I had for Paul. That kind of love comes once in a lifetime."

I slapped the table. "I knew it."

"Oh God," she said. "Don't listen to me. I'm sure some people find that kind of love twice in their lives. In fact, I'm positive."

I laughed. "It's okay. I've accepted that Jack is not Noah."

"You still think of him?"

"Of course. But I have to believe I made the right choice." I pointed to my belly. "Besides, I've put on a few pounds. Doubt he'd want me now."

Mary Rose laughed. "You might be surprised." She looked at the clock. "Is Jack going to wonder where you are?"

"Yeah, I better go." I stood and hugged her goodbye. While walking through the garage, I glanced over Paul's things one last time. His entire life summed up by labeled boxes: shoes, medical supplies, reference books. Then I pictured my labeled boxes: art supplies, more art supplies, additional art supplies. Even the number of boxes would give insight into my personality. Too few boxes might suggest I was either organized or dispassionate; too many—disorderly or sentimental. Paul fell safely in between.

Jack still wasn't home when I walked into the house, so I went straight for the shoebox tucked in the corner of the closet with an old blanket thrown on top. I grabbed the box and sat on the edge of the bed, pulling out the pile of letters tied together with a red, satin ribbon. With a gentle tug, they rained down on the bedspread. All but one was postmarked from Vienna. This letter started, *A letter to my baby, with love*. It seemed so long ago that I had written it. Reaching into the envelope, my throat tightened and pulse quickened. It wasn't time. I tied all the letters back up with the ribbon, then looked out the window at the large snowflakes that now fell from the sky; reinforcing my belief that it was nowhere near time for my spring-cleaning.

Warning Signs

On January eighteenth, I became a mother for the second time, and this time I planned to stay one. Chestnut hair and dark eyes made her all the more mine. Mother would be thrilled that she looked like a Robertson. I cradled my infant girl in my arms and stared at the door, wishing for Jack to walk into the room with an acceptable excuse for missing the birth of his daughter. With each contraction, my previous delivery had come rushing back to me. There was that same empty spot at the bedside where the father of my baby should've been standing, and the familiar silence where his whispers of, "You're doing great, love," and "Just one more push, sweetheart," should've been heard. The difference–this time, the nurses and doctor took pity on me.

"I bet he'll be here any minute," the nurse assured me with each trip to my room. "I'm certain he has a good excuse," Dr. Barrett had said as he gathered his instruments.

Outside, cars were parked in uneven rows as the drivers misjudged the lines underneath the inches of snow. At first, I thought the storm had kept Jack from reaching the hospital. Then I remembered that it only started two hours ago and he should've been here long before. The pressure in my chest became unbearable. I called his office again, hoping for news.

"Yes, Mrs. Templeton, I've left three messages at the courthouse that you're at the hospital," Jack's secretary, Betty, assured me. "If he calls the office, I'll definitely tell him."

I hung up the phone and looked to my comfort, my beautiful baby. "I can't believe this is happening."

Mary Rose rubbed my back. "I wish there was something I could do. He'll regret missing this, Cara, he really will."

I wanted him to do more than regret it. He needed to fall to his knees and beg forgiveness, to beat himself up over it in the days and years to follow, thinking it the worst mistake of his life. How could he have missed his daughter drawing her first breath? I watched gusts of wind like miniature cyclones carry snow across the parking lot. As far as Jack was concerned, the baby and I might as well have been swept away with it.

"I've been waiting forever to find out her name," Mary Rose said. "Is it safe to tell me now?"

"Lily Katherine. Katherine after my Aunt Kate." I smiled at the sound of her name. "I wish she could've been here."

Mary Rose swept the hair back from my face. "I'm sure your Aunt Kate would be honored to share a name with the first girl in the family."

I looked at my dear friend. She didn't know that Lily wasn't the first. I owed it to Jane to claim her as my daughter, to acknowledge her existence. I placed my hand on Mary Rose's forearm and gave a gentle squeeze. "Mary Rose, Lily isn't..." The words still wouldn't come forth.

Why couldn't I tell my best friend about the daughter I had given away? It would've been easier to tell the checkout girl at the grocery, the bank teller behind the counter, or the hotdog vendor at the ballpark. Their opinion of me did not matter. How would I sit across from Mary Rose at the kitchen table everyday, wondering if she thought less of me for walking away from my child? To have her know that I had tossed a loved one aside, while she would give anything to have her beloved Paul back. Now that I held Lily in my arms and felt the frailty of a newborn child, I was even more ashamed of my earlier decision.

Mary Rose tilted her head to the right. "Lily isn't what, Cara?"

"Ever going to meet Aunt Kate, which is a shame," I said quickly.

The knock at the door brought me upright with expectations of introducing Jack to his daughter. Instead, the nurse walked to the bedside. "Husband still hasn't made it?" she asked, checking my IV. "He lost his window of opportunity. I hear the roads are getting worse. They're even talking about shutting them down."

Mary Rose glanced outside. "Oh my. Harper's still at daycare. They may want to close early."

"You need to go," I said.

"I hate to leave you alone."

"You've done enough. Go get Harper. I'll be fine."

The nurse filled my water pitcher and placed it on the nightstand. "Just push the call button if you need anything," she said over her shoulder as she walked toward the door.

Steph stepped past the nurse and stood, brushing the snow from her coat.

Mary Rose grabbed her purse. "Oh good. Perfect timing."

"God, it's awful out there," Steph said. "I called Mother and Daddy and told them to stay put. Good thing I was almost here when the storm hit. I can't stay long, but at least I can see the baby. Andrew will worry sick if I drive home in the dark."

Mary Rose squeezed my arm. "I'll bring Harper over to the house to see the baby once you're home. She'll be so excited."

"Thanks for everything," I said.

"Drive careful," Steph warned.

"I will." Mary Rose shut the door behind her.

Steph turned to me. "So? Boy? Girl?"

I pushed back the knit cap covering her head. "Lily Katherine, meet your Aunt Steph."

"She's gorgeous. Although, I knew she would be. You and Jack could hardly go wrong." Steph plopped down in the chair beside the bed. "Where is Jack anyway? Out buying those expensive cigars?"

"He better be in a ditch somewhere–bleeding profusely–preferably unconscious."

"No. Don't tell me he missed it."

"Yep. I called him when I first went into labor. He told me he had just a couple more things to do. It didn't help matters that my labor only lasted three hours this time."

"Just one more thing Jack and Daddy have in common. If I remember right, Mother said that Daddy had the doctor page him when she was fully dilated so he could squeeze out a couple more hours of work." Steph looked around the room. "And Tory? I thought for sure she'd be here taking charge of the place like the last time."

"She'll probably come to visit once we get home. Since David has left, it seems to be taking all her energy just to get through each day."

Steph laughed. "She must not be too worn out. Lydia tells me that Tory already has another man."

"Lydia?"

"The college student I hired to work at The Annex. She's taking Tory's pottery class at the college. Apparently, the two of them are friends. Reason enough to fire Lydia, I might add, but she's a good employee."

"Tory would've told me if there was someone else. I don't believe it."

"She has someone all right. Women like her don't take long to pounce on their next victim." Steph looked at Lily. "Oh, before I forget, Mother made me swear to get the baby's vital statistics for the birth announcement in *The Plain Rapper*." She took out a pen and copied them off the bassinet.

This time, *It's an outcast* had been replaced with *It's a girl*, and the card bore a real name, a name with a history behind it.

Steph shoved the paper in her purse. "The last time, Mother would've died if anyone found out and this time she's calling the local paper for Christ's sake."

The door swung open. Jack burst into the room and rushed to the bedside.

"Speaking of dying," Steph said. She grabbed her coat. "I'll get out of the line of fire. I'll call you later."

I pointed toward the window. "You can't go back in this weather. You can stay at the house for the night."

"I'll manage," Steph assured me.

"That's crazy. They're closing roads. You can leave in the morning. Andrew would feel better as well. Call him."

"It's not all that bad. Hell, I'm sure Steph has jogged in worse weather than this," Jack said.

She squared her shoulders and puffed out her chest as she did whenever she heard a challenge. "As a matter of fact, I have. I'll be fine. Mother said she'll come to help out when you get home." Steph turned and headed for the door.

I nodded, then glared at Jack as the door clicked into place. "Not all that bad? Then why weren't you here?"

Jack's gaze met Lily. "I'm sorry I missed it, Cara." He ran his fingers through his hair. "An unexpected meeting popped up, then the snowstorm and…"

I looked at the man who stockpiled excuses to fit any situation. If only he knew how self-serving they sounded. Savoring her newborn scent, I placed my cheek next to Lily's skin. "Yes, Jack, I know. Busy, busy day, I'm sure."

"I really tried to head out shortly after you called, but it was one thing after another."

While Lily dozed peacefully in my arms, I stretched out her slender fingers and looked at her tiny nails. Then I traced her hairline with my index finger. A dimple the size of the tip of a pinky graced the center of her forehead. She would be the beauty of my world, my focus, my life. I no longer had time to worry about Jack's misplaced priorities. Perhaps that was the attitude that kept Mother sane all of these years.

"I tried to tell the partners that I needed to free up some time this week in case you delivered."

I ran my fingertip over the small blister on Lily's bottom lip that was from sucking her thumb in the womb. Lily let out a sigh as she nuzzled deeper into the crook of my arm. She began rooting and I swiftly placed her to my breast.

Jack leaned over. "Aren't you going to let me see her?"

I stroked Lily's cheek and she nursed with more vigor.

"Cara."

I looked to Jack. "What?"

"Can I see the baby?"

"You wanted a boy, but it's a girl."

"Well..." Disappointment flashed across his face. "The important thing is that the baby's healthy. She is healthy, right?"

I ran my hand over the top of her silky smooth hair. "She's more than healthy. She's perfect."

He glanced around the room. "Where are your parents?"

"Did you forget about the storm?"

"Oh that...yes."

A familiar clicking sound made its way to the door, followed by a knock. Jack shrugged.

"Come in," I called.

Tory peeked into the room and Jack waved her inside. I pointed to the window. "How did you make it all the way from Mission Bay? The nurse said they've closed down some roads."

"I know, I know. It was stupid of me. But I thought it would do my heart good to experience something happy in the midst of all the crap I'm dealing with back home." She walked over. "Boy or girl?"

"Girl," I said.

She smiled. "Beautiful. How was the labor? Sorry I missed it this time."

"Mary Rose came to help."

She nodded. "Good. At least you weren't alone then."

Jack's jaw clenched; obviously he had caught her mistake as well.

I turned sharply to her. "How did you know Jack wasn't here with me?"

She laughed and shifted her weight from right to left. "Well, it's...it's certainly no secret that Jack's a workaholic. I just assumed with the weather being a–"

"Blizzard," Jack helped. "Speaking of such, there's no way we're going to allow you to drive back home tonight."

"But you just encouraged Steph to leave," I pointed out.

He looked at me. "You know your sister. She would've felt defeated if she'd stayed. Besides, it's gotten worse since she left."

Tory waved off his advice. "I'll just drive slow."

"Don't be ridiculous. You'll stay at the house," he said.

She nodded. "Okay. Just give me a key and I'll let myself in."

"Don't be silly," Jack said. "The least I can do is drive you over, then I'll come right back."

From what Lydia tells me, Tory already has another man.

"Jack," I said, "if Steph is driving all the way back to Mission Bay, I'm sure Tory can make it a couple of miles down the road." I turned to her. "You'll call us when you get there, right, Tory?"

"She may not feel comfortable driving in this weather," he said.

"She's a Michigander," I said through gritted teeth. "Snow is a way of life."

"I'll be fine," Tory said. "The two of you need some time

together with your new baby. I'll head to the house now."

"But you just got here. Why would you drive all this way to stay only a few minutes?" I challenged, recalling New Year's and how she had rushed off as well.

She stuck out her hand and Jack took the house key off the ring, handing it to her. "I should've just waited until you got home to visit. I don't know what I was thinking. At least I got to see the baby. I'll get up first thing in the morning and head for home. I can come to visit once you're out of the hospital." She walked toward the door.

"Don't leave too early tomorrow morning," Jack warned. "At least not before the plows get out."

"Good point." She pulled the door closed behind her.

No, they couldn't have been together. I had no proof. Daddy would call it circumstantial evidence.

Jack paced in front of the window, glancing down at the parking lot. "I think I'll stop by the office tomorrow morning to grab some paperwork."

Women like her don't take long to pounce on their next victim.

My heart turned cold. "Just make sure it's after the plows get out," I reminded him.

As expected, Mother came to visit with one thing on her mind— to take charge of the household. "First, I'll go to the grocery," she said, "then I'll cook and freeze the meals. Enough to take you well into next month. Tomorrow, I'll clean the house, do the laundry, and iron." She glanced around the room to prevent an oversight, while I stood before her wearing the same housecoat and pajamas that had not left my body in the past three days. I was unable to get the simplest of things done, like stopping my breast milk from leaking through my nursing bra.

"You'll have plenty of time to tend to Lily," she assured me. "And to make sure all of Jack's needs are met, too. You know how a man gets when you don't pay him enough attention."

She has someone all right.

"Yes, I believe I do," I said.

Mother pointed down the hallway. "Why don't you clean up and put on a nice outfit before Jack gets home from work? A touch of makeup wouldn't hurt."

I turned on the water and sat down on the shower floor, too exhausted to stand. How hard could motherhood be, I had asked myself on the way home from the hospital. Just name the baby and take her home. People did it everyday. Then came the feedings every two hours, the constant diaper changes, and the mounds of laundry.

With my new mommy clock ticking away, I quickly toweled off, dressed, and headed back downstairs before Lily cried out in hunger. The smell of baked goods called me to the kitchen. "What are you making?" I asked Mother.

"Banana bread, dear. Jack will have something to eat before he runs off to work in the morning."

I shuffled over to the basinet and checked on Lily, then made my way to the table. "Mother, you're used to Daddy's work schedule. Do you have any tips on how I can get Jack to work normal hours? Maybe just twelve-hour days."

"If only I knew the answer." She opened the oven door, peeked inside, and reset the timer. "Your father has always spent long hours at the office. We both know that he wasn't always working."

With the subject out in the open, I decided to pry a bit. "What was your first clue that Daddy was having an affair? You know, in hindsight."

Mother turned sharply toward me. "You don't suspect…"

Why worry her? "Oh, no. Not Jack. I was just curious that's all."

"Well, there's the obvious warning sign–time that's unaccounted for. The myriad of excuses. A traffic jam, client dinner, difficult case, unexpected meeting, court running over. But the most telling sign is that nagging voice warning you that something is wrong."

I had heard that voice, but chose to ignore it. I needed to know more from the woman who had been listening to that voice for years. "What did you do when you first found out about Daddy's affair?"

The oven buzzer sounded and Mother pulled the bread from the rack and placed it on top of the stove. "I cried. That's what I did. For a week straight, I woke up crying and went to bed crying. Of course, your father felt horrible, even stopped seeing her for a while."

"Then what?" I asked.

Mother's brow furrowed. "What do you mean?"

"What did you do after that?"

"Nothing." Her face hardened. "It wasn't that easy back then, Cara. I didn't have a job. I had you and Steph to think about. My parents thought John was the best thing that walked the earth. I was the wife of a successful attorney. What more could I possibly ask for, and what right did I have to complain?"

"What would you do now, if you found out that he was cheating again? Would you leave him?"

She turned toward the window as if the answer lay outside. "We've been together too long and I'm too old to start over." She let out a small laugh while reaching for the cooling rack. "Besides, the women at the club would think I'd totally lost my mind."

How I had wished for a different answer. For her to stand up and scream, "Hell yes, I'd leave the bastard!" But I knew she'd never come close to saying it; held prisoner by a renewed country club membership each January, the latest model Mercedes every other year, and an updated leather sofa with matching ottoman. I glanced at the fine furnishings in my home and then to the massive diamond ring on my finger. Suddenly, years flew by and I was standing in the same kitchen doling out banana bread to Lily, trying to explain away my decision to stay with her adulterous father.

Mother looked at the clock. "Oh my, it's getting late. When will Jack be home, dear?"

Her warning signs echoed in my head. "Anytime, Mother...anytime."

Slice of Heaven

WELCOME, the bright yellow sign announced. The NO TR SP S ING sign sat in a heap with the barbed wire fencing. Daddy, I thought, while continuing down the path.

The sunlight warmed my back, but once the cloud cover moved in, the season's real temperature took hold. Never fooled by the sun's trickery in early spring, I had dressed Lily for the outdoors: leggings, sweater, fleece bunting, hat, mittens. She couldn't budge, but at least she'd stay warm while I took some photos and made a couple of quick sketches. Blythe had requested another painting, baby or no baby.

"See this path, Lily," I said, pointing toward the creek. "A few years from now, you'll know every hole, dip, and curve." The stroller struggled to stay on all four wheels with each push. As a child, how many rocks had I kicked down this bumpy path? How many times had I picked up a stick and written my name in the dirt as if to claim the property? Lily would get to know this land as her own; a place to play, to discover–possibly even to paint one day. The flowers' sweet aroma caught my nose before my eyes. "And smell that, sweetheart? That's a jonquil. A smell so strong that a single flower can permeate a room."

I often wondered who had planted the first of those fragrant daffodils. Had there once been an old homestead on the property? On a crisp, fall morning, did some pioneer woman spend an entire week on her knees, digging each hole by hand and lovingly patting the bulbs into place with hopes of a good return in the spring? When she moved on, did she worry who might care for the flowers in her absence? Perhaps she knew that anything that dared bloom while there was still a chance of a late season snowfall, needn't warrant concern; the daffodils' durability proven time and again each spring.

Lily started to fuss. "We won't stay long," I said.

We stopped in front of the tree where Sadie was buried. An ocean of yellow now sat before her. I parked the stroller and placed

Lily in the infant carrier. Hopping the creek with help from a couple of logs and rocks, we made our way over to the colony. I reached down, picked a jonquil, and held it close to Lily's face. Although the baby book claimed she was too young to see color, her eyes widened and she stopped fussing.

I nodded. "You see the beauty, don't you?"

Five steps to the right brought me to the perfect cluster. The morning dew clinging to the petals would later be transferred from pictures onto my canvas. I took a deep breath and cool air filled my lungs. "Is there anything more beautiful in the world, Lil?"

Peering down into the carrier, I answered my own question; her cheeks brushed pink by the crisp, morning breeze, her eyes peacefully drowsy, and her chest rising and falling in rhythm with the trickle of the creek. I bent down and kissed her perfect scarlet lips; her milk-laced breath smelled as sweet as any jonquil.

Mother had created a special place for her new granddaughter. She stopped short of calling it a nursery, instead, referring to it as the little person's guest room. It was complete with child-sized wicker furniture, a desk with a miniature library collection, and a padded window seat sprinkled with throw pillows.

Mother caught my gaze. "They grow up so fast. She'll be sitting in that window seat reading all by herself before you know it."

I didn't want her sitting alone, curled up with a book. I wanted her in my lap, nuzzled into my chest, saying, "Please read it to me again, Mommy."

"Wait until you see what I bought, dear," Mother said as she opened closets and drawers packed with things that seemed superfluous. She insisted they were every bit as necessary as the store clerk had deemed them to be. The wipes container had a rectangular cloth wrapped around the outside with a white cord hanging down. "See this?" Mother said. "A wipe warmer, imagine that. Tell me a baby who doesn't deserve such a thing." She turned to the crib. "And look here. This little gadget vibrates the crib, simulating a car ride. In my day, Mothers hauled their babies out to the car and drove around the block a few times. Now, you can just flip a switch in the comfort of your home." Mother pointed to the corner of the ceiling. "That video camera was your father's idea. He wanted to see Lily on a screen, rather than trust the ears. You know what he says about video in the courtroom–nearly as good as a confession."

Mother walked toward a wooden chest along the back wall. "Now, for the best part." The smell of cedar rushed out when she opened the lid. She motioned me forward. "Take a look inside."

I glanced down at the hope chest already filled with fine linens, silverware, crystal, and china. If only such a treasury could hold the promise of a loving partner, a faithful husband, a good father, and, if necessary, the strength to leave. "I certainly appreciate all of this," I said, "but you shouldn't have."

"What did you expect, dear? She is our first granddaughter, after all."

Her words cut deep, reminding me of how others saw Lily; the first on the Robertson side. Why was I expecting Jane to count as a grandchild when she had not even mattered as a daughter?

"Wait until you see what your father has set up for college," Mother said. "He spent weeks researching this fund and that fund. Consistent six to eight percent return on investment, he touted. Why, he's already talking Harvard Law." She clutched her chest. "God forbid she decides to become a Yale girl."

We made our way downstairs and found Daddy holding Lily in front of the volumes of law journals lining the shelves in his study, books handed down through four generations of Robertson attorneys. He turned around. "I just had a brilliant idea, Tulip. You can turn on one of those self-instructional Latin tapes while she sleeps. They say the younger they are, the easier it is to pick up a second language."

"How about we just get through dinner first?" I motioned for Lily and Daddy reluctantly handed her over. When I placed her cheek to mine, she felt hot.

"Mother," I said, "she's awfully warm. Feel her."

She reached over and placed her hand to Lily's forehead, and then to her chest. "I believe she's got a temperature. Let me run upstairs."

Within seconds, I heard the screech of the medicine cabinet, my childhood illnesses rushing back to me. Mother believed in old-fashioned remedies, like the ones her Great Aunt Matilda had sworn by. Homemade saltwater spray that made me feel as though my head was being held to the ocean floor as it shot through each nostril. There was the cough remedy with just a touch of whiskey, but enough to sear my throat so badly that I'd forget all about the cough.

Mother returned with something resembling a hot glue gun. "Just think," she said, "in the old days there was only one place to take a baby's temperature." She glanced over the instructions, placed the tip of the thermometer in Lily's ear, and squeezed the handle.

She pulled it out and held it to the light. "Ninety-nine point one."

"Oh God, her first fever." I touched Lily's cheek again. "Our doctor...he's so far away."

"Well, it's not high enough to be overly concerned, but we'll understand if you feel the need to go back home. Won't we, John?" Mother said.

"Yes, by all means," Daddy agreed. "Can't take any chances with our little Lily."

"We better go home. If she gets worse and…"

Daddy patted my arm. "No need to explain, Petunia."

"Let me gather your things." Mother came back with our coats. She tucked the thermometer in the diaper bag. "Just in case."

I swung the bag over my shoulder. "Thanks. I'll call you soon."

"Do you want us to call Jack?" Daddy asked.

"No, he'll just worry. I'll be home soon enough." I kissed them goodbye.

The two-hour drive home gave me more than enough time to obsess about the illnesses that I had dog-eared in the baby book. I committed the worst to memory: epiglottitis, meningitis, roseola, whooping cough. Their symptoms flashed through my mind and she certainly had every one of them. I pushed harder on the gas pedal.

Relief settled in when I reached Piney Cove; a familiar doctor and hospital close by. When I drove up to the house, the garage door was open and I pulled inside. The sound of music greeted me when I stepped out of the Jeep. Since Lily had fallen asleep in her car seat, I went inside to turn down the music before bringing her into the house.

I threw my backpack on the hook in the laundry room and made my way to the kitchen. Two wineglasses sat on the counter, one with a smear of familiar red lipstick; next to it–an empty bottle of Chardonnay. My legs instinctively carried me down the hallway to the master bedroom, while the bass kept rhythm with the pounding in my chest. My breath suddenly caught with the need to sidestep red pumps and brown loafers littering the hallway floor. The bedroom door was cracked open. The lamp in the corner illuminated the trail of evidence leading to the bed: jeans, sweater, bra, hose, panties, Polo, khakis, boxers. With his back to the doorway, Jack straddled her, thrusting in and out to the beat of the music while groping her bronze-colored breasts. Their naked bodies were linked together like a human jigsaw puzzle. She threw her head back and grabbed the headboard to anchor herself as he filled her with pleasure.

I stood frozen with one palm covering my mouth, the other across my churning stomach. My legs suddenly gave way and I stumbled into the room. Jack looked back in horror and jumped to the floor while Tory shot up in bed–my bed–our bed. Glistening with sweat, Jack scrambled to put on his underwear, his foot catching the center, nearly tripping himself. She stood with her underside as golden brown as a pancake, her hands frantically skimmed the floor in search of her clothing.

I looked at him. "How…" Then at her, "*Could* you?"

Before either one could respond, I ran out of the room, racing toward the light in the kitchen.

"Cara, wait a minute!" Jack yelled. His footsteps nipped at me, but I dared not look back; for it would be a sign of partial forgiveness.

I swung the door open, and stumbled out into the cold, damp night. Flinging the Jeep door open, I startled Lily awake. She let out a wail, while I fumbled with the safety seat lock.

Jack opened the door. "Cara, wait. I can explain," he said, then hesitated as if searching for something that would sound believable.

I grabbed Lily and the diaper bag. Cutting across the street without giving a thought to oncoming traffic, I eventually landed on Mary Rose's front porch. My clenched fists met her door with a ferocity that suggested an armed assailant was but a step behind.

"Please, please, please, be home…be home," I said, clutching my crying baby to my chest.

The door opened and light sprawled out across the darkness, shining into my eyes. "Oh God," Mary Rose said, then ushered us inside. "What, Cara. What is it? Is Lily hurt?"

I shook my head and sobbed. "Not Lily. Jack. Tory. In bed. Together."

"Damn it," she whispered, the first swear word I had ever heard her utter. She immediately gave me the direction I sought. "We'll put Lily to bed. Then you'll take a hot bath while I brew the coffee."

Before I took Lily upstairs, Mary Rose checked her temperature and it had dropped back to normal. Mary Rose didn't think a call to the doctor was warranted. "We'll just keep a close eye on her tonight."

After I nursed Lily to sleep, I placed her in the portable crib that Mary Rose set up in the guest room. For the next thirty minutes, I sat in the tub recalling the image of Jack and Tory, the burden of proof now met. I was an eyewitness, able to identify the offenders. The hot water eased some of the tension from my neck and shoulders. But while stepping from the tub, I caught a glimpse of my postpartum body in the mirror: bulging tummy, engorged breasts, stretch marks running the length of my thighs. I tensed up again. How could I compete with Tory's unblemished body? While toweling off, I shamefully cursed the body that had given my beautiful baby life. I checked Lily again, threw on the pajamas and housecoat Mary Rose had placed on the vanity, and made my way downstairs.

I had sat in Mary Rose's kitchen enough times to know which cupboard housed the sugar bowl, which drawer held the teaspoons, and where she kept the mugs. But this night I asked questions, hesitated, out of the need for someone to take care of me. Mary Rose went along with the charade by asking me if I liked creamer and directing me to one of the chairs at the kitchen table. It was easier to pretend that I was a temporary visitor who'd be returning home after one cup. But, as always, coffee had a way of bringing about the truth.

"I knew, but I didn't want to believe Tory and Jack would do such a thing," I said.

"That's understandable," she said. "Who would?"

I cupped my head in my hands. "God, what am I going to do,

Mary Rose?" Tears slid down my cheeks.

"You're going to get through the night. Then we'll worry about tomorrow in the morning."

Mary Rose had become an expert at surviving one day at a time. I nodded, but knew I'd spend the night racked with worry; the questions already formulating. Would I be able to take care of Lily on my own? How would I tell Mother and Daddy? What about finances? Was Tory still at the house? How long had this been going on? Who knew? Were others laughing at my ignorance? Could I ever face Jack again?

Mary Rose must have sensed my angst. "Cara, why don't you go to bed. You're exhausted. Lily will be up before you know it." My friend led me upstairs, her hand tucked underneath my elbow for support. She walked over to the bed and pulled back the covers. "Try to get some sleep. I'll be next door if you need anything." She rubbed my shoulder, then closed the door behind her.

I went over and lifted Lily out of the portable crib, placing her in bed beside me, then turned out the light.

Throughout the night, I repeatedly sat up in bed, relieved for a moment when I believed it to be a dream. I'd suddenly realize that it wasn't my room and a blanket of doom descended upon me. Lily nursed in spurts, relying solely on instinct to survive. My body did the same by inhaling and exhaling, all I could ask at this time.

Every so often, I'd hear Mary Rose shuffling down the hall, stopping at the door to listen, before she made her way back to bed. I waited for the morning sun to confirm that I had spent the night across the street from my lovely home, away from my husband, the father of my baby. After Lily nursed just prior to daybreak, I checked her temperature again and placed her back into the crib before going downstairs.

While passing the piano, I stopped for the first time, brushing my fingertips over the keys, but not hard enough to elicit a sound. How smooth they felt, just like Noah's hands. I pictured him sitting on the bench, flashing that boyish grin; his fingers working their magic, playing the beautiful music he once composed in the attic of his childhood home. I couldn't help but to wonder how different things might have been if he hadn't left for Vienna.

I took a seat near the front window with a full view of my home and pushed open the curtains. The house was dark except for the master bathroom where Jack groomed himself for the day. He rose at five o'clock in the morning, even on weekends. He called it his biological clock–I called it nuts. It was five-thirty. He'd most likely be showered and shaved, maybe even partly dressed. I started when I heard footsteps on the staircase.

"Cara, is that you?" Mary Rose asked.

"You're an early riser," I said.

"I grew up on a farm. Sort of bred into you." She came over and sat beside me on the sofa. "In the wintertime, I'd get up extra early so I could go ice-skating on the pond behind the barn after my chores were done. You should've seen me rushing around, throwing feed to the animals as if the ice were going to melt any second. I'd be skating by six in the morning while most kids were still in bed."

"I didn't know you liked to skate."

"Oh, yes. My mother taught me. We'd skate hand in hand for hours. My father would stand by the barn and holler, 'You ladies coming off that ice any time before spring?' Mother and I would just giggle and make another lap around the pond while he'd shake his head and go back to work. Mother skated competitively in her younger days. Her mother had taught her by the age of four. Of course I plan to teach Harper to keep the family tradition."

Mary Rose sighed. "I haven't skated in quite some time. But, I suppose it's like riding a bicycle, something you never forget." She placed her hand on my knee. "Did you get any sleep last night?"

"Some. In between Lily's feedings and dreams of homicide." I watched as the master bathroom across the street went dark and the kitchen lit up within seconds. Coffee time. Soon he'd open the front door, grab the paper off the sidewalk, settle at the kitchen table with a cup, and flip to the business news. My hand dropped to my side and the sheers fell back into place; a sheathe between me and my old world. "What now?" I asked.

"Well, I guess you have two choices. Forgive him and try to reconcile, or merely forgive him."

"What about the other choice?"

"What's that?" Mary Rose asked.

"The *not* forgive him choice."

"Your forgiveness has nothing to do with whether Jack deserves it or not. It's you that deserves it."

"But I don't see how I can…"

"Not right away, Cara, but eventually." She grabbed my hand. "You know, when I had to sit across from Greg, the young driver who killed Paul, and forgive him...well…" She scooped up a tear that had traveled halfway down her cheek. "That was one of the hardest things I ever did in my life. He was only a child, nineteen to be exact, had his whole life ahead of him. He made a deadly choice when he decided to get behind the wheel drunk.

"At first, I hated him. I hated him for killing the only man I ever loved and for taking Harper's daddy from her. But when I was forced to look that boy in the eye that day, in his parents' home...I don't know...I knew I had to offer forgiveness."

"God, that must've been hard," I said.

"Yes, but as long as I hated him, I would be stuck in the past, in that moment of time when Paul died."

"And Tory?" I said. "Do I forgive her, too?"

She nodded. "Jack and Tory will have to go on with their lives, together or separate."

My head turned in the direction of a sharp cry that winded its way down the staircase, a sudden reminder that Lily and I would have to carry on with or without Jack.

Mary Rose took a vacation day from work to keep me company, but even her presence couldn't fill the large hole in my life. I felt like an old sweater, ready to unravel with the slightest tug in the wrong direction.

We sat down for coffee and heard a firm knock at the door. "Oh, Jesus. That's probably him," I said.

"I'll get it." Mary Rose stood. "Do you want to talk?"

I shook my head while longing to say yes. How I wanted to pound my fists into his chest, to scream at him, to make him feel my pain.

"I think that's smart. You need some time to think." The door opened and I leaned over to listen. "Hello, Jack," Mary Rose said.

"Is Cara here?" he asked.

"Now is not a good time."

"But I really need to talk to her. I need to explain."

"You can imagine the shock."

"But, I really–"

"Not now." I heard the door creek as it started to close.

"Mary Rose, if you could just hear me out," he persisted.

"You have nothing to say that would interest me."

"Can you at least tell her I'm sorry?"

"Why don't you wait and tell her yourself?" she said. "It might lose something in the translation."

"But–"

The door clicked into place, followed by a few residual knocks, then silence.

The next morning, after Jack pulled from the drive, I rushed over to the house to gather some of my belongings. I opted to move out since I knew I could never stay there after finding Jack and Tory together in my bed. My heart quickened the closer I got to the end of Mary Rose's driveway. The house appeared normal. There was no squad car in the drive, no yellow crime scene tape strewn across the front door, and no investigator drawing chalk outlines around the wine bottle, crystal glasses, and king-sized bed. Apparently it wasn't a felony that my husband and best friend had slept together–it just felt like one.

I pulled two large suitcases from the hall closet before proceeding to the bedroom. Inching the door open, I peered inside. The bed that was never that noticeable before, now held dominion over the room. I shook my head back and forth like an Etch-A-Sketch in hopes of erasing the image of Jack on top of Tory, but it remained clear; his pelvis thrusting forward while her lips pulled back into a grimace, enjoying every adulterous moment.

Turning from the bed, I went from room to room, carelessly tossing things into the suitcases like one of those crazed contestants taking part in a timed shopping spree. First, I grabbed the most valuable items: Lily's things, art supplies, my clothing. I went back to the bedroom and took one last look at the bed– her bed–their bed, replaying the betrayal in my head from the moment I had peered through the crack in the door, until I stumbled out into the darkness of night, forever leaving behind a husband and a friend.

I lugged the suitcases to the foyer, then remembered one last thing I needed to take with me. I went into my closet and felt around for the wool blanket, grabbing the shoebox from underneath. With the box of letters tucked safely under my arm, I marched away from my beautiful home.

Mary Rose understood my need to get away, but worried about me being out in the middle of the woods with a baby. "I don't know if this is such a good idea," she said, sitting on the screened porch overlooking the lake.

I glanced at Lily asleep in her bassinet. "We'll be fine. There's enough firewood to keep us warm and enough groceries for two weeks. Want some coffee?"

"Sure."

Mary Rose continued to stare out over the water even after I returned with two steaming mugs of Irish mocha.

"I've never seen anything so peaceful," she said. "I could sit here all day." She stroked Harper's cheek as the child slept on her lap.

Most of the cottages remained closed up from the winter season. In early June, the plastic would be peeled off the windows, the rugs hung on the line to air, and the boats plunked down beside the docks in the water that now remained a layer of ice.

"People ever skate out there?" Mary Rose asked.

"Not that I know of."

"It looks like a perfect lake for skating." She turned toward me. "Are you sure about this? Should I at least tell someone else you're here? Your family may worry."

"I don't need anyone to meddle just yet. I'll call you if I need anything. I swear."

Dusk settled in and she glanced at her watch. "I guess we'll head back," she said hesitantly. "If it wasn't such a long drive…"

"I understand," I said. "I'm looking forward to the relaxation. I might even lie down for a bit while Lily is still sleeping."

She scooped Harper from her lap and took one final look out toward the lake. "Well, if there's anywhere to get some relaxation, this would be it. Like they say–a little slice of Heaven right here on Earth."

I stood on the back step and waved goodbye until Mary Rose's car made its way up the hill and out of sight. I went back inside and darkness enveloped the cottage, the roar of the fire my only company.

I didn't recall the Bible describing Heaven as such a lonely place.

All's Fair in Love and War

I repeatedly tossed from side to side as if a new position would induce sleep. Lily nursed on and off, dozing in between feedings. The digital clock displayed 4:17 in bright red numbers; Jack would be up in less than an hour. Had he been able to sleep through the night? I sat up in bed shivering; the fire no longer burned brightly, just a few smoldering embers remained. My feet hit the cold, wood floor and I placed three logs on top, then rushed back and slid under the covers.

The fire's rekindled intensity reminded me of how little Jack and I had done to keep a fire burning between us outside the bedroom; a passion with resonance, for lust fulfills but one promise. We lived in separate worlds–corporate vs. cultural–worlds so different, there was little common ground. The charade had ended. I no longer had to put on pretenses, straddling two lives. My eyelids gave way to the warmth of the fire, calling up distant memories of Noah and the passion that we had shared.

I awoke to a familiar knock at the door: rap, rap, rap, rap, silence, one thousand one, one thousand two, one thousand three, rap, rap, rap. Throughout my teenage years, it was a unique tune played out on the bathroom door as Steph and I wrestled with hairdryers, curling irons, and tweezers. By the third round of knocks, Mother decided it time for a reprimand.

"Girls," she'd say from the hallway, "this is an important engagement and we mustn't be late. How do you think the host will feel if we don't show up on time?"

"Relieved," Steph would whisper. Then we'd giggle until we cried, catching our tears with our index fingers before we ended up with a black trail of mascara down our cheeks. We'd eventually make our way into the hallway where Mother stood ready for the 'once over'.

The second series of knocks at the back of the cottage sent me to the door. I knew I'd eventually have to face Mother's questions, but we had only arrived yesterday. How did she know we were here? I opened the door and she walked straight over to Lily's bassinet and peered inside.

"Poor little thing hasn't a clue," she said. "That's what I used to think when I watched you and your sister sleep on the nights your father couldn't manage his way home at a decent hour." She made her way to the kitchen and sat at the table.

"Who told you?" I asked, grabbing the empty teakettle from the stove.

"Steph heard it from that employee of hers, Lydia. Apparently, Tory told Lydia after pottery class. Honestly, I don't know why Tory would brag about such a disgrace. We have an unwritten policy at the club." Mother shook her head. "It just wouldn't be tolerated."

"Well, unfortunately, she's not a member, Mother. Does Daddy know?"

"Not yet, thank God. I fielded the call from Jack yesterday."

My throat narrowed. "Oh, he called?" I asked casually.

"He wants you to come back home."

"Really." I choked back tears as I filled the kettle with tap water.

"Whether you go back is up to you," she said. "Only you know what you can live with."

"I can't." I put the water on to boil and joined her at the table.

"Then your father can start the divorce proceedings."

"Wait," I said. "I...I don't know if I'm ready for that."

"Whenever you feel the time is right, dear. In the meantime, your father and I can help financially. You and Lily can move in with us."

"We're staying with Mary Rose for the time being."

"Well, you're always welcome at Laurel." Mother's gaze intensified. "Are you sure about all of this, Cara? Jack seems apologetic."

I nodded. "I'm positive. I married Jack for all the wrong reasons. Unfortunately, love had little to do with it."

She looked at the fire, her eyes misting over. "You're not the first woman to do such a thing, Cara." She sighed. "Herb told me he'd be back to marry me one day, and when he didn't return, I settled for the next best thing."

"Who's Herb?"

"Herb Ellington, my first love. After he was drafted, we wrote each other everyday for months, sometimes two and three letters a day. Then the letters suddenly stopped. I met your father about that time, and we married shortly thereafter. You know your father, able to persuade even the most doubtful. He promised me a good life, a life I would have never known otherwise. Don't get me wrong, I care for your father, but he's no Herb Ellington."

How strange that my life paralleled Mother's in this way.

"And yes, I've made concessions over the years, I admit. At this point in my life, I get what I need out of the marriage. But I'm certainly no fool."

I needed to know more about what could have been. "Where did you meet this Herb guy?"

"The Alexandria County Fair," she said. "While I showed my horse, Renegade, Herb displayed his prize winning zucchini. I don't even like squash, but I never told him that." She smiled. "We spent the whole week together, strolling the fairgrounds with our blue ribbons in hand, sharing a caramel apple on the Ferris wheel, then a corn dog. It was one of the best times of my life."

"I don't believe it," I said, getting up as the teakettle announced its work was done.

"Oh, it most certainly was, dear. I haven't had a day like it since."

"No, not that. I can't believe you ate a corn dog." I brought the cups back to the table along with the tea bags.

Mother laughed. "You do many things for the sake of love, things you'd never do otherwise. I haven't had a corn dog or caramel apple since."

I leaned in for the rest of the story. "So, you just never heard from Herb again?"

"My heart ripped in two the morning I saw his obituary. Still have the clipping, tucked away in the bottom of my jewelry box. I read it every once in a while to remind myself that he loved me, that the letters hadn't stopped for any other reason. According to the newspaper, he spent quite some time in the hospital following the accident."

"Accident?"

Mother pulled a tissue from her purse and dabbed her eyes. "He was killed during a training exercise. They didn't release many details...confidential, being the military and all. I certainly couldn't call his family for information since I'd never met them."

"I'm sorry, Mother."

"Don't be sorry, dear. I wouldn't change a thing. If it weren't for marrying your father, neither you nor your sister would be here. A right turn here or a left turn there and you end up with something different, but it seems there's something positive that comes out of going either way."

"Noah Meyer was the love of my life," I blurted. "He left for Vienna to teach music shortly after I met Jack. I loved him, but then the letters stopped and I...I–"

"Settled," Mother interrupted. "Don't blame yourself, Cara. We need to grab onto something in our lives–security, a better life, whatever it may be."

The truth cut deep, but as I glanced to Lily asleep in the bassinet, I knew that I couldn't regret my marriage to Jack.

"Say, why didn't you introduce your father and me to this Noah Meyer fellow?" she asked.

"Timing never seemed right."

"You can't time love. It has an agenda all its own."

We finished our tea in silence. Memories of Noah and the summer we shared drifted through my mind. Perhaps Mother sat recalling the Ferris wheel ride she shared with Herb.

She stood and carried our empty cups to the sink. "I'd say it's about time to get you and Lily to a warmer place before you both freeze to death. You can stay at our house, or if you prefer, you can go back to Piney Cove."

We loaded up the Jeep and I followed Mother's car to the front entrance of Lake in the Woods. She pulled onto the main road headed toward Laurel. I sat idle for a second, looking right, then left, then right again. The image of Jack and Tory making love resurfaced. I gripped the steering wheel and made a hard right– opposite the direction of my husband.

* * *

Mother eventually told Daddy of Jack's infidelity, but my father never once suggested divorce. Maybe he didn't want to give Mother any ideas. The betrayal was still too raw in my mind to talk about it. Mother stayed busy caring for Lily and sent me to the creek each day.

"I'm not sure what you do there, but if it helps, stay as long as you need," she said.

I packed my supplies and, instead of driving down the street and parking roadside, I walked the long route. I remembered the way: our backyard, neighbor's yard, apple orchard, grape vineyard, asparagus field, tall grass, creek. In the spring, the path was abundant and colorful. The budding orchards reminded me of the bounties of summers past and I could almost hear the chugging and clunking of Farmer Jensen's tractor. The dilapidated tree fort conjured up memories of secret clubs and skinned knees. Seeing everything through the eyes of a ten-year-old again, made me realize my vision had narrowed since Aunt Kate's death; no longer could she remind me to enjoy the sheer pleasure of the journey, to look for the subtleties amongst the obvious. With her prompting, I would've foreseen what was going on between Jack and Tory, that Mitch was married, that Noah was leaving, and that giving up Jane would cause me so much pain. But it wasn't Aunt Kate's job to keep me aware of my surroundings. I needed to take note of my own turf.

I would stop searching for the perfect patch of daffodils, or the best angle within a handful of Poeticus. Instead, I would begin looking at things through a wider lens, no glossing over rougher terrain in search of the easier path. There would no longer be a solitary cluster of daffodils, no more than there had been a single act of betrayal, or a lone heartache.

After painting the entire field of Poeticus as part of the bigger territory in which they bloomed, I put down my brush and leaned back against the oak tree. I watched in wonder as my entire life played out across the clear blue sky like a movie at a drive-in theatre.

Once back in Piney Cove, Mary Rose handed me six phone messages from Jack. I shuffled through them:

Call me.
Come over when you return.
I want to see Lily.
Let's talk.
How about dinner?
Happy early Mother's Day.

Mary Rose pointed to a long, narrow box on the table. "Your Mother's Day gift from Jack."

"A bit early."

"He's taking it seriously."

I recognized the shape and size of the box. "*Hmm.* Jewelry. It would've meant something if he'd remained faithful to his daughter's mother." I turned, leaving the box behind and made my way upstairs to do the important things: nurse Lily, put her down for a nap, unpack.

After she woke, I made my way back to the kitchen where Mary Rose and Harper baked cookies. I stared at the box and nudged it with my finger.

"Oh, go ahead," Mary Rose said. "I won't tell. Besides, you don't have to keep it."

"You're right." I placed Lily in her infant carrier and opened the box to find brilliant sapphires and diamonds. Jack always bought the best of everything. "I suppose it wouldn't hurt to try it on." I held out my wrist and Mary Rose secured the bracelet.

She turned the clasp around to the back. "It's beautiful."

Harper leaned over the counter. "Pretty," she said.

"It is, isn't it?" I gazed down at the dazzling gems. "I'll give it back today when I take Lily over for a visit." I twirled the bracelet around. "I have to face him sooner or later. Impossible to avoid him since we share a daughter. Not to mention, I want to save Daddy some work by grabbing some financial information while I'm there."

Mary Rose looked surprised. "So, you've made the decision to divorce?"

"It's getting harder to forgive as time goes on." I looked at the clock. "I should call and get this over with." I reached for the phone.

"Oh, Jack said you don't need to call, that you could just run over when you got home. He's been waiting...for three weeks, actually. He reminded me daily."

I stood. "This won't take long." I grabbed the diaper bag and put Lily in the stroller. The walk across the street was much too short; I needed miles to prepare for my first meeting with Jack. To make matters worse, he answered the door on the first knock.

"You don't need to knock, Cara. This is still your home." He pulled us inside.

Toys littered the living room floor. "What's all this?" I asked.

"A few things I picked up for Lily."

"Jack, you don't have to buy things to show her that you love her."

"Of course you buy things for people you love," he said, staring at my wrist.

I suddenly realized I'd forgotten to take off the bracelet and tugged at my shirtsleeve to cover it, wishing I could cover the smirk on his face.

"Look, Cara," Jack started, "I'm sorry about what happened."

My chest tightened and my breathing became shallow. "Are you really, Jack? It's more likely that you're sorry that you got caught."

"No, Cara. I'm sorry. Do you actually think Tory meant something to me?"

His self-centeredness conjured up memories of Mitch. My gaze met Jack's with an icy stare. "But she meant something to me, damn it! I not only lost my husband, but my best friend, too."

"Well, I would hardly say that a best friend would—"

"Stop it!" I interrupted. "You're not going to put all the blame on her. *You* invited her into our bed while I was having our baby! How could you?"

He stood speechless. For the first time, Jack Templeton had no answer. After long moments, he said, "I don't know, Cara. I really don't know."

I needed to ask the question. "Why Tory? I'm sure you had plenty to choose from."

A look of persuasion flashed across his face as if he had to convince me of the logic behind it all. "Girls like Tory don't require much. They're simple...needing only one thing...never asking for anything more."

"And what did I ask of you, Jack? Was it asking too much for you to take interest in the baby?"

"You took enough interest for the both of us, Cara. You were in your own world...spending hours in that nursery just staring at the walls."

"I needed to prepare myself, Jack. You knew my past. The baby was your idea, remember? You wanted a family right away. If you felt pressured by it all..."

"I realized too late that it was a mistake, okay? Just like you could never replace Jane by having another baby, I couldn't replace my father by becoming one." Jack leaned back against the counter and folded his arms across his chest.

My God. That's what it was all about? It made sense now; the urgency to start a family so soon, the anger over my inability to get pregnant for months, the way he pulled away soon after I announced the positive test. Why hadn't I figured it out? We'd be the new family to replace the one he'd lost.

"I made a poor choice and now I'm living with it," Jack said.

Why hadn't we talked openly like this during our marriage? We had both suffered losses, yet chose to endure them alone.

Jack straightened as if to toss off the weight of the past. "Anyway, it's too late for all of that now. The damage has been done and I take responsibility. We need to remain civil for Lily's sake."

"Yes. She needs both of us."

He held out his arms to accept her. "Thought I'd drive her over to the park for a walk. Get some fresh air. Clear my head before I settle down to work for the night. I have a huge deal in the making."

His talk of work signaled that his moment of weakness had passed. I nodded. "Sure."

"I'll need the stroller."

"It's out front, but you'll need a lot more than that."

He paused. "Like what?"

I opened the diaper bag and pulled out the first item. "Diapers– remember tabs go in back. Some wipes, a blanket, pacifier, bottle of breast milk, and a spare outfit in case she soils the one she has on. Oh, and a hat."

"Christ, we're not spending the night. How long do you think we'll be gone?"

"Doesn't matter. Two hours, two days–you still need the same amount of stuff. Oh, and don't forget to burp her after her feeding." I followed him to the door. "Check her diaper often. She doesn't like to be wet."

"Who would?"

"Make sure the car seat strap is tight, but not too tight," I added.

He turned. "Anything else?"

"Yes, drive carefully."

He made his way to the car and placed her inside.

"And, Jack?"

He sighed. "What?"

"Oh, never mind."

"You might as well say it, Cara. You won't rest knowing there was one more potential hazard you didn't point out to me."

He was right, but I couldn't stop myself. "Her pediatrician is Dr. Young. Do you remember his number?"

"It's on my speed dial."

"You're making fun of me, aren't you?"

"Absolutely."

I pointed to the door. "I'll go back inside now."

"That would be good." Jack packed the stroller, then got in the car.

"Just one more thing," I said.

He poked his head out the window and I cradled my arms in front of me. "She likes to be held on the left side."

"Any particular reason?"

"No."

"Of course not." He closed the car window.

I watched him drive up over the hill out of view. He'd be gone a half hour tops; one cry and he'd speed home and hand her back to me. Besides, what could happen in such a short time? Thoughts of car wrecks, pedophiles, and child abductors suddenly crowded my mind. I needed to keep myself occupied, so I slipped into Jack's office and started my search for a bank record, 401k retirement plan, life insurance policy, W2 form, a stock or bond report–anything with numbers. My fingers leafed through rows of manila folders before one in particular caught my eye. *Farnsworth Gallery* it read. Inside, a copy of a sales contract. My throat tightened as I flipped the pages, remembering back to Mr. Farnsworth saying that his lawyer had drawn up the contract, helped him finalize the deal. Why wouldn't Mr. Farnsworth have chosen Jack? He was one of the best real estate attorneys in the area.

Jesus, did you even see it coming? Jack had asked me. *It seems to me that Farnsworth could've given you more notice. Well, not to worry, something is bound to come along.*

That something was a marriage proposal; convenient timing, considering my financial concerns and impending unemployment. Jack could've warned me that the gallery was going to be sold, but that would have taken away his advantage–buying my security.

"You bastard!" I threw the file on the desk.

I looked at the sapphire and diamond studded handcuff locked tight around my wrist. With the sweep of my thumb, the clasp snapped open, and the bracelet tumbled to the floor.

Trampstick

One only had to watch Daddy in the courtroom to see that he'd chosen the right profession. The way he paced back and forth in front of the judge and jury like the pendulum of a clock, keeping time with their fleeting thoughts of guilt or innocence. Then he'd stop and grab the rail, making time stand still while he hammered his points across. And the way he paused during his closing argument at just the right moment, creating the feeling that what he said next would prove his client's innocence. While Daddy preferred to keep the divorce amicable for my benefit, there was no doubt he'd be disappointed in giving up the opportunity for a good fight.

Jack had a major disadvantage. Daddy not only believed him to be guilty, but my father knew the nature of the crime. He was familiar with the trail of evidence, the same evidence Mother carried around in her pocket: telephone logs, hotel and restaurant receipts, Visa bills for unfamiliar gifts. The difference being that Mother would never use such evidence against my father.

As a child, I'd climb into Daddy's chair and twirl around behind the mahogany desk, making myself sick with dizziness while white specks floated before my eyes. The desk seemed so big back then, but not half as large as it appeared on this day.

"I'm sorry it's come to this, Petunia." Daddy grabbed his legal pad and pen.

"Me, too." I choked back tears.

Daddy twisted the hand carved fountain pen around in his hands. "As you can imagine, this is quite difficult for me. God only knows why your mother hasn't divorced me. She certainly has grounds for it. In light of things, I've asked her forgiveness and I'd like to ask the same of you. I'm truly sorry."

I leaned back in the chair and crossed my arms. "Sorry? That's supposed to fix everything? Do you know how painful it has been for Mother all of these years? How humiliating?"

He lowered his head. "No, I guess I didn't. Not until now, anyway. Until I saw what it has done to you, to your future, and to Lily. I deeply regret the pain I caused my family, the shame I placed on your mother. The only thing I can do at this point is to say that I'm sorry and hope you'll forgive me." He slowly lifted his head.

"Has Mother forgiven you?"

"Yes. Or, at least she tells me so."

"Will you do it again, you know, once this all blows over?"

"I have promised to remain faithful to your mother."

I nodded, then reached over and squeezed his hand.

He quickly cleared his throat, ready to move on. "Let's go over a few things."

"Sure."

"I have your assets listed here. It looks as though the two of you did rather well."

"Jack brought in most of the money."

"Then he was a fool to throw it away." Daddy tapped the end of his pen on the pad of paper. "Oh, before I forget, who will be representing Jack?"

"He plans to represent himself."

Daddy chuckled. "A bigger fool than I thought. I suppose it will save on legal fees, but if we can't work something out, then we'll move it to court." Daddy smiled. "Then he'll wish that he had retained the services of a real attorney.

"Now, we'll ask for half the savings and investments, nothing out of the ordinary there. I'm assuming both the creek property and the cottage are things you want for sentimental reasons, am I right?"

"Yes. *Especially* the creek property."

"And the house in Piney Cove? Do you and Jack plan to sell?"

"We haven't talked about it, but I'd just as soon sell it. It's Jack's dream home, not mine. Mary Rose said that Lily and I could move in with her."

"You're always welcome to come back to Laurel, Buttercup."

"Thanks, Daddy, but Mary Rose seems to like the company."

"I don't doubt that she does." He placed the pen on the desk and folded his hands. "We'll propose that you get primary physical custody of Lily. With the hours he works, she's sure to be nanny bound. He can have joint legal custody to help make decisions about medical issues, schooling, and such. We'll ask that Jack have temporary custody one day a week, on alternate weekends, alternate holidays, alternate birthdays, and three to four weeks of extended time in the summer when she reaches school age. Right now, an exception will have to be made since you're breastfeeding and she can't be away from you for long periods of time."

I fell back in my chair, panicked from the mere thought of being separated from her at all.

Daddy glanced at the paper again. "We could call his moral character into question."

"No," I said firmly. "Let's leave that out of it. I'm trying to put it behind me."

"Okay," Daddy said. "By the looks of his salary, you'll be getting a little over five hundred dollars for child support."

I nodded. "Five hundred a month is good."

Daddy laughed. "That's five hundred a week, Tulip."

"Oh, well, that's even better."

"Seeing that you quit your job to follow him to Piney Cove–"

"Um," I interrupted, "I hate to bring this up, but I was about to lose my job, anyway."

Daddy pointed to Jack's file marked *Farnsworth Gallery.* "Seeing as Jack assisted in your unemployment status, and given the disparity of your incomes, three hundred a week in alimony is fair. At least temporarily, until you establish a steady income." He jotted notes on the legal pad. "Of course, you and Lily will stay under his health insurance policy, until you obtain that benefit through an employer."

"How long will all this take?" I asked.

"That depends on Jack. If he agrees to our proposal, it will go rather quickly. If he contests, it could drag out a while."

"Give him the house," I said.

"Wait a minute. Does he want the house?"

"He lives for that house. If he'll agree to everything else, he can have it. Lily and I will stay with Mary Rose."

"Are you positive?"

"I'm sure."

Daddy leaned back and folded his hands across his stomach as he always did while contemplating things of importance. Then he shot forward. "Okay, here's how it'll come down. Jack will keep the house until Lily is no longer receiving support. At that time, he will pay you fifty percent of the equity of the house at the time the divorce judgment was entered. You, in return, will not go after any compensation for his law practice."

I suddenly remembered one more thing. "I want the painting."

"What painting?" Daddy asked.

"The one above the mantel. He never appreciated it, anyway."

"You got it. I'll file the petition and Jack will be served." He stood and grabbed his notepad from the desk. "Oh, I've been meaning to tell you that I saw your old boyfriend, Mitch, down at the courthouse the other day. Barely recognized him in a suit and tie." Daddy laughed. "They all find style when their ass is on the line."

"He's not one to be in legal trouble. Do you know why he was there?"

"Haven't the slightest idea. Could be that he's driving that Firebird of his a little too fast. I was just glad he didn't stop to talk to me."

I laughed. "Talk to *you*? He was deathly afraid of you."

"And he should've been." He smirked. "Now, it's Jack's turn." Daddy left the room to talk to his secretary.

I walked around the desk, tracing its rectangular shape with my index finger before sitting in Daddy's chair. After gently pushing off, I gained momentum with each subsequent turn. In no time, I was twirling around, my stomach and head remaining a lap behind. I thought about stopping, but instead spun faster. Soon, I broke through the dizziness, whirling myself into a state of exhilaration.

"One-woman show," I repeated several times, letting it slowly roll off my tongue to savor each syllable. In early December, a collection of my paintings would hang in The Gallery at Pines Crossing.

"It will get the townspeople through the rest of the winter," Blythe Calloway had assured me over the phone. Although the event was several months away, Blythe had it all planned. The exhibit would run for a month, and even though most people in Piney Cove were familiar with my work, she'd advertise in the local paper, including a short biography along with my picture.

"We want to catch the eye of the badgers staying in town that weekend," she had said.

I'd been to many openings, but never as the featured artist. I'd always been just one of the many guests who grazed on cheese, crackers, and fruit while browsing the works on display. Sipping wine and listening to people talk about the marvelous use of color and lively texture, I secretly wished it were my pieces attracting such praise. Now, I would have the chance to explain the inspiration behind my paintings. The guests' heads would be cocked to the side as they hearkened my story, looking for the deeper meaning, then nodding as if seeing the daffodils through my eyes. They'd see that a Lemon Glow was close in color to that of a sunrise along the lake's horizon, that the shape of a Jumblie resembled a hummingbird, and that when jonquils hung their heads so low in the early morning hours that perhaps they really were still sleepy.

The people of Piney Cove would visit the creek without having to travel down the old dirt path.

The sun filtered through the large picture windows of my old studio. I looked out over the water, never tiring of the view of the lake and its ability to pull my focus onto the long stretch of pale blue, before pushing my thoughts back inland with a single wave, only to lure me out again with its shimmering surface. Out and back, out and back; soothing, like a rocking chair for the mind. I broke free from the water's grasp and turned my attention to the eighteen paintings that hung on the walls, then quietly plucked them from their hooks like a professional thief, propping them along the baseboards.

I took one last look at what used to be my special room, the walls now barren; how cold it felt when void of color. My easel held a nearly finished painting–a colony of Thalias, and my palette remained covered with the twelve workhorse colors. The turpentine that once filled the dipper had long since evaporated and cotton rags, stacked by the dozen, sat on a nearby table. I could have slipped back into the abandoned workstation by pouring more solvent, picking up the No. 3 bright to finish the detail work. How convenient it would be to paint over the darkness, the losses with vibrant colors, adding layer upon layer, until the pain underneath was no longer visible–a pattern that had sustained me for years. I glanced down at the row of paintings along the floorboards, the crises lined up next to one another: Mitch, a Barrett Browning; Jane, a Laurens Koster; Noah, a Poeticus. Would the Thalias on the easel become Jack and Tory? No, I told myself, the painting would remain unfinished for now. I flung a nearby sheet over the easel before turning out the light.

Jack waited for me in the kitchen. "What is it that you want?" he said, drumming his fingers on the marble countertop.

"I think you know." I pointed to the papers spread out in front of him like a poker hand. "I believe Daddy outlined it all for you."

Jack frowned. "Not that. What do you really want? To fix it."

I leaned against the wall for support. "It can't be fixed."

"You're wrong about that, Cara. Anything can be fixed. Your father just raised the stakes that's all. Nice strategy, I might add. But even your father knows everything has a price, and I'm willing to negotiate."

"Well, I'm not."

"Oh, I get it. You're teaching me a lesson. That's okay, but I never thought you'd take it this far." He made his way over to me and slid his hands around my hips. My breath quickened as his lips descended upon mine.

"You don't want a divorce, Cara," he whispered.

"Stop." I pushed him aside. "I have to go. Lily needs me."

"You'll soon realize that you need me," he said.

I flashed a smile. "Yes, as a matter of fact, I do need you."

"Really?" His eyes widened.

"Yeah, grab a couple of my paintings from the studio and carry them across the street for me."

My series of losses, brought about irrational fears. I'd often sit next to Lily's bassinet while she napped, my hand resting on her chest, feeling the rise and fall, taking comfort in the grunting noises she made. It took an effort not to check on her throughout the night, to climb out of bed whenever she stirred, or run to her the moment she made any noise that resembled a cry. Things that other mothers would have barely worried about became my obsessions. I soon found myself sleeping on the floor next to her crib, which had been emptied of her stuffed animals and extra bedding to reduce the risk of suffocation.

"What are the odds that she'll have a reaction to that vaccine?" I'd ask the doctor, checking his answer against what the nurse told me but five minutes earlier. "Did you wash your hands before picking her up?" I questioned those who dared to hold her. "Cara, have you moved Lily to her own room yet?" Mother asked whenever she called. "Soon," I'd say.

One person understood my obsessions.

"You know," Mary Rose said, "when Paul died, I became scared to death of losing Harper. I was terrified to let her sleep alone in her crib. Afraid she'd die in her sleep of SIDS. Every night, I'd end up bringing her into my bed." Mary Rose laughed. "Only to worry that I'd roll over in my sleep and suffocate her, that she'd fall out of the bed, or get strangled in the sheets. I don't think I slept for six months straight."

"So, I'm not crazy?" I asked.

"No." She patted my arm. "Just a good mother."

Would she still consider me a good mother if she knew about Jane?

Satisfied that Lily wasn't going to die anytime soon, we packed up the car and headed for the cottage. Harper immediately took to the water. Mary Rose swam beside her while the little girl dogpaddled in small circles. When they stepped ashore, their naturally curly hair was plastered down the middle of their backs, only to spring up above their shoulders when dried. It was the first time I'd seen Mary Rose in a bathing suit. Her body was void of any lasting effects of pregnancy—no stretch marks or varicose veins, unlike my hips and thighs that resembled a road map, thus the reason Lily and I spent our time discovering nature by walking the grounds around the cottage. We enjoyed our frequent trips to the cottage throughout the summer months.

Jack spent the summer settling into his new life without us and reduced his visitation with Lily to a weekly jaunt to the toy store.

Why had I expected him to change just because he was a father? I watched through the front window as he shuffled women through his front door, tossing a glance toward Mary Rose's house as an afterthought. This time he zipped the car straight into the garage and closed the door behind him; the woman would be staying overnight.

"How was your date last night?" I asked while he stood on the front porch the next morning.

"That was no date," he said. "Business meeting."

"Oh, is that right? Must've been a long one."

"Yes, it was. Not to change the subject, but I was hoping you could do me a favor. If I'm not back by three o'clock, would you mind letting the caterer in? Big party tonight." Jack wasn't as discreet about his business engagements. I suppose he wanted me to know that his success continued without me.

"Sure," I said.

"The partners want me to entertain more."

"Uh-huh."

"Quite a guest list, I might add."

"*Hmm*." My lack of interest stopped him short of reciting the menu.

That night, I sat in the rocking chair in the front room, nursing Lily and holding back the window sheer. I listened to the slam of car doors and watched men in suits and women in snug, black dresses make their way up the drive. I looked down at my oversized pajamas and ratty slippers, and felt both relieved and jealous. After several more cars arrived, I lost interest and let go of the sheer, the veil falling down over my old life.

For years I had been John Robertson's daughter, Mitch Sanders' girl, and Jack Templeton's wife. Now I was Cara the mother, the caregiver, the nurturer. After moving in with Mary Rose, my responsibilities had shifted. Since I worked from home, it made sense that I watched both girls on the weekdays. Mary Rose was happy to get Harper out of daycare and back into the comforts of home. There was no pressure to rush Harper out the door, so we stretched out our morning coffee. I painted while the girls napped in the afternoon. By the time Mary Rose returned home from work, I had dinner on the table. The routine of everyday life gave me comfort and we became a family.

On August sixteenth, I waited for Mary Rose to mention a trip to Paul's grave. I finally asked over dinner. "Do you want to go to the cemetery today?"

She looked up from her plate. "Cemetery?" She hesitated, then gasped. "Oh, my God. It's August sixteenth, isn't it?" Her gaze met the calendar hanging on the kitchen wall. "How could I forget?"

"Don't worry. We'll still have time after dinner."

"I can't believe...it's just that..." She buried her face in her hands.

"Mary Rose, it's okay," I tried to reassure her. "We all get busy, forget things."

She continued to beat herself up all the way to the florist and then on to the cemetery. "I don't understand it," she said. "How could I forget?" She opened the door before the car came to a complete stop, then sprinted up the hill to his grave. By the time the girls and I joined her, she was on her knees in prayer, tears streaming down her face. I crouched beside her and rested Lily on my hip. Harper walked around the stone as she'd done in the past, but this time she added her rendition of *London Bridges*. I placed my hand on Mary Rose's back and she opened her eyes.

"Do you think he'll forgive me?" she asked.

"I'm positive he will."

She rested her head on my shoulder and continued to cry.

"It's okay," I whispered, knowing that Paul Townsend could not have been happier that she had forgotten.

The gray, December sky crowded my head like an extra narrow frame. Things should've looked brighter with the divorce finalized. Even though Jack had agreed to the proposed settlement and Daddy claimed victory, I still felt like a failure.

"Jack should've had a big breakfast like me," Daddy touted. "Bacon, eggs, the works."

For nearly two weeks, I carried my divorce papers around the house, pouring over them to be sure the content had not mysteriously changed from one day to the next. That I still had custody of Lily and that the creek property remained in my name.

Mary Rose lifted the documents from my bedspread and placed them on the dresser each night. She understood my fears; she had spent many nights with an accident report glued to her chest. The difference–she had prayed for a change; that Paul's name was somehow erased, or at the very least, the word injury replaced fatality.

She assured me that I'd soon tuck the papers away with other important documents like my birth certificate, passport, and social security card. That I'd stumble upon them every so often when cleaning out the drawer and startle again as if seeing them for the first time. And that eventually, I'd give them nothing more than a glance.

This particular morning however, I had something else on my mind. Blythe Calloway expected me at the gallery to prepare for my show the following evening. I showered, then loaded my paintings in the rental van. When I pulled up to the gallery, badgers lined the storefronts, overflowed from the café, and swallowed up every parking spot.

I circled the block several times, and just when I was ready to adopt Jack's motto, 'Buck the badgers,' a car pulled out and I zipped into the parking place. Then, I made my way inside the gallery.

Blythe walked from behind the counter. "Well hello, Cara."

"Busy place today," I said.

"They've been coming and going since I opened this morning," she said. "Were you able to park near the gallery?"

"It took a while, but I'm right out front. There must be a conference in town. I see all the name tags floating around."

"Yes, but unfortunately, lookers outnumber buyers."

"That's not what I had hoped to hear."

Blythe chuckled. "Perhaps we can change that. Oh, have you seen the ad?" She grabbed the newspaper and handed it to me. "People are talking about the show. Everyone is thrilled that you'll be displaying some of your finest pieces. I'll be anxious to see your favorite."

"I'll go grab the paintings."

"Let me help." She put the doorstop in place and we unloaded nineteen paintings.

I ran my finger over the frame that housed the 40x60 canvas and remembered how grand it had looked over the mantel. "This is my favorite."

"Are you sure you want to sell that piece? It's priceless," she said.

But even your father knows everything has a price, Jack had told me.

I smiled. "Do you think sixty-five hundred would be reasonable?"

The cylinders lined the vanity like soldiers prepared for battle: Passionate Pink, Chocolate Mousse, Sensual Sagewood, Cocoa Wine, Vivacious Violet. Every color of lipstick I had owned over the past five years stood at attention before me. I dabbed on the last shade, Scarlet Ember, and meshed my lips together. I called Mary Rose for a second opinion.

"Does this lipstick scream tramp?" I asked.

She leaned forward to examine my mouth. "No, I wouldn't go as far as to say it's trampstick, but it does hint that with a little wine you could loosen up a bit."

"So much for that one." I wiped my lips with a tissue. "I've gone through them all. Any suggestions?"

"I think I have just the color. I'll be right back." She returned with a brand new tube and handed it to me. "Try this."

"Cranberry Cream. Sounds delicious." I coated my lips and looked into the mirror. "Subtle, yet makes a statement. Perfect color for my dark gray dress. How come you never used it?"

"I had every intention, actually. That evening, Paul and I had tickets for the symphony–*Swan Lake*. It was to be our first official night out without Harper."

"Oh God, I'm sorry." I pointed to my lips. "You sure this won't bother you?"

"Not at all. I can't think of a better occasion." Mary Rose stood in the mirror alongside me, her face was pale and her cheeks sunken.

"Are you feeling okay?" I asked.

"I'm fine, probably just all the excitement over your show. Now, let me look at your lips." She tilted her head and zoomed in close. "That color says, 'I long for you, but I will restrain myself because I have class.'"

I laughed. "Shouldn't it say,' I'm a professional artist?'"

"Everyone already knows that or they wouldn't come."

"Well, here's something they don't know," I said as we walked downstairs to give the sitter her list of instructions and to kiss the girls goodbye.

"And what's that?" Mary Rose asked.

"I'm nervous as hell."

Return to Sender

Self-doubt sent me to the gallery two hours before the start of my show, time I spent pacing in front of each painting, scrutinizing them as if I were a guest. I knew their texture, color, detail, and cast shadows by memory, but now questioned my choices. Had I picked the right colors for the Barrett Brownings? Were the cups of the Romance too large? Should I have hung the pictures in the order of their bloom seasons? Perhaps I should have skipped the lipstick altogether.

I had waited all of my life for this day, for people to get a glimpse of the beauty that rolled around in my mind. For the townspeople of Piney Cove to see there was a place to the south with a landscape so lively, so satiating to the eye that one glance would send a smile to their lips. Would they feel anticipation from one painting to the next, the same foretaste I had every time I crossed the embankment and made my way toward the field of flowers? Could they imagine the flowers' sweet aroma swirling up from the canvas? Would they have the urge to reach out and pick one of the daffodils for a loved one?

Mary Rose saw the worry splashed across my face. She placed her arm around me. "Everything is beautiful. You couldn't have picked better works to display."

Pushing negative thoughts aside, I met each guest as they trickled into the gallery. Blythe introduced me to those I didn't know. Within an hour, the room was full and multiple conversations bounced about. Not wanting to miss a single word during my opening, my attention was summoned in different directions. But panic set in when chitchat replaced art talk. Had they forgotten why they were here? I remembered feeling the same way after Aunt Kate's funeral. She was barely in the ground an hour when, over ham sandwiches and potato salad, the conversation turned to quilting and college football.

Just as Mr. Solomon, the local high school art teacher, and I finished discussing the picture of jonquils painted alla prima in the field, Mrs. Hewitt, the librarian, boldly announced that Bergman's Delicatessen had jumbo shrimp much cheaper than the chain supermarket and twice as flavorful. Three women turned and nodded as if they had just tasted a sample.

"You don't say," another woman said. "I'll have to get over there tomorrow."

Then Mr. Kriegler, manager of the credit union, informed us that his son was old enough to mow lawns this summer.

"I'll have to keep that in mind," Dr. Greenley said. "Can he handle two acres?"

Soon, a single voice rose above the others. I looked up to see Steph making her way across the room. Andrew, Mother, and Daddy lagged a step behind. My sister stopped in front of me, but her gaze continued down the wall of the gallery. "Where did you put the sale pieces? They're not up front."

"Sale pieces?" I asked.

Her hands came down on the armrests she called hipbones. "You certainly can't expect to draw in customers without clearance merchandise."

"This is art, Stephanie, not jogging apparel."

She shrugged. "Suit yourself."

I rolled my eyes.

"Maybe Steph is right," Mother whispered. "Even I can't pass up a bargain bin, but you didn't hear that from me."

Andrew ran his finger over the price of one of the paintings, then peered down the row, nodding that calculator head of his.

Blythe motioned me over from across the room. I turned to my family. "Why don't you get something to eat and drink. I'll be back shortly."

They made their way over to the refreshments while I joined Blythe and the gentleman standing next to her admiring a series of jonquil paintings. My heart raced at the thought of him even considering my paintings.

"Cara," Blythe said, "this is Dr. Blake. A neurosurgeon at County General."

Wouldn't Mother be impressed. "Hello, Dr. Blake."

"Please tell Dr. Blake a little about this series," Blythe prompted.

"Certainly. It's titled *Sleepy Heads*. It was a cold day in April, much colder than usual." I pointed to the first painting. "See how the stem leaves are parallel to the ground? That's because the temperature had dropped down into the teens overnight." Then I moved my hand to the three subsequent pictures that depicted the flowers rising from the ground at different stages. "Daffodils perk up as the sun warms them, eventually they stand upright."

"Ah," he said, "interesting. I didn't know that. An appropriate title then."

"Their heads hung until nearly ten-thirty that morning. I thought they'd never wake up."

"Well, I'm glad they did. The detail is superb," he said. "This series will be perfect for my dining room." The doctor leaned in close to study each one a moment longer, then nodded. "I'll take them."

"Splendid choice for that room," Blythe assured him. Obviously, she had been a guest in his home before.

I smiled as she placed a circular, red sticker next to the paintings to indicate they had been sold; proof positive that someone liked my work. With a large sale behind me, if I failed to sell another piece, I would still consider the show a success.

"Thank you, Dr. Blake," I said. "Enjoy them." As I made my way back across the room, someone tapped my shoulder. My eyes widened.

"Don't look so shocked, sweetheart," Jack said. "You think I'd miss the biggest event to hit this town? Besides, I need to see what it sells for." He pointed to the Poeticus painting. "I have to admit, I'm a bit surprised you're selling it."

"Oh, well...I..."

"No need to explain. It's yours to do with what you please. Part of the settlement, right?"

I nodded. "By the way, I never did thank you for being so amicable during the divorce."

"There was no sense in being difficult."

Translation—he didn't stand a chance against Daddy. "Yes, I

suppose."

The chime on the door announced a new arrival. A man in a beige overcoat with the hood pulled over his head stood in the doorway. His posture and walk seemed familiar. I turned back to Jack. "I better go."

He looked at the door. "Absolutely. Who am I to stand in the way of potential customers? But, you'd do better with Mr. Lawson over there." Jack pointed to an older man admiring a still life. "He owns the Bay O Wolf restaurant that we went to a couple of times. Go seal the deal, sweetheart."

I walked over to the restaurateur. "Hello, Mr. Lawson. I'm Cara Templeton. Can I answer any questions for you?"

He turned toward me, nudged his glasses down, and peered over the frames. "I'm looking for a painting for my lobby, nothing overly elaborate. I believe this one has potential. What variety?"

"Laurens Koster. They possess a simple elegance." *Think sale.* "Just like your restaurant."

"*Hmm*...I like that." He beamed. "I believe you have yourself a sale, young lady. You'll come see it once it's hung?"

"Of course. I'll even try to bring you a fresh bouquet. They have quite a fragrance."

"I look forward to it. Simple elegance," he repeated before he turned and made his way toward Blythe.

Two sales in the same evening. Could it be possible that one day my work would be referred to as a Templeton original?

The gallery remained crowded as Mary Rose busied herself serving coffee and Mother and Daddy socialized in the far corner. I heard Mother announce that I was, indeed, her daughter and that she always knew I had talent. How long I had waited for those words.

Jack and Daddy must've declared a truce since they stood in the same social circle. Steph and Andrew were glued to the sofa along the far wall with a look of boredom pinching their faces. I made my way to the front, scanning the room before spotting the beige overcoat draped over the gentleman's arm. The hood no longer covered the sandy brown hair that now fell loosely across his forehead. His warm, brown eyes met mine.

It couldn't be. I squeezed my eyes shut, then reopened them, expecting the mirage to be gone. But Noah stood there smiling, his boyish grin unmistakable. His hands offered the ultimate proof, hands I'd held while walking near the creek and along the beach. His index finger that cut across the warm summer breeze on the hillside at Pier Pointe while *Chopin's Opus 25, No. 9 Etude* drifted over us. I looked past his wrists and saw no wedding band. I couldn't breathe as he reached me, the familiar scent of his hair swirling up memories of a love-filled summer.

"Noah," I whispered, his name leaving my lips as if he'd never left. "How...when?" was all I could manage.

He gave me a social hug and I felt his reluctance to let go. "I couldn't believe it when I saw the ad in the newspaper. I must've looked at it a hundred times to make sure it was you."

"But...but when did you get back to the states?" I asked, trying to make sense of it all.

"I moved to Chicago about a year ago."

"Chicago? Well..." I choked back my disappointment, picturing the expanse of water that still remained between us.

"When I got the brochure on this teachers' conference, I knew I had to come back to Michigan to try to find you. I stopped at Pier Pointe yesterday and stood on the bluff where we used to listen to the concerts. Even went to the creek, hoping you'd be there. Since it's winter, I knew my chances were slim, but I had to try. Then I opened the paper and there you were."

Why was he searching for me? "But you stopped writing. I just assumed..."

"I wrote, but you had moved. My last letter came back to me." He pulled out an envelope with the words, *Return to sender. No forwarding address*, stamped across the front. "Read it when you have some privacy."

"Oh, God. I forgot to...the post office...that little card." An immediate change of address seemed so insignificant at the time.

His smile faded. "I see your name has changed."

"Oh, that. Yeah. I got married a couple of years ago."

"Your husband must be proud of you." He looked around the gallery as if searching for the man who had stolen my heart.

"We're divorced," I said quickly.

"I'm sorry to hear that."

"Don't be. I'm doing fine. And what about you? Do you have a significant other in Chicago?"

He shook his head. "No. Guess I never found the right woman. Or, perhaps I found her, but let her go."

Mother came up from behind and nudged me with her coat slung over her forearm. "Sorry to interrupt, dear, but I'm afraid we must be going. We have quite a drive ahead of us. What a delightful evening. Bring Lily for a visit soon."

I grabbed her shoulder. "Before you go, there's someone I want you to meet."

She chuckled. "Why, I believe we've met everyone in town tonight."

"Noah, I want you to meet my mother, Gail Robertson."

He took her hand. "A pleasure to finally meet you."

"How do you do...Noah, is it?" She hesitated, then drew a sharp breath. "Oh, for the love of God. It's Noah." She waved over the rest of the family. "Noah, this is my husband, John, our oldest daughter, Steph, and her husband, Andrew." She turned to them. "This is Noah."

Noah smiled. "It's nice to meet all of you."

"Who's Noah?" Daddy whispered to Mother.

"I'll explain later," she whispered back.

Steph sighed. "I believe you've run out of time for your closeout sale." She pointed down the wall. "See how many you have left."

"Well, if they don't sell by the end of the show, I'll just drive the rental van down to the corner gas station and sell them out of the back," I said, then looked at the scrunched up faces as the rest of my family fought to hold back their laughter.

Daddy let loose, followed by Mother. Andrew turned away, a mere smile would insure him a night on the living room sofa.

"Fine. Laugh all you want," Steph said. "You don't see me with last year's merchandise hanging on my racks." She marched them out of the gallery.

Noah turned to me and chuckled. "Closeout sale?"

I smiled. "Don't ask." There were a handful of people lingering near the door. "I better say goodbye to my guests. You're not going anywhere, right?"

"Not a chance."

Blythe and I bid farewell to the last of the townspeople, then she motioned me to follow her toward her office. "I'll keep you posted on any future sales throughout the month. The exhibit was one of the best I've had." She pointed to the wall. "Of course, the Poeticus painting was the sale of the evening."

I caught a glimpse of the red sticker. "Someone bought it?"

"Your father. I believe his exact words were, 'this needs to stay within the family.'"

Daddy knew how important that painting was to me after all.

"He's lucky he bought it when he did since there was another interested buyer."

"You're kidding. Who?"

"None other than Jack Templeton," she said, waving off the absurdity. "He obviously regrets what he's given up. I'll be in touch." She walked into her office.

While I stood not knowing what to think of it all, Mary Rose made her way over. "What a night, Cara. People couldn't stop talking about your work." She smiled. "Serving coffee lent itself to some great eavesdropping."

"I want to introduce you to someone," I said, leading her across the room. "Mary Rose, this is Noah."

She fell back a step. "Noah, as in, *the* Noah?"

I laughed. "Yes, that would be the one."

Noah extended his hand. "Nice to meet you, Mary Rose."

"Listen," Mary Rose said. "I'll go home to the girls. You go out and enjoy yourself. Noah, can you drive her home?"

"By all means," he said.

"Thanks, Mary Rose. I'll see you at the house." After she left, Noah and I stood in the middle of the empty gallery.

"You did good," he said.

"I did, didn't I?"

"So," we said in unison.

"Want to…" we said together, then laughed.

He pointed to me. "You first."

"Coffee?" I asked.

"Sounds great."

We walked down the sidewalk, under the soft glow of the streetlamps. At the corner, our gaze locked before he bent down to meet my eager lips.

He pulled back gently. "Do you have any idea how long I've waited for that kiss?"

"Yes, I believe I do," I whispered.

Snuggling my head into its rightful place on his shoulder, we strolled toward the corner café. "It won't be Viennese coffee," I reminded him.

"That's okay. I never much cared for it anyway."

Once home, I went upstairs to nurse Lily, then came back down to the kitchen table. I pulled the worn envelope from my coat pocket and ran my finger over the rejection stamp on the front. How could I have been so stupid? I opened the letter and started to read.

Dear Cara,

I suppose you've probably given up on me by now. It's been a while since I've last written. Perhaps it was presumptuous of me, but I thought it wasn't fair to keep you waiting for my return. If I stopped writing, I thought you'd put our relationship behind you and I'd try to do the same. But there you are, every minute of the day, even following me into my dreams at night.

As I sit alone in Vienna, I can only wonder how different things might've been if I'd stayed in Michigan. This once in a lifetime opportunity may have cost me a once in a lifetime chance at happiness.

Yes, Cara, I love you. I loved you from the moment we met. It took being away from you to realize that I've made the biggest mistake of my life. I can only hope that it's not too late and I pray that you share the same feelings. Just say the word and I'll jump on the next flight to Michigan.

Love,
Noah

He had wanted to come back to me. He hadn't been kissing a

Viennese woman under the streetlamp. Noah had loved me just as I'd loved him. I placed the letter to my chest and closed my eyes, thinking of how things could've been.

I woke to the sound of the coffee pot. Mary Rose stood at the kitchen counter in her robe and slippers. It was after seven o'clock.

"Gee, I must've fallen asleep here at the table," I said, rubbing the stiffness from my neck. "Did you just get up? You never sleep past five-thirty."

She shuffled toward the table and sat down with a heavy sigh. "I'm exhausted. In fact, I feel as though I never went to bed. Last night wore me out. Speaking of which, you're still in last night's clothing."

I laughed and pointed to the heels on the floor. "All but those. I couldn't wait to ditch them. You know how I despise the things."

"Was the reunion with Noah everything you hoped it would be?"

"Yes," I smiled, "and more."

She raised her brow.

"No, *that* still remains a mystery. And it's partly your fault, you know."

"*My* fault?"

I pointed to my lips. "The change in lipstick. If I had stayed with the trampstick, I might have a different story to tell this morning."

Mary Rose giggled and fell back into the chair. "Yeah, but you might not have sold as many paintings." She looked at the envelope on the table. "Return to Sender. Well, that's never a good thing."

I handed her the letter. "Read it. It gets worse."

She began to read and her hand immediately cupped her mouth. "Oh my. Please don't tell me you would've gotten this before you married Jack." Her finger searched for the postmark on the envelope.

"Yep."

She waved the letter in the air. "But wait a minute. Let's say that you had received this letter and married Noah, then you would've never married Jack and moved to Piney Cove, right?"

"That's right."

"Then you wouldn't have Lily...and we would've never met. So this return to sender was actually a blessing!"

It's all a matter of circumstance, Mother had said. *A right turn here or a left turn there, and you end up with something different, but it seems there's something positive that comes out of going either way.*

I reached across the table and took Mary Rose by the hand. "Yes, it most certainly was."

"Wait a minute," I protested, balancing on one foot like a displaced flamingo. "That's not fair!"

"What's not fair?" Noah asked as he hurled another snowball.

"Are you going to help me find my boot or not?"

"I thought Michiganders knew all about winter's hazards. Besides, you look kind of cute that way." He made his way closer to me with his fingers outstretched.

"Don't even think about it, Noah Meyer. Tickling is strictly prohibited at the creek. Didn't you see the sign?" I pointed behind him.

He turned to look and I chucked a snowball at his head. He swung back around just in time to greet it. "Oh, so that's how we're playing this?" He rushed me, wiping the crystals from his brow.

"Truce, truce," I offered, but he kept coming until I landed on my back with him perched on top of me.

He bent down and kissed me. "I believe the word to be, *uncle.*" He kissed me again.

"If I say it, will you get off me?"

He nodded. "Of course. A true gentleman never offers an armistice, then fails to honor it." His hand brushed the wet strands of hair back from my face.

"Um, okay. Let me see. That word...*hmm*...what was it? Aunt?" I kissed him while his fingers tried unsuccessfully to tickle me through my thick, wool coat. "No, uh…grandma." I licked some remaining snow from his cheek. "Wait–I think it might be cousin." My laughter swirled about in the cold air as his warm lips nuzzled my neck.

"Keep going," he whispered in my ear. "I believe there are several relations to go."

"While that may be true, my jeans are screaming uncle. Snow

pants would come in handy about now."

He rolled off and pulled me to my feet, then looked at my jeans and laughed. "And here you were worried about your sock getting wet." He dug up my boot from beneath the snow, shaking it out before putting it back on my foot. "There. Ready to forge ahead?"

I grabbed his arm and we walked toward the creek bed. "You know, I never thought I'd see you again."

"Really? You didn't believe me when I told you I was coming back?"

"I wanted to believe it. But plans change, people change. I figured you fell in love with a beautiful Viennese woman, a violinist, or harpist. That's when I decided to marry Jack. But I never stopped thinking about you."

"Nor did I stop thinking of you." We stopped near a large oak tree.

"This is where Sadie is buried," I told him, pointing down at her gravesite.

"Oh, Cara, I'm sorry. I didn't know."

I nodded. "And Amadeus? How is he?"

"He's getting up in age. He was certainly happy to see me when I returned from Vienna. My parents took good care of him, but as you know, most dogs are loyal to one person." He placed his arm around my shoulder and winked. "Then again, so are most musicians."

I laughed, then motioned to the other side of the creek. "It should be easy to cross today."

"Yes, I believe it will be. Especially for you." Then he swooped me up and slung me over his shoulder.

"Noah! I can walk...really. Put me down!" I kicked my legs back and forth.

"Better stop. You lose your boot in that creek bed and it will be floating downstream next spring. The police will start a search party for the missing woman that supposedly lost that boot. We don't want to start an unwarranted panic, now do we?" He walked through the bed and up the embankment, then twirled me in circles until the blood rushed to my head. Noah finally let me down.

I stood, gripping his coat sleeves until I regained my balance.

He looked at me and smiled. "If I would've known the creek was this much fun in the wintertime, I would've come back to Michigan a lot sooner."

I slapped his arm. "If you think this is fun, wait until spring. You won't believe it." I pointed to where the flowers bloom. "There's the field I've told you about. You didn't get to see them in bloom last time, but we can have another picnic here...sit under the oak tree...take a walk down the long path."

He fell silent.

"Noah, you are coming back, right?"

"Of course, I will. But, it won't be until school lets out for summer break. By then, I can get a sub for my piano students. I'm just sorry it can't be sooner."

"God, summer seems so far away," I said, looking at the thick blanket of snow all around us.

He lifted my chin up, his gaze meeting mine. "Until then, I promise to call every night and I'll send a letter a week. But you have to promise me one thing."

"And what's that?"

"That you won't move. I had a hell of a time finding you this time."

I laughed. "If I do, you'll be the first to know."

We walked silently, hand in hand, our pace slowed by a wind that threatened to knock us back a step for every one we took forward. Noah stopped momentarily and looked back with wonder at the oak trees laced with crystals. "Simply beautiful," he said.

For the next half hour, he stood at the perimeter of the daffodil field, asking questions about their color, fragrance, and life cycle. He wanted to know what bloomed where, the spot where I stood most often to paint, the location of my easel, and what direction offered the best lighting.

"I'm sure it's hard to picture them with all this snow on the ground," I said.

"I can see them," he said, taking one last look around. Then he turned to me and smiled. "So, you haven't told me about her."

I smiled. "Her name is Lily."

He chuckled. "A flowery name. Why doesn't that surprise me?"

"Well, I thought daffodil or jonquil was a bit over the top, so I settled for the next best thing."

We started back toward the creek bed. "She's wonderful. You know, after the adoption, I vowed to myself that I'd never get pregnant again. But when I found out that I was pregnant, I was happy. Truly happy. Until I suspected Jack was having an affair. That's when I knew that Lily would be my life, my focus."

He nudged me. "Sure there's enough room left in your life for one other person?"

"Plenty. You'll be here this summer, right?" I asked once more.

"There's nothing that could keep me away."

"Once you leave, it will seem like an eternity before I see you again."

"And then some." Noah squeezed my hand as we neared the Jeep. "You look happy, Cara, as well as peaceful."

"I am," I said. "Things are finally going well for me."

He put his arm around my shoulder. "So, you've come to terms with the adoption?"

I sighed. "I still think of her, wonder where she is, how she's growing, what she looks like. But I don't feel the heaviness I used to. Of course, I'll always have doubts. Something I'll have to live with."

He turned me toward him. "You made the best decision you could at the time, and that's all anyone could ask."

I nodded and we made our way toward the Jeep. The snowdrifts that had crawled up its side, served as a reminder that summer was too far away. I closed my eyes, wishing the snow would melt, and I begged God for something I thought I'd never ask–to skip right over spring.

I took my usual seat at the kitchen table, while Mary Rose poured a third cup of coffee. "Please, sit down, Noah," she offered.

He hesitated, then lowered himself into the chair. "I hope I'm not intruding. I know this is a special time for you and Cara."

Mary Rose waved off his concern. "Don't be silly. It's nice to have you here." She gave me a wink. "Well, that's as long as you know the password."

"Password?" he asked.

"Of course," she said, "you don't think we'd let just anyone into our coffee klatch, do you?" She went back to the kitchen counter for the pastries and brought them to the table.

Noah looked at me and I shrugged. "Sorry," I said, "you have to say the word."

He stroked his chin, then tapped his index finger to his lips. "Password...let me see. I'm thinking it has something to do with...let's say...coffee. Not that it narrows it down any."

He sat deep in thought as Mary Rose placed a steaming mug in front of him. "Irish mocha. You can drink it as soon as you come up with the word," she said.

Mary Rose and I picked up our cups and both took a sip.

"Now, how can you two tease me like this?" he asked.

"Easy," I said. "You're a guy."

"Can I at least smell it?" His eyes remained hopeful.

Mary Rose looked at me for direction. "I suppose it wouldn't hurt," I said.

He placed the cup to his nose. "It certainly smells delicious." Then he put the coffee back on the table before letting out a chuckle. "Are you two serious?"

"Most serious," Mary Rose said. "Pecan bun, Cara?"

"I'd love one. Can you pass me a napkin, Noah?" I held the pastry in front of him. "You can see how something so gooey could get rather messy."

"Yes, I can certainly see that," he said, handing the napkin my way. "Are the buns password protected as well?"

"Of course," I said, slicing mine in half. "Wow, would you look at the size of those pecans?"

Mary Rose took another sip of coffee, then cleared her throat. "So, Noah, I hear you and Cara had a little snowball fight yesterday. Although, you had an unfair advantage from what she tells me."

"Uh...yes, I suppose I did," he conceded.

"I heard there was an eventual peace offering, an exchange of pleasantries if you will," Mary Rose said, before taking a bite of her pastry. "*Mmm*...these *are* quite tasty, aren't they?" She looked at Noah. "Any ideas yet on that password?"

He shook his head while cradling the coffee cup in his hands.

"You've outdone yourself, Mary Rose," I said.

"It's an old family recipe. My Great Aunt Gert used to make them. Her husband loved them."

"Her husband?" I asked. "Why, he would be your great...um...great..." I glanced at Noah with raised brow.

He suddenly straightened in his chair and threw back his shoulders. "Uncle," he announced. "The password is uncle."

Mary Rose and I laughed, then she reached for the platter. "I suppose we should give you the largest sticky bun as compensation."

"How about two?" He took a bite. "Delicious."

Mary Rose handed him the cream and sugar. "What did you think of Cara's show? Fantastic, wasn't it?"

"Great show." Noah reached under the table and squeezed my thigh. "You're bound to see an increase in commissioned paintings." He turned to Mary Rose and winked. "I suppose, I'll have to buy one."

Mary Rose pointed at the living room wall. "I was lucky enough to receive one as a Christmas gift last year. Mind you, long before she became the famous artist that she is today."

Noah's gaze followed her finger. "A signed original, that's certainly worth some money."

"Would you two stop it!" I said. "It was only one show. And I don't spot a crowd gathering at my doorstep quite yet."

Noah held up his sticky bun. "Well, that's a good thing. I don't feel like sharing, even if they know the password." Then his focus shifted to the far corner of the living room and his eyes widened. "I didn't know you played the piano, Mary Rose. A Steinway Player. Quite the piano."

"Oh, I don't," she said. "Paul used to tinker on it every now and then. Your typical beginner stuff–*Chopsticks* and *Heart and Soul*. We'd mostly let it play for us. Although, I haven't used it since he died."

Noah nodded in understanding, but I knew from the way he kept tossing glances at the piano, he believed it a shame for it to sit idle.

"Mommy," a voice came from around the corner.

Mary Rose stood and wiped her hands on her apron, then peered into the hallway. "Well, good morning, Harper. We have a special guest for breakfast."

"Oh goody!" she squealed. Harper peeked around the corner, then drew back.

"It's Cara's friend, Noah. Come say hello." Mary Rose motioned her daughter to the kitchen just as a distant cry floated down the staircase."

"Sounds like Lily's up as well," I said. "I'll be right back." I pushed away from the table and headed to her room. I could hear Harper giggling from the kitchen as I made my way to Lily's crib.

"Mama," she said, leaning against the rail with arms outstretched.

Picking her up and holding her to my chest, I brushed my finger over her cheek. "There's someone important I want you to meet this morning," I whispered. "Let's get you dressed." After a diaper change, I reached for a plum-colored dress with tiny, cream roses accenting the waistline and collar.

"A beautiful dress for a beautiful girl," I said, sliding tights over her wiggling feet. I picked her up, but stopped just short of the door.

"We need some shoes." It was definitely a shoe day. I grabbed them from the chest of drawers and pried them on her feet. Lily looked down and frowned.

"I know, sweetheart. Only for the introduction, then I'll take them off," I assured her while heading for the door again. "Oh geez," I twirled around, remembering that I needed to comb her hair. "See what happens when a man walks into your life?" I ran a comb through her locks before returning downstairs.

Harper had taken a seat next to Noah. She listened intently as he instructed her on the proper way to eat a sticky bun. "What you want to do is lick off all the topping first," he told her.

Mary Rose laughed. "Then she'll put it back in the pile and grab another, until she's licked every last one."

"Mary Rose, you weren't supposed to tell Noah what Harper did last night," I said, making my way over to the table with Lily.

"Oh, so that's why you gave me the largest one," Noah said, looking up. "Why, this must be Lily. What a beautiful dress. And look at those fancy shoes."

Lily looked down at her feet and smiled.

Noah turned to Harper. "Should we show Lily how to eat a sticky bun?"

"Yeah." Harper picked one from the pile and placed it in front of Lily, then picked up her own. "Watch me, Lily." Harper zipped her tongue across her pastry and laughed.

Lily immediately grabbed hers and did the same, spreading the topping all over her face.

Then Harper grabbed another from the plate and rubbed it across her own cheeks and nose.

"Girls," I said, raising a brow to Noah, "our guest seems to be teaching you some interesting table manners. Food on your face is not attractive."

"Oh, on the contrary," Noah argued. "I've never seen this many beautiful women in one room before."

"Really?" I said, picking up a pastry. "Let's see how it looks." I brought it toward my face, but quickly changed directions and smeared it across his.

Mary Rose turned to me, then pointed to Noah. "Maybe I need to get a dog and go to the park so I can meet a man that handsome."

The girls howled in delight.

I laughed. "You never know what may stroll along." Then I grabbed a napkin and wiped the topping from his nose. "Seems like forever since we've been together, doesn't it?"

"Yes," he said, picking a pecan from his hair.

"Well, you're here now, and that's all that matters," Mary Rose said. Then she cupped her mouth. "Oh, I forgot. You have to leave again, don't you?"

"Today, but I'll be back," he told Mary Rose. "I know where she lives now."

I laughed. "If you're not nice, I could change that, you know."

"Will you be coming back for the Christmas holiday?" Mary Rose asked.

Noah looked at me and grabbed my hand. "I would love nothing more, but I've already committed to a trip up the coast to see extended family. If I'd have known…"

I placed my hand to his lips. "I understand. You don't need to apologize. Who would've thought?"

"How long can you stay today?" Mary Rose asked.

Noah looked at his watch. "I have about twenty minutes before I have to leave for the airport."

Mary Rose motioned to the piano. "Would you mind? It would be a real treat to hear you play."

Noah went straight for the bench and sat down. The girls sprawled out on the floor while Mary Rose and I stood on either side of the piano. He turned to Mary Rose. "Any requests?"

She fell quiet, her eyes misting over. "*Swan Lake Waltz*. It was Paul's favorite. Do you know that one?"

"It just so happens that Tchaikovsky is my favorite," Noah said, closing his eyes. Then his hands began floating across the keys.

Mary Rose folded her hands and leaned over the piano. The girls remained quiet at her feet. I stood in wonder, studying his every move. While Noah immersed himself in his passion, I wished the song to go on forever. But I knew the last note would eventually be played, and he'd board that plane for Chicago.

A Whisper in the Dark

Each night the phone rang at nine o'clock, and Noah and I spent the next hour reminiscing. The memories were so rich and so vivid that I couldn't help but wonder if distance was the great embellisher. Was it truly as magical as I believed it to be?

His returned letter became a running joke. "Have you checked your mailbox for any returns?" I'd ask Noah.

"If you'd stop enclosing a self-addressed stamped envelope, maybe the letters wouldn't come back to you," Mary Rose ribbed him whenever she answered the phone.

Noah once sent me a stack of change of address cards. The humor somehow eased the pain.

Each night, after he said goodbye, I placed the receiver to my heart until the phone company's recorded message instructed me to hang up. After I did as I was told, Mary Rose called me to her room.

"So?" she asked.

I sat at the foot of her bed with the enthusiasm of a high school girl recalling her first date. "He told me he can't pass the art supply store without going inside. On the weekend, he goes to the local art museum just to wander around. And the greeting card at the Hallmark store with the daffodil on the front, well, you can't even imagine what that does to him."

Mary Rose laughed, then grabbed her side, wincing in pain.

"Are you okay?"

The twinge had stolen her breath and she couldn't speak.

"Mary Rose, what's the matter?"

"Nothing," she finally managed.

"That was hardly nothing." I touched her forearm. "How long has this been going on?"

"I don't know. A couple of months, maybe longer."

"Months? Mary Rose, you work in health care. You know better. Have you called the doctor?"

She shook her head, still clutching her side.

"Why not?"

"I don't know. I suppose the fear of finding out bad news is stronger than my desire to find out any news, so I just pretend it isn't happening. Not to mention, I'm terrified of doctors."

"Terrified of doctors? You were married to one!"

"Yes, and that's why. Paul would come home with all those horror stories. Those poor, unsuspecting patients who nearly keeled over from a heart attack without the slightest warning. Fine one minute, under the knife the next. It was better they didn't know what was about to happen. At least they didn't obsess about it, worry every minute of the day."

"Stop rationalizing. Unless you call the doctor in the morning, *I'll* be worrying every minute. Promise you'll call tomorrow?"

"Do I have a choice?"

"Sure you do. You can call at nine o'clock or ten."

The next morning, Mary Rose called her family physician and went into work late that day. Even though it was the afternoon, I brewed coffee and anxiously awaited her return. As soon as she stepped into the house, I motioned her to the kitchen. The girls stayed busy playing with puzzles on the living room floor; Lily took them apart as fast as Harper put them together.

"What does the doctor think it is?" I asked, grabbing our favorite mugs from the cupboard.

"She didn't say exactly. She referred me to a gynecologist," Mary Rose said.

"Why a gynecologist?"

"I didn't ask."

I leaned back against the counter and sighed. "You were referred to a specialist and didn't ask why?"

"I know, I know. I just couldn't bear to think about it."

"When is your appointment?"

"Tomorrow."

"Gee, that's awfully fast. She must think you need to be seen right away. I'm going with you. Mother can watch the girls."

Mary Rose sat at the table and I brought over the coffee. "You really don't have to go," she told me.

"Oh, yes I do. We need to find out what's going on."

Mary Rose lifted the cup to her lips. "I was afraid of that."

Mother came to the house the next morning and put the girls to work sorting Tupperware by size and shape while she organized the pantry. Mary Rose and I sat in the exam room and waited for the doctor, passing time with idle chatter. How would we celebrate Lily's first birthday? Had Steph recovered from the holiday rush on jogging apparel? Did the local preschools really have a waiting list for enrollment? Every once in a while, I'd glance at the wall lined with posters of the female anatomy, parts that I wasn't even aware I had, with names Mother would've never repeated.

There was a tap on the door, followed by a head poking into the room. "Mary Rose?"

Mary Rose turned toward the voice. "Yes."

A woman made her way over to the exam table and readjusted the stethoscope around her neck. "I'm Dr. Pruitt."

"Hello, Dr. Pruitt." Mary Rose pointed to me. "This is my friend, Cara. She's here for support. I hope you don't mind."

The doctor shook her head. "Not at all. Sometimes patients forget what we've talked about once they leave the office. Having a second pair of ears never hurts." Dr. Pruitt nodded at me, then turned back to Mary Rose. "I see you were referred by your family doctor." She thumbed through some papers. "Here are the lab results...medical history. No familial history of cancer which is good."

The word *cancer* jolted me like a surge of electricity, but Mary Rose didn't flinch. Paul's horror stories must have desensitized her over the years.

Dr. Pruitt skimmed the medical chart again. "You've had complaints of urinary frequency, irregular bowels, nausea, pelvic pain, fatigue, weight loss, distended abdomen, and some bleeding between periods." The doctor drew a breath, winded by the laundry list of symptoms. "After the pelvic exam and pap, I'd like to do a sonogram to be on the safe side."

Mary Rose's eyes were now misted over. Had she heard Paul

lump symptoms together like that whenever he talked about horrible diseases?

I leaned back stunned from the multitude of physical problems Mary Rose had reported to her family doctor. Why hadn't she mentioned these symptoms over coffee? Her occasional comments seemed so benign. The lack of energy, bladder frequency, bloating; all problems that could be explained away.

Dr. Pruitt placed the stethoscope to Mary Rose's chest. "Deep breath." She moved around to the back. "And another."

Mary Rose breathed in and out while staring straight ahead.

The doctor withdrew the stethoscope and patted the end of the exam table. "Okay, if you could slide down and put your feet up in the stirrups for me."

I stepped out into the hall, allowing Dr. Pruitt to finish her exam, then watched as the nurse eventually led Mary Rose to the ultrasound room. After the test, we went to lunch while waiting for the results. When we returned, Dr. Pruitt called Mary Rose into her office for a private consultation.

"Please, come with me, Cara," Mary Rose pleaded. "I need you."

Mary Rose didn't have to tell me how Paul had called patients into his office for consultation when he had bad news to deliver, news so terrible it wasn't right to blurt it out just any old place. It was implied by her quivering voice, her rigid stance, and the fear in her eyes. We entered the office and sat in the chairs lining the front of the desk.

The doctor put down the medical chart and folded her hands with her fingers interlocked, the same way Daddy did whenever he was about to enlighten one of his clients on the reality of the judicial system.

"I knew your husband, Paul," the doctor started. "He was a wonderful man, and an excellent doctor. I'll make sure we complete this workup quickly and get you diagnosed as soon as possible."

Mary Rose smiled. "Thank you."

"Unfortunately, your ultrasound showed abnormalities–areas of mixed solid and liquid which are often indicative of cancer."

I held my breath and placed my hand on Mary Rose's back. She pulled a tissue from her purse.

"I'm going to run a blood test called a CA-125. It helps detect the presence of cancer, measuring a substance in the blood called a tumor marker. I'll also send you for an MRI to get a better look," Dr. Pruitt said. "If the scan comes back abnormal, along with an elevated lab test, you'll need to see a Gynecologic Oncologist–a cancer specialist."

Dear God, anything but cancer.

"Dr. Gingham is her name..."

This can't be happening.

"...best in the area."

Mary Rose is too young, they must be wrong.

"...most likely order further testing."

My God, what will happen to Harper?

"...exploratory lap."

Please Lord, the little girl needs her mother.

"...tissue samples."

I'll do anything. Just make this stop.

"...pathology report."

I'm begging you.

"…treatment options."

Lord, let there be a miracle.

Dr. Donna Gingham's office was on the second floor of the new medical office building located a few miles east of town. The sconce lighting, leather sofas, original artwork, and silk plants proved she was a specialist. The women sitting in the waiting room with wigs, hats, and scarves covering their heads left no doubt that her specialty was cancer.

A couple of brave women wore nothing at all on their heads. Their stark baldness told of the drugs pumped into their bodies to fight the disease that ravaged their reproductive organs, breasts and lastly their hair–this enemy stole the very essence of womanhood.

The door opened and a nurse stuck her head into the waiting area. "Mary Rose," she called.

We followed her down the narrow hallway and into an exam room. I took a seat under the poster of healthy cells versus cancer cells, the bad cells magnified larger than necessary. The nurse took Mary Rose's routine vital signs and asked the basic questions. When was your last menstrual cycle? Ever have a mammogram? Have you recently had a pap? The nurse was careful not to probe too deep, leaving the tough questions for the doctor.

Following a single knock on the door, a young woman wearing a white lab coat bounced into the room, her stride quick, her motions fluid. A cheerleading outfit could have easily replaced the lab coat. She had her thick, brown hair pulled back into a ponytail. I wondered if she liked that hairstyle or if she wore it that way out of courtesy for her patients.

The doctor looked at Mary Rose. "Hello, I'm Dr. Gingham. Most of my patients call me Dr. Donna. We get to be like family around here."

I watched as Mary Rose cautiously looked her up and down. Maybe she shared my thoughts—how could a doctor this young and energetic know anything about such an enervating disease?

"Well, Dr. Donna," Mary Rose eventually said, "this is my friend, Cara."

Dr. Donna turned toward me. "Hello, Cara."

"Hello, Doctor...um...uh...Donna," I finally managed. Daddy had never allowed us to call judges or attorneys by their first names and doctors seemed to fall into that same category.

Instead of grabbing the medical record, Dr. Donna reached for Mary Rose's hands. "I imagine it's been a tough few days. The first time you hear the word cancer it's terrifying. But I'll be honest with you–no one walks away from this office without hearing it several times each visit. Get used to the word. The people that embrace the enemy do far better than those who hide from it."

Mary Rose nodded and tears spilled down her cheeks.

Dr. Donna handed her a tissue, then gently patted the exam table. "Can you lie down for me?"

I cleared my throat. "Mary Rose, I can step out…"

She grabbed my wrist. "Please...stay."

Dr. Donna nodded in approval.

I turned my head toward the window and stroked Mary Rose's cheek as the doctor invaded Mary Rose's most private area with the tools of the trade; the same area that had likely remained untouched since Paul's death.

After the exam, the doctor helped Mary Rose to a sitting position. "According to the ultrasound, the tumor on your ovary is rather large. Unfortunately, the MRI showed tumors on your liver as well. In other words, if my suspicions are correct the cancer has spread."

Cancer. That word again. I couldn't bear the thought of hearing it several more times.

"Spread?" Mary Rose asked, before covering her mouth with her hand.

"Yes, I fear it has metastasized–" She stopped. "Spread."

I fell back in my chair. Was this bluntness all part of helping us to get used to the word?

"I'd like to schedule you for surgery," Dr. Donna said. "Both your white blood count and red blood counts are low and your CA-125 came back extremely high. I want to see exactly what we're dealing with. The sooner the better." The urgency in the doctor's voice frightened me. "Do you have any questions?"

Mary Rose held a blank stare.

I touched her back. "Mary Rose?"

She turned toward me. "Huh?"

"Dr. Donna wants to know if you have any questions?"

"Oh, yes." She cleared her throat. "Why didn't I know I had...had…"

"Cancer," Dr. Donna confirmed.

"How could I have let it go this long?"

Dr. Donna leaned over. "Ovarian cancer doesn't scream at its victims. It's more like a whisper in the dark. We're often so busy with our lives that we don't stop to listen to that faint voice. It's only after it nags you for so long, that it finally gets your attention. And by that time, it's well advanced."

Mary Rose nodded as if she knew all about the nagging.

"I am truly sorry," Dr. Donna said. "My office staff will call you later today with the surgery date. We'll schedule it as soon as possible." She gave Mary Rose's hand one last squeeze before leaving the room.

Mary Rose sat for the longest time, unable to say a single word. Then our eyes met and we threw our arms around each other and sobbed, giving into the sadness of this thing called cancer.

Get used to it? *No way.*

Embrace it? *Never.*

Fairy Tales

When Mary Rose was diagnosed with cancer, I wanted the world to stop, to prove that we couldn't go on after such bad news; yet I wanted things to continue as usual, to keep my mind off the ugly truth. The conversation over morning coffee took on a medical slant. Words like oophorectomy, metastasis, and ascites became as common as creamer, sugar, and muffin.

"We have to keep things as normal as possible, between the blood draws and X-Rays," Mary Rose said. We opted for a quiet Christmas, just the four of us. The girls were oblivious to anything outside of Santa's arrival, which helped ease our minds.

After the holiday, Mary Rose insisted on going back to work part-time each day while I cared for the girls. When everyone was tucked in bed for the night, I spent time in front of my easel.

Every so often, I'd walk past Mary Rose's room and she'd call out from her bed, "How's the painting coming along?"

"Oh, great," I'd say, knowing that I'd just spent two hours mixing paints into a color that fell somewhere between black and gray; my mood swirled around in the center of the palette, staring back at me. My lack of desire to paint reminded me that this new world filled with cancer held little beauty.

While on the phone with Noah, I forgot the cancer, temporarily suspended in a world filled with hope. But after I hung up, my happiness turned to guilt. How could I even think about enjoying my life while Mary Rose fought for hers? I quickly dried my tears and made my way to her room where she patiently waited for me.

She put her rosary beads on the nightstand and patted the bed. "Sit down and tell me something good."

I squeezed in next to her. "Well, Noah's hoping to come during spring break if he can reschedule his piano students. He'll be here for sure once school lets out for summer."

"And when's that?"

"Last week in May."

She hesitated as if calculating the days in her head, then nodded. "I look forward to seeing him again." Her answer gave me hope. "Any talk of him moving here?"

"No, not yet."

"He will," she said firmly.

"What makes you so sure?"

She closed her eyes and took a deep breath. "Love always calls you home."

I suggested we cancel Lily's first birthday party, but Mary Rose insisted on a small gathering at the house.

"You're having surgery tomorrow," I argued.

"Surgery or not, it's her birthday," she said. "Besides, it will do us good to have company. It might lighten the mood."

While shopping for decorations, we had passed the valentine display and Harper insisted we buy strings of paper hearts. We rounded it off with red balloons, red flowers on the cake, and red wrapping paper.

Harper took a string of the hearts and offered an end to Lily. "Hold this." There was a rip, followed by a cry. Harper held it up. "Look, Mommy, my heart is breaked."

"We'll tape it back together," Mary Rose assured her. "Too bad your daddy isn't here. He was a great heart mender." I watched Mary Rose get winded from walking across the room to get the tape, realizing that my own heart broke little by little with each passing day.

Mary Rose ran her finger down the tape line. "Just like new. Now, give this to Aunt Cara and she'll hang it up with the rest."

Harper handed it to me and I added it to the long chain. The tape glistening under the light reminded me how fragile things had become.

"Harper, honey," I said, "can you go up to my bedroom and bring me the bag of balloons from the nightstand by the bed?"

"Okay." She jumped up and ran to the staircase.

Lily stood and motioned for Harper. "Hapa," she said.

"It's okay, Lil. She's coming right back," I assured her. I backed off the ladder. "You know, Mary Rose, we'll have to tell the family soon. They'll want to know why you're having surgery. We need to tell them...that...that it's probably...you know..." How I wished that Dr. Donna were here to say the word for me.

"Not today," Mary Rose said. "It will ruin the party. Besides, tomorrow we'll know more. Why worry them before we have all the facts? If they ask, we'll just tell them it's exploratory surgery for abdominal pain."

"You're right."

Harper came back with the balloons and handed them to me. The doorbell caught her attention and she ran to the foyer. "Gamma and Gampa," she announced, looking out the window.

I walked over and opened the door. "Hey, come on in."

"Well, Hello, Harper," Mother said, looking past me. "We heard there's a birthday party here."

Harper nodded. "Yep. Lily's happy day."

Daddy leaned over and kissed my cheek, then offered to entertain the girls with one of his favorite courtroom stories.

"I can get their dolls out," I said.

"Oh no. They'd rather Grandpa John tell them a story, right girls?" he said.

Harper clapped her hands and gathered at his feet. Lily sat beside Harper and neatly folded her hands in her lap. The big mean judge with the hairy wart on his nose, the wicked defense attorney with secret powers, and the bailiff with magical handcuffs kept Harper tied to Daddy's every word. She squealed in delight when he added trap doors to the judge's chambers. Lily wasn't old enough to understand, but cheered along with Harper nonetheless. After Daddy finished the first story, I joined Mother in the kitchen while Mary Rose stayed seated on the sofa.

"I see you found the finger food," I said as Mother arranged the stuffed mushrooms on a platter.

"You mean the hors d'oeuvres, dear."

"Appetizers," I compromised.

We had agreed on one thing from the start–less was better.

"A big meal seems, well, too grand," Mother had said. "Given that Mary Rose isn't feeling good, it's best not to overdo. Even your father will understand."

Steph arrived and expressed pleasure over the tiny portions. "It's about time. Right, Andrew?" He followed her around the table with his plate held out in front of him, graciously accepting the morsels of food she plucked off each platter.

Mother glanced out the front window. "Here comes Jack." She held the door open as he carried three armloads of gifts into the house.

"Really, Jack. She's only one year old," I reminded him. "She wouldn't have known the difference if you'd only bought her one present."

"But I would," he said.

Mother offered him a seat. "Sit down, Jack. Get something to eat."

He glanced at his watch. "I think I will, thank you."

While the rest of us filled our plates for a second time, Jack nervously nibbled a few carrot sticks in between glances at his watch. He leaned forward in his chair, ready to pounce on any opportunity to leave.

Mother stood and started to clear the table. "We can have cake in a couple of hours."

Jack mouthed the word, "hours," then stood. "I'd love to stay longer, but I've got to meet a client for dinner. I'll call tomorrow." He gave Lily a hug and left.

Daddy watched the door click into place and shook his head. "Please tell me I was never like that."

Steph, Mother, and I looked at each other and laughed. "Absolutely," Steph and I said while Mother kept on laughing.

"Well then, I suppose I need to make up for lost time," he said. "Okay, girls, gather around for another story."

Mary Rose fell asleep on the sofa and I listened in amazement as Daddy wove his magical story into a fairy tale finish. I prayed that tomorrow, Mary Rose's story would have a similar ending.

That night, Noah called and offered to fly in the next day.

"We don't even know if things are that bad for sure," I said. "Hopefully, this will be nothing more than a big scare. She'll be fine.

Besides, your students need you there."

"You sure?" he asked. "I can get a substitute."

"We'll be fine. Mother is watching the girls until Mary Rose is released from the hospital. Not to mention, a snowstorm is on the way and you might get stranded here for days."

"Now, that would certainly be a tragedy," he said.

"To your piano students it would be."

"You actually think they enjoy playing?"

I laughed. "Their parents swear to it, don't they?"

"Sure they do. Especially when talking to the parents of non-piano playing children. Promise me you'll call to let me know how the surgery went?"

"Of course."

"Oh, how was the birthday party?" he asked.

"It was nice. You know I really wanted you here, but Jack was coming and he doesn't know about you and..."

"No need to explain. Jack's her father and he needed to be there. I'll make it next year when things have settled down a bit. By that time, Jack will be used to seeing me around."

"Lily loves the little keyboard you sent her. She tinkers away while Harper dances to the music."

"Wow, she's already playing songs?" he said. "Anything recognizable?"

"Well, if there's a song that's a little classical, a little jazz, with some hip-hop thrown in, then that's what she's playing."

Noah laughed. "One day she'll have to take lessons to hone her skills, and I know this really great instructor."

I smiled. "As long as her piano lessons don't cut into her art lessons."

"Wouldn't think of it. Speaking of lessons, I need to prepare one for tomorrow. Tell Mary Rose I'm thinking of her and call me if you need me."

"I'm sure she'll be fine." After hanging up the phone, I wished I'd taken him up on his offer to come to town. The fact of the matter was, I had no idea if she'd be fine.

The next morning, the snowstorm, along with the nurse's stern order to arrive no later than six o'clock, prompted us to leave earlier than planned.

"I never could figure out why they make patients come so blessed early," Mary Rose said. "Not being able to eat breakfast only makes matters worse. You have extra time to think about how hungry you are. And don't even get me started on skipping my coffee."

"We'll have coffee twice tomorrow," I assured her.

"You didn't have to go without yours, you know."

"It just didn't seem right."

The nurse pushed a gurney into the room. She patted the center. "It's time." She assisted Mary Rose onto the stretcher and I followed behind. The nurse wheeled Mary Rose down a long hallway and stopped short of the automatic doors that read–*Surgery–Authorized Personnel Only*. "Time to say goodbye," the nurse announced. She pointed down the corridor. "Cara, you can go sit in the visitor's waiting room. That's where Dr. Gingham will look for you after she's done."

I bent down and whispered, "You'll be fine."

Mary Rose grabbed my hand. "Promise me, that if anything happens, you'll take care of Harper."

"Of course. But nothing is going to happen."

The nurse unlocked the brake and pushed the gurney forward. I watched helplessly as the double doors swung open and swallowed Mary Rose alive.

The directory overhead sported arrows pointing in all directions like a bad road map. Then I saw it–*CHAPEL*–down the hall and to the right. Through the tiny rectangular window on the door, I spotted an elderly woman in the middle pew, her hair neatly coifed as if she'd come directly from the beauty parlor. She remained perfectly still with her head bowed in prayer as I took a seat behind her.

Dust motes danced about the sunlight that filtered down through the elaborate stained glass window depicting The Beatitudes. My gaze fought through the mixture of particles and light to the empty rows leading to the pulpit. I imagined the place was packed at the end of each shift when hospital staff gathered to rejuvenate their souls after caring for patients like Mary Rose. Most likely, it was from the wooden pulpit that the clergy bestowed a sense of hope, giving them a reason to return to work the next day. Surely, these walls contained all the sadness they could possibly hold.

Outside, snowflakes tumbled to the ground and I remembered the first time I saw Mary Rose standing in her drive with the snowblower. How strong and energetic she had been back then, how weak she looked headed for the operating room. Why hadn't I noticed? And why didn't I demand that she go to the doctor sooner? With my mind so filled with problems of my own, I failed to notice my best friend filling with cancer.

The elderly woman in front of me kissed her rosary and slipped it into her sweater pocket. She gathered her purse and Bible, and turned to leave. Her eyes were red and swollen, but a smile covered her face, perhaps convinced her visit would yield a desirable outcome. With the click of the door, the room darkened as the ray of light disappeared; either due to cloud cover, or the fact that I was less deserving of its presence than the woman who had just left. I looked around in search of an answer like the one she had found. Anything to explain why something so horrible was happening to my best friend.

Nothing.

I fell back in the pew and waited.

Still nothing. How I wished Noah was here to explain it to me, or at the very least, to hold me.

Then the squeak of the door caught my attention. A man in a brown suit made his way down the center aisle. I quickly dabbed my eyes with a tissue and returned my focus to the front. Eventually, I felt his presence beside me. The man's employee badge read, Pastor Dan Woodward. He cleared his throat. "Excuse me, are you here for the nine o'clock service?"

"Oh, um, no. I wasn't aware there was one." I gathered my backpack and stood.

His hand came to rest on my shoulder. "Please, stay as long as you need. When the weather is bad, nobody shows up. I'm sorry to have disturbed you." He walked to the front of the chapel and went through the door on the left.

After a few minutes, I walked the same path. My fist stopped short of the door several times before eventually knocking.

He opened the door a crack. "Have others come?" He peered over my shoulder.

"No…um...Pastor Woodward...I was hoping to have a minute of your time."

"By all means." He ushered me inside his office and offered me a seat.

He pulled his chair out from behind the desk. "Never did like barriers." He folded his hands across his lap and waited.

"I'm Cara. Cara Templeton."

"And I'm Pastor Dan." He pointed to his badge. "But I suppose you already knew that."

"I don't know exactly why I'm here," I blurted.

"Most people don't. Just a feeling, a need perhaps. Is a loved one in the hospital?"

"My best friend is having surgery today. She was recently diagnosed with...a horrible disease and...and–"

"And you're wondering why," he interrupted.

I nodded.

"Good question. I don't know that I have a simple answer." He leaned closer. "What I do know is that we must believe God has a bigger plan. Often, what we see as a tragedy, is merely God's way of bringing His plan into place."

"But she's so young. She has a daughter...she–"

The crack of his hand slapping his knee sent me upright in the chair. "Here's a story. A woman dies in her mid-forties from a stroke. I think we'd both agree that's a tragedy. The following day, another woman who lives four towns over picks up the newspaper and reads the obituary." He leaned toward me. "You follow?"

I nodded, pressing my back firmly against the chair.

"Now, the funny thing is that the two women are the same age. And the woman reading the obituary has been an alcoholic for years, drinking herself half to death. Seeing that obit makes her realize she's headed in the same direction–to an early grave." He hit the desk with his hand and I jumped. "So, what do you think happens next?"

"I...I...don't know."

"She gets on the horn to her husband, that's what–tells him she's ready to get treatment for her addiction." Pastor Dan clucked his tongue. "You know what the best part is?"

"Uh...no."

"She goes through rehab, gets a degree in substance abuse counseling and then goes on to help others lick the same problem. And the beauty of it?" He pointed to me like a teacher calling on a pupil.

"Um..."

"I'll tell you, young lady. The family members of the woman who died are completely unaware of the chain of events that followed her death. But God knows, because it was His plan all along."

Pastor Dan raised his index finger in the air. "But that's not the end of the story, is it?"

"No," I said on a hunch.

"That's right." He smacked his lips. "One of the daughters of the deceased woman goes off to college. And what do you suppose she studies?"

I shrugged, then opted to guess. "Medicine?"

"Now you've got it. She works tirelessly in the laboratory attempting to find a treatment to prevent strokes. Wants to find a way to thwart the very disease that took her mother's life, saving thousands of lives in the future."

Pastor Dan pointed toward Heaven. "So you see, Cara, at first glance, this woman's death was a tragedy. For others, it was nothing short of a miracle." He closed his eyes and bowed his head as if to thank God.

I quietly gathered my backpack off the floor to leave. "Thank you," I whispered.

He jerked his head up and spread his hands out in front of him. "The bigger plan, Cara. You have to believe it's out there."

I grabbed a sandwich from the cafeteria before heading back to the surgery waiting room. Choices that were once easy, proved difficult since my meeting with Pastor Dan. Was the bigger plan for me to get the turkey sandwich instead of the tuna salad? Did God want me to get the coleslaw or the potato salad? Should I have given the cashier the five-dollar bill instead of the ten? Why was I even thinking this way?

Questioning my every move, I turned from the elevator to take the stairs, only to revert back to the elevator. When I entered the waiting room, the receptionist motioned me over.

"Are you Cara Templeton?" she asked.

"Yes." My muscles stiffened.

"Surgery called. Dr. Gingham will be out to talk to you in just a few minutes. Please remain in the room so you don't miss her."

"So soon?" I suddenly recalled Daddy's comments whenever a jury made a quick decision on a colleague's case. "Never a good sign," he'd say. "They thought the guy was already guilty before hearing the evidence. The deliberation was a mere formality."

I sat down and waited for Dr. Donna. Those around me wore worry on their faces. Some had it caked on, while others had a mere dusting; the difference between brain surgery and a knee repair. When Dr. Donna popped into the room and sat in the chair across from me, my face grew heavier by the second.

"Mary Rose is in recovery," she said. "The nurse will let you know when she's been cleared to return to her private room."

"Okay." I knew that plan was too simple.

"Well, as you know, we suspected cancer. When I opened her, I found cancer outside the ovaries and uterus. It had spread to the liver, just as the MRI indicated."

Tears welled in the corners of my eyes.

"I went ahead and removed the ovaries and uterus. We'll have to wait for the results from the tissue and fluid samples, but it doesn't look good. The cancer is very extensive."

I grabbed for Dr. Donna's hand. "You have to do everything you can to help her. Everything. She...she has a daughter...Harper...who needs a mother."

Dr. Donna straightened in her chair. "Oh, I don't recall her having a daughter. But rest assured, I'll do all that I can. Unfortunately, this cancer is an aggressive one and I don't hold out much hope."

I let go of her hand and decided to reach out to a higher power, grabbing the cross necklace around my neck. "Will she need more surgery to get it all out?"

Dr. Donna placed her hand on my forearm. "My guess is that there won't be another surgery. I'll wait for pathology before making a final decision, but I suspect the outcome will be poor. A trial run of chemotherapy could buy a little time, but realistically…"

"If she doesn't have the chemo?"

"Three to six months. Most likely less."

My hand cupped my mouth as I fell back into the chair. Pastor Dan would have liked me to believe that this was all part of a bigger plan. But I didn't much care for this plan. I wanted to hang onto the smaller plan, my plan for Mary Rose and me to grow old together over coffee.

Simple Pleasures

I called Mother while Dr. Donna made her way back to the recovery room to see Mary Rose. As I dialed each number, I wished I'd heeded the doctor's advice and practiced saying the word cancer. I could've whispered it to myself in the shower, or screamed it while driving down the road in the Jeep, allowing the music on the radio to drown out my panic. I still found it impossible to say the word when someone was actually listening.

Mother hung on the line. "Is everything all right, dear?"

I closed my eyes, my finger chasing the trail of warm tears down my cheeks.

Get used to the word, Dr. Donna had warned.

"Mary Rose has…" The word became lodged in my throat.

"Cara?"

I reached for the cross pendant around my neck and pressed it into my palm. "Cancer, Mother. She has cancer."

"Oh, dear Heavenly Father. They were able to remove it all during surgery, right?"

Embrace the enemy.

I leaned against the lobby wall for support. "No. There's too much...way too much. It has spread everywhere."

"There has to be something they can do. With all the technology they have these days–"

"No. There's nothing they can do," I interrupted. "The doctor said that chemo could extend her life some, but regardless, she doesn't have a whole lot of time."

"How much time?"

"Three to six months. Maybe less."

"Sweet Lord, have mercy."

After making a similar call to Noah and Steph, I sat on the edge of the hospital bed for nearly ten minutes before I could speak. "God, what a decision to make."

"There's no decision," Mary Rose said.

I drew back. "What do you mean? Mary Rose, you have options...choices."

"You heard Dr. Donna. Chemo isn't a cure. Besides, there's the nausea, vomiting and..." her hand went up and stroked her thick curls, "hair loss." Then her eyes widened. "I've seen those people in the hospital. That's no way to spend my last few months. I need to be at home with Harper, not sitting in some clinic hooked up to an IV all day."

"Don't you think you should at least try it?" I begged.

Mary Rose took a deep breath and slowly exhaled. "When my mother was ill, the doctor called me from the nursing home and wanted me to prolong her life with a feeding tube. I was lucky she died that night, before I had to make that gut-wrenching decision. I never dreamed I'd have to make a similar decision for myself, but I refuse to extend my life just to prolong my misery."

"All I'm asking is that you think about it, Mary Rose. For Harper's sake." I immediately felt ashamed for using her love for her child as leverage.

"It's stage four cancer." Mary Rose held up four fingers. "Not one, or two, or even three. Cara, do you understand that it's too late?" She placed her head on my chest and gently rocked back and forth. "I had hoped this was all a mistake, that they'd find it wasn't cancer after all. But I'm dying, Cara. It's really happening."

Then Mary Rose not only embraced the enemy, but surrendered. Her soft whimper steadily building, until it became a noise between a moan and a wail, filled with the pain of a leg-trapped coyote. The howl pierced my heart and I pulled her tighter to my chest.

I believed there was only one other time that she made a similar sound; the day she removed the wedding band from Paul's finger.

For the next several days, it felt as though Mary Rose and I did nothing but cry. We sobbed as the coffee percolated, and wept through the last drop. My only solace was the nightly phone call from Noah; a brief respite from the present as we reminisced about the past and planned for our future. Each night, he offered to jump on the next plane to Michigan.

"You have a full-time job, plus you have piano students on the weekend," I told him. "You can come later. I'll need you here...for the...you know...funeral."

"I'll come then, and any other time you need me," he said.

One morning, Mary Rose decided to get her affairs in order, to discuss the inevitable. While the girls remained asleep upstairs, I poured the coffee and she took out a legal pad.

"You know, it's probably not too late to look into chemo," I said, placing the cup in front of her.

"It's too late," she said.

"You might be surprised–"

"Cara, please," she interrupted. "We need to face reality."

Reluctantly, I nodded.

She picked up a pen. "Harper's my main concern. I have no family to care for her and she adores you and Lily. I would like you to be named her guardian, but only if you feel comfortable with such an obligation."

"Of course," I said. "She's like family."

"Now, about my assets. Everything will go to Harper in trust. The money can be used to take care of her needs. The house will be sold after you and the girls have another place to live. I'll have my attorney, Mr. Humphrey, take care of all the paperwork."

Mary Rose jotted notes about the aftermath of her death on the legal pad. Watching her, I realized, ready or not, her life would end.

"When Paul died, I had to plan his funeral in the midst of all my grief. I vowed never to leave that task to anyone, so I went ahead and made my arrangements through the same funeral home. I'll call them to go over the details."

She talked about her death with such an eerie calm that I had to ask. "Aren't you afraid, Mary Rose?"

"Afraid?"

"Of dying."

She leaned back and traced the rim of her cup with her finger. "No, not so much of the actual physical death." She paused. "I'm more afraid for Harper. That she won't understand, that she'll be devastated. I guess we'll need to prepare her soon."

My heart ached at the mere thought of telling Harper that her mother was dying. "How do you tell a child such a thing?"

"All we can do is the best we can do. We'll have to spend a lot of time together these last few months. I need to remember every moment so I can share the memories with Paul," she said.

I suddenly realized what she had known all along and my heart felt lighter than it had in days. "He'll be happy to see you."

She smiled. "Yes. It seems like forever since I've held him in my arms."

Late winter refused to give way to spring's arrival, but the cold didn't change our plans. Mary Rose and I packed the car and headed to the cottage with the girls. The wood-burning stove roared as the girls sat on the nearby rug playing with their dolls. The lake's thin sheet of ice jogged my memory.

"Wait here." I went out to the Jeep for a box, hurried back in, and handed it to Mary Rose.

"What's this?" she asked.

"A present."

"What kind of present?"

"I was saving it for Christmas."

"But Christmas is months..." Her voice trailed off, then she nodded. She opened the box and pulled out a pair of shiny, white ice skates.

I had been so excited the day I bought them for her, knowing the skates would be the perfect gift, now my chest grew heavy, knowing that she would not live to see another winter.

"Too bad the ice isn't thick enough now," she said, "or I'd go out there and skate a while."

"Yes, it is too bad. I'd love to watch." But I knew that even if it were thicker, her wobbly legs would never be able to support her. "I got Harper a pair, too. I figured it was time."

Mary Rose wiped the tears from her eyes. "What a thoughtful gift. Can you help me put them on?" She held out one of the skates. "I can pretend, right?" While I laced them up, she pointed to the opposite embankment. "Always wanted to just glide over to the other side."

She placed her feet on the floor.

"How do they feel?" I asked.

"Perfect." She leaned back, closed her eyes, and moved her feet back and forth across the floor. "Cara, do you ever wish that you lived here year around?"

I looked at the cottages on the far side of the lake. Each year, owners abandoned their summer getaways at the first drop of an autumn leaf and they didn't return until the summer sun thawed the frozen lake.

"*Hmm*, I've never really thought of it. The cottage isn't heat efficient, but that could be fixed."

She opened her eyes and straightened her back. "Why don't we put the house on the market as soon as we get back?" she said. "It would be one less hassle for you to deal with later. Plus, the equity wouldn't be tied up."

"But what if it sells quickly? You know, before you...beforehand."

She looked around the cottage. "Could we move in here? We can winterize the cottage with some of the money. Harper loves it here and so do I."

Mary Rose showed excitement for the first time in recent memory. "Sure," I said.

"Really?"

"Yes, really. Daddy and Mother can help get this place ready after the house sells."

"And, Cara?"

"Yeah."

"I was thinking that even if the house doesn't sell right away, I'd like to spend my last few weeks here...if that's okay." She leaned her head back and stared out over the lake.

I thought back to Paul and how he had died on a cold, metal table, under florescent lights, with no one around but the medical personnel who attempted to save his life. It would be different for Mary Rose. She would die in a soft bed, under the warmth of sunlight, surrounded by those who loved her.

"Of course," I whispered.

That evening, Mother and Daddy drove to the cottage for a visit.

The girls were in bed, exhausted from an earlier nature walk.

Daddy started a fire, then sat next to Mother. "So, where are they?"

I pointed to the bedroom.

He laughed. "Not the girls."

"Where are what?" I asked.

"The marshmallows."

"Marshmallows?"

"We can't very well have a fire at a cottage without them," he said.

I shrugged. "I didn't buy any." Mother and Mary Rose looked at me with long faces. "Sorry."

Daddy smiled. "Up in the cupboard, to the right of the sink."

Surprised, I walked to the kitchen and pulled out the bag, along with some metal skewers.

"You know how long it's been since I've roasted marshmallows?" Mary Rose said. "No matter what I did, I'd always burn them. They'd catch on fire..." She snapped her fingers. "Black in an instant—unsalvageable."

Daddy loaded the skewers and leaned closer to the fire. "It's all in the wrist. You have to wait until the precise moment and," he jerked them out, "voila. Golden brown perfection." He repeated his magic until everyone had some.

Mary Rose sighed. "This is what life is about."

"Life is about marshmallows?" I popped a gooey one into my mouth, then licked the tips of my fingers.

"The simple pleasures," she said. "Things you don't do nearly enough, and you forget how wonderful they make you feel until you do them again."

I thought for a moment. "Like getting cotton candy at the circus."

"Yes," she said.

Daddy smiled. "Gorging on a quart of sweet cherries from a roadside stand."

"Good one," I said.

"Taste testing all the different fudge samples at the shops up north," Mary Rose added.

Daddy nodded.

"Making homemade peanut brittle," I offered.

"Taking part in a taffy pull," Daddy said.

Realizing that Mother had yet to participate, I turned to her. "What's your simple pleasure, Mother?"

She placed a hand to her cheek. "Oh, my. I'm not sure I have one."

I leaned closer. "C'mon. There must be something that makes you feel warm inside just thinking about it."

"Well, now that you put it that way." She wiggled in her chair, then straightened. "A caramel apple at the county fair."

"Those are wonderful," Mary Rose assured her.

"With nuts," Mother added.

"Got to have the nuts," I said.

"Gail, since when do you like going to the fair?" Daddy asked. "We've never been to one that I recall."

Mother folded her arms across her chest. "Well, John Robertson, my life certainly didn't start the moment I met you."

Mary Rose and I fell back into our chairs with laughter. I winked at Mother as I pictured her on the Ferris wheel with Herb Ellington.

"When the fairground opens this summer, we'll make it a point to go," Daddy said, sticking another marshmallow-filled skewer into the fire.

Mother grabbed his free hand. "That would be nice."

Thief in the Night

Mary Rose would never admit to the pain, the thief in the night that robbed her of sleep. She never let on that lifting Harper could bring her to her knees, or that she stopped halfway up the staircase to gather strength to finish the journey.

"You okay?" I asked.

"Me? Oh, sure. I'm fine." She waved off my concern. I imagined she had given her co-workers a similar response following Paul's death.

She snuck into the bathroom and I heard her shaking the pain pills from the bottle, followed by a rush of water from the tap. She hobbled down the hallway and I prayed that the pills would immediately wipe the wince off her face and steal the hesitation from her step. The drawback to those magic little pills–the hazed look in her eyes, the distance placed between Mary Rose and her surroundings.

"I never wanted to see my mother suffer in her old age," Mary Rose once said. "But when they gave her pain medication and she no longer recognized me...well, that about killed me." Mary Rose refused to take the medicine during the day when Harper could notice such side effects.

Although Mary Rose wasn't feeling well, she wanted to visit the creek. "I haven't been there since the wedding," she said. "It's spring and some fresh air will do me good. Besides, Harper wants to hear your father's continuing saga of *The Wanton Witness and the Judge's Jinx.*"

We dropped the girls off at the house in Laurel. Knowing the path I had walked as a child would be too far for Mary Rose, I opted for the shorter route. I drove down the road and parked on the side of the street near the dirt path.

"Are you sure you want to do this?" I asked.

"I'm positive," she said.

I got out and opened her door. She moaned as she tried to swing her legs around.

"Nope. I'm not going to let you walk that far." I shut the passenger door and climbed back behind the steering wheel.

"Cara, I'll be fine. Please...I want to."

I looked at Mary Rose, then at the large opening where the fence used to be and I did what Aunt Kate would've done; placed the key back in the ignition and stepped on the gas pedal. "Hold on."

Mary Rose grabbed my arm. "What on earth are you doing?"

"Getting us to the creek," I said, my eyes focused on the narrow trail.

"Can we do this?" She reached for the dashboard.

"We can do anything we want. It's my property, remember?"

The sounds of twigs and brush rustling underneath the Jeep had me second-guessing my decision. To keep Mary Rose's discomfort to a minimum, I weaved in between potholes. Once in a while, I misjudged and she grimaced.

"Sorry," I offered as rocks shot out from under the tires. We finally reached the old oak tree. "We made it." I pried my hands off the steering wheel.

"I have to say, you navigate well in adverse conditions."

"Don't all Michiganders?" I turned and pointed behind us. "I still have to get us back, you know."

She laughed. "At least you've cleared the way."

I grabbed the blanket and helped Mary Rose to her feet. We walked to the embankment, the water level much lower than normal for this time of year. A few large rocks peeked above the surface.

"You want to try going over?" I asked.

She looked across. "We've made it this far. It would be a shame to stop now."

I followed close behind, ready to catch her if she fell. She gently eased herself onto each rock, looking back for reassurance before stepping to the next.

"Wait," I said, when we reached the other side. "Let me help you up." I stepped in front of her and climbed the embankment, then offered my hand, pulling her to the top.

After catching her breath, she followed me over to the field where I spread the blanket. She looked out over the golden flowers. "I bet you never tire of looking at them."

"Never."

"It's amazing how they pop up each spring–all by themselves, without any help. Blooming in such harsh conditions." She laughed. "Daffodils are self-sufficient little things aren't they?" Then she turned toward me. "That's it, isn't it? Why you admire them so."

"Yes. They've got all the qualities I wish I had, I suppose. I've always relied on others to take care of me. Mitch, Tory, Jack. That's what I love about Noah, he believes in me."

She rested her hand on mine. "You're as strong as those flowers any old day."

"Too bad they don't bloom year-round. Hey, that reminds me. I've got an idea," I said.

"It doesn't involve the Jeep, does it?"

I laughed. "No, but I have to get something from the back of it." I went over and grabbed my easel, canvas, art supplies, and a folding chair. When I returned, I pulled two pencils from my bag and offered her one.

"Oh no. Not me," she said. "That Jeep ride is looking a whole lot better right now."

I set up the easel, put the canvas into place, and patted the seat of the chair. "Come sit. We'll do it together."

She reluctantly lowered herself into the chair and took the pencil.

"Landscape or a small cluster of flowers?" I asked.

"Oh, we should definitely start small."

I rubbed her shoulder. "Okay. Which flowers?"

Mary Rose scanned the colony. Several times she started to point, then withdrew her finger. "Gee, I don't know. They're all beautiful. You pick."

"Keep looking," I coached her. Then her gaze came to rest on a bunch located to the right. I pointed. "Those?"

"I think so." She looked at me. "Are they good?"

"Does your heart tell you they're good?"

"Yes."

"Then they are."

She clutched the drawing pencil, her hand so stiff that her forearm trembled slightly.

"You don't want to hold it so tight." I put my hand over hers and loosened her grip. "More like this."

"I have no idea what I'm doing."

I laughed. "Neither do I, but don't tell anyone." I looked to the flowers, then to the canvas, and back to the flowers once again while guiding her hand. Mary Rose fought me at times, her upper body tense.

"It's okay," I assured her. "Just try to stay loose." I had forgotten the reservation I had when first starting to paint. How I'd shake my wrists to free myself from nerves before picking up the brush, and how I'd take forever to choose my subject matter, second-guessing myself, but always going back to the first thing that caught my eye.

"Open minds are instinctively drawn to beauty," my instructor had often reminded the class. "Those who can't see the beauty will never become artists. But that's okay, we need overpaid scientists in the world, too." Then she laughed while creating a vase overflowing with Gerbera Daisies, a bushel basket of Golden Delicious apples, or a thatched roof hut along the ocean front without as much as a hint of effort.

"Now *feel* the movement," she'd say. "It comes from the inside." She paced behind us, stopping abruptly to peer over our shoulders.

I knew better than to look back; a sign of indecisiveness. Instead, I kept my hands moving–smoothly–deliberately, until I reached a natural breaking point.

"Best in the class," the teacher whispered in my ear as not to offend the others.

Mary Rose and I continued to sketch the cluster of jonquils, our hands sweeping across the canvas.

"I can't believe I'm doing this," she said.

"Why not?"

She laughed. "Well, for starters, I'm not an artist."

"Oh, but you are, my dear friend. You add color to the lives of everyone around you."

* * *

I had always loved the smell of coffee. Even as a child, I pushed a chair up to the kitchen counter and climbed up to the pot, taking in a deep breath. Once, I got up the nerve to ask Mother for a cup. She hesitated before quietly removing a mug from the cupboard. "Just this once," she whispered. She poured a few sips, slid the cup my way, and watched the kitchen entryway as if someone would walk in and discover our crime. Mother was sure I'd take the first sip and spit it out. Instead, I licked the last drop and asked for more.

"It's an adult beverage, dear," she said. "No need to start such a habit at your age. Now, run along."

I remembered how grown up those few sips had made me feel, how much I wanted to be an adult. Now, as I lay in bed, immobilized by the fear of telling Harper that her mother was dying, I longed to retreat under the covers like a child hiding from the boogeyman.

Mary Rose and I agreed it best to take it slow, and give Harper the chance to digest small pieces of information at a time. There would be the move to the cottage, the sale of the house, her mother's weakening state; too much for a girl just shy of four years old to understand, yet too much for her to ignore. I knew we had no choice but to tell her. I got out of bed, scooped Lily from her crib, and we joined Mary Rose and Harper for breakfast.

I strapped Lily in her highchair, then walked over to the stove and grabbed the spatula from Mary Rose's hand. "Go sit down. I'll finish."

She nodded and sat next to Harper. "Aunt Cara and I thought it might be fun to move to the cottage now that the weather is getting nicer. Would you girls like that?"

Harper clapped her hands. "Yea! Fishing, Mommy?"

"Oh, I'm sure Grandpa John would be happy to take you. I'll watch from the dock."

"Can we ice-skate, Mommy?" Harper looked up with anticipation.

While flipping the French toast from the skillet onto a platter, I choked back tears, knowing Mary Rose wanted nothing more than to carry on the family tradition.

"I think Aunt Cara would love to go skating with you next winter," Mary Rose said.

After placing the platter in the center of the table, I patted Harper's head. Then I poured the girls some milk and cut their French toast into small pieces.

All the while, Mary Rose's face strained as if searching for a good way to tell Harper that she was about to lose her mother. "Honey," Mary Rose eventually said, "Mommy has been really sick."

Harper leaned over and kissed her mother's cheek. "I kiss your boo-boo."

Mary Rose held the kiss in place.   "I do love your kisses sweetheart, but Mommy is very, very sick."

Harper smiled. "The doctor can fix you."

"Oh honey, I wish that were true. Mommy went to the doctor. They can't fix me."

I walked back to the stove, unable to bear the thought of Harper's response. Gripping the kitchen counter, I waited for her to refute her mother's illness.

Harper let out a giggle. "Mommy, you silly!"

"Harper, listen to me," Mary Rose pleaded.

I cleared my throat. Mary Rose glanced over and I shook my head, knowing Harper had reached her limit of acceptance.

Mary Rose nodded and reached for her napkin. "Well, breakfast certainly smells good, doesn't it?"

We spent the rest of the meal planning our move to the cottage. The Realtor would list the house the following week and Daddy would arrange the moving truck. The furnishings we couldn't use at the cottage would be placed into storage. If only the move were for happier reasons, it might have been an enjoyable conversation. The girls went to play in the living room, while we finished our coffee.

Mary Rose put down her cup. "Do you think Harper understood any of it?"

"Just enough to make her uncomfortable. She'll ask questions when she's ready. Does she have any concept of death...know that Paul's in Heaven, that kind of thing?"

"We talk about him being there. That he looks down from above and watches over us. In fact, when Sadie died, we talked about her going to be with Paul. That he'd take care of her and keep her company."

I smiled, picturing Sadie with her old, gray muzzle on Paul's lap, and him scratching her favorite spot behind her ear. "I certainly hope that's true."

Over the next several days, Harper rifled off questions: why is Mommy crying, sick with cancer, sleeping all the time, eating in bed, walking funny, not playing with me, sitting on the stairs, holding her tummy, not going to work, praying when it's not night-night time?

I wanted to say that the world is unfair, cruel, mixed-up, unpredictable, without priorities, unforgiving, a rotten place to live. Instead, I bent down and placed my hands on her shoulders. "Because your mommy doesn't feel good, sweetheart. We need to be quiet so she can rest. How about if I play a game with you and Lily?"

Diversion worked on most days; for those other days, Mother and Daddy took the girls to Laurel so Harper didn't have to stand outside the bathroom door watching her mother kneel at the toilet with a cold washrag pressed to her forehead.

"Mary Rose, I think you need stronger pain medication," I said, helping her to her feet.

"Maybe."

"I think we're past *maybe*. I know how badly you want to avoid being drowsy, but you can't suffer like this."

She nodded. "I'll call Dr. Donna tomorrow."

I placed my arm through hers. "Let's get you back to bed."

"I was hoping we could paint."

"That's not such a good idea. You look exhausted. And the smell will send you running back to the bathroom."

"I'll deal with it. We need to finish what we started."

I hesitated, looking down the hall toward the makeshift studio in the spare bedroom.

"Grant me this last wish, Cara." Silence–followed by her soft laughter.

"Damn, you got me again," I said. "You've got to quit doing that."

"I might as well get some benefit from this disease."

We made our way to the studio. "Just to let you know, I'm not falling for you choosing dinner every night, claiming it to be your last supper."

"How about every other night?"

"Fair enough," I said, opening two of the windows, then placing the chair in front of the canvas.

The shadow work had been completed. Mary Rose stared at the palette filled with paints. "Oh my, color…"

"It's easy." I picked up a palette knife and looked at her. "Besides, I've seen you spread orange marmalade on toast without giving it a second thought." I handed her the knife. "First, take a small amount of the cadmium yellows–the medium and the light, and put them in the middle of the palette using the knife."

She pointed to the paints. "These?" I nodded and Mary Rose used the tool to place them in the center, one by one.

"Now," I said, "take this brush with the medium and mix." I handed her the brush and she followed my direction. "Okay, it's just a tad darker than we need. Let's nudge it in the other direction. So, add a touch of titanium white and mix it in."

She moved slowly, hesitantly, then gained confidence as the colors blended, achieving the perfect color for a jonquil. I held out a clean brush.

"Does this mean we're ready to paint?" she asked.

"Yep." I waved the brush at her, but her hand remained at her side. "Take it. Don't fear the brush, Mary Rose."

"What makes you think I'm afraid of it?"

I looked her in the eye.

"Okay, so I'm a little afraid."

I stared at her.

"All right, I'm terrified of the thing."

"The brush won't hurt you. Unless, of course, you poke yourself in the eye."

She grabbed it, then scrunched her body up like an accordion.

"Straighten up," I said.

"I can't."

"What do you mean, you can't?"

She laughed. "I'm too nervous."

"About what?"

"I might mess up."

I shook my head. "Wouldn't that be awful. We might have to do something drastic…like paint over it."

She placed the back of her hand to her forehead and giggled. "I'm being overly dramatic, aren't I?"

"Just a bit. If we screw up, we'll just hang it in some remote area. Remember, if it weren't for bad art, finished basements wouldn't have any décor."

Placing my hand on hers, I dipped the brush, then added color to the petals.

I motioned to put the brush down, then picked up the knife. "We can use this to add some texture. See?" I said, using the edge to add paint to the tip of the corona.

Mary Rose turned, her eyes wide. "Wow. That texture gives the painting such...such…"

"Life–activity," I said. "See how it stands proud from the surface? To think Vincent van Gogh was the master, and still suffered rejection at every turn."

Mary Rose fidgeted in the chair. "Rejection…um…that reminds me. I accidentally let something slip to Jack the other day which might have made him...well...feel a little rejected."

I laughed. "Jack feel rejected? Now, that's funny. What could you have possibly told him?"

She cringed. "About Noah."

I jerked my hand from the canvas. "Oh, God. What did you tell him?"

"Just that Noah was the love of your life before you met Jack and the two of you have recently gotten back together. And that I believe you'll marry Noah one day."

My hands went to my hips. "Is that *all* you told him?" I leaned in and grinned. "So, what did he say?"

"Not one word. He just slithered away."

"Slithered?"

"Yeah, like a junior high school boy used to going back to his chair after a girl declines his offer to dance."

"*Hmm*...interesting. I'll let him slither a while longer. Eventually, I'll have to tell Jack more when Noah comes back to town."

"I hope Jack doesn't go mad and cut off his ear," Mary Rose said. "I'd feel partly responsible."

I laughed. "Jack van Gogh does have a ring to it, but it's highly doubtful. He likes to hear himself talk too much."

Ten days later, Mary Rose's condition rapidly declined and Dr. Donna met us at the hospital. Mary Rose went through a battery of tests and would stay overnight for observation.

The doctor stood at her bedside. "Mary Rose, the tests show that your liver is failing. You've probably noticed the swelling in your hands and feet...your belly and face. The yellow tint to your eyes and skin is another sign of liver malfunction. I need to know how aggressive you want me to be, if at all."

Mary Rose could barely lift her head from the pillow. "No treatment," she whispered.

"But Mary Rose..." I started, before her hand went up to stop me.

"I can't do this anymore," she whispered as tears slid down her cheeks. "This isn't living."

Dr. Donna squeezed Mary Rose's hand. "If you don't want any more tests or treatments to be done, I'll arrange for the Hospice nurse to come out to your home to provide respite care and IV pain medication. You can go home tomorrow and we'll keep you as comfortable as possible."

Mary Rose nodded and closed her eyes.

"I'll be back in the morning." Dr. Donna touched my arm. "Get all of her affairs in order," she whispered into my ear, before leaving the room.

I leaned over the bed and caressed Mary Rose's cheek, while choking back tears "I'm going to go call Mother and Daddy and ask them to keep the girls overnight."

"Okay," she said, her voice thinning.

I left the room and saw Jack walking toward me. "How is she?" he asked.

"Not good. I'm afraid it won't be long now. She's in liver failure. We need to get our belongings to the cottage right away. I'm going to call Daddy."

"Jesus, her condition's that serious?"

"Very serious."

"Can I do anything to help?"

I drew back, caught off guard by the offer.

"Really, I mean it. Give me something to do. At the very least, I can help Mary Rose with her estate planning."

"Her attorney, Mr. Humphrey, already took care of all that."

"Oh," Jack said with rejection splashed across his face.

"Don't take it personally. I think she's used him before, or it seemed that way. Probably when Paul died."

"Humphrey, you say? I've heard the name. Seems to me he has a good reputation." He threw off the rejection with a shrug of his shoulders. "Anyway, why don't I help your father? Between the two of us, we can get you moved to the cottage today."

"Thanks. I'll call him and let him know." I turned toward the elevator.

"Oh," Jack called. "The Realtor was showing the house when I pulled out of the drive. Out of town buyer. Wisconsin plates on their Jaguar."

"Jaguar? Oh my. A little competition for you."

He slapped his hand to his heart. "Jesus. First Noah, now the wealthy soon-to-be neighbors. How will I ever survive?"

I looked toward the room where my best friend fought for her life. "One day at a time, Jack. Just like the rest of us."

Taking Flight

The cool, April breeze formed ripples across the lake and, standing dockside before noon, the air held a nip that made me pull my cardigan tighter around my torso. It would be a couple of months yet, before the water calmed enough to make level-headed men climb out of bed, and take to the middle of the lake as early as three in the morning. For now, the outdoors remained restless, much like my mind. Our arrival at the cottage would be considered incredibly early by most cottage owners, but it seemed preposterously late to me, knowing that the place Mary Rose once called a little slice of Heaven right here on Earth would bring her comfort for such a short time.

Only a few hours after our arrival at Lake in the Woods, the Realtor called with news that the couple from Wisconsin placed a bid on the house. Mary Rose accepted the offer and we completed the paperwork. Expecting the worst, Mary Rose called her lawyer to let him know she wouldn't be able to attend the closing, and that he should execute his power of attorney privilege. She asked me to attend the closing to make sure things went smoothly. Jack and Daddy moved the rest of our belongings into storage, Mother cooked small meals for the freezer, and Steph brought over sweat suits to keep Mary Rose comfortable; her bloated stomach would no longer fit into her jeans. Daddy took an extended vacation from the firm to help around the cottage. In addition to his nightly calls, Noah dropped daily letters into the mail, giving me something to read to Mary Rose before bed.

Hospice arranged for a hospital bed, wheelchair, commode, and shower bench. Mary Rose tried to make light of her illness-induced dependency by referring to the cottage as her infirmary on the lake.

Mother directed the deliverymen where to place the equipment. "The bed should be facing the afternoon sun," she told the gentlemen. "Although, it might get a little too warm...and now that I think of it, maybe it would be best along that far wall, out of traffic." Her hands went to her hips. "But then again, who wants to feel shoved in a corner?"

The men stood still and Mother ignored the intermittent glances at their watches. She finally decided the view of the lake superseded practicality. After the men positioned the bed near the window, she rewarded them for their patience by serving homemade lemon meringue pie.

Daddy carried in logs from outside and stacked them next to the wood-burning stove. The girls crouched over the shrinking pile of firewood in front of the porch and squealed whenever a daddy longlegs or pill bug crawled out from underneath a log.

"Don't let the girls touch those bugs," Mother yelled to Daddy through the living room window while she placed fresh sheets on the hospital bed. She layered two blankets on top of one another, before making her way to the kitchen.

"Wouldn't think of it, Gail," he hollered, then bent down, cupped some kind of crawly thing into his hands, and offered it to Harper.

Mary Rose sat in her wheelchair out on the porch. "Never did make it out on the ice. Paul always wanted to learn how to skate. I'd planned on teaching him–thought I had all the time in the world." She turned her attention to the easel across the way. "Can we paint?"

"Maybe we should wait a day or two. You just left the hospital," I reminded her.

"I'll be fine."

"But, Mary Rose, one day isn't going–"

"We need to finish," she interrupted.

"Okay." I stood and opened two of the porch windows. "If the smell gets to be too much, let me know. I can open the screen door, or we can just stop." I wheeled her up to the easel and poured a small amount of turpentine in the dipper.

Mary Rose smiled at the six jonquils that now spread across the canvas. "Can you believe we're almost done?"

"This session should do it."

Mary Rose took the palette knife and chose viridian, yellow ochre, and cadmium orange for the stems, then mixed the paints.

I patted her on the shoulder. "Good, you remembered."

She dipped the brush and held her hand to the canvas. I gently wrapped my hand around hers as I had done before. After we painted a while, I let go.

She stopped and looked over her shoulder. "What are you doing?"

"I'm letting you go it alone for a minute," I said.

"I don't want to go it alone."

"You'll do fine. Trust me."

"But you've always been there to help," she said.

"Mary Rose, you can do it."

She took a deep breath, then made downward strokes to complete the stem of a flower.

"That's it, good, Mary Rose."

"I'm doing it, Cara. I'm really doing it." After finishing the last stem, her hand dropped to her side.

"Tired?" I asked.

She nodded.

I took the brush from her. "Well, what do you think?"

"It's beautiful."

"Oh," I said. "We need to sign it."

"What are you going to do with the picture?" Mary Rose asked.

"I thought I'd keep it for Harper. A housewarming gift for her first home."

Mary Rose motioned for the brush, then my hand. She wrapped her hand around mine. "First my name." She guided my hand into the word Mom. Then we repeated the same signature. Mary Rose's eyes filled with tears. "I thought I'd be there...to see her grow up...get married...have her first baby."

I kneeled down to her level. "You will be there, Mary Rose. I'll tell her stories about you, about how we met, the things we shared. And I will remind her about her father. I'll never let her forget how the both of you loved her."

"I know you won't. Thank God I have you to take care of Harper." Mary Rose pointed to the bed.

I stood and pushed the wheelchair into the living room. After tucking her into bed, I leaned over and kissed her cheek. "I'll finish cleaning up. If you need anything, let me know."

While I rinsed the last brush, Mother came out to the porch.

"I'm going outdoors to supervise. It seems as though your father has his hands full with the girls."

I laughed. "Progressed to wolf spiders, has he?"

"God only knows." She threw on a sweater and the screen door slapped shut behind her.

As I put away the last of the art supplies, there was a knock at the door. I looked out to see a woman in a nurse's uniform standing on the steps. "Come in." I extended my hand. "I'm Cara."

She took my hand in hers. "I'm Evelyn, the Hospice nurse. Nice to meet you."

"Were my directions okay?"

"Perfect." She pointed to the bed. "How is Mary Rose doing today?"

"Well, she's rallied some since her release from the hospital, and she felt good enough to paint, but that's not a reliable indication of how she feels. She's not eating a thing. I think it's the pain."

"I'll give her a dose of IV pain medication. That should keep her more comfortable than what she's been taking orally." Evelyn made her way over to the bed and gently placed her hand on Mary Rose's arm. "Hello, Mary Rose. I'm Evelyn, from Hospice."

Mary Rose stirred, then opened her eyes. "Oh, hello."

"How's the pain?"

"Sometimes better than others," Mary Rose said.

I motioned toward the door. "I'm going to let Evelyn take over, while I go check on the girls. I'll be right outside."

Mary Rose nodded as the nurse unpacked her bag, setting the blood pressure cuff on the bedside table.

I walked out back and down the hill to where the family had congregated. "My, we've been busy," I said, looking at the glass jar filled with insects.

"If only we could trap them all," Mother said, glancing at her feet.

Daddy nodded toward the unfamiliar car in the drive. "Hospice?"

"Yes," I said, plucking Lily from the ground.

Harper clapped as Daddy placed an ant in the jar. "Yea!"

"Oh, look at this," he said, moving a fallen branch. "A cricket."

He cupped the creature in his hands and helped it into the jar, then quickly secured the lid.

My throat tightened as the cricket jumped, hitting the lid, which in turn made the moth fly into the sides of the jar, frantically searching for that impossible way out. The ant made tight circles in the middle as if he knew there was no use. The spider huddled in the corner, ignoring the insects that he would've eaten otherwise if in his natural habitat; realizing one more meal wouldn't make a bit of difference.

Mother turned to the girls. "Who's up for ice cream?"

"Me, me!" said Harper, while Lily nodded.

"Okay, but we have to leave the insects here," Mother said. "Grandpa will drive."

Daddy looked at his sampling of bugs. "Quite a catch for an afternoon." He placed the jar on the front porch step and came back. "Cara, do you want us to bring you a milkshake or something?"

My gaze held onto the bug-laced death trap.

"Cara?"

"Huh."

"Milkshake?"

I shook my head. "Oh, no thanks, I'm not hungry." I kissed Lily before Mother took her from my arms. "Have fun, everyone."

After the car pulled from the drive, I went over and lifted the jar above my head. The moth now lay still at the bottom. I unscrewed the lid and placed the container parallel to the ground, watching the insects scurry into the grass, the heaviness in my heart lifting with each departure. Some were disoriented, leaving, then crawling back inside the prison walls, until my finger gave them a nudge in the right direction. Only one remained. How I wished the moth to take flight. I dumped out the lifeless body, then sat on the bottom step and cried.

As she had suspected, Mary Rose was too weak to attend the closing on her house. When I returned, I found Mother in the kitchen baking pies with the girls. Daddy had gone to the office for a few hours. I peeked into the living room where Mary Rose sat in bed, staring out the window, her hands folded neatly across the Bible in her lap. While the pump delivered the pain medicine through her IV to ease her suffering, her face wore a look I'd never seen before–rigid, expressionless.

Lily came over and hugged my leg. "Mama."

"Hey, sweetheart." I bent down and kissed the top of her head, then turned to Mother and whispered, "What's wrong with Mary Rose?"

Mother put down the wooden spoon. "Why, I'd assume it's the closing on the house, dear. I'm sure it was hard for her to sell the home that she and Paul had bought together, the place they planned to raise their family."

"Oh God," I said. "How could I be so insensitive? Of course, she's sad. I'll go talk to her."

Mother dried her hands on her apron and motioned for Lily. "Come help Grandma stir this batter."

Lily toddled over and reached for the spoon Mother dangled in front of her.

"Aunt Cara, look," Harper said, pointing to the chocolate mousse pie on the cooling rack.

"That certainly looks yummy." I went over and hugged her. "You're a big helper to Grandma. After I go talk to your mommy, we'll go for a nature walk."

"Bugs?"

"Um...sure, why not?"

She smiled.

I followed the familiar hum of the pump to Mary Rose's bedside. She rolled her head to the side and quickly tucked a piece of paper inside her Bible, then closed it. "Were they nice people?"

"Very nice. They loved the house." I placed my hand on Mary Rose's leg. "They'll take good care of it."

She nodded. "Children?"

"A seven-year-old boy and a four-year-old girl."

"Good. The house needs the laughter of children."

I sat on the edge of the bed and smiled. "More importantly, I think they like coffee. At least they had a cup at the closing. Even asked for a refill."

She drew in a breath, then slowly exhaled. "*Mmm.* I remember those days."

Mary Rose could no longer drink the beverage that had first brought us together. The smell alone made her queasy. She claimed that putting coffee aside was nearly as agonizing as the pain that ripped through her mid-section. "Everything happens over coffee," she had said. "It's like putting your life on hold when you have to go without."

I looked at the small box on the bed and her gaze followed mine.

"Where I keep my special treasures," she said.

I nodded as I thought of the box that held my secret treasures, secured with a red ribbon to keep my past from tumbling into the present.

"Cara?"

"Yes," I said.

She looked out the window, then waved me off. "Never mind."

"You sure?"

"Yes."

I rubbed her shoulder. "Are you in pain? Does Evelyn need to come back this afternoon?"

"No. I'm okay," she glanced at the pump, "thanks to that thing."

"Good. Do you need anything else?"

"Maybe some sleep," she said.

I stood and pulled the blankets up around her neck. "Warm enough?"

"Yes."

"I promised Harper a nature walk. She'll bring you back a few treasures, but I doubt they'll be the kind you'd want to put in that box. Mother's in the kitchen if you need anything." I turned to make my way back to the kitchen.

"Cara?"

I turned and smiled. "Yes?"

"Have I told you what a miracle it is that you came into my life?" Her finger traced the edges of the Bible.

"I don't know if we've ever called it a miracle before. But it's certainly wonderful."

She brought the Bible to her chest. "Much more than wonderful."

"Get some sleep." I walked back to Mother and the girls. "I'm taking Harper on a walk now, Mother. Do you mind watching Lily? She can't walk as far, and the stroller doesn't fare well in the woods."

Lily cried out in protest and Mother took her by the arm. "How about we sort some apples for Grandpa's pie?"

Lily nodded and Harper jumped from her chair. I opened the back door and she skipped into the driveway just as Mitch's red Firebird came toward the cottage.

"Harper," I yelled, "come back." A lump formed in my throat and my pulse quickened as the car zoomed closer.

"Aw," she moaned. "I want to walk, Aunt Cara."

"We'll still go." I patted her head, careful not to take my eyes off the car. "Go back to Grandma until I come get you." I opened the door and ushered her inside.

Mother stuck her head out the door. "Everything...oh, sweet Jesus."

"It'll be fine. This will only take a few minutes." Mitch opened the car door. "Mother go...please. I can handle this."

She hesitated before shutting the door. Mitch climbed out of the car and tucked his sunglasses in his shirt pocket. *Damn. He still looked good.* His black hair sported a hint of gray at the temples and a few lines had been added to his face, in all the right places.

He stopped before me. "How long has it been, Cara?"

"I would think you'd know, you're the one who left. How'd you know I was here?"

"Tory told me your parents bought this place for you, and that you might be here."

I rolled my eyes. "Wonderful."

"She also told me what happened between you two."

"I guess I'm just a magnet for that kind of thing. Let's make this quick, Mitch. What is it that you want?"

"I don't know, exactly." His blue eyes suddenly lost their sparkle and he glanced out over the lake. "My wife divorced me."

"I recall hearing something like that." I walked toward the dock and he followed. When we reached the end, we sat down.

He turned to me. "I've done a lot of thinking since she left. Funny, how it brings your life into focus and you suddenly realize all the rest of your mistakes." He reached for a stone on one of the planks and tossed it into the lake, creating a ripple on the water's surface. "I'd like for us to have a second chance. The three of us."

My chest tightened and my hand went to my throat. "Three of us?"

His face grew stern. "Yeah, you know, my daughter...our daughter. It's time she knew her father."

I jumped to my feet. "*Now* it's time? You think you can just walk back into my life as easily as you walked out–like I'm some kind of consolation prize? Your wife leaves and you want me to fill the hole. Damn you, Mitch! Get the hell out of here!"

He stood. "Cara, it's not like that. I thought about getting in touch with you hundreds of times, but then I saw your engagement in the paper, your wedding announcement, the birth of your other daughter. The timing just never seemed right."

My heart turned cold and I jammed my index finger into his chest. "And do you think the timing was right the day you walked out on me when I told you I was pregnant?"

He tilted his face skyward and closed his eyes. "No," he whispered. He looked back to me. "Cara, please. I want to see her. You don't have to tell her who I am right away."

"No, Mitch."

"What? You want me to beg?"

I looked out across the lake. "You could, but it wouldn't help. She's not here."

"Well, when do you expect her back? I can wait a while, or I could come back tomorrow."

"You don't understand. She isn't here...has never been here...will never be here." Tears fell from my eyes while I locked into his gaze. "I placed her for adoption the day you walked away from that hospital room, Mitch. I don't know where she is."

He stumbled backward. "Jesus Christ, Cara! You placed her for adoption and didn't tell me?"

"Well, it was certainly okay for *you* not to take her home, now wasn't it? Besides, like I told you, she may not even be yours."

He grabbed my forearm. "That's bullshit and you know it."

I jerked away. "I guess we'll never know, will we? If you'd given a damn about me and the baby, I would've never signed those papers in the first place." I dried my eyes with my sleeve and straightened my back. "You knew my family wasn't going to support me, and you were well aware of my financial situation at the time. Besides, with you being married, I thought you'd be happy to be off the hook."

"I had a right to know."

"And my baby had a right to a father!"

He turned sharply as the planks on the dock gave way to Harper's feet. She ran toward us, her curls bouncing with each step.

"Harper, come back," Mother shouted from the cottage.

"I've got her," I yelled, waving Mother back inside. I stepped past Mitch to intercept the little girl. I turned back. "My best friend's daughter. Her mother is dying of cancer."

Harper reached the end of the dock. "Walk?"

I stroked her hair. "Yes, sweetheart." I turned to Mitch. "You need to go now."

He stared at Harper, following her every move. Then he looked to me, his face filled with rage. "This is pathetic for even you, Cara." Mitch turned and walked toward the drive.

Harper and I made our way over to the cottage and Mitch glared at me one last time, before sliding into his car.

Harper tugged on my arm. "Bugs?"

I ran my fingers through her ringlets, taking a deep breath as Mitch disappeared over the hill. "Sure. Let's go see what surprises we can dig up."

Old Roads

After our walk, Harper met Daddy dockside for a fishing lesson. I watched from the porch with Lily pressed tightly to my chest. Mother walked in every few minutes, claiming to be looking for this or that.

"I'm okay, Mother," I finally said.

"That may be, but I think you should tell your father that Mitch came to visit today."

"There's no need. He's gone."

"What brought him here anyway?" Mother wanted to know.

I didn't want to worry her. "Nothing, really. Just to talk about his divorce. You know how people cling to the past when they're in a crisis."

"I can't say I ever liked the man." She pointed toward Mary Rose. "You've got other concerns now. Leave the past where it belongs. Don't allow him to dredge up what happened years ago."

Jane's adoption didn't require any dredging. Aunt Kate had often said, "Traveling old roads can bring about surprises." But Mother was right–this was one journey I would rather avoid. I nodded and Mother's shoulders relaxed.

"Your father and I thought we'd take the girls home tonight. Mary Rose said she doesn't mind."

"I don't know. It might not be a good idea for them to be gone. For Harper to be too far from her mother."

Mother glanced at Mary Rose, then back to me. "I think the two of you need time alone…without the children. They'll be fine. Not to mention, they need a break, too. And, if anything happens, we'll rush Harper back over."

"Okay, but before you leave, have Harper kiss her mother goodbye. In case…"

"Of course," Mother said.

I lifted Lily's head from my chest. "Lil, Grandma is going to take you to her house. You'll come back here tomorrow." She rubbed her sleepy eyes, and I kissed each cheek before Mother scooped her up.

"I've packed the girls' overnight bags and dinner is on the stove. Anything else I can do?" Mother asked.

"We'll be fine." I followed them to the back door as Harper ran to Mary Rose's bedside. Mary Rose held her hand and they kissed.

"Bye, Mommy," Harper said.

"Bye, sweetheart." Mary Rose reached up to brush the locks from her daughter's eyes. "I love you."

"I love you, too."

After Mother led the girls out the back door, I started a fire to keep the place warm for the night. Mary Rose had drifted back to sleep. I pulled a chair next to her, straightened the blankets, checked her IV line, then placed my hand on her chest to feel its steady rise and fall. Mary Rose had comforted me during my divorce, and I would care for her now. She slept for nearly an hour, eventually stirring.

I pointed toward the kitchen. "Are you hungry?"

She shook her head. Her hands felt along the bedrail, before looking to the nightstand. "Hand me my Bible, please."

"Sure."

She opened it and pulled out an envelope, holding it in her hand and smoothing out the crease where it had been folded. "This is something you need to share with Harper when she's older. I never meant to read it before she did...but since I won't be there when she does..." Mary Rose handed me the envelope with tears sliding down her cheeks.

By the light of the fire, I managed to make out the words, *Adoption Letter*. My breath quickened and my fingers ran over the surface. I looked to Mary Rose in disbelief, before easing the letter out. The first line read, *A letter to my baby, with love*. Pressing it to my heart, the memories of my hand hovering over the blank page, the pile of crumpled papers at my feet, the kiss placed at the bottom of the letter, all came rushing back to me. I fell back in the chair, shaking my head. "This can't be."

"Yes, Cara, believe it." She placed her hand on my knee. "All this time, we've shared a daughter."

"But how long…" was all I managed.

"A couple of days. I recognized the handwriting the moment I opened it. I couldn't believe it myself, but then it all fit together." She reached up and stroked my hair.

"But, it doesn't make sense. Harper's birthday is May twenty-second. My baby was born on April seventh."

"May twenty-second was the day the adoption was finalized. It was only then, we felt Harper was ours to keep. The day she was born into our family."

I glanced at the letter now splattered with my tears. "What about the name Harper? You said it was your maiden name."

Mary Rose smiled. "A way of making her mine." She turned toward the fire and grew quiet. After long moments, she said, "All our mornings together, all that we shared, and yet, you never told me about your baby. Why?"

"Oh, Mary Rose," I grabbed her hand. "I wanted to tell you...even tried a couple of times. But seeing how much you loved Harper, I felt ashamed. How could you understand that I walked away from my baby? And it seemed like everyone I told, ended up leaving me." To think Mary Rose sat across from me each morning sharing coffee; our lives so intertwined that they almost became one. Now, I needed to know why. "And you, Mary Rose? You never told me Harper was adopted."

She rubbed the back of my hand. "Before Paul died, we talked about when we'd tell Harper. We thought when she was ten...maybe a bit sooner. But after he died, I had second thoughts about telling her at all. I know that goes against all common sense, but she'd lost her birth mother, birth father, her adoptive father. How much could a little girl take? I know it must sound selfish, but if I decided not to tell her, the more people who knew, the bigger the risk that she would find out."

I nodded and Mary Rose wiped the tears from my cheeks.

"Do you know how often I prayed," Mary Rose said, "asking God to bless Harper's birth mother? To watch over her, to ease her pain. I wanted to meet her, to thank her." Mary Rose cupped my face in her hands and looked into my eyes. "I can never thank you enough for my time with Harper. They've been the best years of my life." She winced, then her hands reached down and reluctantly pushed the button for a dose of morphine.

I needed to tell her my feelings, before her mind yielded to the drug. "Over the years, I've felt so guilty...wondering if I'd done the right thing. Now, nothing in the world seems more right. Thank you for caring for her when I couldn't." I leaned over and kissed Mary Rose on the cheek. "I'm honored to be the birth mother of your daughter."

"Our daughter," she whispered, fighting to keep her eyes open. Eventually, they closed as the medication worked its magic.

I felt for the pendant hanging from my neck. While sitting by the warmth of the fire, my thoughts drifted to Pastor Woodward's advice.

So, you see, Cara, at first glance this woman's death was a tragedy. For others, it was nothing short of a miracle.

Coffee for Two

The sun glinted orange while climbing from the water's edge. I drew my knees to my chest and rubbed the back of my fog-dampened jeans. The cottage remained swaddled with a fine haze, the sun not yet strong enough to burn off the lingering mist. Activity surrounded me; the sounds of the fish and birds taking advantage of the opportunity for an early breakfast. A wave of sadness washed over me, knowing the only activity inside the cottage this morning was Evelyn placing a stethoscope to Mary Rose's chest for the last time, of her making a final notation in the medical record.

Just before dawn, I had called my parents, Noah, and Steph to tell them of Mary Rose's death. Mother offered to keep the girls the rest of the day, allowing me time to gather the strength to tell Harper. Noah made flight reservations to come to town for the funeral.

Eventually, Evelyn waved me back inside. Stopping at the kitchen counter, I poured coffee for two, and made my way to the living room.

"The people from the funeral home will come soon," Evelyn said. "I was just about to get her ready."

"I'll do it," I said, making my way to the bedside.

"Cara, it's part of my job."

"It's the least I can do for her," I said as I glanced at my best friend, who had drawn her last breath wrapped in my arms.

"Okay. Let me know if you need any help, or if it becomes too much." Evelyn squeezed my shoulder.

I looked to the basin of water, soap, washcloths, and towels that she'd prepared. "Thank you, but I'll be fine."

"I'll be in the kitchen. Come get me when you're finished."

"Okay. Help yourself to some coffee. Cups are in the cupboard to the right of the sink."

She nodded and left.

I placed both mugs on the bedside table. "Hey, Mary Rose,

brought you some coffee. Hazelnut–your favorite." I dipped a washcloth into the water basin and lathered the rag with soap. "You know," I said, placing it to her forehead, "I don't know why I didn't notice that Harper had Mitch's blue eyes and his thick, black hair. An artist should notice such things." I moved the washcloth around her face, careful not to get soap near her eyes, before drifting to her neck. "Aunt Kate would've noticed, that's for sure."

Why hadn't I noticed? Had I so distanced myself from the pregnancy that I lost the motherly instinct to recognize my own child?

"And look at the way Harper wields a paintbrush. That definitely should've been a clue." I rewet the washcloth and gently lifted Mary Rose's arm.

"Well, to my defense, I had hoped she would look like me. What mother wouldn't? Mitch told me in the hospital that she resembled him, but he's always had a flexible relationship with the truth." I placed the cloth in the basin and grabbed my coffee, nursing it slowly. "It's not all bad for her to look like him. He seems to be aging well." I put the cup down and lifted her dirty nightgown over Mary Rose's head. Slipping a clean one over her shoulders, I let it rest on her stomach while finishing her bath.

"You're probably wondering about Mitch–why he left me standing there with my stomach sticking out a mile." I smiled, recalling the first time I'd seen him from across the room, the way he gazed at me, making me feel like the luckiest girl in the world.

"The man was everything my parents didn't want for me, but I loved him. After he walked out on me, *did* I get the lecture. And that was before they found out he was married.

"So, the next time, I followed *their* rules and married Jack, and look what happened. Of course, they conveniently forgot the lecture." My thoughts drifted to Noah and I smiled. "Next time, I'm marrying for me."

I pulled the gown down past Mary Rose's knees. "Can you believe it? Here I thought I missed my daughter's milestones, her birthday, the holidays...and I'd been there all along." The wedding ring on Mary Rose's finger caught my attention, and I remembered it was to go to Harper. I slid it off and placed it on the nightstand.

Mary Rose's body was now cleansed, restoring some of the

dignity the cancer had stripped away. I reached for the ice skates. "I just realized that I'll have to get Harper signed up for lessons soon." I put the skates on Mary Rose and tied the laces into perfect bows, before leaning over and kissing her on the cheek. "To help you glide to the other side," I whispered, before the phone's ring startled me.

Evelyn called out, "Do you want me to get that?"

"It's probably the funeral home needing directions. I'll grab it." I picked up the phone. "Hello."

"This is Attorney Stan Humphrey," the voice said. "Mary Rose Townsend told me she could be reached at this number."

I suddenly panicked, realizing I hadn't informed everyone of her death. "Um, I'm sorry, but Mary Rose passed earlier this morning. This is her friend, Cara Templeton. Can I help you with something?"

"Oh, yes, Cara. I recall the name. Mary Rose named you legal guardian for her daughter. Well, this will definitely be of concern to you. A problem with Harper's adoption process has surfaced."

"Problem?" I groped for the chair behind me, my legs giving way.

"The biological father has filed an objection to the adoption based on the fact that he was never notified at the time," he said.

My chest tightened as I recalled the anger splashed across Mitch's face when he left the cottage. I looked at Mary Rose, hoping she'd already made it to the other side and didn't have to witness this.

"It appears he wants custody of the child," he continued.

"Oh God," I choked out, before falling into the chair.

"We should meet soon," Mr. Humphrey suggested.

"How about tomorrow morning?" I asked, feeling an urgency to fix the problem I'd created.

"Aren't you busy with the funeral plans?"

"It's the day after tomorrow and Mary Rose had all the plans in place for herself...you know...when Paul died."

"That's right, she did. Well, how about eight o'clock?"

"Fine. I'll be there." I hung up the phone, immediately picked it back up, and dialed eleven numbers from memory. He answered on the third ring.

"Noah," I whispered. "I need you *now*."

In the Beginning

Harper skipped down the dirt path, unaware that her mother had died–news that stuck in the middle of my throat, unable to surface. It was at the creek that I'd find the strength to tell her. She ran from one side of the trail to the other, kicking rocks, picking up twigs, and looking for bugs. Aunt Kate would have been proud. Harper enjoyed everything nature threw her way. Her black curls shimmered in the sunlight and her blue eyes sparkled as she looked to the creek; she favored Mitch even in my surroundings. Had he noticed her resemblance to him on the dock that day? How she inherited his strong cheekbones and the long torso that made her tall for her age. Had he thought I was lying about the adoption, that I was keeping him from seeing her? Was this his way of getting even with me?

"C'mon, Aunt Cara," Harper called over her shoulder.

"I'm coming," I yelled after her.

Harper had yet to see the field of flowers I'd so often talked about. Over the years, I'd fantasized about this day, bringing her to this special place, to share my passion. Never did I imagine that day would come like this.

Harper ran toward the creek bed. "Wait for me," I called, before catching up to her. I watched with delight as she pointed at the rocks and logs, trying to figure out the best way to get across.

"I'll carry you piggyback." I took off my backpack and strapped it onto my front.

She hiked her leg up on my hip and swung the other leg around, then I stood. Harper draped her arms around my neck. "Horsey ride!"

Giggling, we hopped from one rock to the next. Eventually, we made it up the other side and I lowered her to the ground.

"Again?" she asked.

"On the way back." I pointed at the field of jonquils. "Look over there."

"Pretty!"

"Let's get closer." I took her hand and led the way. At the colony's perimeter, I pulled the blanket from my backpack and spread it on the grass. "We can sit for a while, but first let me get you one." I reached over and picked her a flower.

Harper held it up. "*Mmm*." She sniffed the flower as she scanned the field. Little did she know, there'd be even more to see. The next time, I'd take her the long route–through the orchards where we'd sample the apples and grapes. I'd point out where Farmer Jensen once rode his tractor and she could play hide-and-seek with Lily in the tall field grass. My girls could learn to observe the creek through the eyes of an artist, even paint here one day.

"Aunt Cara, where's Mommy?" The little voice pulled me back to the real reason for our visit.

I wished Mary Rose had left me the words to say, and that I had her soothing, rhythmic voice in which to say them.

Tears welled in my eyes as I took Harper's hand. "Sweetheart, you know that your mommy has been very sick." She nodded and buried her head into my chest as if she knew what was coming next. "This morning her body stopped working...and her heart stopped beating."

Harper dropped the flower to the ground and looked at me with furrowed brows. "Is the nurse fixing her?"

"No, sweetheart. Your mommy...she...she died."

Harper gave me a puzzled look before drawing her attention across the field. "A bunny!"

Why had I thought that such a young child could understand? Then I realized the jonquils would help me.

I stood and grabbed Harper's hand. "Come here a minute." I led her over to a small bunch of wilted flowers. Pointing at them, I said, "You know, Harper, these flowers will only live a short while longer, then they will die." I pointed at a solitary flower amongst them, still erect and holding its true color. "Do you think that you can remember how beautiful this flower is, even when it starts to die like those flowers around it?"

"Uh-huh."

"We'll never forget its beauty when it's gone, just like we'll never forget your mommy and how beautiful she was. She'll be in our hearts and minds even though she's not with us anymore."

Harper's eyes widened. "Like Daddy?"

"Yes, like your daddy. Both your mommy and daddy are in Heaven now."

"With Sadie?"

I smiled. "Yes, with Sadie."

"Will I go to Heaven?"

I wrapped my arms around her waist. "Not for a long time, honey. You're going to stay here with me, Lily, Grandma, and Grandpa."

"We go fishing and look for bugs?"

"Sure," I said. Knowing she didn't fully understand that her mother was gone, I decided it was enough for now. She would have plenty of questions later.

"Let's pick some flowers to take to the cemetery tomorrow."

"Okay."

"I'll show you how. Grab them at the base of the stem. See...they snap right off."

Her tiny hands grabbed one jonquil, then another, and she handed them to me. After she had picked a dozen, I told her to stop, giving her the first lesson on creek etiquette. "We never pick them all, or there won't be any to look at the next time we come."

She nodded and cradled the bouquet. "Mommy and Daddy will like them."

"I'm sure they will."

Unlike my father's traditional decor of rich mahogany, brass lamps, and paintings of foxhounds, Mr. Humphrey's office had an urban feel: glass tabletops, leather sofas, halogen lamps. Though I'd never been in his office before, there was something familiar about Mr. Humphrey. I slid into one of the sleek, black chairs in front of his desk. Despite the situation, he sat calmly, giving me hope that he had resolved the issue with a mere phone call. He reached for his pen and scratched his balding head with the tip. The action transported me back to the courtroom where I had permanently relinquished my baby. *That's it!* Mr. Humphrey had represented Mary Rose and Paul for the adoption.

"Thanks for coming so quickly," he said. "As you know, the gentleman who claims to be the father insists he was never notified of the original adoption proceeding." He leaned back in his chair. "In lay terms, he feels his rights were violated. At the time, it was my understanding that the biological mother didn't name the father because she wasn't absolutely sure who the father was."

"Is he going to relinquish his rights?" I asked, hoping to redirect.

"I'm not his attorney, but if he's making a fuss after nearly four years, then I'd assume he has something different in mind."

"Isn't there a statute of limitations?"

He nodded. "Yes, but he's still within the time frame allowed."

"Can't I object?" I pleaded.

"I wish it were that simple."

I slumped in my chair. "What's next?"

"There's a hearing scheduled for June fifteenth."

Nausea swept over me. "What happens to Harper in the meantime? She just lost her mother. She won't have to go into foster care, will she?"

He raised his pen to his head once again. "No. Right now, you're her legal guardian. The supposed father has no rights to her at this time." He pointed the pen at me. "Which reminds me, he wants to establish paternity before the hearing. You'll have to take Harper for blood work. Mr. Sanders and the biological mother will also have a blood draw to complete the DNA testing. I'll let you know which lab when I find out."

"It's all my fault" I wiped the tears spilling from my eyes.

"Cara, there was nothing you could've done to avoid this unfortunate occurrence."

I suddenly realized that Mr. Humphrey didn't recognize me from the adoption hearing. "Mr. Humphrey," I said, "I'm Harper's biological mother. I met you in court when I placed Harper for adoption."

He whipped off his glasses, rubbed his eyes, then studied my face.

"My maiden name is Cara Robertson."

"I remember now."

"Mary Rose and I just discovered that we shared a child. We lived together and didn't know until just recently."

"Wait. Wasn't that a closed adoption? How on earth did you even meet each other?"

"After I got married, I moved to Piney Cove," I said. "I know, it's crazy."

He shook his head. "In all my years as an attorney, I've never witnessed anything like this before." He leaned across the desk, took a deep breath, and exhaled slowly. "Can I ask why you didn't name the father?"

I lowered my head in shame. "At the time, I thought he didn't deserve it."

"Probably still doesn't, but the law is the law."

"It was complicated...he was married–"

"Didn't your attorney advise you to name him?" he interrupted. "He didn't tell you the repercussions of withholding such information? I remember pressing your attorney to get the father's name, but he assured me there would be no problems."

I panicked as I felt our relationship changing with Mr. Humphrey's adversarial tone. "Well, he asked me several times, but I didn't realize what was at stake. Believe me, if I could go back..."

"Unfortunately, that's not possible. I know you meant the world to Mary Rose and she desperately wanted to keep Harper in your care, so let's hope we can resolve this matter." He reached for a file folder and his mood seemed to lighten. "For now, just sit tight until I call you."

I motioned for his pen and wrote down the phone number to the house in Laurel. "You can reach me at the cottage or at this number."

Mr. Humphrey took the piece of paper and placed it in the file. "I'll see you at the funeral."

"Oh, yes," I said, not expecting to face him again so soon.

Suddenly, I realized the need to face another attorney, and Daddy had even less tolerance for mistakes in the courtroom.

The night before the funeral, Mother prepared a large dinner at the house in Laurel to bring the family together. The next morning, we'd drive to Piney Cove to bury Mary Rose. The girls ate an early dinner and went to bed. I stared at the comfort food sprawled across my plate: meatloaf, gravy, mashed potatoes, dinner roll.

"Cara, aren't you going to eat?" Mother asked.

I shook my head. "God, I don't know where to start."

She pointed toward my plate. "Anywhere would be fine, dear, as long as you get some food in your stomach. The meatloaf would be the most nutritious."

I fell back in my chair. "No, I don't know where to begin with what I have to tell everyone."

"Starting at the beginning is always nice," Steph said, before taking a bite of salad.

Everyone snickered, but I found myself even less tolerant of Steph's attitude. Noah stroked my leg under the table and gave me a nod of encouragement. Steph had always gotten away with being direct, so I decided to try her approach. "Harper is my daughter."

Daddy looked up from his plate. "Well, Tulip, technically you're her guardian."

"No. She's my daughter, the baby I gave birth to nearly four years ago."

All eyes turned to Daddy who sat speechless for long moments, before clearing his throat. "Let me get this straight," he waggled his fork at me, "Mary Rose's Harper is the *same* baby you placed for adoption?"

Mother clasped her chest. "Sweet Lord, have mercy."

Steph nudged Andrew. "Well that's a hell of a beginning."

Noah slipped his arm around me, while I waited for Daddy's next response. Then I realized he needed more evidence. Grabbing the envelope from my pocket, I passed it to him. "It's true. Right before she died, Mary Rose handed me the letter I'd written to my baby."

Daddy stared at the envelope, his face held steady.

"And that's not all," I blurted, wanting to get the worst out into the open.

"Christ, there's more?" Steph said.

"There's a problem with Mitch."

Daddy jerked his head up from the letter. "What kind of problem?"

"I think he wants custody," I said. "He requested a court hearing to set aside the original adoption order."

"But we know that won't happen," Noah tried to reassure me.

"Why would he request...unless..." Daddy's voice trailed off as his face reddened.

"He was never notified," I confirmed.

Mother looked to him for help. "John? Is it possible he wasn't told?"

"If the mother named him as the father, he would have been informed. Tell me you *did* name him," Daddy said, his voice raising a few decibels.

I bowed my head like a shamed schoolgirl and Noah tilted my chin up. "You can do this," he whispered in my ear.

"Don't be so hard on her, John," Mother said. "I'm sure it was just an oversight." She patted his hand. "Nothing that can't be fixed, right?"

"It's not that easy, Gail," he said. "Unless Mitch isn't the father?"

"He *is* the father!" I said.

Daddy pounded the table with his fist. "Then why didn't you say so, damn it!"

Noah squeezed my shoulder and I met Daddy's eyes with an icy stare. "Don't you think I've been asking myself that same question?"

Daddy shook his head. "And Henry...that incompetent sonofabitch. He said everything was taken care of. No problems whatsoever. I should've known better than to let him handle things so close to his retirement. Why didn't he tell me you didn't name the damn father?"

"I believe that to be the attorney-client privilege," Steph beamed.

Daddy leaned toward her. "No shit, Stephanie." He turned back to me. "Henry's mind was either in the South Pacific or up his ass. I should've farmed the case out to another firm."

I jumped up from my seat. "It wasn't a case! It was my life. Stop talking about me like I'm just another client. I'm your daughter. Besides, it wasn't Henry's fault. He asked me several times who the father was and I didn't tell him. I never realized what trouble it would cause, until now."

Mother looked at Daddy. "Is it possible that Henry thought you had already explained the risk of withholding such information?"

Daddy threw his napkin on the table. "So, now this is my fault? That was his job, not mine!"

We all shifted in our chairs, followed by long moments of silence. A thread of helplessness sewed us all together like different patches on a giant quilt of despair.

Mother pushed from the table and stood. She pointed her index finger at each one of us. "We *will* stand by Cara and the decision she made years ago. We *will* assume there was good reason for her not to name the father at the time, and we *will* figure out a way to keep custody of Harper. We have to...for Cara, for Mary Rose, and that precious, little girl asleep upstairs. Have I made myself clear?"

While everyone stared wide-eyed at Mother, I snatched the letter from the table and darted to the guest bedroom

The knock on the door sent my heart pounding. I ducked my head beneath the covers to avoid Daddy's stern lecture. Relief washed over me as Noah spoke.

"Cara," he said, "why don't we go to the living room and talk? Everyone has cleared out."

Too exhausted to stand, I threw my arms into the air and his body filled the gaping hole. "I can't face my father, Noah."

"He went to bed."

"Did you see how angry he was?"

"I think frustrated better describes how he's feeling." Noah took my arm and led me out to the sofa in the living room.

I sat beside him and buried my head into Noah's chest. "What am I going to do?"

He ran his fingers through my hair. "First, you're going to get a good night's sleep. Then you'll get through the funeral. After that, you can focus on Harper. The hearing isn't for several weeks, so you'll have plenty of time to call Mitch."

I bolted upright. "Call Mitch?"

"To tell him the whole story, how you came to be Harper's guardian. That you took care of Mary Rose and Harper over the last few months. It would be different if Harper had been living with an adoptive family you'd never met before. He might be able to take Harper away from strangers, but he won't take her from you. Just speak from your heart."

"You don't know Mitch," I said.

Noah kissed my forehead. "I don't have to know him. Besides, I wouldn't be surprised if this isn't just his ego talking. He wants to get back at you for taking the control away from him. He'll realize it isn't worth the effort."

"You think so?"

"I'm positive."

Whether right or wrong, I felt comforted by Noah's confidence.

"Are you ready to go back to bed?" Noah asked. "You must be exhausted."

"Where did Mother tell you to sleep tonight?"

"She put me in the guest room two doors down from you."

I frowned. "Two doors is a long ways away."

"Yes, it certainly is." He caressed my cheek. "But you need your rest for tomorrow. Come on, I'll tuck you in."

"I don't want to be without you," I whispered.

"Then sleep here." He motioned for me to put my head on his lap.

"But you won't be comfortable trying to sleep sitting up like that."

His finger came to rest on my lips. "Now, there's where you're wrong. I'm with you, aren't I?"

Loving arms engulfed me and he bent down to kiss the top of my head. I closed my eyes and inhaled slowly, surrendering to his scent, letting it carry me off to happier times.

Forgiveness

I hadn't been to a funeral in years, the last being Aunt Kate's. I remembered little of her service, just the sadness I felt, standing at her freshly dug grave while cars pulled from the cemetery. And how I wanted to yell, "That's it? It's over? You're all going to return to your lives just like that?" Those same words pooled in my mouth as the last of Mary Rose's co-workers pulled from the dirt road. The men who would bury Mary Rose stood underneath a nearby oak tree, occasionally checking their watches. Noah had taken the girls for a walk, while Daddy and I remained at the gravesite.

Daddy rested his hand on my shoulder. "I'm going over to the restaurant to greet the guests for the luncheon. Steph and Andrew have already headed over. I can grab Harper and Lily from Noah and take them with me."

"Sure," I said.

Daddy turned to leave, then spun back around. "Tulip, about last night."

"It's okay, Daddy. We're all under a lot of stress."

"Doesn't matter. I was out of line and I'm sorry. Mitch won't win this. I've been in touch with Humphrey and we're going to fight it. Mitch won't stand a chance."

I nodded, wanting to believe him. Daddy left to gather the girls.

A few minutes later, Noah stepped up behind me and rocked me in his arms. "How are you holding up?"

"God, I miss her so much." I turned to him. "What will I do without her? And when you leave..."

He held me tighter. "Maybe it's time I move back here."

"Really?"

"Really." He spun me around and cupped my face in his hands. "I love you, Cara."

"I love you too, Noah." I finally said what I had wanted to say for so long. "So," I smiled, "when will you be moving?"

"There will be plenty of time to talk about our future. Right now, it's time for you to say a final goodbye to your best friend. I'll give you a few minutes."

I turned my attention back to the flower-covered casket and realized that I'd forgotten the daffodils. "I left the jonquils in the car."

"I'll go get them," Noah said. Within seconds, I heard footsteps behind me.

"That was quick," I said, turning to accept the bouquet. But it wasn't Noah. I stared at her in disbelief. The low cut blouse, skintight pants, and three-inch heels that were once signature Tory now made my stomach churn.

"Cara—"

"You don't belong here," I interrupted.

"I don't plan to stay long. I just wanted to tell you how sorry I am that you lost your best friend."

"Which best friend would that be?" I fought back my tears; she didn't deserve them.

"Both." Tory's wet eyelashes glistened in the sunlight. "I miss you...us."

I threw my hand out in front of me. "Stop! You should've thought about that when you decided to screw Jack."

Tory lowered her head. "Look, maybe I should go. This was a bad idea."

"Yeah, it was." But before she left, I needed to know. "Why'd you do it?"

She shifted her feet, then looked out across the cemetery. "I don't know. I was drunk."

"That's the best you can offer? Did you ever believe that excuse when your mother used it?"

"No," Tory whispered, her bottom lip quivering. "She called and wants me to move to Florida with her." Tory raised her brow as if asking my opinion.

"I think that would be a good idea."

She nodded. "I think it will be a fresh start for both of us."

When Tory turned to walk away, it was most likely the last time I'd see her. I longed to scream after her, to tell her what an awful person she was, to hurt her as badly she had hurt me. Then I remembered Mary Rose telling me I'd have to forgive Tory in order to get on with my life, just as Mary Rose had forgiven the young boy who killed Paul.

"Godspeed, Tory," I whispered.

She tossed one last glance over her shoulder, before disappearing down the hillside.

Noah walked from behind a tree and handed me the daffodils. "That looked intense. I didn't want to interrupt." He placed his arm around me. "You okay?"

"I'll be fine. That was my old friend, Tory," I said.

"Oh. What brought her here?"

"Closure, I suppose." I kissed the bouquet of daffodils and placed them on the center of Mary Rose's casket.

Noah left for Chicago to return to work, promising to come back every chance that his schedule permitted. In the meantime, we'd have to settle once again for nightly phone calls. Two days after he left, I returned to Lake in the Woods. The cottage felt larger once emptied of the hospital bed and other equipment. I stood in the spot where Mary Rose died and looked out the window. The dock beckoned and I wondered if she saw Mitch the day he came to visit, if she noticed his resemblance to Harper. The roar of an engine pulled my attention to a shiny Firebird in the driveway. I walked through the kitchen and opened the back door.

"Come in, Mitch," I said, my throat tightening. "We can go out on the porch. It's nice out there."

"Sure." He followed me and we sat in the wicker chairs.

I folded my hands across my lap and thought of the speech I'd prepared. It sounded so mechanical, so forced, now that we were face-to-face.

Just speak from your heart, Noah had said.

"You're probably wondering what this is all about...why I called you here," I said.

"I have to admit, it surprised me," he said. "I'm assuming it has something to do with the court hearing. Don't know if I should have come."

"Mitch, can we forget about court for a minute?"

He thought for a moment, then settled deeper into his chair.

"Do you know who your daughter is, Mitch?"

His eyes narrowed. "The little girl with the dark hair. It's her, isn't it?"

I nodded. "Harper."

"You said she was your friend's daughter. That her mother was dying. I knew you were lying, but then I found out you really did place the baby for adoption when I did some investigating. Now, I don't know what the hell to think."

"Her mother did die. Mary Rose and I lived together after my divorce. We had no idea that we shared a daughter up until right before she died, I swear."

He stood. "I'm supposed to believe that shit?"

I grabbed his arm. "Please, Mitch, sit down. It's the truth."

His eyes held the same coldness as that day in my hospital room. "If you're all for telling the truth, then tell me this—is she really mine?"

I took a deep breath and slowly exhaled. "Yes, she's yours."

He sat back down. "Positive?"

"Positive. There was nobody else. I was true to you."

"Why should I believe you?"

I picked up the envelope from the coffee table and removed the letter, my hands trembled as the past overtook the present. "Maybe this will help you understand." I looked at the first page and began to read aloud, my voice quivering.

A letter to my baby with love,

Forgiveness would be asking too much. Instead, I'm asking for understanding. I can't say that I understand it all myself and finding the right words to explain it to you isn't easy. All I can do is hope that this letter conveys my love for you.

By the time you read this, you may have your own opinion of why I chose not to keep you. You may blame me, or worse, blame yourself. I need you to know that the decision did not come easy. Guilt and self-doubt have been my constant companions of late.

My life will be forever changed the day I give birth to you. I'll peer into every stroller that goes by, wondering if you're tucked inside. I'll never drive past another playground without taking a second look at the child sitting on the swing. Every time I go to the creek, I'll wish you were there, to see the beauty of the daffodils and to lean how to paint.

My heart tells me I'll feel this way for the rest of my life. But my mind knows that I could only make this decision based on my life, as it is, at this moment. And at this moment, I see your life being so much more than I can offer you as a single mother. I wish that I could ask my family for help. My heart is breaking at the thought of giving you up, but I realize I can't do this alone.

Your father was caught in the middle of two lives and had to commit to the one that didn't include you and me. I will forever wish things were different, that we could've been a family. You deserve better. A two-parent family who can give you a life filled with love and laughter. Most of all, the example of their love for one another, an important gift for any child.

My wish is that you can look back over the years and never regret being adopted. To know that your life could not be any better and that you can't imagine being loved anymore than you are by your adoptive family. Perhaps it's self-serving for me to wish this–that it serves only to reduce my guilt.

While my decision may appear to be a selfish act, it is only through my love for you, and my hope to give you a better life, that I'm able to let you go.

Love,
Your Birth Mother

I waited for Mitch to tell me that he couldn't imagine taking Harper, now that she had finally returned to me.

Instead, his expression hardened. "That doesn't excuse you for not telling me about the adoption."

"I know," I whispered.

We sat quietly for several minutes. My increasing nervousness prompted me to fill the silence. "How did you know it was her?"

A faint smile crossed his lips. "I told you in the hospital that she looked like me. She still does."

"Yes, she's certainly beautiful," I said, hoping to stroke his ego.

"That's quite unbelievable. The two of you, hooking up after all this time."

"Yes, fate, really. There's no other explanation."

"You always did believe in that." He checked his watch. "Well, I better get going." He stood and ran his palms down his jeans, before slipping them into his pockets.

Panic swept over me and I moved between him and the doorway. "Wait…um…you don't have to go so soon."

"Yes, I do. It's a bit of a drive."

"Well...uh...do you still plan to go to court?"

"Haven't decided yet."

"Oh, okay. I'll be sure to let my father know."

"Your father's getting involved?" A look of concern crossed Mitch's face, the same expression he wore whenever his favorite football team was behind in the fourth quarter.

I straightened and threw back my shoulders. "Of course. Why wouldn't he?"

"I suppose I should've expected that," he said, before stepping past me.

This time, the familiar slam of the door brought a smile to my lips.

For the first few days following my meeting with Mitch, I looked out in the driveway for anything red and shiny, waiting for him to come tell me he'd lost interest. By the fifth day, I started to worry. Maybe he still planned to pursue his parental rights. Perhaps I was too confident when he left, and that going up against Daddy didn't concern him as much as I thought. I brewed some coffee to help me relax, only to discover I couldn't drink it alone. After putting the girls to bed, I decided to take my old approach to handling worry– start a new painting.

When I captured just the right color, I called out, "Mary Rose come look at..." before catching myself. When the phone rang, I put down my paintbrush, and darted to the phone. "Hello, Mitch," I said in anticipation of hearing his voice.

"Excuse me?" A voice came on the other end.

"Oh, I'm sorry. I thought you might be someone else."

"Cara, this is Mr. Humphrey. I was hoping to catch you. There will be no hearing on the fifteenth."

I pressed my back to the wall. "Why the delay? I don't think I can take worrying much longer. Can't you do something? Each day I have to wait is–"

"No, Cara, it's been cancelled...permanently. Mr. Sanders dropped the petition."

I caught up with the breath that had escaped me. "So, there's no hearing...ever?"

"That's correct," he said.

"That's it? It's over? Just like that?"

"Just like that. Call me if you have any other questions. You've been given a second chance with your daughter. Enjoy her, Cara." Mr. Humphrey hung up the phone.

I pressed the receiver to my chest and breathed deeply. "It's over. It's over," I said, savoring Mr. Humphrey's words. Then I walked to the bedroom, my pace quickening the closer I got to the door. Standing over Lily, I pulled the bedspread up under her chin and kissed her while thanking God for my little girl. I turned and knelt down beside Harper's bed. Grabbing my cross pendant in one hand, and stroking her cheek with the other, I thanked God for giving her to me–not once, but twice.

A Path Well Traveled

I stopped at the crest of the hill. After a year, her grave still startled me. Harper took my hand in hers, and Lily's in the other, and we forged our way to the gravesite. Noah followed a few steps behind.

"Do you think Mommy and Daddy are looking down on us, Aunt Cara?" Harper asked.

"Yes, sweetheart, I do."

"I bet Mommy gives Sadie kisses for you."

"When she's not kissing your daddy," I teased.

Harper giggled. "Yuck."

"It's not so yucky." I looked back at Noah and winked.

"I miss Mommy," she said.

"Me, too."

There would come a day when I'd have to explain it all to Harper, just as I had the day I wrote the letter. But this time, the question was not why, but how. How could one little girl touch so many lives?

After we all knelt and prayed, I pointed down to the dirt path that led around the cemetery. "Why don't you girls go for a walk with Noah while I finish my visit?"

"Okay. C'mon, Lily," Harper said in her big sister voice.

The two ran down the hill and Noah hurried after them. I bowed my head once again. "God, I miss you. I'm finally able to drink coffee again. I have a cup of coffee for you every morning." I wiped my tears with the back of my hand. "You probably already know all of this, but in case you've been too busy with Paul..." I placed my hand to my forehead. "Wow, where do I start?

"The girls have really grown, and Harper loves being the big sister. She's become quite the fisherman, too. Daddy entered her in a local contest and she won second place. Not to mention, the ice-skating classes are going great. She took right to the ice—no fear, that girl." I opened my eyes and grabbed the gardener's spade and the large pitcher of water sitting next to me.

"Can you believe I'm opening my own gallery? The building needs a few repairs, but it has lots of potential. Even Mother can see past the cracks in the walls and the dust on the floors." I chuckled. "And do you believe I asked my parents to help finance it? I've finally realized that it's not a bad thing to ask for help."

Unfolding the newspaper, I carefully removed the daffodils inside, one by one, as I made my way around Mary Rose's grave, transplanting each bulb from the creek to its new home. Although I hydrated them with water gathered from the creek, the flowers drooped, as if they, too, were in mourning. Luckily, rain was forecasted for the evening and soon they'd stand tall once again.

"Oh, we got a new puppy from the shelter. A Golden Retriever mix named Caramel. The name was Mother's idea, of course.

"The best news–Noah found a teaching job here in town, and he's putting your piano to good use in his studio. He has quite a list of students already." I glanced down at my hand and smiled as the sun shimmered off each facet of the diamond. "Look at this ring. We're going to marry next year...a spring wedding...but I bet you knew that."

After forty-five minutes, I patted the last of the soil into place. The daffodils would get used to their new home and flourish here just as they did at the creek. I'd be their keeper, nourishing them, just as they had fed my soul for so many years.

I gathered my tools and pushed to my feet. "There. They'll be gorgeous tomorrow." I turned and waved my hand in the air, motioning for Noah and the girls.

They eventually made their way up the hill. "Nice visit?" Noah asked.

"Yes," I said as we started back down the dirt path, a path I knew would be well traveled over the years. And just like my daffodils, I'd reappear each spring like an old friend wanting to share a cup of coffee.

While Noah and I walked hand in hand, the girls giggled, racing to the car.

"Wait for…" I started, then waved off my concern.

"They aren't going anywhere," Noah assured me.   "Besides, they're not old enough to drive."

"Oh, Lord. I don't even want to think about that day."

"We'll have plenty of years to warm up to the idea."

"Plenty of years. Now that sounds nice," I said, resting my head on his shoulder and breathing in the wonders of spring.

Noah, the girls, the sunlight sprinkling through the oak trees, and the branches rustling in the breeze, all reminded me of the season's promises and of those yet to come.

Meet the author:

In my childhood home, we didn't have books, take trips to the library, or subscribe to magazines. Reading was not encouraged, or even mentioned. While in college, however, I fell in love with the written word. Then life distracted me. Seventeen years passed before I dared try writing.

At thirty-five I began this new journey. After tucking the children into bed, I'd write into the early morning hours. Fatigue elbowed gourmet meals aside. The words, "Would you like a lemon-basil marinade on your chicken?" soon turned to, "What would you like on your hotdog?" Scrapbook pictures piled up along with the laundry. Hairstyles and cosmetics became optional. I pecked at the keyboard night after night and soon had my first fifty pages in hand. They felt like the start of something real.

This new world beckoned and, surprisingly, writing came naturally. I looked at life through a writer's eyes and listened with a writer's ears. I pulled out threads from all of life's experiences and wove them into a rich tapestry. In those late hours, my words opened windows and I flew into a long denied horizon.

Recently, I married a man who shares my passion for writing. My husband and I immerse ourselves in reality during the day, but each night escape to worlds we create. Afterwards, Michael and I sit on the porch drinking coffee and talking about literature, our novels, and our children. With our blended family, we've firmly planted ourselves in O'Fallon, Missouri.

I'd like to think of this as my final destination. It certainly feels like home.

About the Artist:

The photographic images of Barbara J. Kline usher us into a romantic world of fantasy and mystery.

Born in Niagara Falls, New York in the 1950's, Kline chose to pursue her dream of a career in photography in the state of Florida. After college and a two- year position as a commercial photographer, she became an assistant to the well-known surrealist fine art photographer Jerry Uelsmann. After a four year association with Uelsmann, Kline embarked on a new life in the state of Idaho and began to concentrate on her own artistic career. Although Kline has employed the technique of multiple imagery in her work since in her work since 1984, she only began hand-coloring her photos in 1993, after a trip to Mexico inspired her to incorporate the hues of nature into her work.

Two of Kline's images have recently been chosen to grace the covers of significant publications. Alice Walker's book "The Same River Twice" and "Sacred Practices for Conscious Living" by Nancy J. Napier both displayed Kline's work on their jackets. Her work has been included in over fifty exhibitions since 1989, from Venezuela to Yugoslavia, she has won many awards, including the Festival of the Masters at Walt Disney World. Her photographs are included in many prominent corporate and private collections.

Settled and happy in the mountains of Idaho, Kline continues to find beauty and magic in places many of us would take for granted. We at Hanson Gallery welcome you to the world of Barbara Kline.

View Barbara J. Kline's work at
www.barbarajkline.com

Coming

October 2005

Paula J. Egner

If There Be None

Women's Fiction

*Brethen, I do not regard myself as having
laid hold of it yet; but one thing I do:
forgetting what lies behind and
reaching forward to what lies ahead.*

Philippians 3:13 (NAS)

Charley Sue scrunched her toes, and her patent leather shoes scuffed against the dirty gravel. "It's not fair," she grumbled, and stared down at the dusty road. The toe of her shoe connected with a rock, and it shot out ahead of her.

"You stop that kickin', young lady!" Aunt Mattie scolded from where she walked a few feet behind her two great-nieces.

Seven-year-old Edie–the younger of the two girls–darted a "glad-it-was-you-and-not-me" glance at her older sister and snickered.

"Yes, Ma'am," Charley Sue mumbled, and stuck her tongue out at Edie, shielding the gesture from her great-aunt's line of vision with her hand.

Aunt Mattie believed it was a sin to drive her car on the Sabbath, so the threesome walked the mile or so to church every week. Charley Sue didn't understand why they had to go every Sunday, anyway. She hadn't gone with her mama and daddy. When she still lived with them, the whole family'd slept late on Sundays. They'd stayed in their pajamas until well after noon, and each week her mama'd made a late breakfast– pancakes smothered in homemade blackberry preserves.

But this morning, as every Sunday morning for the past three years, it wasn't even nine o'clock yet and Charley Sue'd already led their tiny parade past the Lilliard pasture. The field wasn't far from the house where she and her sister lived with Aunt Mattie, but their aunt'd given them strict orders to stay away from it, except, of course, while on their Sunday trek.

"That dirty Lilliard heathen'll steal you little white girls, for sure!" she'd warned. "It's a cryin' shame, anyhow, how decent Christian folks in Markus got nothin', and that darkie got all them acres to farm." She'd shaken her head and mumbled something about Jesus helping us all.

But Charley Sue liked Mr. Jonas, which is what Mr. Lilliard told her his first name was. The back of his pasture butted up against the woods behind Aunt Mattie's house, and Charley Sue'd met him one day when she'd snuck over there alone to play. He'd been out checking on his cows, and she'd run between two of the heifers. She hadn't even known he was there, and would've run into him, had he not grabbed her to stop her momentum. She'd screamed so loud it made her throat sore.

"Hol' on, li'l girl," his voice was garbled, and the words were barely distinguishable. Charley Sue'd twisted and turned to free herself from his grasp, with Aunt Mattie's warning screaming inside her head. Her heart hammered, and she'd struggled to catch her breath.

"Which Channing are ya, anyway?" he'd turned his head sideways, and spit a stream of brown liquid onto the grass, still holding tightly to Charley Sue's arms.

When Charley Sue recognized her last name, she'd paused in her struggling. "You know me?" she'd squinted at him, and could see a wad of tobacco swell under his lower lip.

He released her arms, and gave a muffled laugh. "Not you, li'l one, but I knowed your daddy when he wasn't no bigger'n you." He'd smiled lopsidedly, and his lower lip remained swollen by the chew hidden behind it, "It look like he coulda just spit ya out, ya favor him so much."

"You knew my daddy?" No one ever talked to her about her daddy anymore.

"Sho did. Ol' Lester's son, Charles."

"I'm named after him 'cause I'm the oldest," she'd squared

her shoulders, "My name's Charley Sue."

"Well, Miss Charley Sue," he extended a brown, leathery hand, "Jonas Lilliard, but you can call me Mr. Jonas."

His fingernails were jagged and yellowed, and longer than any woman's Charley Sue'd ever seen. She'd stretched her hand out to meet his, feeling very grown-up, and smiled, "Nice to meet you, Mr. Jonas."

He'd assured her that she and her sister were welcome to play on his land anytime. "Just don't rile up my ladies here," he'd waved his arm in the direction of the cows. Charley Sue'd giggled and promised not to bother them.

She'd kept her meeting with Mr. Jonas a secret from Edie for several weeks afterward. She liked the freedom her imagination gave her when Edie wasn't around to spoil it with reality. One of her favorite times was when she'd pretended she was Jane, lost in the wild, and Tarzan was trying desperately to save her. She'd gathered the tree's callous green fruit, and envisioned they were coconuts–her only means of survival. She'd run through the field with her stash, and dodged the wild animals, camouflaged as Mr. Jonas's cows. As she'd maneuvered, she was certain she'd heard Tarzan's rescue yodel in the distance.

But today was Sunday, and the only call Charley Sue would hear would be Brother Tyler's whooping call to glory, then Aunt Mattie's echo of "Hallelujah!"

They neared the entrance to the Second Pentecostal Church, which was really just a converted old farm house. From what Charley Sue could tell, the sanctuary was where the living room and kitchen had been, with a wall removed. The tiny former bedrooms were used for Sunday School classes.

Charley Sue didn't know why it was the *Second* church instead of the *First*, and she'd asked Brother Tyler about it once. But he'd just chuckled, tousled her hair, and began a conversation with Aunt Mattie, who'd been standing behind her.

Up ahead, she saw Brother Tyler at the entrance of the church (or on the front porch, depending on which way you looked at it), greeting the early arrivals. He appeared to be leaning forward, and Charley Sue wondered if the weight of his belly–most of which had already sunk below his belt–was pulling down the rest of him.

She sighed as they entered the sanctuary. There would be no Tarzan today.

The service wouldn't start for another thirty minutes, but even so, once in the Lord's house, Charley Sue knew no words were to be uttered unless done so in prayer, singing, or when praising the Lord. She never praised out loud, though. Aunt Mattie insisted it wasn't acceptable for a child of nine.

She watched Aunt Mattie crane her neck around from where they sat on the front pew, each time she heard another member enter. Her aunt's dark brown hair was dusted with white, like shallow snow on bare soil, and was pulled back into its usual ponytail. Charley Sue'd noticed that it swished, as if swatting at flies, whenever Aunt Mattie turned too fast.

"Welcome, saints of the Lord," Brother Tyler mounted his perch behind the pulpit, and opened his arms wide as if gathering in his flock. "Can I hear a, 'Praise the Lord'?" Even without the luxury of a microphone, Charley Sue felt his booming voice as much as heard it.

The little congregation gave Brother Tyler the response he was looking for.

"Can I hear an *Amen*?" He raised up on his tip-toes and peeked from behind the pulpit.

Amen's smattered back.

"Say it like you mean it!" Brother Tyler thundered a fist down onto the pulpit, and the strands of gelled hair that stretched across the top of his balding head bobbed up and down in starched unison.

This time, the resounding *Amen!* blanketed the sanctuary like a homemade quilt.

"Are you *happy* to be a child of God this morning?" He jumped up and down, jowls jiggling.

The congregation followed suit, clapping, raising their hands, and shouting praises.

Charley Sue's mind wandered. This kind of worship didn't scare her anymore, but if she'd just concentrate on something else, the hours'd pass more quickly. Still, she had to be careful to stand when Brother Tyler instructed the congregation to stand, and to sit when she was supposed to sit, or Aunt Mattie'd make her wish she had. Other than that, she could be anywhere else she wanted to be in her mind, which was just about anywhere else but here.

Today, though, her thoughts fixed on her mama, and she squeezed her eyes shut. But no matter how hard she clenched them, she still couldn't see her mama's face. She recalled the deep brown eyes, though, so brown they were almost black, and the dark, waist-length hair that matched those eyes perfectly. But Charley Sue didn't have a real picture, only the one she felt in her heart. Aunt Mattie'd burned all the real pictures when her Mama'd first left.

Charley Sue sighed and glanced sideways to where Aunt Mattie sat, just one child away. If Aunt Mattie knew that her eldest niece was thinking about her mama, she'd get a belt lashing. And it was even worse if Aunt Mattie caught the children crying about their mama.

Still, sometimes late at night, lying just across the tiny hall from Aunt Mattie's bedroom, Charley Sue missed her mama so much! One time, after listening to her aunt's moans (Aunt Mattie's way of snoring) for what seemed like hours, Charley Sue'd cried and cried. And not the silent-tear-trickling-down-the-cheek type, either. This'd been the sobbing kind, that'd started in the pit of her stomach and threatened to turn her inside-out. She'd promised God she would be good forever if He'd just keep her aunt asleep so she wouldn't catch her. And He did. Ever since, Charley Sue'd been convinced that it was only a matter of time before He also answered her other prayer–the one where her mama would come back to get her and Edie.

Once, about a year ago, she'd asked Aunt Mattie where her mama was. Charley Sue'd seen her aunt's jaw clench, and the grease crackled as Aunt Mattie'd turned over one of the salmon patties she'd been frying.

The older woman'd looked over at her niece who was sitting at the kitchen table. The red vinyl chair Charley Sue sat on had long before cracked open to hatch the gray cotton stuffing inside, and she'd lifted one leg and then the other to ease the scratching on the back of her thighs. Aunt Mattie'd sighed, "She ran off with some fella, Charley Sue, and she ain't comin' back," she said matter-of-factly, as if she'd just explained that her mama'd run down to the Piggly Wiggly for some milk. She'd flipped over another patty, "And as far as I'm concerned, it's for the best. At least with me, you and Edie'll get a good Christian raisin'. Don't be askin' such questions again, ya hear? From now on, I'm your mama."

Charley Sue, incensed, had jumped off the chair, a cotton tail stuck to her thigh, and screamed, "But you *ain't* my mama! My mama's comin' back to get me. You'll see!"

Aunt Mattie's eyes'd brimmed and she'd turned away, mumbling something about her poor dead sister and her poor dead sister's son. Then she'd looked up and began talking out loud to the ceiling–very loud. Charley Sue'd realized she was praying when she'd heard her aunt declare deliverance from all the evil that Jezebel'd brought onto her poor dead nephew's children.

While Aunt Mattie'd watched the ceiling, Charley Sue'd snuck outside. She'd run as fast as she could to the gnarly oak tree in the backyard, and climbed up to her favorite limb–the one that stuck straight out sideways–and straddled it hard with her knees. The bark was like a razor washboard against her bare flesh, and she'd watched a trail of blood as it'd trickled down her calf like an endless teardrop. "My mama's name ain't Jezebel!" she'd cried, "My mama's name is Liza Mae Channing!"

Printed in the United States
26954LVS00001BA/46-153